MW01140104

Advanced Praise For
You Might Feel A Little Prick

"Anyone who has ever run afoul of the medical establishment or the bloodsucking insurance industry will savor Reuben Leder's blistering satire, *You Might Feel a Little Prick*. Screenwriter Leder's first novel is graced with vivid characters—some endearing, some loathsome—and a diabolically satisfying plot. The book deserves to be compared to Paddy Chayefsky's Oscar-winning black comedy, *The Hospital*."

Stephen Farber—film critic and author of *Hollywood on the Couch* and *Outrageous Conduct: Art, Ego, and the Twilight Zone Case*.

"Leder's novel is a scathing look at the medical industry…The author delivers the story with comic panache…The pace…is a whirlwind and surprises abound. The ending, like the story, is a delightful surprise." —*Kirkus Reviews*

"Welcome to Cleveland Mercy Hospital, the place where 'do no harm' is more of a punchline than an oath. Reuben Leder's *You Might Feel a Little Prick* straps up into Dr. Toad's Wild Ride and whiplashes us through a medical system more interested in big money than alleviating pain. Wielding a satirical sword reminiscent of Paddy Chayefsky, Leder makes our worst hospital nightmares come true in this fast-paced, darkly humorous novel. The "little prick" cuts deep and deadly, exposing that most inexcusable of betrayals: the trust a patient place in his physician. Leder has crafted a savage page-turner that will reverberate with us all the next time we walk into a doctor's office."

Carla Malden—novelist, memoirist, screenwriter, and author of *Search Heartache and Shine Until Tomorrow*.

"The descriptions, language, and story progression of *You Might Feel a Little Prick* are outstanding...Expect the unexpected... Compellingly original."—**Midwest Book Review**

"If there are fifty shades of gray, why not fifty shades of black? And the Blackest of the Filthiest shade may well be Reuben Leder's devilishly scourging of some of the self-appointed white-clad deities of American Medicine in *You Might Feel a Little Prick*. Not since Moliere's *Imaginary Invalid* has the lampooning of the stethoscope-adorned elitist class been done with a more mordant poison pen. For everyone who has waited three hours on a cold vinyl couch for the pleasure of having various orifices and appendages pried, probed, dyed, and scraped, here is your literary sweet revenge."

John Lisbon Wood—writer of *By Love and Art Scarred*, winner of the Heart of England Film Festival, actor, director, and multiple award-winning playwright.

"*You Might Feel a Little Prick* is a suspenseful medical thriller that incorporates dark humor into its peek behind the surgery room curtain...Unpredictable twists move the...narrative toward its cohesive conclusion, which leaves ethical questions in its wake." –**Forward Clarion Book Reviews.**

You Might Feel a Little Prick

A NOVEL BY
REUBEN LEDER

FriesenPress

Suite 300 - 990 Fort St
Victoria, BC, V8V 3K2
Canada

www.friesenpress.com

ISBN
978-1-5255-7308-8 (Hardcover)
978-1-5255-7309-5 (Paperback)
978-1-5255-7310-1 (eBook)

1. *FIC060000 FICTION, HUMOROUS, BLACK HUMOUR*
2. *FIC035000 FICTION, MEDICAL*
3. *FIC052000 FICTION, SATIRE*

Distributed to the trade by The Ingram Book Company

For Etyl and Paul Leder

PART ONE

"He was not born to shame;
Upon his brow, shame is ashamed to sit"

William Shakespeare
(*Romeo and Juliet*)

"Nothing dries more quickly than a tear"

Apollonius Molo
(some Ancient Greek rhetorician)

CHAPTER 1

Emission

The keening wind blowing off Lake Erie weaponized the snow, turned it horizontal—a Christmas Eve more appropriate for balaclavas or burkas than reindeer sweaters. Or better yet, to stay inside. Unless inside meant Cleveland Mercy Hospital; then all bets were off.

Snow drifts piled against this twelve-story monument to Rust Belt Gothic. Even the snowman in the children's park adjacent to the hospital was buried up to the coals of his eye sockets; carrot nose long ago eaten by raccoons, while the rats had to settle for gnawed bits of scarf they carried away over half-buried swings and slides. Most of the Cleveland Mercy windows, ground to top, were dark or dimmed, but all were strung with Christmas lights, giving the ancient hospital the look of a once grand luxury liner floating on a tranquil sea of white.

Ice clung to a pair of stone gargoyles sculpted high over the plowed entrance to this venerable metro institution. Their hollowed eyes had witnessed the comings and goings of the dead and dying for more than a century. But not like they would this night as a death scream cut through the hissing wind, accompanied by a body propelled out an open window of the top floor.

Man overboard.

More like, snowman overboard. In keeping with the Christmas motif, the figure wore a rotund Frosty suit as arms and legs flailed against the inevitable; his screams of terror (and some anger there too) were silenced as he sliced feet first through the snow next to the actual snowman, who didn't notice a thing.

Three, four, five seconds later, then all was as before, like it never happened. No one came running. The blizzard continued to seethe, snow drifts continued to swirl, and the lights of the luxury liner twinkled in the moonlight.

CHAPTER 2

Admission

(Eighteen Hours Ago)

Nick Glass was positive he hadn't signed a Consent Form.

At least, not a Consent Form for *this*.

Okay, he got it. He knew his brain wasn't functioning optimally and remembering the events of two hours ago was ... what was that word?

Challenging.

Right. Remembering stuff was challenging.

Nick knew he was still awake. He could tell because the top of his right hand throbbed like hell from being needle-jabbed over and over again by that ginormous Samoan nurse in Pre-Op; like somehow it was Nick's fault the dude couldn't locate the money vein. Maybe that's what was keeping him awake, the pain from the botched IV. Or maybe the oxygen mask that smelled like Lemon Pledge. Or ...

No! Stop! Quit meandering and focus! Don't be distracted by the drugs drag-racing through your bloodstream and think. Think how to get out of this! They never disclosed what was in that final Consent Form, which means they can't keep you here against your will. So quit lying on this O.R. gurney like you're paralyzed, while all these people who look like rejects from Grey's Anatomy are getting ready to inflict some seriously evil shit, and stop them!

Not so easy. Because Nick Glass *was* paralyzed. And even though attempting to retain a sliver of memory was like swimming through a sea of cotton candy, Nick struggled to remember what had gone down with that freaky Admitting lady, the one with the holiday-dyed, red-and-green Bride-Of-Frankenstein hair who kept him captive in her claustrophobic cubicle. She'd worn a Santa cap as unseen speakers played cloying holiday carols on an endless loop. The cubicle was decorated with pastel paintings and …

Stop! Stop! Stop! What the hell is wrong with you? Forget "Jingle Bell Rock" and remember what was in that last Consent Form! The one you didn't sign.

Or did you?

*   *   *

Nick concentrated as the Bride-Of-Frankenstein Admitting Lady prompted him to keep up, to keep scrawling his initials on the digital signature pad. Over and over again. Illegibility was not a disqualifier.

As he signed, Mrs. B of F explained everything in a faux conspiratorial tone that was so weird even she joked how she sounded like the verbal fine print on a TV pharmaceutical commercial.

"Of course, if you think about it, just about anything can lead to impotence, incontinence, and death, right?"

She didn't wait for Nick to answer. She wasn't expecting one and babbled on in her two-pack-a-day rasp. "Jiminy. You could be flattened by a runaway RTA bus crossing Prospect and Huron on your way to The Jake. Oh, right; hasn't been The Jake since 2008. Almost ten years on, it's still Progressive Field. Progressively more expensive!"

Her cackle echoed like a demented goat inside Nick's head as he lay on the gurney in the freezing O.R. and fought to retain the rest of his Admitting experience. But the remnants of memory were going fast and the cotton candy had become a suffocating cocoon, wrapping itself around Nick's pre-frontal cortex. Soon, there would be nothing left to remember at all.

Nick battled against the darkness he knew would come. He again visualized himself back in Admitting, scribbling his initials on the signature pad. As he okayed each document, digital ant farms of words disappeared only to be instantly repopulated. The ant armies were the myriad legal documents created by the cyber vermin from EZ♥Care Health Solutions®, the makers of these eco-friendly, timesaving, fraud-fostering devices.

As Nick well knew.

After all, EZ♥Care was also his employer.

"Totally routine," Mrs. B of F reassured him. "Just think of all the trees you are saving."

Screw the trees; it was all he could do to get his initials down fast enough. He paused to run a hand through his sandy hair. A nervous tic he'd recently developed. Not that he had much to be nervous about today. A pork in the wok, the Doc had reassured. Something like that, anyway.

Mrs. B of F's drone became white noise, punctuated by sentence fragments here and there. Like: and oh, by the way, would Nick want printouts of what he just signed? Except why on earth would he? Kind of defeats the purpose, she sniggled, like it was their shared joke. Like she didn't use the same line on every patient she processed onto the conveyer belt that would transport them deep into the bowels of Cleveland Mercy and crap them out the Other Side. One way or the other.

Nick guessed Mrs. B of F could count on the lime-speckled fingernails of one hand the amount of times she'd had to cough up hard copy for some analog patient. Hardly ever happened, because once she had them in her cubicle, they were hers. Already in a world of hurt, they couldn't initial fast enough to score the coveted plastic wristband designating them as Official Guests of Cleveland Mercy.

He recalled how he'd done his best to not only take the fight to the digital ant armies but also, once they'd defeated him, to understand the terms of his surrender. He never had a chance; those pricks were relentless. Each Consent Form popped up without warning, like a Whac-A-Mole game where the prize wasn't a stuffed tiger with one quizzical glass eye and a dozen years of dust, but instead a dozen years of exorbitant co-pays. Which beat the alternative: Claim Denied.

Despite Nick's best efforts to understand the rules, the game was rigged. Every patient a loser. They just didn't know it yet. As he labored to keep pace, Mrs. B of F provided a running play-by-play:

"This one's 'Acknowledgement of Insurance and Financial Responsibility.'"

Whack!

"Here's EZ♥Care's 'Patient Bill of Rights.' That's a short one."

Whack!

"'Consent to Surgery: Known and Unknown.'"

Whack!

No! *Not whack!*

Nick paused, stylus poised in mid-air.

"What is it, hon?"

"What's an 'Unknown' surgery?"

"That's the thing; no one knows. Even though we have the bestest scanning equipment in the world, MRIs, CTs, Molecular Imaging, blah blah blah, it's not until you're split open like an Easter hog and the blood and guts get wiped away, that the surgeon knows for sure what *really* needs fixing. And that's why it says, '*Unknown.*'"

The look on her face told Nick the look on his face wasn't exactly convinced.

"Why do I get all the pains in the poophole?" Mrs. B of F muttered. Before Nick could ask her to speak up, she reconjured her cheery voice: "Nick, I know you're a guy and all, but you ever watch that cooking show *Chopped?*"

Nick shook his head and wondered if he'd already had his surgery. Maybe this was a narcotic-enhanced post-op dream? No, he knew better. He was still naked under a flimsy hospital gown in the arctic O.R. waiting for the operation to begin.

"Well, *Chopped* is my fave. Pretend you're this master chef. It's the Dessert Round and you've knocked off all those other master chefs with their stupid lip rings and tattoos; and there's just one more to beat. Now here comes the dessert basket and you're expecting ingredients like, say, pizza dough, ginger, and oh, how about Bing cherries? Except the host, that pipsqueak Ted, throws you for a loop because when you open the basket, under the Bing cherries there's a disgusting half-dead hagfish."

"Excuse me?"

"A hagfish. They're like eels, except when they're ticked off, instead of giving you an electric shock, they shoot out this disgusting slime. But somehow the master chef still has to make a gourmet dessert, even though that pissant Ted threw in that nasty hagfish."

"I don't think I'm following, ma'am."

"What I'm trying to explain to you, hon, is the *magic* that makes every Cleveland Mercy surgeon world class. Say you're fast asleep on the table as the scalpel slices an eight-inch opening in your back and Dr. Trout looks at the screen, expecting to see pizza dough, ginger, and Bing cherries, but on top, there's also this yucky hagfish who not only doesn't belong in your spine but worse, the sucker's sliming your Bing cherries. Well, what's Dr. T going to do? It's life and death, and he's got half a second to figure it out. Does he panic?"

Nick had no idea; he was still coping with the concept of a slime-spewing hagfish living in his back, like he was a Reel Two victim in *Alien IX*.

"No, what he does is transform the slime of the hagfish into egg whites to make the best darn dessert ever! And just like the last master chef left standing on *Chopped*, he wins! And you, like every other Cleveland Mercy patient, you win too! And that's what the 'Unknown Surgery' clause is. So Nick, initial your okay for Dr. Trout to work his wonders on that nasty hagfish. Time's a wasting."

"Yes, ma'am."

"Alright! Just about done." She clicked her mouse and submitted a new ant colony for his approval. "This one's a consent to waive your right to an attorney and go straight to Arbitration if your surgeon, like that would ever happen, had a brain cramp and turned you into a turnip."

Whack!

"Acknowledgement said surgeon may or may not have a 'Proprietary and Fiduciary Interest' in the EZ♥Care Medical Devices, which may or may not be inserted into or about the patient's spine."

Nick paused in mid-whack, his stylus again quivering in space.

"Now what, Mr. Glass?"

Nick noticed he'd been demoted him from *hon* to *Nick* to *Mr. Glass*, but nevertheless held his ground. "Ma'am, I'm sorry, but isn't this a potential conflict of interest? You know, Dr. Trout being part owner of the medical device company? Just asking."

Mrs. B of F flung off her Santa cap. Brittle tufts of green and red hair popped vertical as a Category-Five blast of indignation blew his way. "Do you really think the world-famous Doctor Templeton J. Trout would associate his good name with some fake titanium junk from a Malaysian metal shop?"

"No, but—"

"And Mr. Glass," she allowed the last part of his surname to hang in the air like an epithet, "if Dr. Trout, who's the best darn orthopedic surgeon in Northeastern Ohio, has invested his own do-re-mi in the hardware he's putting in your spine—hardware that will be there *permanently*, long after the cemetery's flooded and the titanium is floating past your grandkids' house—well, I think you'd be hollering down from Heaven and thanking him! Now sign the dang screen!"

"Ma'am. Dr. Trout's not having the surgery. I am."

She glared at him in full Bride-Of-Frankenstein fury. "You got that right, sweetie. So either sign the thing or go ahead, punk, and get outta my cubicle."

Nick tried to meet her gaze and not blink. Or laugh. Two botched iconic movie catchphrases in the same sentence? However, neither laughing nor leaving was an option. He had no options, period. The pain burning in his back told him that. His resolve melted somewhere around the fifth lumbar vertebra and he picked up the stylus.

Mrs. B of F's tongue sucked away a trace of lipstick from her front teeth as she relished victory. "Very good, Nicky. Now just sign this one last little screen and you're good to go."

Nick initialed his acquiescence on the one screen he should've paid more attention to.

And as he lay on the gurney in the O.R., feeling himself drifting away, the remnant of one last memory cut through his brain cocoon: Nick could not recall Mrs. B of F mentioning—or him agreeing to—a Consent Form that allowed Betsy Nguyen of 19 News to *video* his spinal fusion and put it on freaking TV. And social media.

Hell no!

But before Nick could formulate, much less articulate any further objection, the cocoon closed around his brain and the light behind his eyes went out, leaving him in a cold, fathomless void.

CHAPTER 3

In Dreams

A Sony NEX-EA50EH camera aimed by scrub-wearing Derek Blach, ace Cleveland 19 News shooter, was focused on star reporter Betsy Nguyen, who happened to be the last person Nick saw before the sevoflurane and fentanyl sent him to his angry parcel of dreamland.

Betsy also wore scrubs but since she was the on-air talent, hers were form-fitting and diaphanous, as if designed by a Hollywood wardrobe department. Even her surgical cap was translucent, allowing the TV viewer a glimpse of Betsy's trademarked caramel hair streak that cleaved through her lush and layered midnight do, the Veronica Lake bang she whisked out of her left eye when live on location. Whether exuding outrage in front of the rank Cuyahoga River, or waist deep in a downtown dumpster showing love to a blind pit bull and her adopted litter of orphaned kittens—Betsy's insouciant hair flick was her thing.

Nick's thing too, as for the last five years Betsy's hair swirl was the match that lit his TV crush, the crush that immobilized his finger on the remote. The crush Julie always teased him about. He never should have opened his trap the night that Betsy had somehow made the story of a local steel mill shutting down— causing two-hundred union coil-slitters and furnace-operators

to lose their jobs to a child labor factory in Chongqing, China—
sound arousing. But as of three minutes ago when his eyes closed,
Nick's crush was over. How dare she do this to him?

Derek looked at his viewfinder and counted down, "Three, two,
one …"

With perfect timing, Betsy coaxed the caramel streak off her
eye and said, "Hello, Cleveland, I'm Betsy Nguyen and in our
continuing series of specials celebrating the workaday lives of
Forest City's everyday heroes, 19 News is privileged to be in the
operating room, or should I say operating theater, because after
all he is the Lin-Manuel Miranda of surgeons: Dr. Templeton J.
Trout, Cleveland Mercy's finest."

In the dim background, indistinguishable O.R. personnel in
soft focus prepped for surgery. Instruments were placed on trays,
checklists were murmured. The surgical team sounded like extras
in a foreign movie awaiting the arrival of the star.

Betsy held the sterilized mic just below her collagen-enhanced
lips. "Dr. Trout has allowed us exclusive access to document him
and his team as they perform a complex spinal fusion on local
Clevelander and former Kent State baseball hero, Nick Glass.
Per our arrangement with Cleveland Mercy, the video will also be
featured on the hospital's YouTube Channel as well as affiliated
websites, including EZ♥Care Health Solutions dot com. Oh, a
warning, you might want to ask the little ones to leave the room.
Dr. Trout tells me this one could get quite graphic.

"So, without further ado, I give you Dr. Templeton J. Trout."

A spotlight snapped on and Derek racked focus to reveal,
basking in its radiance, Dr. Trout, who favored the camera with
a poised smile. A handsome, video-friendly African-American of
fifty, Trout's very presence invited, *inspired*, trust. He could, and
someday hoped he might, be featured on a United States Postal

Service *Forever* Stamp. Trout, goggles pushed up over a flawlessly chiseled face, a face accentuated by a retro leading man pencil-thin mustache, commanded the camera's attention. And when he spoke, the viewer could imagine it was God himself doctor-splainin'.

"Thank you, Betsy. It's a pleasure to have you with us. Today, we have a real treat for your audience as we are going to perform an anterior/posterior lumbar decompression and stabilization. In English, this means we'll be effectuating a spinal fusion by going through the patient's front *and* his back. Not everyone is lucky enough to get one of these in their lifetime. But, after all, this is the giving season."

Sycophantic dork snickers rippled from his team as Derek panned down from Trout's twinkling eye to the surgeon's distinctive Harvard Medical School lapel pin. A pan back revealed the twinkle had vanished. Trout quieted the room with a flick of an eyebrow before returning his gaze to camera.

It was a gaze that would be frozen in time, a gaze forever searchable—no matter how many attempts were later made by the I.T. geeks to scrub it from the web. It was a gaze assuring the viewers, i.e. potential patients, that they'd found the one surgeon and the one hospital that would bring an end to their pain and suffering. Thousands of clicks would seek him out in perpetuity.

Of course there was no way for Trout to have known it in the moment, but those thousands of clicks would be seeking him out for all the wrong reasons.

"The Patient, a pleasant twenty-seven-year-old, presented in clinic with intractable low back and right leg pain, the result of a mishap during a company softball game. X-rays were not definitive; but since ninety percent of back pain improves on its own after thirty days, I prescribed anti-inflammatory medication, ice, and a few weeks of just good old kicking back. After a month,

The Patient returned to clinic with no improvement; his pain, in fact, had significantly worsened. The next step was an MRI, but those results were also inconclusive. Same with a CT scan. The Patient's EZ♥Care Insurance is excellent, so I sent him to a second imaging facility, because studies have shown not all MRI machines are created equal. One will identify a herniated disc while another will present as a bad acid trip."

More chuckles from his acolytes. Trout frowned but his subsequent wink to all of cyberspace gave away the gag; he thoroughly enjoyed the sucking up.

"However, after giving The Patient an NCS and EMG—and no, those are not television shows," Trout paused for the laugh with the timing of a late-night TV host, "both the Nerve Conduction Study and Electromyography confirmed the weakness and pain in The Patient's right leg was caused by lumbar disc impingements." He picked up a model of a skeletal back from a countertop and tapped the lower discs on the skeleton. "Here, here, and possibly here. Even though the scans wouldn't give away all their secrets, I knew from manifest experience that discs L-4, L-5, and S-1 were the main culprits. I prescribed a conservative course of treatment, beginning with eight weeks of physical therapy: massage, core exercises, electrical stimulation. And, of course, traction …"

*   *   *

Wait! Hold on! How the hell am I hearing this? Oh, right. Julie told me hearing is the last of the five senses to go. Although, she said it's really more like twenty-one senses. Whatever, I'm supposed to be out cold but I'm hearing every word the Doc's saying. And I'm feeling everything.

Yo. Could someone look into this?[*]

*   *   *

There was no way the "pleasant twenty-seven-year-old male" on the table could *hear* Trout, much less feel the scalpel and saws. Not logically. Yet, buried deep in Nick's auditory cortex, Trout's muted words, faint fragments of syllables cascading over a lingual waterfall into the mushy swamp that was Nick's superior temporal gyrus, triggered memories.

Memories of a year in a Hippocritic Hell.

[*] Someone has, Nick. Studies have estimated that twenty to forty-thousand patients in the US *alone* remember being awake during major surgery. Michael Wang, a British psychologist, wrote in a 1998 paper: "It is difficult to imagine a more exquisite form of torture than major surgery with consciousness, pain perception and complete paralysis. Clinical psychologists and the patient's family are then left to pick up the pieces."

CHAPTER 4

In Memoriam

At Traction

Alone in a physical therapy room, lights down low and Sinatra's suicide ballad "Everything Happens to Me" floating from in-wall speakers, Nick, looking stronger and optimistic, was strapped via harness to a state of the art DRX-9000 (Decompression Reduction Stabilization System). This high-tech contraption was the evolutionary zenith of the entry-level torture rack first popularized in the Spanish Inquisition. But instead of the session being administered by a hunchback cleric with little self-control, this device was programmed to operate on its own and shut down at a prescribed time. Nick lay on the table, arms grasping overhead handles as a pneumatic cylinder shifted the two sections of the table apart and then back together to provide a stretching of the spine, alternated with blessed relief.

Rinse and repeat until it was time for the PT Aide to return to the traction room and undo the restraints.

Despite knowing nothing could go wrong because he'd been through computerized traction a dozen times now, Nick's eyes grew wide with panic as the DRX, flexing its software like a Muscle Beach show-off, extended his spine to the utmost limits of decompression.

And wouldn't retract.

Nick's mouth opened in a silent scream as an alarm blared.[*]

* * *

The idea of Betsy Nguyen hosting a surgery performed by the famous Doctor Trout originated with Josh Przybylowicz, the young, hard-charging CEO of Cleveland Mercy, who pitched it to Betsy's bosses at 19 News. The concept was beautiful in its symbiosis. In exchange for a primetime New Year's ratings bonanza full of sex (Betsy) and violence (Trout on Nick), Cleveland Mercy and Trout got to troll for patients on the web. Forever.

Everybody wins.

Josh was the fidgety guy lurking in the corner of the O.R., watching his vision unfold. His sole regret was that the drab scrubs they'd made him wear hid the Brunello Cucinelli suit he'd scored on a quick jaunt to Barney's in the Big Apple last weekend. It would've looked great on TV. *He* would've looked great. Why hadn't they told him he had to wear scrubs in the O.R.? Not only that, he also had to wear a stupid surgical cap over his eight thousand painfully earned hair grafts. Hell, his boys needed to breathe! On the other hand, maybe there was an upside to the scrubs and cap; maybe the audience would think he was a doctor too. Maybe he could get Betsy to interview him after the surgery. Maybe he could even score her digits.

As Josh indulged his fantasies, Trout pretended to peruse Nick's chart before looking back up to camera: "Continuing the strictly conservative treatment protocol, The Patient was given a twelve-week course of acupuncture. Frankly, studies have been all over the place regarding the efficacy of this ancient Eastern art of healing;

---

[*] In 2016 the Quebec Superior Court authorized a class action lawsuit to proceed against thirteen chiropractors and their insurers. The complaint notes that the College of Quebec advised chiropractors to stop advertising and using the DRX 9000 in 2013. Subsequently, nine of the thirteen chiropractors were disciplined.

however, forty Alternative Medicine visits were allowed under The Patient's generous EZ♥Care Insurance Plan so we thought it worth a try. The good folks here at Cleveland Mercy are open to anything that might work, because, as you know …"

Trout leaned closer into the camera and recapitulated Every Surgeon In The World's Mantra:

"Surgery is always our last resort."

I of the Needle

Nick, eyes closed and motionless, was nude on his stomach on a stainless-steel tissue-covered med table. Thumbtacked to the wall behind him hung an acupuncturist's chart of the human body displaying the twelve primary meridians. The wispy, white-bearded Chinese acupuncturist with the unfiltered Chesterfield dangling from his lips, had used at least eleven of them, as Nick had more needles sticking out of him than a porcupine in full quill erection. As the acupuncturist selected a final needle from a knock-off Ming Dynasty cloisonné and inserted it above the bridge of Nick's nose, a bit of glowing ash drifted onto Nick's hair. The old man blew it away and headed for the door.

"One hour," he said. "Do not move."

* * *

"Unfortunately, the acupuncture proved to be no more effective than the traction. Worse yet, The Patient developed a staph infection from a tainted needle placed in his gluteus maximus. This infection was discovered to be MRSA, necrotizing fasciitis—known colloquially as the Flesh-Eating Virus. The Patient required a month of hospitalization, a course of intravenous antibiotics, and ultimately, we had to rip us off a little piece of ass."

More giggles from the surgical team. Trout concealed a micro grin as his reproving eyebrow again silenced them. "Happily, The Patient recovered and we were able to move on to the next phase of our conservative spine treatment plan."

*   *   *

No! No! No! I never signed on for this! This embarrassment, this humiliation! If I ever get out of here alive, I'm going to kill him. I swear, I'm going to kill him!

*   *   *

"We tried in-home Transcutaneous Electrical Nerve Stimulation, known as a TENS device. Also, I prescribed a custom-fitted via handheld-laser back brace, along with a course of biofeedback combined with cognitive behavioral therapy. But all to no avail. We even tried a chiropractor. Now I know what you're thinking and you would be correct—if this were five or ten years ago. Although the medical profession historically has frowned upon chiropractic intervention, there have been recent studies as well as anecdotal incidences of positive outcomes.

"As Franklin Delano Roosevelt once said in an address at Oglethorpe University in Atlanta, witnessed by my great-grand-father, the first Dr. Templeton J. Trout, 'If it fails, admit it frankly and try another. But above all, try *something*.'"

Trout chuckled, "So what the heck, we sent The Patient to a gentleman known in chiropractic circles as 'Rambo from Ramallah.'" He pushed back his goggles, tickled. "I always get a kick out of that. And, of course, EZ♥Care covered it."

A Minor Adjustment

Nick, shirtless, sweatpants pulled down to his butt crack, lay on yet another medical table in a darkened room as an Unseen Voice commanded, "Close your eyes, bro!"

Nick did so, as a robotic machine on rollers approached the table. A telescopic pointer emerged from the metallic mouth and shot a red laser beam that danced up and down Nick's back, like a sniper with Parkinson's. All this to the accompaniment of Pandora's Persian Pop Station. The Unseen Voice echoed through the darkened room.

"So Nick, tell me what do you feel?"

"Uh, nothing?"

"Excellent. For it is your damaged cells that are doing the 'feeling' as photons from the cold laser pass through the dermis and affect the tissue at the cellular level. There, they are absorbed in the mito-chondria of the cell, creating physiological changes such as rapid cell growth, increased metabolic healing, and most important of all, anti-inflammatory action. And I totally wasn't reading that."

Nick glanced toward the window where the sun streaked through dusty blinds, revealing a 7-Eleven on the opposite side of the strip mall. As Nick wondered if he should get a Chrome Dome versus a Mango Chili Slurpee, the red laser vanished and the room lights turned on, revealing a buff guy, about thirty, wearing a tahini-stained white doctor coat.

Behrouz Rahimi DC powered down his Bio-Probe 2000xK Elite via touch screen and walked over to Nick.

"Don't move."

Without warning, Behrouz's gym-strong hands snapped Nick's neck. The adjustment sounded like a desert thunderclap. Nick hyperventilated as Behrouz helped him to a sitting position on the sweat-drenched med table.

"Nick, my man, I love my cold laser but when all is said and done, there's nothing like going OG. Am I right?"

Nick wasn't yet able to speak. He'd also changed his mind about getting the Slurpee as he felt a sudden need to void his bowels.

"Yo, bro. Didn't that feel better." It was a demand for affirmation more than a question.

"Yeah, was magic."

"Fantastic!" Behrouz beamed. He squeezed Nick's bicep and frowned in dismay. "Nick. You're losing your fitness. Your arms look like my grandmother's Reshteh noodles." He gestured to shelves full of vitamin supplements for sale. All had the brand label EZ♥Joint on the color-coded containers. "Are you keeping to your supplement regimen?"

Nick nodded without conviction.

"Then I would imagine you are almost out."

"No, I'm okay, Behrouz."

"Hey, no more Behrouz; it's Bobby. We're brothers. I keep telling you."

"Definitely. Bobby. I'm good with the supplements."

Behrouz leaned forward and lowered his voice, "If it's a matter of money …"

"No, Beh … Bobby … really, I'm—"

"I want you to get well. And that begins with your body's defenses. Your back problems are a manifestation of a vulnerable immune system. Thank God they were able to get rid of the MRSA infection. But at what cost? Permanent antibiotic resistance? And after your back is stabilized, what next? Your cardiovascular system? Or 24/7 oxygen because of a compromised respiratory system? I lose sleep over your kidneys as well."

"Really?"

"Of course. What is more important than secretion and excretion? If you don't breathe a word, I can knock fifty bucks off an entire case: the Alpha Lipoic acid, the Metabolic Detox Protocol, all of it. I don't want to see you suffer, and you know the Western Big Pharma crap they're forcing you to take isn't helping at all."

"Fifty bucks?"

"Did I say fifty? I meant seventy-five. It kills my *ravaan*, my soul, to see what they're doing to you. Also, if I move just fourteen more units this month, EZ♥Joint is going to send me for a weekend at Sandals Grande Antigua. Sweet, huh?"

Nick agreed, "Sweet."

* * *

The regret on Dr. Trout's face, as seen through Derek's lens, was indeed Oscar® worthy. In fact, if Trout ever had the chance to see the video, it would no doubt confirm his theory that doctors-playing-doctors were way better actors than actors-playing-doctors could ever hope to be.

"The result, from what proved to be cans of lawn clippings sold by our Rambo from Ramallah, was a bout of Gastroesophageal Reflux Disease, six weeks of violent diarrhea, and four cases of Depends."

* * *

No! Stop! Stop humiliating me or I will jump off this table and slit your fucking throat! Can you hear me, you bastard? Can you hear me! Because I sure as shit can hear you!

Trigger Point Injection #13

Nick was again on his stomach on an exam table in another medical office, this one right out of a 1950s *Saturday Evening Post* cover. The doctor's surgery was chock-full of early twentieth-century paraphernalia: an old-fashioned height-and-weight scale, wooden instrument cabinets full of glass jars, and a replica human skeleton in the corner. Adjacent to the skeleton was a G-rated anatomical chart. Below Nick's exam table, the marbleized black-and-white inlaid linoleum sparkled.

The door opened and a white-haired doctor wearing a starched white coat and kind eyes entered. A middle-aged, no-nonsense nurse handed him a thick-gauge syringe that seemed more appropriate for equine use.

"Thank you, Irma," said the elderly doc, so old he could have mentored Marcus Welby.* "Go ahead and relax, son, I'll just be a moment or two setting things up." Except the Welby wannabe mounted a surprise attack and jabbed the syringe into Nick's lower back and held it there. Nick cried out in surprise and pain.

"Do not move a millimeter, Mr. Glass," hissed the old doc, as he released the contents of the syringe into Nick's back.

Nick bit his lip as his fingers ripped through the flimsy paper on the exam table.

"You lied!"

"No shit, Sherlock. I've tried to give you this damn shot twelve times now and you keep squirming like this is your first day in

---

* A compassionate sixties TV doctor played by Robert Young† (†never mind), who made house calls and apparently was never paid for his work. Probably the only debatable decision Dr. Welby ever made was in the episode entitled "The Other Martin Loring" where he advised the titular middle-aged patient to resist his homosexual impulses.

prison. Jesus Christ on a popsicle! When are you going to get it? Pain comes with the territory!"

*   *   *

Trout, working without notes, resumed his recitation of The Patient's marathon dance to Big Medicine's Greatest Hits.

"I hate to keep using this word, but unfortunately the trigger-point injections provided little relief. In fact, The Patient's muscular-skeletal pain *increased*. Therefore, we had no choice but to escalate to a procedure called a rhizotomy. Which sounds scary but is in fact a harmless outpatient procedure."

White Russian

Nick was face-planted on a cold steel table in a sleek O.R. equipped with the requisite gleaming and beeping props. The sanitary paper beneath him felt thinner than a slice of Arby's.

Even though Trout wasn't in this Outpatient O.R. and never had been, his basso profundo permeated Nick's waning consciousness and grafted onto his memories. Memories of "procedure" after "procedure." Memories of futility, misery, and always present pain.

And hope.

Sure. Hope. Always had to hope. Otherwise, why go through one numbing disappointment after another?

Except why was he being forced to relive every excruciating detail? He wished the slick Pakistani anesthesiologist he met in Pre-Op would amp up his meds. But how to tell the dude when he couldn't even open his mouth?

"A rhizotomy is a neurosurgical procedure that burns to death nerve roots in the spinal cord, effectively cutting off pain signals to the brain. So, who better than to have scorched those suckers than the orthopedist assisting me today, the Rhizotomy Queen of Cleveland Mercy, Doctor Irina Demidova."

Demidova was towering-tall and featured a heart-shaped Slavic face, its paleness accentuated by ice blue eyes. Her height and slim hips also suggested the body of the ballet dancer she once was. Her snowy blonde hair, pulled back under her surgical cap, was evocative of the Alpine peaks of the Urals. In sum, Demidova looked like the love child of Vladimir Putin and the staring center of Dynamo Moscow. She approached Nick's table, flanked by a surgical nurse and the x-ray tech who would manipulate the fluoroscopy screen.*

"Good morning, Nicholas. Not to worry, petal, this will be over before you know it." Demidova pulled down her goggles and inserted a hollow needle into Nick's spine. The needle contained a catheter and heating element that blitzed through layers of fat, muscle, and tendon, and into the nerve root. The procedure took place with Nick under minimal sedation so he could be alert enough to respond to Demidova's questions. Like, does it hurt when I do *this?* Or how about *that?*

Yes to all of the above was the correct answer.

A door slammed and Trout re-entered Nick's brain. The pompous blowhard hadn't even bothered to knock this time.

"The risks of a rhizotomy include nerve damage, disc trauma, infection, and paralysis. But the success rate *can be* up to seventy-five percent.† However, those pesky nerves tend to regenerate and the procedure needs to be repeated. Unhappily, in this case, the procedure did not work.

"Any of the three times."

* * *

* A live, real time, x-ray.
† Verbal fine print. Fifty percent is more like it. An expensive coin flip.

Back in the oh oh O.R., Trout glanced away from Derek's video-cam to see if his team was ready. His surgical partner, the spooky Doctor Demidova, held up five fingers. Trout nodded and turned to camera. Derek was almost asleep on his feet at this point and Betsy was scrolling through her phone. Trout's voice commanded their attention:

"Unfortunately, and there's that word again, due to the sheer volume of cortisone absorbed by The Patient over a short period of time, he developed osteoporosis—a dramatic and dangerous weakening of the bones, most often seen in post-menopausal women, not in a young man of twenty-seven. I suppose we could debate the merits of all those procedures, but I stick by them because, as you know, I consider surgery …"

"… a last resort," Betsy and Derek mouthed along with Trout's audibilization.

No worries about Trout noticing their smartass mockery, for he only had eyes for the seductive lens. "Therefore, we had to get the osteoporosis under control before proceeding any further. I sent The Patient to the head of the Rheumatology Department here at Cleveland Mercy, a sufferer of the scourge herself—as well as a Board Member at EZ♥Care Health Solutions. If the internationally renowned Dr. Lillian Goorwitz-Clarke, possessor of the Presidential Gold Medal Award of the American College of Rheumatology, couldn't get The Patient's bones back from brittle to brutal, no one could."

Styx and Stones

Nick, a frown creased over a haggard face, arms folded, sat across a desk from Dr. Lillian Goorwitz-Clarke, whose flowing white hair settled upon a tie-dyed lab coat which was personally autographed (as she pointed out to every patient) by the late Brian Jones, a founding member of the Rolling Stones. The walls were decorated with framed posters of long-forgotten tours by bands who are mostly remembered as answers on Trivial Pursuit cards, Boomer Edition. The only place in her office that indicated Goorwitz-Clarke was, in fact, a doctor and not an aging plaster-caster,* was the trophy wall behind her desk. A shrine in black, white, and bronze, it featured a lifetime of medical awards and plaques—testaments to career longevity, prodigious networking skills, and a life well-prescribed. Trout's YouTube Voice narrated the encounter as she dashed off a prescription:

"Dr. Goorwitz-Clarke prescribed Fosamax and when that didn't help, Actonel. Both are bisphosphonates: medications used to treat osteoporosis in said post-menopausal women."

She handed the script to a reluctant Nick.

"This one will work?" he asked.

Goorwitz-Clarke answered with a thinly disguised edge, "Young man, it works for me so why wouldn't it work for you?"

"Maybe because one size doesn't fit all?"

"I'll see you in eight weeks, Mr. Glass."

Nick placed the RX in his pocket, rose, and left the office. He walked a bit hunched over, with the beginnings of a limp.

Like an old man.

* * *

Trout, who had invested hundreds of hours in front of the bathroom mirror, displayed his best "rueful" look to camera: "Regrettably, and unknown at the time to the medical community at large—including Dr. Goorwitz-Clarke who's presently

---

* Parental guidance: only Google this if you are over twenty-one.

on indefinite sabbatical and no longer affiliated with EZ♥Care Health Solutions—this class of medications, which were heavily lobbied by their pharmaceutical manufacturers to a compliant FDA, were not without unforeseen and bizarre side effects. Hips spontaneously fractured in places where hips had never fractured before, likewise arms. Bones became infected. The Patient's heavy use of bisphosphonates led to osteonecrosis, or 'Jaw Death' as the melodramatic media calls it. The Patient's upper jaw became infected and to prevent sepsis—a condition where the infection enters the bloodstream and shuts down vital organs, resulting in death—an emergency bovine bone graft was performed by an oral surgeon to save The Patient's life, so he'd still be around for me to fix his back."*

Hello Yellow Brick Road

Trout's words were no longer fathomable; instead they sounded like distant thunder, rumbling above puffy white clouds that blanketed a verdant field of black-eyed Susans, asters, and sunflowers. All the place needed was a yellow brick road.

And Nick was walking on it. His jaw was swollen and bandaged. His eyes vacant. He paused as he heard the melancholy moo of a cow. Another moo and Nick entered a maze of bright flowers. He came upon a clearing where a black-and-white dappled cow munched on some yellow daisies. The cow sensed Nick's presence, looked up and ambled closer, staring at him with deep soulful eyes.

"Moo," repeated the cow.

"I don't understand Cow."

* Fosamax, Actonel, Boniva and the like are still on the market. In addition to osteonecrosis of the jaw and serious bone fractures, their use has been linked to DVT (Deep Vein Thrombosis), pulmonary embolism, atrial fibrillation, severe musculoskeletal pain, and increased risk for esophageal cancer.

"Maybe you can understand this." The talking cow turned sideways to give Nick a good look at her hide which was festooned with bandages and crisscrossing stitches.

Nick brought his hand to the side of his bandaged jaw. "Oh, jeez. This is from you? I didn't know. I'm sorry."

"Yes, you're sorry. Sorry they took the milk meant for my children? Sorry they cut and removed chunks of my bones, all to heal you? And once your jaw is good, how sorry will you be when you eat me between a sesame seed bun garnished with tasteless onions, genetically modified cheese, and secret sauce? I'm guessing, not that much."

"No. Wait. Mrs. Cow, I promise I won't eat you. I swear."

Nick's vow was rendered moot as a blinding white light flashed and thunder boomed. The cow and the meadow vanished and Nick found himself back on the yellow brick road.

Trout's voice echoed from above like an angry god. "It became abundantly clear we had to become more proactive in attacking The Patient's pain. The jackbooted DEA be damned!"

Nick gazed at a signpost on the yellow brick road that advertised a "Pharma's Market" just around the bend. He followed the arrow that directed him to:

An outdoor market where he was the only customer. On each side of the road were tented stalls. Each stall featured tables with woven baskets that overflowed with multi-colored pills. Instead of farmers, every vendor was an old-fashioned pharmacist. All white-coated, green-visored, and hard-selling:

"Hey there son, check out my Vicodin," called one. *The guy in the next stall topped him with,* "No doubt lots to like with Henry's Vikes but they've got too much acetaminophen. Bad for your innards. Try my extra-strength Norco instead! Price is right! Just a four-buck co-pay for EZ♥Care customers!" *Nick's gaze swiveled to the other side of the yellow brick road where another pharmacist peddled Percocet. His*

neighbor, sucking on a corn-cob pipe, beckoned to Nick. "No, what you want, boy, are my Oxycontin 'Blues.' 160 milligrams, the max dose they make."

A red-suspendered pharmacist shook his head in disdain at that. "Used to make—those 160s were so strong the FDA pulled them off the market. So, unless you want to OD, I suggest you try my Fentanyl patches with 24/7 sweet relief. No ups and downs, all the bliss and none of the abyss!"

The babble of voices was overwhelming. The Pharma's Market was an addict's Nirvana. But Nick wasn't an addict. No, Dr. Trout had told him he was merely 'physically dependent.' Once Nick was better, weaning off opioids would be as easy as giving up popcorn, pizza, or porn.

* * *

"In addition to massive amounts of pain medication, anticonvulsants such as Depakote and Neurontin for nerve-specific pain were prescribed. However, central nervous system depressants, including Wellbutrin, Lyrica, and Cymbalta, had to be added to help The Patient cope with the roller-coaster ride of the anticonvulsants. But in order to control the side-effects of the CNS depressants, the cocktail grew to include anti-anxiety meds such as Klonopin and finally high doses of Xanax."

Trout bounced Nick's weighty chart on a counter, turned to camera and let the world in on a little secret. "To cope with the anxiety caused by the anti-anxiety medications, I tried medical marijuana. Or, I should say, The Patient did."

More obligatory titters from the team as Trout allowed himself a smile. Good one, Templeton.

Hard Rocks

Nick, earbuds on, book in hand, sat in bed. At last, he was not on an exam table or gurney in an operating room but in a safe place: his and Julie's home. Although home was a cluttered apartment with books on boards and concrete blocks, Hopper prints on walls, and a deflated football that served as a candleholder in the sleeping area, it was, however humble, not a damn medical facility. Nick squinted as he tried to concentrate on the book entitled *You Are Not Your Pain* while the tinny sounds of the Beatles singing "I Am the Walrus" emanated from his buds.

As the Beatles urged Nick to smoke pot, he reached for the bong on the wooden night table next to him, a table populated by a dozen prescription bottles that crowded the surface like pharmaceutical soldiers standing sentry around a half-empty glass of water. At ease, men. Nick lit up. The rock ember glowed deep as he embraced the THC. His eyes were distant and glassy. He exhaled, the book slipped out of his hands and his eyes closed. His head lolled to one side …

… onto the shoulder of a worried young woman, who in another era would not have been out of place singing and dancing while painting a barn in a Mickey Rooney/Judy Garland programmer. Julie wore pajama bottoms, a Cavs sweatshirt, and a look knotted with worry. She removed the dying bong from Nick's tenuous grasp and placed it on the night table on her side of the bed. She deftly, almost surgically, extracted Nick's earbuds without waking him and placed them next to the bong. She straightened their blankets, leaned over and whisked a lock of sandy hair off a gaunt cheek, brushing his lips with a kiss. She took Nick's iPod off the bed, placed it on the table, and turned off the lava lamp, leaving only their huddled silhouettes visible in the candlelight.

* * *

In the O.R., Derek finally got to move his camera, like real cinéma vérité. He followed Trout to a computer on a side counter where the surgeon paused and regarded his intimate friend, the lens.

"Penultimately, The Patient underwent a mildly invasive microdiscectomy, an extraordinarily successful out-patient procedure.* If you'll allow me, I've put together a little demonstration. '*Microdiscectomy For Dummies*,' I call it."

Trout poked the touchscreen and an animated depiction of a microdiscectomy played. Over it, Trout explained to potential candidates how easy this surgery was: "As you see here, metal retractors, clamps, separate the skin. A small piece of bone, the lamina, is removed with this burr tool, which I like to call a surgical plumber's snake." Trout, basking in his wit, had to hurry to keep up with the animation: "Then this grasper gets what the burr didn't, including a portion of the herniated disc. Voila, a microdiscectomy."

To put a fine point on success, a cartoon Happy Face was superimposed over the surgical area. How difficult could this surgery be was the message, especially if success could be limned in a fifteen-second toon? Derek swish-panned back to Trout. The O.R. now electric with anticipation.

"Unfortunately, none of the conservative measures I have delineated—including the microdiscectomy—were effective in eradicating The Patient's pain."

---

* Nominally, 84%. Although, Tiger Woods might beg to disagree. He had three of them, the first causing him to pull out of the Masters in 2014.

Derek got a quick shot of the computer screen again as an animated Sad emoji pushed aside the loser Happy Face.

Trout held the moment like Olivier doing *Richard III* and said, "Therefore, we have no choice but to go full ISIS on the young man."

On cue, every light in the operating room smashed on, bathing the theater in searing brilliance.

There was Nick on his side, the operating area prepped and ready, his face hidden behind a sterile surgical curtain. Kind of like the cleanest camping tent ever. The O.R. team was in sharp focus for the first time. They included Demidova, the anesthesiologist, nurses, surgical assistants, and an x-ray tech. Josh Przybylowicz and Betsy Nguyen were off to the side, and hovering over all of them was Derek, the man with the cam.

Demidova, eyes flashing in anticipation, slapped a sapphire scalpel in Trout's palm. A video veteran now, he pivoted to camera, waited for Derek to zoom in for his close-up, and said to the world, "Enjoy the show."

CHAPTER 5

Are You Listening?

Stop the surgery! I want to get off!

Nick screamed as loud as he could, but they couldn't hear him. None of those jokers in their holiday-themed scrubs who were about to slice him open like a twenty-pound Butterball were paying attention. Why couldn't they hear him? Anesthesia was not supposed to work this way. He was supposed to be asleep, for fuck's sake.

But he wasn't. He was hearing everything. Why?

Because the delicate cocoon enveloping his primary auditory cortex had only partly closed. Blame it on the prefrontal cortex, the area of the brain that allowed Nick to not only receive information from the auditory cortex but also enabled him to remember what was said, even remember other people's facial expressions. Worse, it had permitted him to revisit the emotions related to those conversations.

Nick's eyes were taped closed; he wore a surgical cap; there was a breathing tube down his windpipe; a blood pressure cuff attached to his arm; a sensor to measure blood oxygen levels pinched an index finger; EKG leads crisscrossed his chest. As far as the surgical team was concerned Nick was asleep, unaware of the carnage about to be inflicted on his body. He was, for all intents and purposes, in a state the ancient Greek docs called "Absence of Sensation."

Well, Hippocrates and his white-robed, Birkenstock-wearing, nude-wrestling posse were a bit off about that one, because what Nick felt under twenty-first-century anesthesia was an unquantifiable hyper-sensation *and no one in this O.R. knew it.*

Just make it go away please

Connie Smith, Board Certified RN, veteran of a zillion surgeries, picked up an iPod, tapped once with a scalpel and Buffy Sainte Marie's (very) deep track "I'm Gonna Be A Country Girl Again" twanged out of the Bluetooth O.R. speakers. Betsy Nguyen stuck a mic in Connie's face.

"Does Dr. Trout always play country music during his surgeries?" asked Betsy.

"Well, no. Not really. He's more into Barry White and those seventies R & B guys with growly voices, but I won the trivia contest last night at *'Scalpels & Sponges'* across the street so I got to pick the music for this surgery."

"Well, good for you," said Betsy.

"Thanks. I'm Classic Country all the way."

Just kill me now

Derek, now wearing a body-mounted camera rig, gazed into an LCD monitor as he held the Sony high over the action. Even in the frigid O.R., he was sweating through his scrubs as he adjusted frame to reveal the Big Fish in his element.

Surgical loupe pulled over his eyes, Trout glanced into his monitor, which played the grisly fusion in real time, as he cut into Nick's abdomen where the road to "First Do No Harm" had come to a dead-end. A nurse hoovered up Nick's blood as Trout and the staff sang along with Buffy about how they wanted to be country girls again. Trout broke it off, and called out to the room, "Remember folks, Christmas-Kwanzaa-Passover party, my office suite upstairs tonight. We're going to party like rhinestone cowpersons!"

I'll   bring   the   moonshine   Quackman

Sweat sprayed off Derek as he three-sixtied around the table, shooting down onto the progressing surgery where Trout wielded a mallet on a titanium cage screwed into what was left of Nick's lumbar spine. Backbreaking work, this. Breathing hard, he passed the mallet to Demidova and turned to camera.

"Think track and field, as in a relay race."

No   think   about   how   much   this   hurts   Hurts   more   than   anything   has   ever hurt   in   my   life   Where's   that   anesthesia   guy   Need   him   need   him   need   him need   him   pleeeease

The dashing young anesthesiologist, Dr. Marwan ("Call me Marty") Ganapur, moonlighting from his regular gig as hospital Pain Management specialist, wasn't paying much attention to his monitors—and Nick's carbon monoxide levels—because at the moment he was hitting on the hot medical student he was supposed to be training. "Did you know my *Dadabu* used to be the Head of Cardiology at the Aga Khan University Hospital in Karachi?"

"Wow. How cool. So he's retired?"

"More or less. The Taliban blew him up."

"Oh my God!"

"He was a great man. A proponent of secularism and a woman's right to bare her head—except in the O.R."

They shared a quiet laugh as Ganapur confided, "I learned I was next on their list and that's why I immigrated."

"So how do you like Cleveland Mercy?"

"Outside of the biased M&M Reviews, yeah, it's fine. I mean, excuse me, but sometimes a patient dies on the table. There can be a thousand-and-one reasons it happens, yet it's always 'blame the anesthesiologist.' At the last *Death and Doughnuts,* they forbade me to give Propofol during colonoscopies for six weeks. Can you believe it?"

I can

"Oh wow, Dr. Ganapur?" The student pointed at one of the monitors. "Look at that brain electrical activity. The patient's barely under."

Marty Ganapur looked at the monitor and made a couple of quick adjustments. Nick was soon flooded with a cocktail of painkillers and paralytics. Goodnight and good luck. Ganapur allowed himself a small sigh, before smiling at the medical student and whispering, "No harm, no foul, yeah?"

With that one correction from Ganapur, consciousness and the feeling of helplessness that had been Nick's constant companions vanished in a millisecond. At last, Hippocrates' "Absence of sensation" prevailed.

But there was no correction that could banish Nick's Id. That troublesome sucker was free to hang around.

* * *

As Demidova tapped away at Nick's new discs like a woodpecker on soft cedar, Trout lifted the loupe above his eyes and found Derek's lens. "Here, we are finalizing the grafting of cadaver bone to the hardware. The benefits of cadaver material as opposed to harvesting The Patient's own bones, usually from the hip, are a marked decrease in surgical time, recovery period, as well as significantly less post-operative pain. All in all, a win-win for The Patient."

Betsy held up her sterile mic to Trout. "Is there any chance the body could reject the cadaver bone?"

Derek, sensing a dramatic moment, zoomed in for a close-up.

Trout sensed it as well. "That would be a Black Swan event. In other words, the chance of cadaver bone rejection by the host is next to negligible."

Back at it, Trout tightened the screws in Nick's titanium cage like a dad assembling his kid's first bike. Connie reprised Buffy Sainte-Marie on her iPod and the entire team belted out the chorus in close harmony. Even Betsy joined in. After all, isn't TV News a participatory endeavor?

Perhaps so. Perhaps that's why Nick's Id didn't want to be left out. The medical term for this phenomenon is called Post-Operative Cognitive Dysfunction.

'Terror' also works.

Behind the screen concealing his face, Nick blinked. Or tried to, as he realized his eyelids were taped shut. He wondered where he was; he wondered who he was.

He managed to remove the tape from one eye, which was drawn to a monitor displaying the HD butchery wreaked on his spine. WTF! Nick ripped the tape off the other eyelid and, unnoticed by the singing surgeons and chorus, also yanked out his breathing tube and cried for help. But, as before, no one heard him. They were too busy crooning.

Nick screamed. The changes to his markers beeped and displayed on Ganapur's monitors, but Marty was taking a solo on the next verse, trying to impress the medical student.

No one noticed a thing until Nick, defying medical and any other kind of reality, burst through the surgical drape that had concealed him from Derek's camera.

With one hand attempting to hold in his oozing pink-and-red speckled guts, the other grabbed a scalpel off a nearby tray. Nick leapt off the table, howling like a horror movie scream queen. His eyes ping-ponged about the O.R. and settled on Trout, who advanced toward him, bloody mallet raised.

"Get your ass back on the table, boy!"

Nick slashed his throat. A clean surgical slice. Trout, eyes disbelieving, collapsed to the floor as blood gushed from his gullet as if sprayed through a garden hose. Nick, brandishing the scalpel, lurched past Trout's convulsing body and received a blood shower as he headed for the O.R. exit.

Demidova, Ganapur, and the rest of the team froze, as Nick, naked save for surgical cap, clutching his blood-and-guts leaking abdomen, fled out the pneumatically opening doors.

The first to react was Derek as he aimed his camera at Nick's fleeing figure (replete with the MRSA virus scar on one concave butt cheek) and took off in pursuit, shooting on the run, only pausing to capture a quick close-up of Trout's blood-spewing throat and beneath that, his red-stained Harvard Medical School lapel pin. Betsy for once did not flick her hair streak as she was right on her cameraman's heels.

The pneumatic doors closed behind Nick as he stumbled out of the O.R. Still trying to keep his innards from sloshing all over the floor, he fled down an empty corridor. The passageway was decorated with non-offensive "Happy Holidays" banners and drooping streams of dull

*glitter. Alvin and the Chipmunks' version of "Winter Wonderland"
emanated from the hospital P.A. system asking the musical question:*

"Are you listening?"

*Nick was not. He was running, leaving a trail of bloody viscera in
his wake. Behind him, it was all Derek and Betsy could do not to slip
and fall in the gunk.*

*Nick reached an intersecting corridor, only to be knocked to the
floor by a gurney, wheeled by a tatted-up, skeletal, eighteen-year-old
candy-striper who wore black lipstick and a hospital I.D. tag reading,*
"Hi, my name is Raven. How can I show you some Cleveland
Mercy today?" *Raven's dyed jet-black hair and bangs matched her
name. Mortified at what she'd done, even though it was an accident,
she came around the gurney containing an unconscious post-up patient
and bent to help stanch the blood and entrails pouring out of Nick.*

"Dude, I am so sorry."

"No … my fault," *said Nick. Embarrassed, he covered his blood-
doused member.* "Excuse me. It's nothing …"

"Yikes, I better take a look at that." *She brushed his hand away and
reached for his bloody penis just as a gunshot reverberated through
the hallway. Raven and Nick turned to see a pair of burly security
guards, each wearing reindeer antlers attached to their rent-a-cop
caps, aiming their weapons at Nick. One of the guns was still smoking
from the warning shot the guard fired into the ceiling, bagging a*
"Happy Hanukkah" *banner in the process. As the guard flung
the Hanukkah banner off his antlers, Alvin and the Chipmunks
asked again:*

"Hey, are you listening?"

"Drop the knife, dirtbag," *said the guard who'd fired the warning shot.*

Nick put his hands on Raven's shoulders and begged, "Please help
me." *He was unaware the scalpel was inches from her neck.*

"*Absolutely.*" *She patted the motto on her I.D. badge: "That's what I'm here for." Raven was likewise unaware of her neck's proximity to the scalpel.*

"Said drop the damn knife!" the security guard with the itchy trigger finger demanded. His partner reacted to the sound of clattering footsteps, turned, and saw Derek hustling up the hallway, with Betsy Nguyen right behind. The guard, jazzed, whispered to his partner. "Hey, it's the News! Betsy freaking Nguyen! Oh man, I am so into her hair!"

As Derek videoed the confrontation, Betsy whispered into her mic, "Are we live?" The answer came through her earpiece; she gave Derek the thumbs-up, and in one continuous motion brushed the streak out of her eye. When she felt the camera land, she switched on her modulated reporter voice and described the action.

"We are live at the scene of an unfolding hostage situation at Cleveland Mercy Hospital where just a few moments ago, a patient in the midst of major surgery, seemingly anesthetized, came to life and without warning leapt off the operating table and savagely slit his surgeon's throat. We are unable to give the surgeon's name pending notification of next of kin but we can give you a couple of hints; the surgeon was a Pisces who was working for ten thousand times scale."

"Last time, loser! Put down the knife!" said the lead security guard.

Oh. The scalpel. *Nick realized maybe this wasn't a good look.*

As did Josh Przybylowicz who had pushed his way through to the security guards and hissed in their ears. Both nodded. They got the message.

Raven looked at Nick with compassion. "Not a good day, huh?"

"Please … tell them … I just want my life back. They took it from me and I want it back. Please … tell them …"

As Nick bared his soul (and everything else) some of his blood dribbled into Raven's mouth. She squished it around her palate like a first-growth Bordeaux. She swallowed and said, "Earthy, but accessible. AB Positive?"

"Negative."

From the lead security guard: "Ain't gonna tell you again, numbnuts! Drop it!"

Nick, still in inelegant embrace with Raven, still gripping the scalpel, glanced back to the guards. Behind them, thanks to social media, the previously deserted corridor was filling with scores of onlookers: doctors, nurses, patients, hospital workers and visitors.

Betsy whispered into her mic, "The patient says he wants his life back. Although, I personally witnessed him taking a life."

Josh took a look at the gathering crowd, most aiming smartphones, and signaled the security guards. "Take the shot!"

Nick realized he was about to be executed.

"No, please. Don't! I just want my life back. I want my back back! I want to go to the Tremont Farmers' Market with Julie on Saturday morning; I want to—"

The guards fired. Two entry wounds blossomed on Raven's forehead and she slumped to the floor, dead. Bullets also ripped through the unconscious patient on the gurney. The couple-hundred onlookers, plus millions worldwide watching on screens, gasped.

Josh almost passed out as he saw the contrails of his career flash before his eyes. Derek, on the other hand, couldn't believe his luck as Betsy moved the streaked swath of hair off her eye and coolly reported, "Hospital security guards have just shot an unconscious patient and a candy-striper, a selfless volunteer, a young woman whose only crime was caring too much."

Josh's wail drowned out whatever Betsy was going to say next. "Him, you assholes! Shoot him!"

The chastened guards emptied their clips and Nick went down in a fusillade of bullets. As Nick bled out onto the linoleum, Alvin and the Chipmunks asked again:

"Are you listening?"

CHAPTER 6

"Dreaming Dreams No Mortal
Ever Dared to Dream"

Edgar Allan Poe
(*The Raven*)

"Are you listening?"

All he could hear was the barrage of bullets, but instead of booming like they were coming from a subwoofer the size of a Smart Car, the gunshots sounded faint and trebly, as if crackling from a transistor radio. Wait, what's a transistor radio?

"Nick, are you listening?"

He wasn't listening because the gunfire in his head returned him to the hospital corridor where he felt the bullets tearing through his flesh, the hot steel spinning him around as the security guards with the reindeer antlers on their ball caps, those trigger-happy Rent-A-Rudolphs, emptied clip after clip into him like Sonny Corleone getting lit up on the toll bridge …

"Nick. Can you hear me?"

Nick, trussed and wired-up in a hospital bed, stirred and fought to escape the godfathers and gunshots of his dreams as he became aware someone had been asking him a question.

Someone.

Julie?

"Julie?"

"Welcome back, Nicky."

He blinked a few times until his eyes stayed open for good. Oddly, the tinny gunshots in the background were still rat-tat-tatting but he didn't care; they were sublimated because right in front of him, sitting in the shadows on the edge of the bed, was the woman who'd kissed him goodnight all those murky evenings when he had passed out from the harsh rocks of medicinal pot; the woman whose girl-next-door smile wouldn't have been out of place in the Mickey Rooney/Judy Garland flicks they used to binge on the classic movie station.

Julie.

Instead of pajama bottoms and Cavs sweatshirt, Julie, her light-brown hair now tied back in a ponytail, which enhanced the soft contours of her face, wore a white doctor coat over institutional scrubs. And the photo on her Cleveland Mercy I.D. badge didn't do that smile any justice at all.

The badge that read: Julie Toffoli, M.D.

"You were talking in your sleep."

"I was?"

"Oh yes. Quite entertaining. The parts I could understand, at least."

She dampened a cloth from the water pitcher on the bedside table and dabbed his face. Behind her, a steady evening snowfall was visible through the cracked-open window. On the inside of the moistened glass, thanks to the humidity created by a mid-century cast-iron radiator bolted to the floor, Julie had drawn a steamed heart with her finger. Inside the heart were the initials, *N & J*, with an arrow going through the center of the heart.

"Did you do that?"

"No, all hospital rooms at Cleveland Mercy are accessorized with personalized steamed Cupid hearts on the windows. Only in the winter, though."

"Oh." He tried to say more but instead his head slumped and he drooled on his chest.

"Hey, stay with me, Nicky. I've got to get back to my floor soon before they miss me."

"I missed you," he mumbled.

"I missed you more." Julie leaned over to kiss him but instead reacted with annoyance to yet another flurry of the staticky gunshots. She looked and saw they'd been coming from the wall-mounted TV.

"Where did you put the remote?"

"What?"

"I need to turn down this stupid TV. There's nothing but guns going off all the time. It sounds like when Sonny got it at the Long Beach toll plaza in *Godfather One*. Oh, here it is."

She squeezed his hand, grasped the multi-purpose remote attached to the bed, and aimed it at the TV, about to click it off but didn't, as the visuals on screen brought a horrified look to her face. She turned up the volume of some kind of wildlife documentary, except the shaky video could be better described as a dead wildlife documentary. Caribou. Grizzlies. Giant Dall sheep. A narrator intoned:

"*… This footage, which depicts clandestine 'trophy hunts' in rural Alaska, was covertly shot by courageous Inuit and Yupik guides employed by wealthy clients from the Lower forty-eight. These so-called sportsmen range from captains of industry, to corporate lobbyists entertaining government officials, to Silicon Valley billionaires. This is what a hundred grand buys them.*"

Julie and Nick were unable to look away from the faces of the executioners, posing with the majestic animals they'd killed. One guy had his tongue splayed on a grizzly bear's bloody cheek. Another joker in a camo Patagonia parka stood behind a caribou's regal sixty-inch antlers and, with glove off, rendered the "horns" behind the animal's trophy horns. A third hunter bared his capped teeth, mimicking the death snarl of a grey wolf he had gunned down.

"... *They swoop into pop-up hunting camps that are here today and gone tomorrow. Because of NRA and Safari Club lobbying, President Trump had nullified the Obama-era 'Predator Control Laws,' the result being the massacring of hibernating animals in their dens, hunting from planes, or luring grizzly bears with food for point-blank kills. In many cases, the guides take the hunters out on the same day they land in their private aircraft. Then, after a night of celebratory partying, they fly out the next morning with their trophies secured in freezers, leaving the carcasses of these magnificent animals to birds of prey and other scavengers.*"

On screen, goggle-wearing guides wielding buzz saws decapitated the corpses. The trophy heads were wrapped, dropped into portable freezers and taken to waiting private planes. The planes took off from the tundra, leaving the bodies bleeding red on a blanket of white.

"*These slaughters are antithetical to the ethos of the Native Alaskans who for thousands of years have used each part of the animals they hunt for subsistence. To feed and clothe ...*"

Zap.

"I can't watch anymore of this." Julie dropped the remote back on the bed. Tears welled in her eyes. She shook her head as if trying to expel the horrific images. "Hunting innocent animals is bad enough, but you know what this is? It's speciecide. How can these rich creeps get away with this?"

"Because they're rich creeps?" The room became quiet, save for the pings and beeps of the monitoring equipment. Nick reached with his free hand to touch her cheek, but the effort was too much. As he let it drop, he woozily said, "Jules, I need to tell you something. Seriously."

"What?" she asked, although her head was still in Alaska.

"Betsy Nguyen put my operation on the news."

"What?"

"She was there. With a cameraman."

"Yeah. Right."

"I swear. She was."

"Nick, I'm not in the mood for any jokes right now."

"Jules, I'm not joking."

"Really? Betsy Nguyen was in the O.R."

"With a camera guy."

"Come on. How could that be?"

"I don't know. It was a big deal."

"Wait. You didn't give her permission, did you?"

"No."

"Did you speak with her?"

"No."

"Did you sign anything?"

"No." Nick paused, squinted, amended: "Maybe."

"Back up. How do you even *know* she filmed your operation?"

"I heard her talking into the TV camera. You know how her voice goes ... *'Hello, Cleveland, I'm Betsy Nguyen and 19 News is privileged to be in the operating theater of the Lin-Manuel Miranda of surgeons, Dr. Templeton J. Trout, Cleveland Mercy's finest.'* Something like that."

Julie grinned. "Ha. Are you certain you didn't dream this?" Her grin became a snide smile. "Because I know for a fact this isn't the first time you've dreamt of Betsy Nguyen."

"Hey, it was only once and I didn't mean to dream about her; she just kinda showed up."

"Actually, Nick, it was twice. And Mr. Happy was dreaming right along with you." Julie shuddered, "Which totally creeped me out. And for the record, that was the worst Betsy Nguyen impression ever."

"Jules. It wasn't a dream. She was there. And Dr. Trout was explaining everything they were doing to me, and everything they'd done to me in the past. Every test, every procedure."

"That's impossible. You were under general anesthesia."

"I even heard a nurse say how she got to pick the surgery music. She won a trivia game in a bar."

"Stop, Nick. You had to have dreamt this."

"No. I remember everything. Listen." Nick proceeded to render a raspy imitation of Trout's basso profundo: *The benefits of cadaver material as opposed to harvesting the patient's own bones are a marked decrease in surgical time, recovery period, as well as significantly less post-operative pain. All in all, it's a win-win for the patient.*"

"He probably said that in one of your pre-op visits and you just think it happened during the op."

"Julie, I heard him in the O.R., telling this to 19 News."

"How, Nick? How exactly could you have heard *anyone?*"

Nick frowned as the "how" eluded him. The cocoon he visualized so clearly while on the table had become indistinct, a shimmering simulacrum now faded into a narcotized mist, just out of reach.

"Because …" His eyes began to close again. "Because …"

Julie glanced at his morphine drip, took out her iPhone and did some quick dosage calculations.

Nick's head lolled to the side. "What's an M&M?" he slurred.

"Peanut or plain?"

"An M&M in doctor talk?"

Julie looked up from the phone at Nick like he just crawled under a rope line and snuck into an exclusive club. But how did he get past the bouncer? "An M&M is short for the weekly 'Morbidity and Mortality Conference.' Why are you asking that?"

"Because I heard the anesthesiologist dude tell somebody how he got out of Pakistan because his grandfather got blown up and now that he's here at Cleveland Mercy, he has to go to all these M&Ms. He called it *'Death and Doughnuts.'*"

"Marwan Ganapur was your anesthesiologist. He's from Pakistan. And I say this in the strictest of confidence, but he's been the subject of a number of M&Ms."

"Told the peeps in the room to 'call him Marty.'"

"He tells everyone to call him Marty. I'm trying to wrap my head around this. You *really* heard them say all that? In the O.R.? While you were under general anesthesia?"

"I keep telling you."

"This is beyond weird."

"No kidding. I yelled at them to stop because nothing in my life ever hurt so bad. They were cutting me with knives and banging on me with hammers, and no matter how much I screamed, they wouldn't stop." A tear trickled down his cheek. "Jules, you gotta believe me."

Julie, crying too, dabbed at his face with a wet cloth.

"Yes, I do. And I'm sorry for doubting you. I am so sorry."

"S'alright. I love you. But you need to hear what happened next."

"There's more?"

"Promise you won't flip out?"

"I won't. Unless it's something gross concerning you and Betsy Nguyen. Keep that to yourself."

"No. Nothing like that. What happened was I woke up in the middle of surgery, jumped off the table and killed Dr. Trout. I slit the bastard's throat."

Julie's belief in Nick's story just did a one-eighty. "Ha. You really had me going there." She looked to an imaginary nurse and said, "I'll have what he's having."

"Jules. I'm telling you what I remember."

"Right. Of course you are. So what happened after you slit Dr. Trout's throat?"

"I panicked. I ran outside the O.R. And that's when the guards with the reindeer antlers shot me. No, wait. They shot me after they killed the candy-striper."

"The candy-striper? Nick, you are on some powerful meds and the subconscious projecting stuff is common."

"She kinda looked like the chick in *Amélie*. Remember that French movie we saw at the Cinematheque?"

Julie scooped a portion of chipped ice from a paper cup and slid the slush into Nick's mouth. "Suck on these and don't say anything else. I don't want you getting dehydrated."

Nick did as ordered but only for a second, as he tried to speak through a mouthful of ice chips. "You don't believe anything I said."

She dried his face with a towel. "Nick, keep the ice in your mouth and please stop talking. You're still under monumental amounts of anesthetic. You've had a monster operation, you're trussed up in a rigid back brace which doesn't allow you to breathe, and you're going to have to wear it almost 24/7 for the next six months, so—"

"—so you don't believe me."

"Well, I don't believe you killed Dr. Trout."

Julie pulled the privacy curtain closed, leaned over, kissed him fully on the mouth and whispered, "Because if you did, I'd have to call the police. Reluctantly. Because I love you."

"I love you too, Jules," Nick whispered back, eyes dulled by the cumulative effects of the surgery and the pain meds coursing through his body. "Except I know I offed the dude."

Julie put her arms around him but before she could reply, the privacy curtain was swept open from the outside, revealing Dr. Trout wearing a snowman costume beneath his white coat.

Beside him was Dr. Demidova, dressed as the tallest and most sexy elf ever. And behind her was a Santa's workshop full of interns and medical students, all wearing green elf tights under their white coats and conical feathered caps atop their domes. Trout graced Nick and Julie with a bountiful display of leering white teeth.

"I was going to ask how you were feeling, Nick. However, the answer is evident. Impressive, young man. Damn impressive."

CHAPTER 7

A High C On The Butt Trumpet

Julie leapt off the bed and stuck the landing in her sensible New Balance hospital sneakers. She tossed a sheepish glance at Trout and Demidova and wondered if they'd noticed the lipstick trace she'd left on the corner of Nick's mouth. Demidova had, and smirked as she also clocked Julie's finger-drawn heart on the humid window.

Nick's dilated eyes stared at Trout in confusion. *Didn't he just slit this guy's throat?*

"Sorry," said Julie. "I was just checking on—"

"Yes. We saw you 'checking.' You are who, exactly?"

"I think cute heart on window explain all, Doctor," Demidova said as she walked over and closed it. Julie's Cupid heart, framed by the evening snow, began to dribble down the glass.

Julie ignored the sniggers from Trout's elves. "I'm Julie Toffoli. First-year intern and Nick's fiancée. Presently on pediatric rotation."

Trout frowned, as did the elves with stethoscopes who took their cue from the boss and imitated his patronizing mien. Not an easy thing to pull off when looking like a road company of *A Midsummer Night's Medical Center.*

"Then I'm sure the infirm little tykes on the fourth floor are eagerly awaiting your ministrations, as is your Attending. That would be Kasper Klepstein?"

"It would. O-kaay then, well thanks for taking such good care of Nick, Doctor Trout."

Julie waved goodbye to the semi-sentient Nick and turned to go. She paused at Dr. Trout and whispered, "How did it go?"

Trout didn't reply, instead eyebrowed Julie to follow him. They passed through the clutch of med students who were thanking their lucky stars it wasn't them who were being taken to the woodshed. Like, who was she to ask Templeton J. Trout how well he'd performed a surgery?

Trout paused outside the room near a framed black-and-white photograph mounted on the corridor wall. The stark image featured a circa 1950s operation taking place in a cavernous amphitheater attended by a hundred white guys in skinny ties and starched white coats. The female patient, lying on her back, her breasts only partly covered by a sheet, was unconscious and unaware of the collective male gaze.

I sure the hell bet they didn't have photo waivers back then, thought Julie.

"'How did it go?' You really asked *me* 'How did it go'?"

"Sorry. I didn't mean …"

"Really? Then what exactly *did* you mean? Your fiancé's condition is highly problematic and he was damn lucky I took him on. If you really want to know 'how it went,' catch 19 News tomorrow night. Betsy Nguyen will tell you. It went great, although I'm sure you're aware, Dr. Toffoli, that any surgery is a crapshoot."

"Sure, but—"

"Who lives, who dies, or who next week is busting The Electric Slide. Despite one's expertise, there's always the specter of the known unknown. All you can do is your best, then move on." Trout gestured to the photo on the wall. "The most profound advice the venerable Doctor Jackson Ambrose, President Emeritus and patron saint of this hospital, ever gave me was to develop an immunity, not only to viruses and whatnot, but to the whispers of self-doubt. Banish them."

Julie squinted at him, thinking, *Oh my God, Nick was telling the truth. At least about his surgery being videoed. How could they do that?*

"Of course, I have no doubt your young man will be just fine, as he was in expert hands. Mine. I'll allow you to crawl back into bed with him tonight. However, for the first forty-eight hours, I request you refrain from any amorous activities. You did notice the catheter in his penis? Which is what we call a 'known known.' Good day, Dr. Toffoli." Trout turned on a Bruno Magli and re-entered Nick's room.

Julie realized she'd been artfully shown the door and outside of the patronizing snark, Trout had given her zero hard info. No time to work up a good fume as a shadow crossed her face, a shadow that was more like an indoor eclipse of every buzzing fluorescent light in the corridor. She looked up at the cause of this darkness.

"'Scuse me, sistah. Late for my patient."

Carmelo Iakopo, a three-hundred-and-fifty-pound scrub-wearing RN, who went about six-six, maybe six-nine if you counted his luxuriant head of hair, pulled up into a vertical man bun, hovered over Julie.

"Oh, sorry," said Julie as she took in his sleepy psychopathic eyes, gleaming gold tooth, and serpent tattoos crawling on his cheeks. She stood aside as he eased past her into Nick's room.

"Sorry," Julie repeated to his back and turned into the corridor, only to be almost flattened by a high-speed gurney pushed by a power-walking candy-striper.

"Beep beep," chirped the volunteer in the candy-cane striped dress.

Julie doubletaked as this raven-haired wisp blew past her. A raven-haired wisp who could have been a double for the French actress in *Amélie*. An undead ringer for the deceased candy-striper Nick had described in his drug-fueled dream.

"Sorry," Julie said and wondered why she was apologizing to everyone in the world. She watched as the candy-striper barreled towards the elevator bank. There's no way a gurney pusher would or should be moving a blanket-covered patient at high speed. A gurney moving that fast would be accompanied by a pack of doctors and nurses holding IV bags and trailed by an EMT barking vitals into a crackling walkie. That was the one cliché the TV medical shows got right. And that's why there were never any shows about black-lipstick-rocking candy-stripers racing gurneys solo. No, something wasn't right here at all. Julie tried to come up with one good reason what this poseur with raccoon eye make-up was doing in Nick's batshit dream, and couldn't. That had to be quite a conclave of crazy inside Nick's head.

Julie turned to go but stopped as she realized she'd stepped on something—an institutional sandwich that had fallen off the gurney. She picked it up; the saran wrap had come undone and Julie wrinkled her nose at a dicey looking tuna salad sandwich with a week-old eat-by date. She hustled towards the elevators to return it to the candy-striper, who was banging on the Down button as if that would make a car arrive faster. Julie approached the elevator and it became obvious that the head-to-toe blanket-covered "patient" on the gurney was either a four-hundred-pound corpse or the candy-striper was absconding with massive amounts of stale tuna salad sandwiches and God-knows-what other contraband.

"Hey! You dropped your lunch."

The candy-striper ignored her as an arriving elevator chimed, slid open, and she pushed the gurney inside. The look on the candy-striper's face was no longer chirpy and cheerful.

It was more like, *oh crap, busted.*

Julie could only watch as the elevator door closed and the candy-striper was gone. She looked up at the Art Deco brass floor-indicator arrow which manually ticked one hundred eighty degrees counter-clockwise *past* the Ground Floor and all the way to the last stop: B-3. Which meant the car had stopped at Basement Level Three.

Which Julie realized was impossible, because the sign above the elevator call panel read:

ELEVATOR DOES NOT GO PAST THE GROUND FLOOR.
ALL BASEMENT FLOORS PERMANENTLY CLOSED.

Below, the faded date affirmed:

HOSPITAL ADMINISTRATION - MAY 21, 1978

Julie, baffled by the mystery of how Goth Girl had absconded with eight zillion tuna salad sandwiches to a basement floor that supposedly no longer existed, turned to enter the adjacent elevator car but was bumped into by a white-coated Art Garfunkel doppelganger (circa 1969) who exited, face down in his phone. The tall, balding doctor with poufy side hair indicating a mid-life crisis follicly out of control, flashed an angry look that became a poorly concealed leer as he realized who he'd bumped into. Ever the gentleman, Dr. Kasper Klepstein, Julie's boss, put his hands on her hips to "keep her from falling."

Julie backed away but Klepstein went with her, like a spontaneous tango had just broken out. Except Julie didn't feel like dancing.

"Dr. Klepstein."

"Toffoli."

Julie looked for help. But the throngs of nurses, doctors, patients, pharmaceutical reps, and other healthcare detritus all seemed to have their eyes fixed somewhere else—anywhere else except on the middle-aged doctor with his hands on the young intern's hips—as if apprehensive that a viral #MeToo moment might break out. Julie returned the senior doctor's bemused gaze with a glare. Besides the Garfunkel hair, she noticed he also had a pronounced butt chin. She'd once read a study about those deep dimples, with the primary takeaway being that those so-endowed were notable for their deep insecurity along with voracious sexual appetites.

"Dr. Klepstein. Your hands?"

"Of course. Didn't realize."

Like hell.

Klepstein slid his paws off her. "So, tell me, my favorite First Year, when are you finally going to relent and share a meal with me?"

"How about now?" Julie plopped the leaky tuna salad sandwich into his wandering hands and darted into the elevator, which whooshed closed behind her. Klepstein stared after her as the mayo-soaked slime dribbled through his fingers and came to rest in an asymmetrical stain on his crotch. He bit his lip and scowled at the others in the corridor, none of whom saw a thing.[*]

*   *   *

[*] From 1996 to 2008, medical students at UCLA completed an anonymous survey after their third-year and reported how often they experienced physical, verbal, and sexual harassment. The most common perpetrators were fellow physicians of higher hierarchical power: attending physicians. One anonymous doctor stated: "Medical residents have fewer labor protections than Chinese factory workers."

"Nicholas, please to tell me on scale of one to ten, what is current level of pain?"

Dr. Irina Demidova pointed to a wall chart opposite Nick's bed. The pain levels were depicted by emojis that ranged from the happy-faced Number One, escalating to higher numbers featuring less cheerful faces with captions like *"Hurts A Little More"* to *"Hurts A Lot More"* to finally the Number Ten which was a suicidal death mask captioned *"Worst Pain Imaginable."*

Nick, teetering on a slender tightrope above the underworld, examined the pain chart like it was the Periodic Table of Elements and he had to memorize it for a test in Mrs. Lauberscheimer's Chem class next Thursday.

Wait, was that test next Thursday? Or was it today? No, no. Get a grip, Nick. There's no test. High school was nine years ago. And instead of the doddering Mrs. Lauberscheimer, the lady quizzing him was some Slavic sexpot with faulty syntax whose stethoscope dangled just below her bursting cleavage while her silver blue eyes twinkled as if he wasn't wearing any clothes.

Holy crap! Was he not wearing clothes?!

Nick blinked, took in the room as it came back into focus and wondered what the hell he was he thinking. The so-called Slavic sexpot was wearing demure scrubs and an elf cap. The skyscraping Dr. Demidova looked just like the rest of the medical rabble in the hospital room. Only way taller.

Hospital room?

Oh yeah. His hospital room.

Which he was occupying because he just had a spinal fusion. Right, Trout's "Full Isis." His nuclear option after countless failed therapies and procedures. Nick also remembered Julie being here at some point; they'd been talking and she didn't believe he'd slit Dr. Trout's throat.

Oh fuck! Trout! *Did* he slash the guy's throat with a scalpel? No, of course not. Because there he was. Alive and well in a snowman suit standing next to Mrs. Putin, the two of them hovering over his bed.

Julie was right—it was a dream. Except it sure hadn't seemed like a dream. As he untensed, the post-op pain flooded over him. Jesus, this hurt. But okay, whatever; at least he understood the where and why of his present circumstance. He was also conscious enough to realize his hiked-up hospital gown was riding perilously close to his junk which …

Holy shit! There was a tube coming out of his dick! And flowing through the tube was a river of piss. Which meant the tube thing was a catheter!

"Nicholas?" repeated Demidova, "What is pain level?"

Nick struggled to speak, "Um, eighteen? And when I breathe, it's more like fifty." A cough caught in his throat, already sore from the intubation tube, and he began to choke.

In an instant, like creating a hole for a running back, the O-line sized nurse with the serpent tattoos separated himself from the medical huddle, rushed to Nick's bedside, and proffered a fresh cup of ice chips. Nick sucked on the ice and his cough quieted.

"Thanks man," said Nick, squinting. There was something familiar about this guy. But what exactly?

Carmelo Iakopo leaned in close. Nick thought he saw the serpent tattoos squiggling on the guy's pockmarked face as Iakopo said, "No problem, brah. Now tell the doc a number between one and ten."

"It's eighteen. At least."

Iakopo flashed rage, a transient fury only Nick seemed to have noticed. Wheels began to turn inside Nick's head, but they were stuck in the memory mud as Nick whispered to the nurse, "I know you, right?"

"Yeah, you know me," Iakopo whispered back.

"From where?"

"Don't worry, it'll come back," Iakopo said softly, so only Nick could hear. "In da meantime, I'm gonna take real good care of you. Dat's a promise."

Iakopo stood and spoke to Nick in normal volume for the benefit of the room: "Now tell the doc your pain level, from one to ten."

"Ten?"

Trout held up three fingers to a med student taking notes on an iPad. The student nodded and inputted the Number 3 as Trout took a step forward. "Nick, listen to me. Listen and concentrate, son."

"I'm listening, Doc."

"Excellent. Now tell me, beyond the *expected* level of post-surgical pain, how do you feel? Specifically, your right leg? The one that's been numb and weak these many months." Trout cocked his head back to his crew. "Quite often, post-fusion, the majority of my patients notice an instantaneous cessation of referred nerve pain. Somewhere in the range of seventy percent. Well above the norm."

Demidova, her voice echoing from somewhere up Trout's ass, added, "The difference is famous Templeton J. Trout touch."

Trout smiled his thanks (she would get that famous Templeton J. Trout touch later) and resumed to Nick, "So, what do you say, champ? How's the leg?"

The med students watched the scene closely, each one committing to memory Trout's every move, mannerism, and vocal inflection, ensuring that Trout's modality of arrogance and feigned empathy would be passed on to the next generation of cutters.

Nick concentrated hard but shook his head in defeat. He felt terrible about letting the great surgeon down. "Sorry, Dr. Trout. But inside it's like everything's still numb and tingly."

Trout glanced to Demidova, who placed a stainless-steel instrument that featured various needles; a spiky, jagged wheel; and a reflex hammer into his waiting palm. Basically, a neurological Swiss Army knife.* Not their first rodeo.

"Close your eyes, Nick, while I try something. You might feel a little prick. And no, definitely not mine." The acolytes dutifully tittered. "Close your eyes."

Nick didn't have to be told twice; his eyes, heavy-lidded to begin with, crumpled closed with assists from pain, gravity, and opiates.

It was a good thing Nick wasn't watching. Because Trout jabbed one of the needles into his calf. On the street, minimally a misdemeanor; here, a medical test. But Nick didn't feel a thing. "When are you going to do it, Doc?"

"Next time, son," said Trout, slipping the Neuro7 back to Demidova. "On second thought, you've been through a lot today and it's quite early in the process. Don't worry, your nerve issues will resolve within twenty-four hours." Trout patted Nick's shoulder, "I guarantee it."

Nick, dry-mouthed, again on the verge of dipping back into unconsciousness, whispered something inaudible.

"What is it, Nick?"

Nick forced himself to find the strength to speak. "When can I go home?"

The elves rolled eyes and stifled smirks. Demidova shut them up with a glare as Trout looked at Nick with ill-disguised frustration.

"As soon as possible. I get it. You don't want to be here and

---

* Called a Neuro7 Neurological Device

likewise EZ♥Care doesn't want to pay a penny more for your bed than they have to. Because your bed not only includes you, it includes the costly equipment you're hooked up to, the unionized nurses who monitor the equipment; the techs who input the info, and the software analysts who dissect the data to develop smarter programs so the next generation of patients will receive improved cost-effective care. Bottom line, Nick, a spinal fusion in the old days used to mean at least a week in the hospital. But as long as you remain infection-free, I'll release you as soon as you can hit a high C on the butt trumpet."

Nick squinted at him, confused. His brain not ready to process any Oscar Wilde just yet.

"You must expel gases through your anus, Nicholas," Demidova translated.

Trout, who'd had enough of this, cued Iakopo who opened the connecting hub on Nick's peripheral IV line and injected him with the warm glow of Dilaudid.

"Go to sleep, Nick," said Trout. "By the way, when you wake, it's imperative you get out of bed and do some hallway walking. You don't have to go far, but you do have to walk. Nurse Iakopo or any of the staff will assist you. If you want to get out of the hospital anytime soon, you must walk. Shake those insides loose. Got that?"

Nick nodded like a drunk. A drunk with a sudden moment of clarity as he realized what was familiar about Iakopo. But just as quickly, his eyes closed. Trout and elves pivoted out the door to their next patient. The room was emptied save for the sounds of the monitoring equipment, the lingering scent of aftershave and ammonia, of perfume and piss, and the soft moan from Nick as he dreamt of where it had all gone wrong.

CHAPTER 8

Last Year At Lakewood Park (I)

Smoke from a spring barbeque dissipated into a pale sky that cloaked Lake Erie in gray. Beyond its white-capped wavelets jutted the downtown Cleveland skyline where chrome and steel duked it out with stone and brick, with the loser being an architecturally unified civic vision. But unless that was Frank Lloyd Wright peering through a pay telescope from the curving Solstice Steps, who cared? The view was still breathtaking. It was still C-Town.

The sounds of Lakewood Park were an aural kaleidoscope where the shouts and screeches from the fortresses of Kids Cove and the thump of tennis balls on the hard courts didn't stand a chance against "Hang On Sloopy"—the official song of Cleveland's three major sports teams—as banged out by a teenage cover band on the bandshell. Never mind the brutal harmonies and out-of-tune guitars, the boys sang the anthem of their fathers and grandfathers with the exuberance that comes with playing one of the greatest garage band jams of all time.

Over the bandshell, smoke from the nearby BBQ drifted past a banner which read:

"WELCOME TO THE EZ♥CARE
ANNUAL COMPANY PICNIC"

Not far from the stage, an apron-clad chef wielded a pair of stainless-steel tongs over a Fire Magic Echelon Diamond Grill, replete with infrared burner, 1056 inches of cooking area, and a remote-controlled hood with a "Magic Window" to regulate temperature. Negating all that high-end gadgetry was the low-end chef himself: Jimmy Tom Muscat, EZ♥Care Health Solutions CEO. Muscat, an ex-jock gone to jowl, a bottle-blonde alpha dog sniffing at the fire hydrant of his fifth decade, wore a ketchup-splattered apron that read *"Jimmy Tom The CBO, Chief Barbequing Officer Y'all!"* He enjoyed playing the role of benevolent monarch, chef, and first baseman at the annual company picnic and cutthroat softball game. Problem was, Muscat didn't play well with others and was even worse at faking benevolence. It was much easier being himself: a crude, competitive control freak with intractable anger management issues. What normal humanoid, even a "CBO," would barbeque countless burgers and dogs for his wage serfs while pimping a seven-figure Louis Moinet "Meterois" watch[*] as if it were a twenty-buck Timex? Jimmy Tom Muscat, that's who. Muscat didn't give a good goddamn about smoke and grease damage to his ostentatious wrist ornament since today he was A Man Of The People and he wanted the people to know it. During the week, it was another story—Muscat would terrify boardrooms or bitch slap any state senator who had the temerity to ask him to testify about his monopolistic business practices—however today, Jimmy Tom Muscat was all smiles. But, good God, they sure made his jaw hurt.

Muscat always had one hundred percent attendance at his annual simulation of corporate magnanimity because his employees and their plus ones and twos and threes, all knew who paid

---

[*] A very limited-edition watch comprised of very limited pieces of the moon, an asteroid, and a Mars meteorite.

their mortgages and fed them—even if each year Muscat burned everything to shit. Wouldn't have mattered if he used the magic grill or rubbed two sticks together, since Muscat ascribed his annual scorched creations as "Cajun Style À La Muscat."

Year after year after year, the burgers looked like flattened cow patties and the links like shriveled dog pee-pees. At least, that's what Edith Wheaton, paper plate in hand, at the head of a long line of EZ♥Care employees, was thinking as a beaming Muscat gestured her to the grill. Edie was of comfortable late middle-age and wore Coke-bottle sunglasses that obscured a narrow face framed by a short, silvery hairdo. Fortunately, the sunglasses also obscured her look of revulsion at the incinerated roadkill Muscat had plopped on her plate.

"Hey, Aggie. Hope you like your wieners Cajun Style À La Muscat: sweet, thick, and juicy!"

Muscat laughed at his joke, as did the first ten employees in line. But not Edie. Possibly because Muscat didn't seem to know who the hell she was. "Excuse me, Mr. Muscat. I'm *Edie*. Edith Wheaton. I work in your outer office. Twenty-six years now. Aggie—*Agnes*—is a Senior VP in HR."

Muscat didn't miss a beat. "Damn! Of course! Edie! Yes! By God, it's you! Guess I'd better get me some peepers too!" He mimed taking Edie's glasses off her face and putting them on his. That slice of Marceau elicited more laughs, more forced this time, from the line. Bathed in chuckles, Muscat mimed replacing the glasses. "Well, so glad you could make it, Aggie. Totally touched, hon."

Edie was about to correct him again but Muscat was already looking past her. "Okay, darlin', see you around. Let's keep it moving, folks. Chop chop!"

Edie, dismissed, moved to the condiment table as the couple who were the twenty-first and twenty-second in line looked on and moved up two spots.

The couple is Nick and Julie.

One year ago.

One year ago, when the future was theirs. At least that had been the assumption.

One year ago, Nick walked upright on this earth; his body, at six-one and one-seventy-five, strong and vital; his back straight; his eyes bright, eager, alert; his face unlined and devoid of the dread that would come to define the later diminished versions of himself. One year ago, Nick's journey and destination were inevitable; why would he even think that his internal GPS might need some serious reprogramming?

One year ago, Julie by nature optimistic and an indefatigable striver, had felt empowered—no, had felt she'd the absolute right, the *obligation*—to speak her mind without worry or consequence. Like now, as she watched that ass clown Muscat committing slow-motion murder. No, not to the creatures on the grill; it was too late for them; but to his employees, future customers all, as the charred animal flesh he served seeded microscopic malignant cells inside their bodies with latent, patiently waiting Death.

"Did you see what he put on her plate? That's not barbeque; that's biohazard. I'm not touching it."

"Uh, Jules. We had an agreement, remember?"

"I'm reneging. That crap smells worse than the lake."

"I don't disagree and I totally respect your moral code. But you've got to respect I really want that promotion to VP Claims."

"So you're okay with me blowing off my principles so you can move up the ladder of this greed-driven "health" cartel, personified by the creepiest man in the world? Principles that are the bedrock of who I am?"

"Maybe just one or two of them. I mean you've got loads of other principles."

"This, Nick … this is how fascism begins." Julie did her best not to laugh. This was too easy.

"Fascism begins with a hot dog? Jules, this guy thinks he's the lovechild of Bobby Flay and Paula Dean. Just toss it in the bushes when he's not looking."

"Did you just ask me to toss a decaying piece of animal pulp in the bushes?! Oh my God. You did! Ladies and gentlemen, I give you this year's winner of the BFF Of The Earth Award: Nicholas Glass!"

"Whoa. Jules. You're kidding? I won? I really won?" Nick feigned an Oscar® nominee's fake surprise on hearing their name called. "I am literally speechless. No, wait, I am not literally speechless. I have it right here." He took out his phone and pretended to read an acceptance speech from the screen. "I'd like to thank the Academy Members of the BFF's Of The Earth and all my team who've supported me through thick and thin. You know who you are, even if I don't. Also, I cannot leave the stage without giving a special shout-out to a certain white-striped skunk who, during the After Party, will scarf down the dog dick Julie Toffoli tossed in the bushes. I like to think of Julie's selfless act as doing a solid for a skunk who wasn't born with the privileges the rest of us have. Wait … what's that music I'm hearing? I'm being played off?"

The cover band had moved on to assassinate "Louie Louie."

"No! I will not be silenced! Because I still need to thank the love of my life, my inspiration, my ethical core, my … Damnit, Jules! The rat bastards cut off my mic!"

Nick put his arms on Julie's shoulders which were shaking in laughter. "Hey, I'll take out a half-page ad in *BFF Of The Earth Monthly*. That's a promise." Nick removed his hands from her shoulders and waved to the waiting line, "Goodnight everybody! Goodnight and God Bless!"

Everyone applauded as Julie tried not to lose it; she loved playing him like that. And he loved giving it back. The two of them, soulmates since before they'd ever heard the expression, and once they had, banned it from their vocabulary. Because platitudes like "soulmates" didn't come close to defining the essence of how they felt about one another. *Soulmates, lovers, betrothed*: all inadequate to categorize the magic that had bonded them since the eighth grade.

Julie faked a pout. "Alright, Nicky. Since you are this year's BFF Of The Earth, I won't get you in trouble with your cretin of a boss."

"Honey, you can't even try to get Nick Glass in trouble," said Agnes Umphrey, the lady in line behind them, who had slow-clapped Nick's "acceptance speech." Aggie, like Edie, was of late middle-age and also had short, silvery hair and Coke-bottle glasses. The difference was she was African American. So perhaps Muscat was merely colorblind when he confused his two longtime employees, or, more likely, he had defaulted to his baseline state-of-being: a clueless creep.

"Your boy is gold with Mr. Muscat. Trust me, I know of what I speak."

"Gold? Really, Aggie?" said Nick. "I don't think I'd put it quite like that."

"Me neither," said Julie. "I'd say more like pyrite or chalcopyrite. AKA 'Fool's Gold.'"

Aggie shot a look over to Muscat at his grill and lowered her voice. "Herb Smyly, Executive Senior VP HR, told me Muscat's got Nick fast-tracked to VP Claims."

Julie beamed. "Wow. How cool. Definitely better than BFF Of The Earth. I mean just ten months ago you were in the mailroom working your way up from Hitler Youth to …"

Aggie shushed them, "Keep this on the down low. Act surprised when it happens. And Nick, it'd be good if you could get a couple hits in the game later. Maybe a homerun. That would seal the deal. You know how he is."

"Yeah. I know how he is," said Nick as Muscat's voice commanded, "Next! Who's next?"

"That's you two," said Agnes. "Good luck."

"Nick! Get your butt over here!" said Muscat, clocking Julie as he spoke. "And bring that super fine young lady with you."

As they left Aggie for Muscat with smiles of thanks, the older woman's own smile was tempered by her knowledge of the price of that promotion. But maybe those two had it in them to get over, she mused as she watched the young couple face down the Devil.

Muscat's gaze lingered on Julie's *Médecins Sans Frontières* tee as he asked Nick, "How ya doing, son?"

"Great. Thanks."

"What is that, Greek or something?" Muscat pointed at Julie's chest.

"It's French for 'Doctors Without Borders,'" said Julie.

"Ah, them fellas. Talk about a hard way to make a buck. So Nick, where's your manners? Aren't you going to introduce me to your lady friend?"

"Actually, my fiancé, Mr. Muscat. This is Doctor Julie Toffoli."

"Doctor?"

"Well, almost …" Julie's explanation was cut short as Muscat let Blanche Dubois into the house.

"Doctor!" Muscat swooned, feigning dizziness. "Thank the Lord there is a doctor in the park, because all of a sudden I'm feeling rather poorly." With a limp wrist he fanned the smoke rising from the BBQ. "Perhaps it's the vapors," he fluttered.

"I'm not a doctor yet, Mr. Muscat. Nick's jumping the gun a bit."

"By what? Three weeks. Julie's about to graduate from med school."

Muscat returned to being Muscat. "Say hey, that's just great! Congratulations, young lady." He regarded Julie with a calculated admiration. "Where're you doing your residency, Miss Toffoli?"

"Right here in town at—"

"One of the famous medical centers at University Circle?"

"Actually, Cleveland Mercy."

"Ah, today's opponent in the Big Game. My good buddy Josh Przybylowicz or however the hell you pronounce that eyechart of a name, is CEO there. We do business—except today he's my arch enemy."

"Well, since I'm not officially at Cleveland Mercy yet, I'll be rooting for Nick and you guys."

"I darn well hope so. Anyways, I like that hospital. Even though she's a prehistoric decaying edifice. Kind of like my first wife." Muscat clanked a rim shot with the tongs on the flaming grill. "Baa-dum!" The intense smoke sent him on a coughing jag as he croaked, "The thieving bitch." Rallying from almost singeing his eyebrows off, he looked back to Julie and theatrically rolled his eyes.

"They say that old hospital's haunted, you know."

"I hear that's a myth perpetuated to keep interns in line."

"Maybe, maybe not. Hell, half the place has been condemned since the seventies. What with that vermin-ridden unused basement: a waste of commercially viable space, if you ask me. Nonetheless, I wish you all the luck, young lady."

"Thanks."

"You're most welcome. By the way, call me anytime. I'd love to sit down and chat about your future with EZ♥Care, Doc."

"Well, there is the slight matter of me completing my years of fellowship first," said Julie who shot a horrified glance to Nick as Muscat turned to get a dog off the grill.

"I'll wait," said Muscat as he plopped his charred creation on her plate. "The one thing I have is patience. And the one thing you'll have are patients. Enjoy now."

"Thanks." Julie dry-swallowed and did a quick turn to the condiment station.

Muscat watched her go, or more accurately watched her backside go, as he winked at Nick and lowered his voice, "Nice going, son. Not only a truly awesome ass and a pair of chesticles that'll poke your eye out, but a friggin' doctor too. Score!"

Nick resisted punching his boss's lights out and instead held out his plate. However, there was no carcinogenic protein forthcoming.

"Sorry, Nick. No pups for you." Muscat pointed to the cooler full of beers next to the grill. "And no suds either. First pitch is in one hour and I don't want my best player, my former MAC Player of the Year, bloated and blasted."

"Don't worry, sir. This is softball."

"It's *fast-pitch* softball. Besides, the term softball is a misnomer; they're as hard as regular baseballs, just a bit bigger." Muscat leaned into Nick and went from genial to fierce in a flash. Grease, sweat, and vehemence dripped from his face. "Look, I don't care if it's a fucking beachball; the point is I want to win. Like I do every year. Don't suffer any illusions, Nick. You're employed at EZ♥Care because of your bat and waning celebrity. Any monkey can push a pencil. I'm expecting you to win this damn game and carry us on your back through another undefeated season. Got that?"

"Yes sir." Nick noticed people starting to stare.

As did Muscat. He pulled back from Nick, smiling like a socially maladroit alien who'd unwittingly let his humanoid mask slip to reveal his true grotesque form. He clapped Nick on the back.

"Great. Go help yourself to a kale salad or whatever healthy shit they got at the next station and drink a couple of cans of that energy drink I got you. See you at warm-up."

"Yes sir."

Nick split toward the next station but as he passed the BBQ, unnoticed by Muscat, he snagged a brat off the warming rack.

Muscat, oblivious as a dissolute tsar in his end days, called out. "Next! Who's next?"

Aggie replaced Nick at the altar of the grill. She stared at Muscat without expression. If Muscat realized he'd earlier mistaken the white Edie with the Coke-bottle glasses for the black Aggie with the Coke-bottle glasses and same trim hairstyle, he wasn't going to let on.

Aggie clucked her tongue and without innuendo said, "I'd like my wiener Cajun Style À La Muscat: sweet, thick, and juicy."

Muscat scrutinized her. Was this woman making fun of him?

Her expression, though, remained a cipher. "Hold the spunk," she added as fat dripped onto the gas jets and spewed flames like hellfire into the air.

CHAPTER 9

Hold The Junk

Nick lay in the darkness of his hospital room, swimming in the shallow end of the post-op Dilaudid injection. His sallow face, which bore so little resemblance to his keen presence at the BBQ, was beaded with rivulets of sweat, his hospital gown drenched as a ragtop spindling through a carwash with the top down. A carwash that, instead of featuring the fake new-car smell, used the less popular Lysol-and-urine fragrance.

Dried spittle crusted on Nick's unshaven chin as he half-grinned and murmured, "Hold the spunk," and croaked a dry-mouthed laugh.

His eyes closed as he was again returning to the void when a familiar voice intruded, "What? You asking me to hold your junk?"

Nick's eyes cracked open to see an insulted Carmelo Iakopo RN hovering over the bed. He had placed a tray of equipment on Nick's bedside table. "You think I'm some kind of *māhū?* Hold your junk? Okay, brah. If dat's what you want. I'm here to serve." Iakopo snapped on a pair of gloves as Nick tried to cry out, but his larynx was dry as a Cali drought.

Nick stared at Iakopo's disfigured face. It nagged at him: there *was* something familiar about the guy who was about to squeeze the life out of his not-so-privates. And not just familiar from here in the hospital. But where? It still wasn't coming.

"Check out dem ceiling cracks, brah. Dey look like Baby Jesus with a woody to you?"

Nick fell for it. As he looked up, Iakopo lifted up Nick's gown, stuck a ten-milliliter syringe into the balloon port of Nick's catheter, deflated it, and yanked the catheter out of his penis.

Nick's screams echoed through the ward as Iakopo shrugged. "Guess not."

"Oh fuck oh fuck oh fuck," Nick moaned as Iakopo tossed the used catheter into the biohazard trash receptacle and gave Nick a plastic urinal from a countertop.

"Piss in dis. But don't pour it out. I gotta measure how much you go, for the Doc. And don't worry if there's a little blood. Or some pain. Pain's a good thing, let's you know you're alive."

Iakopo's cell buzzed. He checked out the Caller ID and answered, turning his back to Nick, who couldn't have cared less because it felt like a plumber's snake had just been run through his dick. After listening to the question on the other end, Iakopo glanced back to Nick before whispering into the phone, "He's feeling awesome. You couldn't be happier." Iakopo ended the call and watched Nick writhing in his sodden bed. He looked to the whiteboard on the wall that showed what meds were given to Nick and when. He produced another syringe from his equipment tray and bent over Nick, who recoiled in terror.

"Hold still, brah. Dis one you're gonna like." Iakopo opened and inserted another dose of Dilaudid into Nick's IV line. Nick calmed as the narcotic spread through his bloodstream and bathed him in a warm, safe feeling like no other; a feeling better than sex, better than hitting a baseball, better than …

His eyes closed.

"*Mele Kalikimaka*," said Iakopo as he removed the syringe, closed the line, made an entry on the whiteboard, and lumbered out the room.

Nick's last fragment of clarity before the blackness came was the realization of just where he had seen this sick fuck before.

CHAPTER 10

Last Year at Lakewood Park (II)

A softball, traveling an astounding eighty-nine miles per hour delivered from a pitcher's rubber only forty-six feet away, smacked like a gunshot into a catcher's waffle-grill-sized mitt.

"Yeah! Dat's what I'm talkin' 'bout!" shouted Carmelo Iakopo, catcher for the Cleveland Mercy Healers softball team, as he hocked a loogie. "Bring it, brah!" he said, ignoring the brown spittle dripping down the steel grates inside the mask that he'd neglected to lift before spitting.

Standing behind Iakopo, an elderly umpire wearing gray pleated slacks, an old-fashioned "balloon" chest protector over a navy blazer, and a cap with the initials CDP, hollered "Play Ball!"

In the on-deck circle, the waiting batter tapped the knob of his bat onto the reddish clay dirt. The weighted doughnut slid off the bat and improbably rolled to the third-base dugout like a caveman's beta wheel, where Jimmy Tom Muscat, wearing a faux-Yankees pin-striped uniform with **EZ♥CARE KILLERS** stenciled across the chest, picked it up and exclaimed: "Awesome! A sign from the Baseball Gods! We're going to roll those bitches!"

The scores of his employees packed on the bleachers over the dugout mumbled uncomfortable agreement, as Muscat bellowed towards the field, "Take that mammerjammer's head off, Nick!"

Nick, the batter in the on-deck circle, flinched.

As did Julie, who was sitting in the first row with Edie and Aggie. The ladies' expressions were stoic; Muscat's taunts were nothing worse than what spewed out of his mouth every day at work. Julie, though, couldn't hide her distaste for this narcissistic shitheel. She watched as Nick settled in the left-handed batter's box.

Nick fussed with the Velcro on his batting gloves as he regarded the Cleveland Mercy pitcher, a hotshot orthopedic resident named Montana, who had elicited oohs and aahs from both sides of the crowd with the electric speed of his warm-up pitches. Nick knew he could hit Montana. He'd hit guys with dumber names and smarter stuff back in the Minors. Before Cleveland released him.

See the ball, hit the ball. Every coach he'd ever had—from the aggressive Little League dad (not his Dad; no, never his Dad) to the bantam rooster at Kent State, where Nick starred for the Golden Flashes—had recited Pete Rose's oft-repeated mantra: *See the ball, hit the ball.* And Nick could hit the ball. Better than anyone in the Mid-American Conference East Division, three years running.

Nick knew that old saw about hitting worked; but it worked for him so long as he could clear his mind of the stakes. Back at Kent State, the stakes hadn't been *whether* Nick would get drafted by a Major League team, but in what round? He was that good. His future, his earning potential, had depended on where he was picked. Were he chosen in the first couple of rounds, he likely would've been fast-tracked to the Majors. At least, had a good shot. But if he was a low pick, an afterthought, his career track would've been nothing more than cannon fodder to fill out a Minor League roster, a body to play against the budding stars who were supposed to make it. Nick's baseball journey would've been a decade of eight-hour bus rides, a gut-load of Big Macs, sleeping two to a room in every Motel Six on the circuit, and finally, when age and apathy had eroded his skills to the point where he couldn't cut it any longer, it would have been time to find a real job. One of those plentiful Rust Belt jobs that correlate to no skills, no life.

Well, that was … before.

In the here and now, the payoff of excelling in what should be a stress-free company softball game was essentially his second shot at the Major Leagues. The Major Leagues of Healthcare. And although the game was fast pitch softball and this Montana guy (Montana who? Billings? Missoula? Bozeman?) was nothing like the MAC hurlers Nick had dominated a few short years ago, the orthopedist named after the forty-first state could definitely bring it.

The ump pointed to Montana, who threw a blur of a riser that Nick punished with an even quicker swing. The ball flew high and deep down the right field line, most likely never to be seen again …

If it hadn't collided with one unlucky Great Black-backed seagull, the largest of its kind in the world. An instant ago, the gull had sported a magnificent six-foot wingspan; now it was vaporized.

A diffuse cloud of reddish-stained feathers, most still attached to bits of seagull glop, parts of intestines, and contents of said intestines—including what appeared to be an undigested Cajun Style À La Muscat link—rained on the field, mostly onto the bewildered Josh Przybylowicz, Cleveland Mercy right fielder, CEO, and born again ornithophobist. A collective groan rose from both sides of the bleachers, as more than a few spectators lost their lunch. Julie was horrified. Edie clutched Aggie's hand as a surreal stillness settled over the ball field, with players and fans in collective shock.

But not the white-haired ump. The creaky geezer was unfazed. "Ground-rule double!" he barked and pointed Nick to second base, where an acne-blighted teenage base umpire brushed a feather off his shoulder.

Nick dropped his bat and trotted to second, as a vein-bursting Jimmy Tom Muscat stormed home plate.

"Blue! That was a homerun!"

Muscat went grill to mask with the ump, who was not intimated. "Get out of my face, buddy."

"One, I'm not your 'buddy' and two, you can't call what was going to be a homerun a ground-rule double!"

"I just did. Next batter."

"No no! Hold on, old man. Are you freaking blind?"

"Not yet. And my hearing aids work just fine. I suggest you calm down."

"Calm down!?"

The ancient ump apparently wasn't aware that no one told Jimmy Tom Muscat to calm down. The CBO began to kick dirt and wave his arms like the crazy old-timey baseball managers he'd seen on TV. "Listen to me, you fucktard. That ball had homerun distance! Not only would've it exited the playing field, my boy hit it so hard it would've traversed the Earth five fucking times before coming down! That, Blue, was one glorious homerun and you fucking know it!"

"Except a seagull got in the way. The rules are clear. The fowl was fair. Ergo, ground-rule double." The ump bent on arthritic knees and with his whisk broom brushed home plate clean of pieces of seagull beak and feathers. "And call me a fucktard again, you're out of here. Next batter."

Muscat, out of control, lunged at the ump, only to be grabbed by Iakopo, who tossed his mask away and spoke to him in calm, soothing tones.

"Hey, brah. Yeah, you gotta point. Dat woulda been a homerun if da bird didn't interfere, but think about it. It ain't worth getting thrown out over. Your boy's in scoring position and we're just getting started, so let's play the game. Just sayin.'"

Muscat, locked in embrace with the massive soft-spoken catcher, acceded. "Okay, son. You make sense. I'll drive him in myself." Iakopo let him go and Muscat nodded his thanks, before turning and spitting at the feet of the old ump. "Just so you know, Blue, I'm calling the Superintendent of Rec and Parks to make sure you never so much as call a tee-ball game ever again."

"I'm quivering in my jock." The ump clipped the whisk broom to his belt with one hand, while the other reached inside his blazer and emerged with a manila envelope, which he handed to Iakopo. "Would you be so kind as to give this to Mr. Muscat? Appreciate it."

"Yeah. Sure."

If Iakopo got a glimpse of the gun in the ump's shoulder holster when he took the manila envelope, he kept it on the down low. None of his business.

"The fuck is this?" Muscat reacted to the envelope Iakopo put in his hands.

"Probably da rulebook."

"I don't need no stinking rulebook!"

"Don't worry; it's not a rulebook." The ump removed his mask, revealing a deeply creased face topped by a full head of close-cropped white hair—the same brush-cut he'd sported since he left the Navy over four decades ago. "Giving you a rulebook, Muscat, would be a waste of time, since you don't have much respect for rules of any kind. No, what's in your possession—in front of the witnesses present—is an Official Summons, served to you by a disinterested party as required by law. Jimmy Tom Muscat: I'll see you in Civil Court."

"Court! What the fuck for?"

"Wrongful Death."

Mission accomplished, the ump dropped his mask and chest protector on home plate and limped off the field toward the parking lot. The base ump, prepped for his promotion, trotted toward home plate, picked up the equipment and said, "Runner on second, no down. Next batter!"

Muscat, holding the Summons, glanced at the departing ump.

"Who is that guy?"

"Him? He's the guy who paid me a hundred bucks to ump this game. Play ball!"

Nick stood on second base as a breeze swirled dust devils containing feathers and gull particulates about the diamond. He watched Muscat stomp to the plate and play to the crowd by taking vicious practice swings with his gold-plated bat. Nick didn't have to look to the bleachers above the EZ♥Care dugout to know Julie was disgusted. If it were anyone else who'd struck the gull with that lethal blast she would have left immediately; hell, she wouldn't have come to this joke of a picnic in the first place because it was no secret in the medical community that Jimmy Tom Muscat's monomaniacal buffoon act was simply that—an act. No one could have amassed the all-encompassing regional medical empire he had without being a zillion times more ruthless than anyone else. Shoe on the other foot, though, Nick would've done anything for Julie. That went without saying.

The teenage ump had enough of Muscat's showboating. "Sir, if you don't get in the batter's box, we're not going to get all nine in before curfew."

"Why don't you shut the fuck up, Pizza Face."

"You already have a Court Summons; you want a Forfeit too? Don't matter to me; I already got paid."

"Hey, cool your jets." Muscat stepped into the right-side batter's box. "Let's do it."

The ump pointed at Montana to pitch. Iakopo settled into his crouch as Muscat clenched his bat like a murder weapon. The pitcher windmilled a bullet of a riser that whooshed high and inside, headed straight at Muscat's head. The CBO's body Gumbied to avoid decapitation and wound up in a tangled heap on the dirt. Adding violation to humiliation, the ball harmlessly clinked the knob of Muscat's bat for a foul strike.

"Strike one!" barked the ump as he clapped his hands in an up-and-down motion, the signal for a foul tip.

Muscat gathered himself, rose, and glared at the kid, who ignored him and pointed to Montana. The pitcher took his sign from Iakopo and threw an even faster pitch that slammed into the catcher's mitt before Muscat could get his swing started. Again, he lost his footing and crumpled in front of the plate. When he made it back to his feet, whatever dignity Muscat had left didn't make the trip with him because there was a bloody Great Black-backed gull feather stuck vertically to the top of his helmet. He looked around—and even though he had two strikes on him, Muscat thought it pretty cool that almost everyone in the park had their phones out and were videoing him at the dish. Well, he'd give them a moment no one would ever forget—footage they could upload to the internet. Go viral, yeah. He would get the I.T. geeks to put it on the homepage of the EZ♥Care website. Because Muscat *knew* he had this pitcher's velocity timed now. He gave a thumbs up to the fans and got ready to hit. This time, though, instead of going for the downs, he'd choke up, shorten his swing, meet the fastball, line a single the other way to drive in Nick, and give the EZ♥Care Killers the lead.

With the bloody feather still sticking out of his helmet, a demonic gleam in his eye, teeth clamped so hard he'd likely wind up with terminal TMJ, Muscat readied for the pitch.

Montana took his sign from Iakopo and went into his fierce windmill delivery …

… only to let go with a school-zone MPH change-up that Muscat, swinging out of his old-school sanitary socks, was miles in front of. The fluttering pitch landed in the catcher's mitt like a barn swallow gliding into her chicks' nest.

"Stee-rike three!" shouted the ump.

Muscat, at the apex of his violent swing, lost control of his golden bat, which went flying, handle over barrel, straight towards the EZ♥Care bleachers like a boomerang.

But this boomerang wasn't coming back.

The whirling cylinder whizzed past Julie, missing her by a sliver, and instead slammed into Edie's exposed right knee. Her shrieks echoed throughout the park along with the sickening sound of multiple bones shattering. Edie instinctively tried to stand, but her demolished leg couldn't support her and she pitched forward, smashing her skull onto the iron railing below. The impact of cranium meeting unforgiving metal sent Edie somersaulting over the rail, where she landed on a weighted practice bat in front of the dugout. Streams of blood sprayed all over the pinstriped uniforms of the EZ♥Care players as the poor woman, caked in red clay and blood, wailed in agony.

Edie's cries harmonized with the chorus from the shocked crowd. At home plate, Muscat got up, dusted himself off, and ignoring the commotion, confronted the kid umpire. "Blue, you realize I *did* check my swing." That's when he realized: "Hey, where's my bat?"

The queasy kid pointed behind Muscat, who looked back to the dugout. Edie's shattered body was being tended to by Julie.

Muscat feigned concern and reminded himself to say "Thoughts and Prayers" but then saw the sheer multitude of smartphones aimed his way. Shit. The hell with thoughts and prayers; the main thing he had do was make sure no part of this shit-show got on the internet. Especially if he'd killed the woman.

* * *

Fans and players of both teams stood with caps over their hearts in silent salute as EMTs lifted a gurney containing Edie into the rear of an ambulance parked down the third base line. Aggie, about to follow them inside, paused as Julie, disheveled and covered with blood, touched her shoulder and handed her Edie's smashed and blood-streaked glasses.

"I'll go with you. Do what I can do till we get to the ER and the real doctors."

"Bless you, honey, but you are a real doctor. And a fine one at that." She looked to Nick standing on second base. "What about Nick?"

Julie glanced out toward a concerned Nick who gestured *would she like him to go with her?* Julie shook her head *no, it's okay*, and turned back to Aggie.

"I'll text him. He can drive home. I'll Uber from the hospital and—"

Julie was interrupted by the braying Muscat standing at home plate with his arm around the shoulder of the teen umpire, like a terrorist with a hostage. "Look, could you get Aggie and that meat wagon outta here so we can finish the damn game?"

Aggie glared at him and shouted, "I'm Aggie! *She's* Edie! And you are a disrespectful punk ass bitch!"

Muscat's initial instinct was to tell her to fuck off. But his concern that the injured Edie might hire some high-powered litigator and sue his ass released his better angels from their solitary confinement in the Supermax buried deep in the part of his brain where ersatz empathy resided. He shook his head somewhere in the neighborhood of contrition-adjacent and said, "I apologize, Aggie. I lost control of my emotions—and my lucky bat. You tell Miss Edie I will make this right. Swear to God."

Aggie ignored him and followed Julie into the ambulance. An EMT shut the doors and went around to the driver's side. A quick blast from the siren, the rooftop cherries flashed, and the ambulance drove away.

Nick, standing on second base, frowned as Muscat returned to the dugout where he kicked over a bucket of Gatorade.

*   *   *

The sky had grown slate-gray, and the light towers buzzed as moth clouds made bad choices. The nearby bandshell was deserted. Sloopy couldn't hang on, and neither could the plus ones and twos and threes. The scoreboard showed the game was headed into the bottom of the ninth inning, with EZ♥Care leading Cleveland Mercy six runs to three. Muscat, about to head to his position at first base, pounded his mitt and shouted encouragement to his troops. "Three down and we're outta here. Then I want everybody to come by to my modest little manse in Chagrin Falls and celebrate. Don't broadcast this to your ladies, but select members of the Hard Knockers from the Burning River Roller Derby will be in attendance. Par-taay!"

"Mr. Muscat?"

Muscat turned to see Nick, still on the bench and untying his spikes.

"Hey, Nick. We still have three outs to get."

"Yeah, well that's the thing. Could you sub someone in for me? We still have five guys who haven't even played."

"What the hell are you talking about? What do you care about my scrubs?"

"You're right. It's not about them. This is about me. I'm done."

"For the inning?"

"For the season. I'm going to focus on being more than a pencil pusher."

"Whoa, Nick. That was a joke. You can't quit on me."

"Not on you. The Game. It's not fun anymore."

"Because you killed a seagull or because the Tribe cut you?"

"I don't know. I just know I'm done."

Muscat's expression, usually transparent as a toddler's, flashed rage—but if you blinked you missed it. "Okay, Nick. I don't like it, but I get it. You do what feels right for you. That's Rule Six in my book on personal growth which you got a copy of when you started the job. Far be it for me to stand in your way. But if you could just finish this last inning, help us seal the win, I swear to God I'll never ask you to play ball for the rest of your life. You okay with that, son? Three measly outs."

Nick began re-tying his spikes. "Thanks. I appreciate it."

"Hey, you gave me two great seasons. Go out a winner." He fist-bumped Nick who grabbed his glove and hustled to his position at shortstop.

*   *   *

Even though Cleveland Mercy had a runner at second base, all EZ♥Care needed was one more out and the abomination that had masqueraded as a game would at last be over. Muscat shouted encouragement to the EZ♥Care pitcher, a stout guy in his forties built for short bursts of dominance, not for nine humid and stressful innings. He was pitching on fumes. "Come on, Dewey. Put the big guy away and it's Hard Knockers for everybody! Let's do it!" Easy for Muscat to say, when the batter for Cleveland Mercy was the gigantic Carmelo Iakopo, and the bat in hands was the size of a SWAT battering ram.

Dewey blew out a breath and tried to put a little something extra on the pitch. But he was fresh out of extra. Iakopo flicked his bat and sent the offering deep into the night, never to be seen again. As Iakopo jogged passed first, he shrugged an apology to Muscat who whispered something back. Iakopo nodded as Muscat called to the ump: "Time!"

"Time," acknowledged the ump as Muscat walked to the mound and gestured for Nick to come in and replace Dewey. Nick passed a downcast Dewey, who took Nick's place at short.

At the mound, Muscat gave Nick the ball. "Just get this last out for me, son, then you're done. Jimmy Tom Muscat keeps his word."

The next Cleveland Mercy hitter, the guy with a chance to keep the game alive, to be a hero even, was Josh Przybylowicz—which meant he had no chance at all. Not that he was talentless, just that Josh had no intention of winning. Because losing to Jimmy Tom Muscat was a good thing. Losing would mean more lucrative EZ♥Care contracts for Cleveland Mercy. Winning would be losing those contracts. That's the way Muscat rolled. Not a hard decision. Josh stepped into the batter's box and prepared to make a credible out. He dug in, faked aggression, and waited for the pitch from Nick.

The pitch he knew would end the game.

Josh strode into the ball, jamming himself. The intended result was a weak pop-up to the pitcher's mound. A sure game-ending out.

Nick waved off the other infielders as he called out, "Got it!" He looked up into the hazy, halogen-tinged sky at the white ball which was spinning toward his waiting glove. Just to be sure, Nick repeated, "Got it!"

"No! It's mine!" roared Muscat (a former Youngstown State third-string linebacker) who was charging hard from first base.

Those three words were the last thing Nick remembered before everything went black.

* * *

Later, Nick would wonder why Muscat had tried to make that catch. The play had clearly been Nick's. In a logical world, the ball would have fallen into his glove, EZ♥Care would have won, and Muscat would've been happy.

Except Muscat would not have been happy. He wouldn't have been happy at all, because Jimmy Tom Muscat wouldn't have been remembered as the visual punctuation point of the win; he wouldn't have been part of the reason there was another golden trophy in his display case. All anyone would remember about the game would be local hero Nick Glass's majestic blast obliterating a majestic seagull; Muscat duped into accepting a lawsuit by an old man posing as an umpire; and most horribly (and virally) Muscat's lack of compassion after seriously injuring longtime employee Edith Wheaton with an errant baseball bat.

That's why Muscat needed to, why he *had* to, catch that final out.

That and the small issue of payback. After all, who on God's green playing field says No to Jimmy Tom Muscat and doesn't think there'll be consequences? Which is why, in attempting to snag the ball before Nick could, Muscat knocked him out cold.

File what happened next under Unintended Consequences, as the violence of the collision caused Muscat to take his eye off the ball for a millisecond, just long enough to lose it in the gauzy lights. Long enough for the spinning sphere to thump off Muscat's dome and carom into the darkness of foul territory beyond first base, as if the ball couldn't wait to exit this dumbass game along with everyone else.

As Muscat scoured the murk for the wayward ball, Josh, despite his best efforts to fake a leg injury, limp around the bases, get thrown out, and still lose the game—he even considered feigning a heart attack—couldn't help but score.

"Game!" called the ump as Josh reluctantly crossed home plate. "Curfew has arrived, the park is closed, and the game ends in a tie. Kissing your sisters is optional!"

*   *   *

Nick, alone, lay face down on the pitcher's mound. His mouth was dry and his tongue coated with dirt. He couldn't move. His back was on fire; worse, each time he inhaled it felt like a knife being plunged in to the hilt. He heard Julie's ringtone on his cell in the EZ♥Care dugout. It might as well have been on Mars. Nick closed his eyes, but there was no escape, only searing pain.

Maybe he was out for a minute, or ten, or an hour. It didn't matter because he still couldn't breathe without the knife cleaving through his spine. At first, all he could hear was the sound of cars gunning out of the parking lot. Really? They were just leaving him here? Only then did he hear the two voices. Shimmering, ghostly voices in the dark.

What do you want to do about da kid?

He's dead to me.

Looks like he's dead, period.

I don't give a flying fuck. No one quits on Jimmy Muscat. Ever.

Still. He don't look so good. I checked his vitals but—

Don't worry about it. I called my security guy to pick him up and drive him home. Let his cute doctorette take care of him. This is about you. There's been a recent opening in my line-up and Josh graciously offered me you.

What about my job at Cleveland Mercy?

You keep it. Except I pay your salary now. Whatever it is, it just doubled.

Awesome, brah. What do I gotta do except hit homeruns and shit?

I want you to be my eyes and ears there. I call you for a favor, you do it. Discreetly. You feel me?

Mos def.

Let's go, I'll buy you a Kona Brewing Company Longboard.

One life, brah.

Goddamn right.

Nick heard them walk away and opened his eyes. He saw Iakopo and Muscat stroll through the darkened park towards the parking lot like Bogart and Rains at the end of *Casablanca*, as Julie's ringtone played the final fanfare.

CHAPTER 11

Respect The 10

The phone kept ringing. Julie's ringtone. Nick's eyes opened but were unable to focus. He was still face down on the pitcher's mound at Lakewood Park.

No, that wasn't right. He was … where exactly?

Oh yeah, he was twisted on his side in the hospital bed. On his side, because it hurt too much to put pressure on the fusion sites. By the time the signal from his brain reached his hand, the phone on the bedside table had stopped ringing. He let his hand slump back to the dank sheet, sticky from jello and scratchy from cracker crumbs. He thought about calling for the nurse to change the sheet—until he remembered just who his nurse was.

Of all the gin joints …

Nick remembered the catcher and his boss walking away in the haze of the Casablanca Airport. No, was Lakewood Park.

I think this is the beginning of a beautiful friendship …

How could he have forgotten Carmelo Iakopo? Maybe because it was just one game. Just one life-changing game, that's all. His eyes again grew heavy.

He had no idea when they opened again. But open they were and he was staring at the Pain Chart on the wall, the one with the emojis representing the various pain levels from one to ten. Nick scrutinized their stupid faces, contorted in levels of wretchedness ranging from discomfort to death. The one thing they all had in common was they appeared to be mocking him.

No, they *were* mocking him.

And to prove it, Nick watched as the little fuckers jumped off the pain chart and sprung to animated life.

As they did, a reverby announcer intoned, "Ladies and Gentlemen, give it up for *'The Tormenting Ten,'* the all-singing, all-dancing, direct from Osaka, Japan, Pain Chart Emojis!"

Colored spotlights flashed in all directions, applause filled the air, as the ten pain emojis gracefully separated like dancers in a Busby Berkley musical and frolicked in front of Nick's face.

Nick closed his eyes to make them go away. This had to be another dream, another hallucination. But when his eyes blinked open again, they were still there. Flying all around him. They sounded like Alvin and the Chipmunks from his surgical nightmare, singing "Winter Wonderland" through the hospital P.A. while the security guards with the reindeer antlers had executed the candy striper, then him. But unlike his dream, they had a new set of lyrics:

> *How ya feel, Nicky? Don't your back feel icky?*
> *No time to feel glum, there's more hurt to come;*
> *No time to be Zen, pick One through Ten,*
> *Cuz your Dancing in a Pain Wonderland!*

The emojis came together for The Big Finish like the Rockettes. High-stepping, high-kicking, giving it their all.

> *Cuz your Dancing in a Pain Wonderland, Oh yeah!*
> *Dancing in a Pain Wonderland!*

Nick gaped as the Worst Pain Imaginable Emoji, Number Ten himself, the Star of the Show, stepped out in front, head-butted him right on the nose and said in a Chipmunk voice:

"Respect the Ten, bitch!"

Nick recoiled, closed his eyes once again, but when he summoned the courage to open them and confront those evil little pricks, they were once again inanimate and back on the wall chart where they belonged. Like nothing had happened.

He looked to the window; it was still snowing, and the Cupid's heart in the window with Julie and his initials was now just a smudged streak.

CHAPTER 12

Julie's Crucible

The sign above the hospital room door read "Room 421 East—Pediatrics." The laminated cards inserted into the slots on the door were more telling. In bright red letters on a white background, they read:"STOP! DANGER! INFECTION HAZARD! REPORT TO NURSES STATION BEFORE ENTERING!"

Inside the darkened room, Julie, wearing a mask, sat on a loose-legged plastic chair at the side of the patient's bed. Referring to hieroglyphics scrawled on a whiteboard, she transcribed the info into her iPad. She ignored the electronic dissonance from the machines that kept the patient alive as she inputted the medical markers with a meticulosity that bordered on obsessive.

But even obsessives need sleep; Julie's eyes grew dull and closed right in the middle of typing. Her head slumped and her right thumb slid across the keyboard like a narcoleptic Jerry Lee Lewis falling off the piano bench in the middle of a gliss. It was her twenty-eighth straight hour without any sleep. For this was one of the crucibles for first year interns, the infamous every-third-night thirty-hour shift.*

---

* Dr. William Halsted, the first Chief of Surgery at Johns Hopkins in the 1890s, considered the founder of modern medical training, required his interns to be on call 24/7, 362 days a year. Easy enough for the manic Halsted since he was addicted to morphine and cocaine, whereas Julie had to rely on stale, burnt coffee.

Most hospitals had done away with this archaic punishing baptism. It had only taken about a hundred and twenty-five years, as the dangers to residents and patients alike were obvious. Except not so much to Josh Przybylowicz. Josh skirted the Fed guidelines with the tacit support of the more influential doctors on the Cleveland Mercy staff, among them Trout and Klepstein, who kept alive the tradition of pushing newbies up to and beyond their limits. That rigorous rite of passage had been good enough for *them* when they were training. Residents could always regenerate; and if the rare collateral damage occurred, a patient lost to medical error committed by a fatigued trainee, then so be it. The final diagnosis would be a simple RBG, short for *Received By God*, followed by a discreet transfer to ECU, the *Eternal Care Unit*.

Above the bed a party banner read: "HAPPY BIRTHDAY, CHARLIE! FROM YOUR REALLY COOL NURSES ON 4 EAST!" Tied to the banner were balloons. It was the sharp hissing of a balloon gone rogue, zooming around the room, that snapped Julie back awake. She deleted the glissando on her screen and closed the tablet.

Julie glanced at the wall clock: 7:28. A compulsive look at her watch confirmed that. Time to go. She rose, picked up her iPad, about to leave, but instead put it back down. Grabbing a pair of nitrile gloves, Julie took a last look at the patient, Charlie.

He was a ghost-white twelve-year-old whose undersized body was accessorized with a spiderweb of wires, leads, and tubing; his breathing, raspy and weak, was assisted by a ventilator; his eyes were open, but vacant; his thin hair, matted to his head; his chest, concave. Julie wanted to flee but the more powerful impulse was not to take her eyes off him. She walked to the sink where she moistened a towel. As she wiped the boy's forehead she murmured, "Stay tough, little guy." Charlie's open eyes registered nothing. Julie leaned in to him, whispered through her mask, "You know, parents? Way overrated. Take it from me."

She exited Charlie's room into the deserted corridor but stopped in her tracks as the familiar sound of wheels clanking on linoleum signified a fast-moving gurney, not far away. A second later, around the corner came the mysterious candy-striper wheeling yet another overstuffed cart past her, headed toward the elevator bank. This gurney either had another obese corpse under the sheets or, more likely, another consignment of "borrowed" stuff. This time, the candy-striper (didn't she ever go home?) was accompanied by a thin young man in generic medical garb, with a thatch of long, stringy hair stuffed under a hairnet. His ID badge was turned backward. The kid had the coordination of a Halloween skeleton as he tried to help Raven maneuver the gurney over the lip of an elevator entrance. The wheels bumped against the lip, and a white cardboard box fell out from under the sheet. The kid tried to catch it, failed, lost his balance and fell backward into the elevator car, yelping. Raven kept her cool, picked up the box and pushed the cart inside.

Julie, curiosity thoroughly piqued, strode toward the elevators. Why and what was this candy-striper still doing here at night? And what contraband was she and Skeleton Boy transporting? And to where? As Julie double-timed it toward the elevator bank, she realized those weren't her real questions. She had just one, the same one; what the hell was this chick doing in Nick's dream?

Julie was almost at the elevator when two words from the intercom brought her to a standstill.

"Code Blue."

The Operator's voice was a flat monotone, a delivery designed not to alarm the civilians or remind them they were in a place where terminal outcomes occurred with some frequency. "Four-Two-One East. Code Blue. Four-Two-One East. Code Blue …"

The elevator door closed, but Julie had already turned and was sprinting back down the corridor. Four-Two-One East was the room she had just left and Charlie, her patient, was coding.

* * *

The monitors that told the continuing story of young Charlie's fluctuant life were no longer beeping and pinging: they were screaming. Julie's adrenaline trumped her exhaustion as—masked, gowned, and gloved—she performed chest compressions on the inert boy. She remembered a med school professor of a certain age who'd taught her class to think Disco when performing chest compressions. The Disco Doc's tune of choice was the Bee Gee's "Stayin' Alive" and the awesome thing about it was it worked. The prof had encouraged his students to sing it out loud because it kept you on beat. Which is what Julie was doing right now. "Stayin' Alive" had never been sung with this kind of desperation.

With Julie were the first responders of the Code Team—at the moment, Consuelo Goquiolay RN and three tense and tired medical students.

Josh Przybylowicz made it a point to recruit Filipino nurses as much as possible. They were well-trained but more importantly, excellent for his operating budget, and they didn't bitch about working nights and holidays. Also, they would never be so impudent as to correct a physician who'd made a minor mistake or become a whistleblower—because they knew Josh would have their asses deported back to Quezon City in a heartbeat. On the downside, mastery of the English language wasn't a strong suit for some, and that included Consuelo Goquiolay RN. She was often too embarrassed to speak up and therefore tough to hear or understand. Still, Nurse Goquiolay was all focus as she squeezed oxygen from a balloon into a tracheotomy tube while the med students, stumbling to get out of each other's way, affixed defibrillator pads onto young Charlie's chest. Through it, Julie continued the non-stop compressions, singing:

"Ah, ha, ha, ha, stayin' alive, stayin' alive."

She glanced at a monitor that had nothing but bad news on it, broke off the tune and ordered, "Get me a central line!"

"On it!" said Dimitri Inciarte, a senior med student who hadn't shaved in days, not because he craved hip-looking stubble but because he craved sleep after twenty-nine straight hours on his feet. In an attempt to steal a few minutes of down time, he'd been deep in his personal coma on a cot in a broom closet when the jangle of his pager alerting him to the Code call had woken him.[*] Inciarte ripped open a catheter kit and slathered antiseptic soap on Charlie's groin.

"Hey, Dimitri. Put on a gown," Julie said, continuing the compressions. "And let's get a drape on him. This isn't a practice dummy."

"Right. Sorry." Inciarte secured his gown as another student got the drape unfolded and situated. The third student began a transcription of the care given to Charlie: meds, timings, etc., the official record of everything that happened.

Julie continued with the compressions. A grueling one hundred a minute. Her forehead glistened as she looked at the monitor again: still nothing but tiny squiggles above the baseline. She knew the compressions weren't working but kept going as she yelled at

---

[*] No, Inciarte wasn't still living in the 1980s nor was he dealing drugs. Pagers have the ability to get through the heavily shielded walls of a hospital that cellphones can't. About 85% of hospitals still use them and no way was Josh going to invest in new technology that had no profit potential.

Inciarte, "Come on! Get that line in!" She resumed her singing, a prayer in rhythm.

Visible outside the door was the Attending, Kasper Klepstein—the doctor with the ultimate responsibility for Charlie and the guy whose predatory actions toward Julie were responsible for his earlier public humiliation by way of a leaky tuna sandwich. His insecurity-fueled anger burned hotter than the Code he could see was going down in flames.

This was the first time he'd seen Toffoli since the insolent bitch had pulled that stunt by the elevators. He could tell by the averted faces in the corridors and the ill-concealed giggles in the cafeteria the story had already made the rounds as fast as fingers could tap Send.

Well, fuck her. Payback's also a bitch.

Klepstein, dressed in sweats, dropped his gym bag with the handle of his E-Force racquet sticking out the top, puffed up the sides of his Garfunkel hair like a warrior going into battle, stepped inside the room, slid on gown and mask, snapped on a pair of gloves, and made his presence known.

"Sweet Jesus, Toffoli! Shut the fuck up!"

Julie stopped her chanting of "Stayin' Alive" as Klepstein roared two inches from her ear, "What the hell are you doing?! Don't you know Disco is dead? Go harder on those compressions, goddamnit!"

"I don't want to break his ribs."

"Then for fuck's sake, I will! Move aside."

Julie, exhausted, withdrew as Klepstein took her place. She looked at the monitor: still nothing. The look of failure on her face was jolted into one of shock as Klepstein ordered, "Light him up!"

"Everyone clear," said Nurse Goquiolay at a volume only those closest to her could hear.

This included the fumbling Dimitri Inciarte on the other side of the bed, who was still working on getting the central line threaded into Charlie's femoral vein. He shouted, "Wait! I don't have the line in yet!"

"Leave it, junior! Stand down!" said Klepstein.

As Inciarte backed off, Julie shouted: "Clear!"

Everyone took a step backward as Nurse Goquiolay pressed a red button on the defibrillator.

As the current shot through him, Charlie's matchstick body spasmed. Julie looked to the monitor but there wasn't even a squiggle now. Charlie was flatlining.

Klepstein barked, "Give me a round of epi, lido, and amiodarone. Epi first!"

Julie reacted viscerally. "What! No! That could kill him!"

"When I want your advice, Toffoli, I'll call Barry Gibb."

"It's too much, Doctor."

"Go fuck yourself, Toffoli."

Julie, about to snap back, instead jumped to get out of the way of a young medications nurse, Marietta Cuyegkeng, newly arrived to the Code and Cleveland Mercy as well. She maneuvered her way through the crowd and injected Charlie with a syringe of epinephrine. As Nurse Cuyegkeng backed away, she bumped into Inciarte who was trying to extricate the catheter line. In the process, he inadvertently elbowed Cuyegkeng, causing her to drop the uncapped syringe onto the bed. Inciarte didn't see it as he removed his own from Charlie. Blood flew everywhere from it as Inciarte uselessly held the catheter line in his hand.

"Shit! I blew the line!"

Klepstein, not looking at him, responded: "You. Leave the room. Toffoli. Put in the line. Think you can do that?"

"On it."

Inciarte, shamed, backed away. As Julie pushed past him, her only focus was on wiping the blood off Charlie's thigh and groin, getting the line in, and saving the kid's life …

… which is why she didn't notice she had pricked her gloved finger on the uncapped syringe, dropped by Nurse Cuyegkeng when she and Inciarte had collided.

As Julie re-inserted and began running the line, Klepstein continued with the compressions on the bruised, lifeless Charlie.

"Still fibbing," said Nurse Goquiolay in a quiet voice.

"Fuck! Charge the fucking machine! Now!"

Goquiolay's finger was already on the defibrillator's red button in anticipation of this move, when a teary Inciarte approached Klepstein. "Doctor Klepstein, I'm really sorry …"

"Why the fuck are you still here?!" Klepstein's outburst drowned out Goquiolay's timorous "Clear," as she pushed the button on the defibrillator.

Charlie's body again convulsed.

Julie wasn't ready for the second defib. Concentrating on the delicate threading of the line, she hadn't heard Goquiolay over Klepstein's bellowing at the apologizing Inciarte. The upshot being, as Charlie shuddered from the charge, Julie's masked face—but uncovered eyes—were on the receiving end of a blood burst from the recalcitrant line. Needing both hands to thread the line, she was unable to wipe away the blood. "What the hell! Someone wipe my eyes?"

Nurse Cuyegkeng slid under someone's outstretched arm and dabbed at Julie's face with a towel, as another voice cried out, "Still fibbing!"

"Goddamnit! One more time!" Klepstein ordered.

"Wait!" Julie called to Klepstein. "I'm in! Look at the screen!"

"We're out of time! Light him up! Now!"

"Clear," said Goquiolay as she hit the button again.

Julie watched, horrified, as everything modulated down for her. All sounds were slowed to the point of unintelligibility, like a seventy-eight vinyl playing at thirty-three rpm. She imagined Charlie's body levitating over the bed, as if he were ascending to a higher plane. Then she realized what bullshit that was. Her patient had simply died.

She closed her blood-flecked eyes. When she opened them again, Charlie was still a corpse and a red-faced Klepstein had ripped off his mask. He tossed his gloves and gown onto the floor and headed for the door. Nothing more to do here. Julie, breathing like she'd just run a marathon, gown and face soused with blood, watched his abrupt exit in bewilderment. That's it? Klepstein felt her gaze and paused. "What is it, Toffoli?"

Julie had plenty of questions, but she asked the easiest one. "Is there a family member or—"

"I'll deal with the family. Congratulations on a delightful clusterfuck. Call it."

He looked at his watch and frowned. Late for his game. He scooped his gym bag off the floor and was gone.

* * *

The detritus from the unsuccessful Code was scattered about Charlie's trashed room. The monitors were silent, the "Happy Birthday" banner lay trampled on the floor. Bits of blue balloons commingled with discarded EKG leads and IV lines, left for the cleaners to remove.

This is what failure looked like. Julie's first.

She sat on the wobbly plastic chair, inputting the details of Charlie's short life and forever death. Details she knew no one would ever bother to read. There were no advocates for Charlie;

no one required explanations or excuses. Julie stopped typing, sucked in a deep breath, and almost choked on it as her body trembled and tears fell unabated.

*   *   *

Julie didn't know how long she'd been crying but she knew that it wouldn't get the paperwork finished. She brought her tablet back to life and resumed. As she began typing, she noticed a drop of blood on the keyboard and realized her finger was bloodied. Where the hell had *that* come from? Zombie-like, she rose, walked to the sink and washed her hands. As she did so, she looked at her reflection in the mirror and also noticed a cluster of dried blood around her left eye. She stared at the face staring back at her. A fearful face. Julie scrubbed her hands and face until her skin was burnished coral pink. She flushed her eye with saline solution. Finished, she searched a cabinet for a band-aid and placed it around her finger.

Only as Julie walked back to her iPad, did she notice the uncapped syringe lying on the bed, where she'd been working on the catheter line. She put on gloves, tossed the syringe into the biohazard receptacle, sat back on the chair and resumed typing.

After a few words, she stopped. She stared at her notes on the screen. The words "HIV Positive" read like a Breaking News chyron. Julie closed the computer and noticed the small stain through her band-aid. She closed her eyes and tried to reconstruct each moment of this night, as if she could conjure an alternate ending.

CHAPTER 13

When Snowmen Fly

"Pa-rum pum pum pum," sang a distinctive baritone from inside a roly-poly Snowman costume.

Trout-as-Snowman lay back on a confetti-strewn, award-winning Vaya ergonomic office chair (because God forbid Trout himself would ever need back surgery) crafted by the same designer who had conceived the interior of the Porsche Boxster and also the Ferrari P4/5 for Enzo Ferrari. However, Trout wasn't driving anywhere in his Vaya chair, since he was handcuffed to it. The chair had been kicked out from behind an impressive desk and sat square in the middle of the debauched mess that was the aftermath of his Christmas party in his Cleveland Mercy/ EZ♥Care Penthouse Suite. Empty champagne glasses, vodka bottles, and party streamers abounded. Trout's snowman nose was aimed at the ceiling when a scrabbling noise interrupted his vocalizing.

"Aaaiiii! Where is snowman zipper?" asked a naked Dr. Irina Demidova as she popped up from the floor, a latex tress whip in her hand, and an askew angel halo on her head.

"There is no zipper. They're buttons, three of them on the pouch." Trout tried to keep the impatience out of his voice.

"*Da*. I try again." Demidova brushed the whip across his snowman face and dropped from sight. Pa-rum pum pum pum.

* * *

Trout's office hadn't always been a Penthouse Suite.

For almost a century, the top floor of Cleveland Mercy housed a warren of squalid and cramped wards that were frozen in the winter and sultry in the summer. These rabbit hutches were reserved for the poorest of the poor until Josh Przybylowicz—then the Cleveland Mercy marketing whiz and before that PR intern for the Browns—had a brainstorm. Josh, with his knock-off Kiton K-50 suits and under-the-basket floor seats at the Q, was always looking for new ways to monetize illness and death. All he needed for his latest scheme was an investor. Which was how he found himself hosting EZ♥Care's Jimmy Tom Muscat at a Cavs-Warriors game. The evening with Muscat turned out to be a stunning success—even the part where a seven-foot Latvian center, diving for a loose ball, knocked Josh batshit senseless. Because when Josh regained consciousness, not only did he have a thirty-buck cup of craft beer soaking his lap and a subdural hematoma soaking his brain, but, best of all, he had secured Muscat's funding.

Josh shut down the money-losing charity ward pronto and hired trendy architects and decorators to do a makeover. When his rebranding campaign was complete, he had an overflowing wait-list for the **EZ♥CARE PENTHOUSE SUITES @ CLEVELAND MERCY**, exclusive fiefdoms for the hospital's star physicians. The exorbitant rent plus the annual Suite Licenses eagerly remitted by social-climbing docs like Trout and Ganapur, dwarfed the pittances Medicaid paid for the parade of indigent patients' noxious one-night stands in the old charity ward. Hell, from now on those recidivist losers could go to Metro Health, who *had* to take them.

The renovation shot Cleveland Mercy from 363rd to 114th place on the U.S. News & World Report list of best hospitals and shot Josh Przybylowicz straight from Marketing to COO. Then—after a couple of years of nimble politicking and, when necessary, a well-placed blade in the back of a Board member supportive of something called "Patient's Rights"—he was crowned CEO.

Cleveland's historical house of healing was his. So was the brand-new medical office building across the street for the less high-flying docs. Josh's most satisfying triumph, however, was that his under-the-basket floor seats at the Q were moved to center court, where he belonged.

*   *   *

Along with the status befitting a Lord of the Penthouse Suites came another prized perk: total privacy. Which allowed Trout to be cuffed, flogged, and blown by the gorgeous Irina Demidova, his angelic dominatrix, while singing Christmas carols in his Vaya chair. He gasped out the last of "The Little Drummer Boy" as Demidova slithered up his snowman gut, showering him with kisses until she scraped her cheek against Trout's Harvard Medical School lapel pin, attached over his snowman heart.

One would have to ask a shrink why Trout so felt the need for professional validation that he would bother to take the time to stick his Harvard lapel pin onto his snowman costume. Since there was no shrink present, Demidova, not thrilled about having her lip pricked, asked Trout himself.

"Aaaiiii! Do you have to wear stupid Harvard pin on *everything?*"

"Yes."

"Why?

"Because it's part of me. It *represents* me."

"You need psychiatrist." She leaned over to collect the rest of her angel costume from the floor and slipped into it, one wing at a time.

Trout coughed. "Irina, could you uncuff me, baby? I'm hot as Hades in here."

Demidova did so. "You are hot everywhere, my Snowboy,"

Trout lifted off his snowman's head, gasped for air, and stumbled toward the coffee table where sat a glass bong painted with depictions of stethoscopes in bright African colors. He snagged a lighter off the table and fired it up.

"Jesus Christ. How are you supposed to walk in this dumbass costume?"

"Super careful." Crack! Demidova's whip slapped his snowman ass. "You want I take selfie of you and me? For next year Christmas card?"

"Hell no!" Trout, horrified, pressed his lips inside the rim as he milked the bong until the chamber was white with smoke. Holding in the hit, he passed the bong to the now mostly decent Demidova.

She demurred. "*Nyet, spaseeba.*" She wrinkled her nose as she glanced about the smoke-filled room. "We must air out place before cleaning crew come, no?"

Before Trout could reply, Demidova tottered toward the French doors that led out to a purely decorative Juliet balcony and pulled open the antique Bouvet door handles. Bad idea. A blast of wind and lake-effect snow blew her halo off and knocked her onto Trout's prized zebrawood desk, custom-cut from an endangered Cameroonian jungle. Party streamers swirled as bottles, glasses, and crystal smashed into walls. Demidova lifted herself off the desk and lurched back to the French doors. "Maybe is better I close."

"Nah, leave it. You're right. We need to ventilate this place or I'll be doing yet another song and dance for HR. How many times can I blame the Guatemalan janitors for getting high in my suite?" Trout chuckled before being hit by a depressing realization. "Dammit!"

"What?"

"I forgot to dictate my Surgical Note. You know, for the TV Special. The poor sonofabitch we made bionic. What the hell was that chump's name?"

"Nicholas. Nicholas Glass."

"Glass. How appropriate."

* * *

Outside the office, Nick paused in mid-knock as he overheard Trout's bon mot via the open transom above the door. He clung to his IV pole, struggling to catch his breath. His hospital gown and Kent State Baseball t-shirt, around which was fitted a rigid, constricting back brace, was stained with sweat. The exertion it had taken to walk from his room to the elevator, and from the elevator on the penthouse floor to Trout's office, had wiped him out. But Trout had ordered him to walk. And walk he had. Besides, Nick had a few questions for his surgeon.

Now, he would have loads more.

"Did not Bionic Man have superpowers after operation? This boy, Nicholas, he has superpowers of ten-year-old Rumanian glue sniffer."

"We did the best we could. Considering."

Demidova's drunken giggle culminated in an unladylike snort. "Templeton, you saw what I saw. His spine was like thousand grains of sand. Like sawdirt!"

"Sawdust," Trout corrected.

"*Sawdirt, sawdust, call it what you want but is impossible to grow new tree from sawdirt. That boy did not need six-figure spinal fusion. Of course, YOU do, my kotik; your ex-wife does; present bitch wife does; your girls' Hathaway Brown private school does; your Lamborghini Reventon dealer does; Marcel, my shoe consultant, does; but what that poor zadrota really needed was lifetime Pain Management and you know this. Back in Mother Russia, Nicholas would disappear to sanitarium in Siberia like that!*"

Her declaration was punctuated by a sharp thwack that sounded like a whip to Nick. He recoiled.

* * *

Inside the suite, the wind blowing through the French doors continued to send party streamers flapping like psychedelic bats. Demidova guzzled a shot of Stoli Elit.

"Also, Templeton," Demidova said as she wiped her mouth with her forearm, "Do not lie. You wished to be on TV news and internet. I saw how you look at reporter whore when she do thing with hair. You get big эрекции in pants."

"I got no such thing!"

"Not anymore," Demidova licked her lips and passed the bong back to Trout, who'd become somewhat pensive.

"I don't know; maybe you have a point. Maybe I should've sent the kid straight to Marty Ganapur and his Pain Management Chamber of Horrors right after I saw the first scan." Trout air-quoted the words *Pain Management*.

"Too late now." Demidova, shivering in her skimpy angel costume, knocked back another shot for fortification.

For fortification, yes, Trout thought, but also because drinking till unconscious is part of her Slavic DNA. He wondered how he was going to get her out of his office so he could get home to his wife and kids before it was technically Christmas.

"Also," Demidova grinned, "does not hurt you are equity partner in EZ♥Care OrthoTec, creators of titanium cage we put in Nicholas's spine."

"Hell, Irina, yeah, there's that—but if I didn't take him all the way downfield to the end zone, somebody else would've. Shit, every cutter in Northeast Ohio would've been standing in line to work with Jimmy Tom Muscat, their scalpels raised like … what do you call them in Mother Russia? Scimitars?"

"Your morphology is incorrect. Scimitars were used by Turks. Still, is vivid imagery, Templeton. But best you leave 'surgeons with scimitars' out of Surgical Note," she laughed, and threw back another shot.

"Don't you worry about that."

"Good, because the truth would be unwise, Templeton. Tragic, yes, like Tolstoy novel. But wise, not so much."

* * *

In the corridor, Nick was deflated; his eyes red and puffy. He'd been crying. *Had* been crying. Now, he was angry. He glanced to his hand which held his iPhone. The blue line moving from left to right indicated the Voice Memo App was recording every word said in the office. If Trout loved Russian Lit so much, Nick wondered if he'd appreciate a copy of Nabokov's *Invitation to a Beheading* for Christmas? Because it sounded like he'd already binged through *Lolita*.

* * *

Demidova, feeling a second wind—both from the still-open French doors as well as from the insane amounts of Stoli and spliff—began stroking Trout's snowman pouch. "Shall we pa-rum pum pum pum one more time, like hooligans in Gorky Park?"

Trout tossed her a regretful look and rose to his feet. "Next time, baby. I need to dictate that damn Note."

Demidova pouted and headed for the mahogany coat stand, as Trout wheeled his chair back to his desk and picked up a micro-recorder. "Just call me the Hunter S. Thompson of spine surgeons. Only difference is my prose will be colorful fiction and I'm not going to blow my brains out over it."

"Who is Hunter S. Thompson?" Demidova pulled a full-length Russian sable fur coat from the coat rack and was able to get most of it wrapped over her indecent angel costume. Indecent, in the sense that Trout couldn't remember any Biblical images from his childhood church days that had angels with one tattooed breast popping out.

"Never mind. Not important."

Demidova leaned over the front of his desk and laid a sodden kiss on him. "I go now. But first, Templeton, I wish to ask for little Christmas present."

"Irina, you're wearing your present. Do you know how much that sable—"

"No, something else. Something sweet and Романтический."

"What?"

"Templeton, I wish for you to think very serious about leaving bitch wife." She kissed him again on top of his head. "*Da?*"

"*Da,*" Trout replied as Demidova, with the scent of Clive Christian Imperial Majesty and sex wafting behind her, staggered to the office door and out into the hallway.

Trout waited till the door closed before muttering, "*Da fuck* you thinking, bitch!"

* * *

Demidova exited Trout's office, too baked to notice she didn't securely latch the door behind her. Instead, she scanned the hallway for anyone who might see her, anonymous as she was in a sable coat half-covering her fallen angel costume. She was in luck. No one there, nor should there have been on this exclusive floor at this late hour. Reassured, Demidova serpentined her way towards the elevator bank.

On her way she passed a tall Christmas tree. If she had paused to admire it, she might have noticed the top of an IV pole emanating from the "topper" ornament, a twinkling star.

But she didn't. She barely had it together enough to hit the DOWN button on the elevator on the third try. The car, already waiting there, chimed and opened. Demidova stumbled into the elevator, dragging the sable behind her. Bummer was, she was too slow and the door closed on the trailing end of the coat like a deli slicer. A Cossack curse echoed from within the departed elevator as a sliver of Demidova's sable coat was left behind, like a slice of uneaten pastrami.

Ripped sable coats were of no concern to Nick who emerged from concealment behind the Christmas tree. He dragged the IV pole with him as he padded back toward Trout's office, wearing a newly acquired look of resolution. The look of someone with backbone to spare—which wasn't quite the case.

* * *

Julie, changed out of her blood-streaked scrubs, eyes puffy, shoulders slumped, pushed the UP button at the fourth-floor elevator bank. A ping announced the arrival of a car. Before Julie could step in, Demidova tippled out. She clocked Julie, recognizing her from somewhere. But where? Who cares, no matter. She was still furious about having her sable snipped by evil elevator. She would make Templeton get her new coat. No, perhaps not yet. Now was more important he leave bitch wife.

Julie appraised the sauced Tatar. Any normal evening she would've been taken aback by the sight of a disheveled staff physician wearing an (almost) full-length Russian sable fur coat over an angel costume, albeit an angel costume more appropriate for jumping out of a cake at a Shriners convention. But this moment, this whole damn evening, wasn't even close to normal. She stood aside as Demidova lurched out of the car. Ignoring her, Julie entered.

Julie pressed the eighth-floor button; the door began its rapid close only to stop as the plastic angel halo was thrust inside. As the door re-opened, Demidova, halo in hand, stared at Julie like a dumbstruck physicist who had just figured out cold fusion.

"You are intern, yes? Girlfriend of Doctor Trout's spine patient? Nicholas?"

"Yes." Julie flinched as the elevator alarm clanged.

"Maybe you should get new boyfriend."

Julie, confused, shouted over the din, "What? What did you say?"

Demidova made like she was zipping her lips shut and withdrew her angel halo. The elevator door closed, the alarm stopped, and Julie was launched upward.

* * *

Trout sat at his desk, still in his snowman costume, sans head, and concentrated on the Surgical Note. He remained unconcerned about the open-air environment; it would take a cyclone to get the stench of sex, drugs, and alcohol out of his office and besides he needed to clear his head. The one on his neck, not the stupid snowman cerebrum inanely grinning at him across the desk. He clicked on the micro-recorder and pretended he was addressing the Nobel Committee for Physiology and Medicine: "Mr. Glass tolerated the procedure well. He was extubated in ICU, kept under observation until 15:00 when he was transferred to a private room where he is resting comfortably."

Trout frowned, tapped Pause, looked around the office. Did he just hear something? Some scraping sound? Well, whatever it was, it wasn't doing it now. Must've been the wind. Trout resumed recording.

"As long as Mr. Glass adheres to his post-op protocols, including wearing his thoracolumbar sacral-orthosis brace for six months before beginning PT, I see no reason why he can't have a normal, productive life. The fusion was a complete ..."

But Trout couldn't continue because he was laughing his ass off, laughing not only at his sexy Teddy Pendergrass voice addressing the Nobel Committee, but also his unsexy prognosis, ending his description of Nick's surgery the same way it began: selling an earthly Elysium of a future, albeit a future rife with fine print. His laughter ebbed and he hit Record again: "The fusion was a complete ... a complete ..."

"A complete waste?"

Trout, startled, looked up. The imaginary scraping noise he'd thought he heard?

Well, it wasn't imaginary.

Because letting the office door swing shut behind him and wheeling his IV pole across Trout's hand-scraped hickory hardwood floor, was the subject of his Note.

With a murderous glint in his eye.

* * *

Julie entered Nick's darkened room. She called his name, but no answer and no Nick. Next thing she noticed was the absolute quiet. No beeps and pings. All monitors disconnected. His bed a mess. It was like Charlie's room after …

No. Don't go there.

But Julie couldn't help it as the worst possible decoding of Demidova's barb resonated: *Get new boyfriend.* What was *that* about? Julie slumped on Nick's bed. Where was he? Did they take him back to an O.R.? Or worse?

No. Don't go there.

She was squinting at the whiteboard for a clue when an outsize shadow obscured it. Spooked, Julie looked back to see a giant backlit figure in the doorway. Like some kind of fifties horror movie monster.

But this monster spoke in an incongruous sweet and melodious countertenor. "Who dere?"

"Julie Toffoli?"

Iakopo turned on the room lights and gazed at her with recognition. "Ah. Spine Boy's *wahine.* I'm Carmelo Iakopo. 'Member me?"

Like with his disfigured melon supporting about fifty pounds of man-braids, she could forget. "Yes, of course. When Dr. Trout did his rounds. Also, you played in that softball game last year when …"

"Your boy crushed that seagull."

Julie winced at the memory.

"Bingo. Dat's me."

"Where's Nick?"

"Don't know. I was glommin' some zzzs. Dis be my second twelve-hour shift in a row cuz Jasmyne Dimasalang called in sick at the last minute. Which is bullshit. I know for a fact she's trickin' at 'Liquid' on West 6th, da bitch."

"Well, that sucks. Look, about Nick?"

"And da bouncers dere, don't get me started on their entitlement issues …"

"Nick. Do you have any idea where they might have taken Nick?"

"… *banning* me. Dey just asking for an ass-kickin'. Wait …" His eyes fixed on Julie as his brain processed the next thing, which was the last thing: Julie's previous question. "Maybe they took him to x-ray?"

"There aren't any orders on his chart."

"Hey, he could be in a half-dozen departments and they just forgot to enter it. Look, Doc, don't worry 'bout it; I'll check around." He took in her depleted mien. "You look like you can use some down time. Go ahead, chill here. Your boy will turn up. I mean, where's he gonna go, messed up like he is, right?"

"I don't know." Julie slumped on the bed, fighting the dissipation of the adrenalin she'd been riding on all day and night. "Thanks, I appreciate it."

"I find him, I'll bring him back to you."

Iakopo turned off the lights and exited, leaving Julie alone in the darkened room. Alone, exhausted, but unable to sleep.

*   *   *

"Sawdust."

"What are you talking about, son?"

"*Sawdust.*"

Nick stood in front of Trout's desk. He clung to his IV pole to stay upright, but his resolve and anger transcended his pain and diminished motor skills. At least for the moment. "You said my spine was like sawdust."

"I didn't say that. Dr. Demidova said that. And she was feeling no pain. Besides, I'm your surgeon, not her. She was in the O.R. to assist."

"Sounds like she assists pretty good, Doc. Still, she said *sawdirt* and you corrected her and said *sawdust*."

"I was giving her a damn English lesson. All that should matter to you is that your spine is fixed. I've fused all your lumbar levels, plus while I was in there, a bonus if you will, I performed laminectomies on two of your thoracic discs as well." Trout beamed like a used bone salesman. "No extra charge."

Nick wondered in what world a headless snowman dictating surgical lies about him, in an office that had its own weather system and where some kind of orgy had taken place, could have any credibility? No, this was all wrong. Nick, whose default state of being, a dutiful patient, still died hard, tried to reconcile Trout's words with the cynicism and cruelty of what he'd overheard only moments ago. But he couldn't. It didn't compute.

"I call bullshit."

"No, it isn't bullshit. And you, pardon me, are fucked up. But your back is not. Follow the rehab protocol and in ten months a jackhammer couldn't break through that fusion. Once you heal, you're going to have a whole new life. A life you never dreamed possible."

"That's probably the truest thing you've said. Because I never dreamed I'd be a permanent patient. I never dreamed that when I woke up every morning the amount of pain I was in would define my day. I never dreamed that I really belonged in Dr. Ganapur's Pain Management Chamber of Horrors for the rest of my life. No, I never dreamed any of that."

"Nick, calm down. You're building a career. EZ♥Care is a Fortune 500 company. And the new back I gave you will allow you to enjoy that career. Not just anyone gets to work for Jimmy Tom Muscat."

"Which is lucky for me because Muscat's the psycho who wrecked my back in the first place."

"That's between you and him. All I know is the surgery I performed on you will enable you to have any white-collar future you want. Not to mention giving you the ability to enjoy the pleasures of that pretty intern. Of course, she'll have to be on top, but hell, I could get used to that. You know what we call foxy interns like her around here? IILF'S. Interns I'd like to—"

"Shut up, Trout. You don't talk that way about Julie. *Doctor* Julie Toffoli. You don't."

Trout held out his hands in a peace offering. "Okay, Nick. I confess; I'm a bit buzzed. I apologize. Okay? I wish you two a wonderful future." As he spoke, Trout rose from his chair and moved around to the front of his desk to confront Nick; he wasn't going to remain in a submissive posture to this drug-addled punk. "Now what brought you up here?"

"You told me to walk, remember? So I got out of bed and walked. Thought I'd come and say thanks. But now, how about thanks for an unnecessary surgery. Complete with your own titanium, you double-dipping—"

"You walked? Are you crazy? You're supposed to walk with the assistance of a nurse."

"You mean the nurse who ripped the insides of my dick out? Well, fortunately he wasn't there. No one was there. But I'm here." Nick concluded with a clumsy attempt at a Russian accent, "My precious Snowboy."

"Look, Nick, whatever you thought you heard, you were eavesdropping on a privileged conversation between medical professionals."

What passed for a sarcastic grin creased Nick's pained face. "Privileged conversation? Sounded like you were enjoying some pretty kickass privileges to me."

"Nick, you're still under powerful anesthesia and clearly you are imagining things. Crazy things. I'm going to escort you back to your room and put you to sleep."

"Really? You'd do that for me? The Hunter S. Thompson of spine surgeons—except what you do is 'colorful fiction'? You're going to *escort* me back to my room? Put me to *sleep*? No thanks. I'm going to HR, camp outside the door and wait for someone to show so they can listen to *my* colorful *non*-fiction."

"Hey now, that was a silly ass joke. I was playing for Miss Grey Goose. You know how that goes."

Nick shook his head. Who did this quack think he was? Treating him like he was just another loser patient who didn't know shit. After everything he'd been through, and sure it might've taken too long, but Nick now knew when a charlatan in a white coat—or in this case, a white snowman costume—was conning him.

"A joke? No, the joke is you did an unnecessary six-figure surgery on me to pay for all your wives, your girls' private school, your Lamborghini dealer, your girlfriend's shoes. Some joke, Trout. You just needed to make bank. And you didn't care what lines you had to cross to get it."

"Nick, you have no idea what you're saying. Let's go back to your room. I'll give you an extra blast of Auntie Em. You won't remember a thing."

And that's when Trout noticed the iPhone in Nick's hand. Nick grinned like a TV private eye who'd just tricked the bad guy into a confession.

"Maybe I won't remember, but this will."

Trout's amiable facade disappeared as fast as his career and privileged life would if that iPhone ever got into the wrong hands. Which would be just about anyone's.

"Give me that phone."

"What? No!" Nick clutched his IV pole and felt a strong gust of wind blow through the French doors. It sliced through his hospital gown and shriveled his nuts like a pair of sun-dried raisins. Trout took advantage of the distraction and grasped for the roller clamp on Nick's IV pole.

"Give me that phone!"

With his other hand, Trout lunged for the phone. Nick simultaneously grabbed the snowman head off Trout's desk and rammed it on Trout's noggin. *But backwards.* He hadn't meant to do that, but there it was.

"What the fuck!" Trout's voice boomed from within the snowman head. He couldn't see, and since the head was jammed on backwards, also couldn't remove it. "You asshole! Take this off me! I can't see!"

"Good! Then you can't hurt me!" Nick instinctively rolled away from Trout. His backward path took him toward the open French doors.

Trout stumbled blindly in the direction of Nick's voice. "Hurt you? I'm not going to hurt you, you fucking piece of shit! Take this thing off my head. Now!"

"No! I'm going to HR!"

"Goddamnit!" roared the snowman as he charged in the direction of Nick's voice.

Nick sidestepped the sightless Trout, who flung himself at what he thought was Nick. But instead, Trout flung himself through the doors and onto the decorative and totally inadequate Juliet balcony.

Nick grabbed at him but Trout had momentum and Nick was too weak to gain much purchase on the snowman costume. He couldn't hold on and in one inevitable instant Trout was gone, screaming into the night. Nick slid his IV pole to the edge of the balcony and looked out.

He saw the original coal-eyed snowman in the children's park. And adjacent to that, a fresh hole in the snow. A hole that became harder to see as the blowing snow enshrouded the playground. Nick's face framed his disbelief. Maybe this was another one of his weird dreams. Or wish fulfillment. No, he knew better.

He knew better because in his hand was Trout's Harvard lapel pin. It had torn off the snowman suit when Nick grabbed at Trout to keep him from falling. The pin had pricked his palm and the droplets of blood proved this wasn't a dream at all.

Nick was standing in Trout's Penthouse Suite and the best surgeon in Northeast Ohio wasn't.

CHAPTER 14

Western Blot

Ignoring a warning sign tacked up in 1999 by hospital administration forbidding cellphone use—because Y2K scientific consensus had believed electro-magnetic signals could cause ventilators to shut off or pacemakers to explode—Julie sat on Nick's bed texting non-stop.* But he wasn't answering. Still, she kept at it until she heard a *scrape, creak, scrape,* and looked up to see Nick dragging his pole into the room. He was drenched in sweat and more or less passed-out on his feet.

"Jules," he croaked through parched lips.

Julie shot up from the bed and grabbed him just as he let go of the pole.

* * *

Nick, in bed and log-rolled onto his side by Julie, opened his eyes as she stuck a disposable thermometer in his mouth. "Where have you been? It's after midnight. What happened to you?"

---

* The only known case of injury via cellphone use in a hospital took place in a Wareham, Massachusetts ER in 1998 when a man was pepper-sprayed by police for refusing to end his call. However, *doctors* with cellphones can be dangerous: one study showed that 85% of cellphones taken into sterile operating rooms by surgeons had pathogenic bacteria on them.

machine-gunned Julie, scaling the heights of mania for the third time this evening.

"Mmmrrrggghhh." Nick tried to make himself understood with the thermometer in his mouth. Julie yanked it out, checked the reading, tossed it in the biohazard receptacle, and entered the info in his chart.

"The sign," said Nick, pointing, "It says you're not supposed to use your phone here. We might blow up."

"Boom!" Julie ripped the warning off the wall and tossed it in the trash. "This sign is bullshit. It should've been taken down decades ago. Just like this damn hospital. Where were you, Nick? What happened?"

Only now, did Nick have it together enough to notice her face: cheeks reddened from scrubbing and eyes swollen from crying. "You tell me. What's wrong?"

She shook her head. *Not now.* "I asked first. Where were you?"

"You know how Dr. Trout told me to walk?"

"No, I don't. He kicked me out of your room. So, although walking is customary protocol after most orthopedic surgeries, I don't know that for a fact."

"Well, he made a big deal of how I had to walk tonight."

"But not alone. You're supposed to be supervised."

"I didn't want any supervision. I walked to the elevator, took it up to Trout's office. I wanted to ask him about the surgery. I'm about to knock on his door when I overhear him yucking it up with the Russian doc about how my fusion wasn't even necessary! How he just did it for the money. And to be on TV. So I went inside and confronted him about it."

"I'm sure that went well. What did he say?"

"He died."

"He died. In his office? By your hand?"

"More by his feet."

"And Dr. Demidova just watched? Or did she help you, with her angel halo?"

"Julie. I'm serious. Yeah, she was part of the conspiracy, but she split before I went in there and—"

"Nick. Stop. I don't want to hear another one of your drugged-out dreams. Not tonight. Maybe your pain meds need to be adjusted."

"Meds had nothing to do with it. Trout is dead."

"I'm going to give you a Valium. You need sleep."

"You have Valium?"

"I'm a doctor. At least, for now." She grabbed a cup of water from his sliding bed tray and handed it to him along with a pill. "Take this and close your eyes."

Nick did so, but all he could see was a Technicolor image of Trout in his snowman suit sailing through the night and screaming to his death. The moment was indelibly hardwired. He opened his eyes.

"Jules, you don't understand. He was gonna hurt me."

On fumes, she sagged into the chair next to the bed. "Look, I'm not in the mood to hear more of your absurd dreams about you killing Dr. Trout. By my count, that's twice you've whacked him. Maybe tomorrow you can make it a hat trick. Nick, I'm going through some bad stuff tonight, so please shut up and go to sleep."

"What bad stuff? What happened?"

"Go to sleep."

"Not until you talk to me. What did you mean you're a doctor 'at least for now'? Jules, what happened?"

"I lost a patient tonight. Which, if what you're saying is based in any kind of reality, would make us both a couple of killers."

"You didn't kill anyone."

"Maybe I did. I don't know. The kid wasn't going to make it anyway. But I don't think tonight was his night to go. Or maybe it was. Whatever, he's gone. But it gets worse."

"What's worse?"

"I'll explain when your mind returns."

"I can understand you fine."

Perhaps the Valium was having an opposite effect as the look on Nick's face reflected a growing acuity. "Julie, you proposed to me in the eighth grade. I made our engagement rings out of barbed-wire from a construction site and had to get twenty-seven stitches—"

"Twelve. It was only twelve stitches."

"Whatever. Talk to me. Please."

Julie's left leg twitched. She didn't look at him, her gaze somewhere off in the distance. "Mainly, what's worse is my future. And yours too if you still want to hang around. I mean you have an out; the rings don't fit anymore and—"

"Julie. Stop. What else happened?"

"After tonight, there's no way I'm going to be a pediatrician."

"What? Why?"

"The kid had HIV. It never should've happened, but I caught tons of blood in my face, my eyes specifically. I was like Carrie getting doused by the pig's blood at the prom. And to double down, I got pricked by an uncapped needle full of blood." She showed him the band-aid on her finger.

"How does that even happen?"

"When you work with a crew of exhausted students, nurses too intimidated to open their mouths, and a self-important martinet who has it in for me, chaos occurs, mistakes are made."

"Jules, even I know that doesn't mean you'll get infected. HIV happens either through doing it with an infected person or sharing needles, right?"

"Mostly. It's unlikely I could've gotten the virus through a cut because usually the virus dies when exposed to air. But through the eye, well, that's like hitting the lottery. If enough blood goes through the mucous membrane and into the bloodstream …"

"Was there enough?"

"Enough to make me go downstairs to the lab and have them do a 'Rapid' Test. It's protocol. Except I told them the sample was from a Jane Doe, an indigent patient."

"Why Jane Doe?"

"Because I didn't want Klepstein knowing about it, and if it turns out to be something, well, I'll just deal with it."

"So what were the results?"

"Poor Jane Doe."

"Jesus, Julie. Have them re-test it."

"I did, and the result was still positive. I ordered anti-retrovirals and, just to be absolutely certain the rest of my professional life is over, I sent Jane Doe's sample to an outside lab for a Western Blot."

"A what?"

"Further verification. Absolute-for-certain-there's-no-hope-verification. I'll know in about a week. And I'm sorry I told you to shut up."

"I don't remember you saying that."

"Liar."

Nick took her hand and tried to raise himself up. It hurt like hell, but he wasn't going to cry out and he wasn't going to grimace. "Okay. Worst case? These days people live forever with HIV, right?

"Yes. It's high maintenance, there are side effects; still, you take the right cocktail, you live. My problem is the kind of life available to me. Which won't include being a pediatrician."

"But if you take all the right precautions and everything?"

Julie lost it: "Jesus Christ, Nick! Would you take your kid any-where near a doctor with HIV? *Our kid?* The kid we shouldn't bring into this world?" She let go of his hand, rose and paced the room. "Goddamn it to hell! That asshole ruined my life!"

"Who?"

Julie stopped and whirled back to Nick. "Klepstein. Dr. Kasper Klepstein. My Attending. I swear, Nick, I could kill him. I really could kill him." She sat on the bed.

"Or I could," Nick whispered.

He opened up his other hand. In it was Dr. Trout's Harvard Medical School lapel pin.

Julie stared at the pin, recognizing it. She also recognized its significance.

"Nick. Tell me what happened with Dr. Trout."

CHAPTER 15

Ms. Clean

A slice of moonlight illuminated an indentation in the snow near the base of a slide in the children's park. Hard to see, even if one knew it was there. And as the moon went behind the clouds, it couldn't be seen at all. Ultimately, a moot issue as the hollow forged by Trout's return to Mother Earth was filled in by the snowfall, which returned with anthropomorphic vengeance. Local TV called it the largest accumulation in a Cleveland December since 1978. So much snow fell, so fast, that come dawn the entire playground would become a mountain of white and steel.

A scene so shadowy and stark, it would've made a great Expressionist Christmas card, Julie mused, as she peered over the Juliet balcony of Trout's office, his defenestration off-ramp.

She wondered if he could really be down there but knew there was no way to tell now. What she no longer wondered about was whether Nick's story was reality based. Too much of what he'd told her about his overheard Trout-and-Demidova conversation rang true—especially once Julie had factored in the timing of her encounter with Demidova in the elevator, when that sable-killing slut told her in a moment of inebriated honesty, that maybe she should "get new boyfriend." Also, look at the mess inside: the residual after-party rubble in Trout's suite, the bottles of Dom

Perignon and Stoli Elit rolling on the floor, the shattered glasses, the stethoscope-themed bong, the wind and snow blowing through the open French doors, sending crepe paper streamers fluttering to and fro above the wreckage. No, Nick hadn't dreamed this.

He'd been here. And so had Trout.

Which also meant there'd be an excellent chance Nick would be recuperating from his fusion in a prison hospital. It would be the dead and deified Trout's "word" against Nick's. They might as well throw away the key.

Which is why Julie, wearing gloves, was using surgical pads to wipe all possible areas where Nick could have left his fingerprints.

As Julie scoured, the wind continued its yowling through the open doors. She ignored it; there was nothing left that could frighten her. At least, not until she bent to wipe down Trout's zebra-wood desk, when *Oh-Holy-Mother-Of-God* she felt the creepy wisp of a touch on the back of her neck …

Julie gasped and whirled to face her attacker. And blew out a sigh as she removed a windblown streamer that had wrapped itself around her neck.

"Wimp," she said and renewed her sanitizing but stopped a moment later when she heard the unmistakable sound of a *hand opening the office door from the hallway.* This time Julie knew she was busted. Streamers might wrap themselves around your neck, but they could not open doors.

Had to be Hospital Security, who, in about two seconds, was going to jack her up. Fleeting thought: Julie wondered if she and Nick could do their time in a co-ed prison? Did they even have co-ed prisons? Did—

The door opened. But instead of security guards with reindeer antlers attached to their caps, it was Dr. Irina Demidova, still dressed in her indecent angel costume, only half-covered by the unbuttoned sable coat. Demidova, still tanked, gripped the door-knob for support as much as for entry. She looked around and sing-songed: "Templeton? Where are you, my Snowboy?"

Um, how about buried under tons of iceberg? thought Julie, who was scrunched under Trout's desk and hoping to hell Demidova wouldn't look down.

Or fall down.

Demidova closed the door and lurched about the office, becoming more and more agitated. "Where are you hi-dink, Templeton? We must talk." She peered behind the couch. Maybe he was passed out on the floor. *Nyet.* "Ah, maybe you are in WC 'dropping deuce'?"

Without regard for propriety, Demidova flung open the door to Trout's private bathroom, but no deuce, just a baggie of cocaine on the Calacatta marble sink.

"Ah! He did go home to bitch wife!" Demidova snarled. Therefore, she felt entitled to pocket the bump. She stuffed the baggie in her coat. Re-entering the office proper, she whacked a bottle of Stoli off the coffee table onto the hickory hardwood floor, where it splintered into glistening shards. "МУ Дак! You asshole, Templeton!"

Julie flinched and wondered if this deranged woman was going to leave, and further wondered, if she *didn't* leave, whether they had a vegan menu in her fantasy co-ed prison? But no time for further rumination as Demidova was headed her way, straight to Trout's desk. Julie held her breath. Demidova's spottily shaved legs, supported by six-inch stiletto heels, stopped inches away from Julie's face as the Russian doc leaned over the desk.

The desk upon which lay the bottle of alcohol and pads of surgical dressing Julie had been using to erase Nick's prints.

Crap.

Julie, teeth clamped together, found herself staring at a scab on Demidova's ballet-dancer muscular legs. Julie hoped she wielded a scalpel with more precision than she did a razor.

Wait! What the hell was the Russian doing on the desk? What was that scratchy noise she was making?

Oh! She was writing! Perhaps leaving Trout a note.

Well, good luck with him getting around to that.

Julie allowed herself a brief exhale. Maybe she would get away with this yet. Then again, maybe not, as Demidova's angel halo dropped onto the rug adjacent to Julie's hiding place. In seconds, Julie would be discovered. She flicked at the halo and moved it a couple of inches out from the edge of the desk. An instant later, an impeccably manicured hand appeared in Julie's eyeline and picked it up. The sounds of the chicken scratches began again.

And went on. And on. What the hell was this woman writing, *Crime and Punishment?* No, maybe it was *The Idiot*, Julie riffed to herself because she knew for certain she was going to be discovered any second. Maybe in co-ed prison she could re-read her fave, *Doctor Zhivago.* She remembered blubbering like a baby when her Dad took her to the Cedar Lee Theater in Cleveland Heights to see a revival of *Doctor Z.* But it wasn't only the nine-year-old Julie bawling; it was *everyone* in the theater. Betcha that'd be a cool psych experiment: why, at sad movies, is one audience member prone to cry when another does? A totally imperfect stranger? And then another, and another, until the whole damn theater becomes one mass sob fest? Except for her Dad. He wasn't crying; he was looking at his watch, as he had a date later with one of Julie's future ex-stepmoms.

Julie's reverie ended as the scratching stopped. Demidova had finished her missive and walked around the corner of the desk. She reached past the bottle of alcohol and surgical dressing for some scotch tape; Demidova was so immersed in her anger and the contents of her note that the few working brain cells she had left were not sufficient to notice, much less question, these out-of-place, out-of-context items. As if Trout always had crime scene clean-up essentials at ready.

Julie was now afforded a frontal view of Demidova's gams, which featured a pair of matching rug burns (further confirmation of Nick's story) as she leaned over and taped the note to Trout's chair, grabbed her halo off the desk, and meandered back to the office door. Julie again allowed herself a breath of relief, but it was a breath too soon as Demidova, just short of the door, turned on a stiletto heel, lost her balance, and crashed onto the debris-strewn floor. Demidova cursed, got up, brushed herself off, lurched *back* to the Vaya chair, ripped the note off the chair, and proceeded to perform a freaking re-write.

Julie remained huddled in a ball as Demidova worked on her second draft. Violent cross-outs, arrows down the margins to new material, until, finally satisfied, she re-taped it to the Vaya and once again wobbled towards the office door, put her hand on the knob, and …

… once again stopped, swung herself around like a drunk around a lamppost, and again headed back to the desk.

She must've seen me, Julie thought. How dumb can this woman be, blitzed or not? Christ, all she has to do is look down.

Demidova paused at the desk.

Okay, now I'm dead.

No. At least not yet. Demidova paused at the desk only long enough to place her angel halo next to the cleaning stuff and flounder to the still-open French doors, where the wind and snow continued to air out the office. What? Was she going to jump too?

Yes! Do it! Please!

In the scope of the great Russian tragedies it'd be right there with *Anna Karenina* or *Rocky IV*. But no; instead, Demidova grabbed the door handles with both hands and brought them to a banging close. And just to be sure, she turned the key and locked them.

Leaving her fingerprints everywhere.

Which, when you think about it, was still a tragedy—for Demidova—who, forgetting the angel halo, at last sable-swayed her ass out of the office.

Julie allowed herself a bit of a smile. In addition to arthouse movies, Julie also watched a lot of eighties TV cop shows with her Dad. And what Demidova had just left on the doors was what the cops in their tight jeans and *Members Only* jackets called a Smoking Gun.

Julie untangled herself, got to her feet, and looked at the note re-taped to the Vaya chair. It read:

> My Dearest ~~Big~~ Snow Boy, if you do
> not leave bitch wife immediately, ~~we are~~
> ~~through~~ I will call and tell stupid
> ~~money sucking~~ cow everything!
> EVERYTHING!!! Also, I will go to Humane
> Resources and TELL THEM EVERYTHING too!
> Pa-rum pum pum pum!
> Love always, Irina

Julie stared at the note, then at the closed French doors, and remembered what her Dad always used to say around Christmas time: Even though this might not be the greatest Christmas, there are always people in the world who are less fortunate, and Julie should think of them before complaining.

Can't argue with that.

CHAPTER 16

Veritas

(Harvard University motto, since 1696)

Morning revealed the children's park buried in high mounds of snow. The top of a tether-ball pole protruded through the sea of white like the periscope of a U-boat in a North Sea hunting ground. Under all that snow and ice, Snowboy might as well have been encased in one big Sub-Zero, at least till Global Warming turned on The Big Defrost.

*   *   *

"Where is Doctor Trout?"

Demidova, flanked by the elfin band of medical students, some wearing ratty Santa caps and blood-stained tights,[*] pondered the same question, the question that had kept her up the entire vomitous night. The inside of her head felt like a pack of running dog Trotskyites chipping away with hammers and sickles in Perpetual Revolution against her Bureaucratic Incrementalist cerebral cortex. It was all she could do to look at Nicholas in his hospital bed, staring at her with innocent eyes, and reply, "Doctor Trout is off today, Nicholas. I asked, what is your pain level this morning?"

"Way better," Nick lied. "Maybe a four. No, make that a three. Given that, when can I go home?"

---

[*] The memo to all hospital staff from Josh Przybylowicz informed that the wearing of tights, caps, and antlers was mandatory through New Year's Day. They should then be promptly returned in laundered condition.

"You give me bowel movement, petal, you go home. We will see tomorrow." Demidova, her face a porcelain mask of pale, turned and left the room. The elf posse trailed behind.

As Nick watched them go, the look of fake cheer he wore became way less fake as he realized: *She doesn't know. She doesn't have a fucking clue. In fact, she's sweating Stoli over her Snowboy.* Nick could see it. He could *feel* it. The edge of panic in her voice, the bloodshot eyes, the sloppy makeup. *So if she doesn't know where Snowboy is, no one does. And no one will for months, until the ice melts. A drunken Christmas Eve suicide over a failed affair, the cops will think …*

Well, good. That greedy, egomaniacal, philandering piece of crap deserved it. Putting me through a year of hell and for what? To make himself an obscene amount of bank and leave me worse off than before. A *cripple for life*, he said. A life doomed to Doctor Ganapur's Pain Management Chamber of Horrors. So screw Trout and the snowman suit he rode out on.

Nick squeezed his morphine pump (because his pain was really still about a seven) and giggled at the thought he was going to get away with murder.

No! Stop with that! What happened wasn't murder at all. *Per se.* At worst, a good lawyer could plead down to Involuntary Defenestration. No, not even that. Not anything. Nick wasn't a murderer of any ilk.

What he was, was a survivor of assault and malpractice.

"Hey, brah."

Nick's latest giggle died stillborn and his face became a profile in terror as he remembered the penile pain delivered by the mercurial Iakopo. And now the ugly giant was back.

"'Sup, brudder? What's so funny?"

"Nothing. Think I was dreaming."

"Or maybe you was laughing at me."

"No, no. I wasn't laughing at you. Fo'realz."

"What did you say?" Iakopo, expression darkening, loomed large over Nick's bed. "You just say *fo'realz?* What? Did I give you permission to speak Pidgin? That's my birthright, brah, not yours."

"Hey, Melo, I didn't mean anything—"

"Fuck you did. Lissen, I'm a proud Samoan, raised in Hawaii; I'm a fuckin' RN, a medical professional—and you are a bitch Haole, stealing our land and shit."

"I've never even been to Haw—"

Iakopo jammed a thermometer in Nick's mouth. "Keep that under your tongue. Pretend it's your Mama's dick."

As Nick gagged on the thermometer, Iakopo entered the readings off Nick's monitors into an iPad. "Your blood pressure sucks, brah. High as a midget on a ladder. What you got to be stressed about?"

Nick tried to talk with the thermometer in his mouth. "I'm not stressed. Other than from surgery. Besides that, I couldn't be *less* stressed. Really."

Iakopo put his paw on Nick's wrist to take his pulse. Nick noticed Iakopo moved his lips as he counted the heartbeats. "Dude, your pulse is like a runaway train. Maybe I'll ask the Doc to get you some Ativan or somethin'. Chill you out."

Nick was thinking it was Iakopo who could use the Ativan—like a whole bottle of it—when the nurse noticed Dr. Trout's Harvard lapel pin on Nick's side table. He picked it up, clearly recognizing it.

"You an Ivy League boy? Didn't know dat."

Shit. *Trout's pin.* Why hadn't he hidden it? Maybe because he *had* been too stressed out after committing involuntary defenestration. No, what was stressing him was what had happened to Julie. He was always able to be there for her. No matter what. Except right now, he was stuck in this hospital bed and knew he had to maintain as this freakshow of a nurse was capable of anything. Iakopo yanked the thermometer out of his mouth.

"Ninety-seven point four." Iakopo tossed the thermometer in the biohazard receptacle and entered Nick's numbers. "You know, brah, I went to Harvard too. *Veritas.*"

Nick was nonplussed. *Veritas?* What was he talking about?

"Da Harvard slogan, brah. Says so right on your pin."

Right on Trout's pin that Iakopo was holding in his hand.

"Hey, what a coincidence," Nick vamped. "Harvard. You too? It was the most enriching time of my life."

"Dat's what I thought it was gonna be too. Dey recruited me outta Saint Louis High in Honolulu. Football scholarship. Full ride. O-line. My four-point-one GPA didn't hurt either."

"Really? Cool."

"Da fuck it was. Bitches threw me out after one semester. Anger Management issues." Iakopo put Anger Management in air quotes. "But dat's what football is, right? Anger. Anger and pain."

"So why'd you became a nurse?"

"It's where the pain is, brah. And they pay you."

Iakopo's cell rang. He looked at the caller ID, turned away from Nick, and lowered his voice. But not low enough. Nick could still hear as Iakopo whispered into the phone. "No idea. Nobody does.

Like he disappeared off the face of the earth. Don't worry, I keep you in da loop." Iakopo clicked off and turned to exit.

Nick called out: "Excuse me, my Harvard pin?"

"Oh yeah." Iakopo flipped the pin on Nick's chest and exited laughing. "*Veritas*, Harvard boy. *Veritas*, all-you-all Ivy League motherfuckers!"

CHAPTER 17

Angry Birds

It was after the breakfast rush. Julie was sitting alone in the mostly deserted, mostly trashed, and minimally hygienic Cleveland Mercy cafeteria. She was at a corner table, away from the remaining knots of visiting friends and relatives. Paper-hatted busboys clattered away dishes and spread bacteria around table surfaces with soiled towels, as Julie pushed some soggy fruit salad around her plate. Her hands had reddened and bruised from the compressions, and her attention was on the paperback she was reading:

The First Year: HIV: An Essential Guide for the Newly Diagnosed by Grodeck and Berger

As Julie highlighted a passage with a yellow Sharpie, she heard the scrape of a chair pulled out across from her, along with the last voice she wanted or expected to hear:

"May I." It wasn't a question.

Julie looked up to see bat-wing-haired, butt-chinned Kasper Klepstein, the Pediatric Attending who was the cause of her reading this horror story of a book in the first place. He stood with a mug of coffee in his hand, just another colleague wanting to hang. Yeah, like hell. She slipped a section of the *Plain Dealer* over the HIV book and hoped Klepstein couldn't read upside down. All the while thinking: *Why don't you leave me alone? Haven't you had enough?*

Apparently not, as Klepstein slouched his angular frame in the plastic chair catty-corner to her. He sipped his cafeteria coffee, winced, put down the mug, and fluffed out the sides of frizz that framed his bald dome.

Julie remembered him doing the same thing last night in the hallway, just before he burst into her Code Patient's room.

Code Patient.

Julie wasn't being insensitive. She was attempting to process the advice Trout had given her in the hallway after Nick's surgery: Develop an immunity. Not only to viruses and bacteria, but to the whispers of self-doubt. Banish them!

Yeah, well how's Trout's posthumous wisdom working out for you, Jules? Then she realized Klepstein had been talking to her.

"What? Sorry," said Julie. "What did you say?"

Klepstein glanced at the *Plain Dealer*. The previous reader had left the Sports Section on top. "I asked what's your take on who's going to be under center for the Browns next Sunday?"

"Excuse me?"

"You're reading the Sports. Which is odd because I hadn't pegged you as a pigskin fan, Toffoli. Especially of a once proud team, now comprised of chronic losers and habitual criminals playing out the string of another pathetic season."

Julie didn't respond. Klepstein eyeballed her like a malevolent carny clown—he didn't even need the make-up—and took another sip from his mug, winced again, and poured the remainder into Julie's water glass.

"So, tell me, Toffoli, who do you think it'll be? The rookie snow-blower from Butt Fuck A&M or the forty-one-year-old Bible-spouter they plucked from the Canadian League?"

"I don't know."

"Aw, come on. Play along. Pretend you know something about it. Like you pretended you knew what you were doing last night." He waved at her not to interrupt. "Don't worry about the book; whatever you've stashed under the paper is none of my business. My curiosity is not piqued. Unless it's lesbian porn. Oh, sorry, that was a joke; however, it would explain your lack of sociability. Oh damn, please don't report me to the Office of Fair Practices."

Julie facial muscles tightened but her mouth stayed shut.

"That was also a joke. I don't give a rat's ass if you whine to OFP nor am I interested in what you're reading. Because it certainly couldn't have been a medical book."

Julie didn't rise to the bait. She wasn't going to give him the satisfaction.

"The Code last night? Was that your first one?"

"No."

"I mean the first one that you led, albeit briefly?"

"Yes."

"Well, like the song goes, 'Good Time Charlie's Got the Blues.' In his case, permanently."

Appalled, Julie lost her crafted attempt at composure. "That's just sick, Dr. Klepstein."

"Excuse me, Toffoli, let's get a couple of things straight. One: my name is Klep-*stine*. Not Klep-*steen*. 'E' before 'I' is always pronounced as a hard I." He grinned humorlessly. "You can also leave the grammar lesson out of any complaint you may be contemplating to OFP. That was not a sexualized pun; I was correcting you as to the proper pronunciation of my surname. Two: this is a hospital. Death happens here. Often, in fact. And yes, young Charlie was circling the drain. Came into this world with in-utero heroin addiction. HIV. In and out of hospitals most of his life, draining societal resources. Hell, we've had him the last four. The patient had the immune system of a Haitian homosexual and the lifespan of a mayfly. Sooner or later, Darwin was going to win. Yet, I still can't help thinking you did your best to speed up the process."

"What? Me!"

"Yes. Fucking. You."

"That's simply not true."

"Oh, it is. You were the one who left it to a medical student to insert the cardiac catheter. You should've been doing that. You should've delegated a nurse to do the compressions. You were the team leader. My God, you did everything ass-backwards—which I allow is part of the learning process. But the worst thing you did was absolutely avoidable."

"Which was?"

"Questioning my judgment in front of staff and students."

"What!"

Klepstein, aware they were drawing looks, lowered his voice, but not his intensity. "Really? How fucking dare you?"

"Because I had a valid point. And I'll argue it at the M&M. No, my biggest mistake, Dr. Klep-*stine*, was not throwing you out of that boy's room."

"Excuse me?"

"Look. You barged in and didn't ask one question as to status. Instead, you screamed out orders, guaranteeing a lack of communication. No one could hear anyone else. I couldn't hear the nurse say 'Clear' because you were barking like a Hitler wannabe."

"As a Jew I resent that!"

"As a human I resent you being the cause of me getting a blood facial!"

"Ah, the Blood Libel Card. Let's see who wants to go to OFP now, Toffoli."

"You intimidated those kids to the point where they botched the handoff and couldn't concentrate on inserting the line. Some of those students had been without sleep for thirty hours."

"Boo fucking hoo. We've all been there."

"I had the Code covered."

"Right. Except the only thing covering that boy now—my patient—is a shroud."

"You're going in circles. What's your real point, Doctor? Besides your ego bent out of shape because I wouldn't 'share a meal' with you?"

"Ah. *That*. One: that was an innocent invitation. As an intern, it might've been somewhat helpful to glean some insight from your Attending. Two—"

"*That* was a joke, right? You've made it pretty clear for weeks what you wanted to 'glean' from me."

"I won't dignify that. Two: my 'real' point is that your attendance at the next M&M will not be required."

"I have a right to defend myself."

"No longer. You'll get the official notification next week, but I spoke with Dr. Wilkes, your Program Director who's vacationing in Saint Barts or Saint Farts or somewhere warmer than this ice-hole, and he's agreed with my assessment: your Residency here will be terminated."

"What?! Why?!"

"I think the language goes something like, '*Behaving unprofessionally and risking patient management.*'"

Before Julie could respond, a young cafeteria worker, rail-thin, long hair tucked under a sanitary cap, appeared at Klepstein's side, a coffee pot in his hand.

"Fresh coffee, Doctor Klepstein?"

The kid pronounced Klepstein incorrectly. Klepstein fumed at the perceived insult. He waved permission. "Exactly half empty."

Julie thought the nervous cafeteria worker looked familiar. His white skin was almost translucent, as if never touched by the sun. From the side, as he poured, she could almost see through his narrow nose. Klepstein whirled on him.

"Stop! What are you, high? I said exactly half."

"Sorry, Doctor K. I can pour some out," the kid stuttered and his white skin sprouted red blotches like a time-lapse tropical blossoming. It looked to Julie as if the kid's and Klepstein's red faces were having their own conversation.

"No, just get me some half-and-half."

Julie wondered where everything had gone off the rails. How could one horrible event have so unalterably changed her life? Yesterday, she was Florence Nightingale Junior. Today, she was Florence Nightingale with HIV and no future. How could this have happened? She looked at Klepstein, fluffing out his bat wings as his nostrils literally flared. The latter, a trick her Dad used to perform at parties while he did his Peter Lorre imitation of Ugarte's pleading for Rick's help in *Casablanca: "Rick, Rick, help me ..."* At that point, her Dad would switch to his Bogie: *"I stick my neck out for nobody."* Except, right now, Julie *was* going to stick her neck out. For Charlie. For those students who were doing the best they could. And for her career.

However, before she could, the skinny kid returned with Klepstein's half-and-half and Julie realized where she'd seen him before. He was the klutz who'd accompanied Raven, the mystery candy-striper, last night, helping her wheel the overloaded gurney into the elevator headed to a basement floor that supposedly was inaccessible. Julie had been about to confront the pair just before

Charlie's Code Blue came over the P.A. But this morning, it no longer mattered.

"Hey, rail ass. Second thought, just get out of here. And check yourself into a rehab center while you're at it. Like I can't tell. Yeah, go ahead: you can take me to OFP too."

The kid, whose name Julie would later learn was Tick, was no doubt high—just look at his eyes: red, white, and dilated. He mumbled an apology and backed off. On the way, he tripped over the chair behind him and spilled the rest of the coffee on the floor. He tried to hold back his panic.

"What's your name, Bones?" asked Klepstein.

But Tick was quickly back on his feet and fled the cafeteria. Klepstein looked after him. "Fuck him. I'll have a word with his supervisor." He returned his focus to Julie. "More importantly, you and I are not through."

"You're correct about that, Dr. Klepstein. I'm going to fight this."

"Appeal away. But I doubt you'll feel so feisty when I'm finished here."

"What? What else did I do wrong, outside of questioning your judgment? Isn't that what we're supposed to do here?"

"Well, since you bring it up, this matter of questioning—that's what I did when the Lab called me. My question to them was: *Did one of my interns really test positive for HIV?*"

Julie's lips parted. *How the hell did he know this?*

"I'll tell you how. I'm banging a lab tech on the graveyard shift. Oh, damn. That's another one you can take to OFP if you want. But I digress. The tech told me about the results of your test."

Julie was reeling. "That's an invasion of my privacy."

"No, it's an invasion of 'Jane Doe's' privacy; that was the name on the test. Not yours. What you did, by not identifying yourself, was a serious breach of protocol. A fireable offense."

"Dr. Klepstein. I was alone. Charlie was dead. I panicked."

"Indeed." He leaned across the table into her face. She felt more than her space was being invaded; he was invading the essence of who she was, her goals and dreams. Take those away and what was left?

"As of this moment, consider yourself prohibited from treating patients. Finish the Sports Section or whatever you're hiding under it, then find a desk. Write some resumes, play *Angry Birds*. I don't give a fuck. Just kill time, instead of patients, until Dr. Wilkes returns."

Klepstein rose from the plastic chair, kicked it out of his way and exited the cafeteria, not giving a shit about the stares he was getting. Including the one from Julie that bored through his back. What he couldn't know, was the bright crimson color her palm had turned from gripping her table knife so damn hard.

Hell, she didn't even realize it.

PART TWO

"*Blow, blow, thou winter wind!*
Thou art not so unkind
As man's ingratitude."

William Shakespeare
(*As You Like It*)

CHAPTER 18

Lieutenant Sikorski Has A Question Or Two

I hate friggin' hospitals. They always remind me of—guess what?—death. You got the living dead, the wish-they-were-dead, and of course the actual dead downstairs in the Morgue where I just was, watching that ghoul Ganesh Chatterjee going to town with his Black & Decker. It's like sightseeing in the back of a butcher shop, the part the public never sees. And even after forty-some years it's all I can do not to toss my tacos. Especially when Chatterjee is slicing open some bloated stiff that's been floating in the Cuyahoga for three months and stinks like a bunch of gaseous turkey turds.

So's not to confuse you, the gases from a corpse is different than the gas I take my Prilosec for. I'm talkin' about the gases that makes every human being who ever walked this earth the same at The End. The part that concerns me is how they wound up on that cold slab in the first place.

And, at least today, one of them wasn't Templeton J. Trout M.D.

Think about it, was kind of nutso that they even called me. Me, the legendary Lieutenant Artemas Sikorski, Cleveland Division of Police - Homicide. By the way, just so you know, I don't allow anyone to call me "Ski." Ever. I guess it's a tribal thing, but "Ski" always sounds like one of the stock ethnics in every WWII movie bomber crew; the one where you got the tobacky-chewing kid from Tennessee, the tough punk from Philly, the corn-fed doofus from Iowa who misses his favorite cow, the studious Jewish kid from Brooklyn with his big schnoz always in a book—whatever, fill in your own stereotypes, but the common thing they share is all of'em are pulling for the same noble cause. Which is bombing the shit out of Krauts and Nips. Catch is, there's always a price. But that price is never the star. The price is always "Ski," the wisecrackin' tail gunner on the B-17 Flying Fortress. See, the Captain, it's either Gregory Peck or Spencer Tracy or, say, Richard Greene if they didn't have the budget, who realizes "Ski" ain't answering his radio after the bombing run. Then they cut to the shot of lovable "Ski" slumped over his fifty-caliber machine-gun with a half-dozen bullet holes in his plexiglass. Point is, "Ski" is expendable. But never Gregory Peck. So that's why my family, my colleagues, and a couple of the less asshole-ish assistant DAs call me Artie. Never "Ski."

And the ballplayers at Lakewood Park where I did some part-time umpiring, they just called me "Blue."

Whatever, I digress. Here I am six months short of mandatory retirement; forty years of putting mobsters and murderers away and they call *me* to check out some fancy-pants doctor who's not even been missing twenty-four hours, a guy who either wrapped his Lamborghini around a phone pole or is shacked up with some gash listening to some heavy breathing through his doodlescope. Whatever, the guy's not even technically vanished but he's a VIP at this carcass of a hospital and my Captain said he had huge pressure from up high to find him.

Which is what I was doing downstairs with Chatterjee and his collection of cadavers: guys who are no longer worried about tax deductions or forgetting to put down the toilet seat, or remembering to call their mothers on Sunday. Yeah, everybody's got regrets, until they don't. Hell, I was just glad to be outta there, and even though my personal doc told me to cut down on the java, I was headed to the cafeteria to sneak a cup when I run into Artie (same like my name) Garfinkle's double, the spitting image. You remember Simon and Garfinkle? They used to be somebody. Garfinkle was the one with the frizzy hair who sang like his spuds were sandpapered off in seventh grade Wood Shop, and Simon was the squirt who played guitar and more or less sang like a regular guy. Hey, they were pretty records, even if the words were pretentious crap. "*Can analysis be worthwhile? Is the theater really dead?*" How the hell do I know? All I know is it don't mean a thing if it ain't got that swing.

The Garfinkle look-alike was exiting the cafeteria as I was coming in, so I badged him and asked about Dr. Trout. He said Trout was in a different department and they don't particularly travel in the "same circles" and at any rate he had patients who "desperately needed him" so unfortunately, he couldn't help me "to any further degree."

Like I was looking for a thermometer. A simple "no" at the get-go would've sufficed; this fuck had some kind of attitude on him I didn't appreciate. I mean really, the first thing he did when he saw me limping up to him on my beechwood cane with the nickel-plated alligator's head handle my ex son-in-law, the tasteless sonofabitch, got me on one of his "business trips" to Florida, was to try an end-around on me.

Obviously, seeing an old guy with a cane, no matter how snazzy, Garfinkle thought I was a patient—and not one of the ones who "desperately needed him." I mean I get it: why would a doctor talk to a decrepit dude like me who looked half-dead, when they've got much more important things to do? Like getting BJ's from those perky pharmaceutical reps with the rolling briefcases and big white teeth. Oh shut up. Like you never wondered why every single one of them chicks peddling free samples of happy pills was under thirty and dressed to sell. You know what I'm talking about. Artie Sikorski's been around.

After getting the bounce from Dr. Garfinkle, I went into the cafeteria for the joe. I wasn't expecting the Algonquin Round Table but hell, the habitués of the bone house downstairs were more loquacious than this group of somnambulants.

The only non-civilian in the place was a sad-looking young lady sitting in the corner all the way in the back. A pretty kid in scrubs. She wasn't wearing makeup, but I didn't need to see mascara running down her cheeks to know she'd been crying. The other giveaway she might've been a tad upset was the knife she let drop to the floor as she stared at the last of Dr. Garfinkle. A lovers' quarrel? I doubted it. Even though I noticed there was two coffee cups on the table.

"Mind if I rest my dogs for a minute?" I asked, but didn't wait for an answer as I badged her before grabbing a chair.

For a second, I saw the flash of a frightened look in her green eyes, like I was about to bust her as an accessory to a murder or something else felonious. Or maybe it was the emerald eye gleaming out of the alligator head in my cane that spooked her. But she recomposed and pulled her newspaper closer to her. A none-too-subtle message about not feeling particularly conversational. Yeah, whatever. After forty years, I can make anybody talk.

"So how about those Browns?" I said, noticing she was reading the Sports. "Who do you think they'll start at QB? The washed-up Bible beater from Saskatchewan or Blow Boy from A&M?"

"I have no idea. I also don't care."

"Know what you mean. Comes a point where getting invested in losers just ain't worth it. 2017's about to end and they ain't won one single game. By the way, I noticed you didn't examine my badge too carefully. Which you should've because you never know who's gonna try and pull somethin' on you."

"Yeah, you never know."

I took my shield out again and let her have a nice long look. It was in the sleeve right next to the high school yearbook shot of my granddaughter, Kimmy, the snap I always keep in my wallet.

Always.

"It says Lieutenant Artemas Sikorski, but you can call me Artie."

"Hello Artie," she said, as she gathered her stuff to make a getaway. They all do. Innocent, guilty, or somewheres in between, nobody likes making small talk with a cop; mainly, because it's never really small talk.

"Hang on a sec, Ms. …" I had to squinch to read her nametag. "Excuse me, *Doctor* Toffoli. My apologies. They say the eyes are the first thing to go."

"That must be a problem when you moonlight as an umpire at softball games. How's that lawsuit against Jimmy Tom Muscat going?"

Holy crapola! She was at the game where that lefty with the sweet stroke hit a ground-rule double off a seagull and I used a little subterfuge to … well, never mind about that. Yeah, of course: that murdering scumbag Muscat's EZ♥Care ringers was playing the Cleveland Mercy team. So that's why she had that squirrelly look when I came over and flashed my shield. A Rec and Parks ump with a badge? Who wouldn't wonder about that?

"Good memory. You're pretty observant."

"Observation and memory. My job. More or less."

"Mine too. More or less." I gestured to the cane. "Except I had to give up umping. Seems like the second thing to go was my hip. Third thing was my left knee. But to answer your question, that suit's been tied up in depositions and delays for a year now by Muscat's boatload of high-priced lawyers, with no end in sight. That sonofabitch is, pardon my French—"

"Pardoned."

"—is counting on me croaking before the case gets in front of a jury. Anyway, Dr. Toffoli, I'm here in my day-job capacity to ask you a question or two."

She smiled for the first time, and I had to laugh a bit as well.

"Yeah. No one's ever accused me of being original."

"What do you want to know, Artie?"

"I'm looking for a doctor."

"Just throw a fork."

"Specifically, an orthopedic surgeon named Trout."

Boom. She flashed the deer-in-headlights look again. I wondered why she was so skittish. To mix mammals-with-hooves metaphors, she was like a high-strung thoroughbred making her first start, the gate boys coaxing the nervous filly into the inside hole in front of ten-thousand screaming fans with their two-buck show tickets on the line. Or … I could just stick with deer-in-headlights. They both applied.

"I'm guessing you know him," I said, my eyeballs on the squint—my default expression when the little voice inside me tells me I struck a nerve.

But instead of striking a nerve, all I did was strike out, as she said, "Trout's the doctor who just performed a spinal fusion on my boyfriend. Nick was the batter who accidentally hit that poor seagull. So yes, I know Dr. Trout."

"How well?"

"Just from being Nick's doctor. I don't work with him; I'm a pediatric intern and Dr. Trout's a famous orthopedist."

Whoa. I just got whiplash from how quick her deer-in-headlights vibe morphed into Bambi on steroids telling me, *Yeah, you might crash into me, but I'm gonna mess up the grill of your Caprice but good.* Whatever, sweetheart, I'm the one behind the wheel here.

"When's the last time you saw him?"

"Yesterday afternoon. After the surgery."

"Where was that?"

"In Nick's room. Dr. Trout was doing his post-surgical rounds. With his team—Dr. Demidova, along with some orthopedic interns and medical students."

"What's your boyfriend's name?"

"Glass. Nick Glass."

I took out my field notepad to jot it down, when it happened again. The deer-in-headlights look squared. At the time, I attributed it to nerves. Concern. Turned out I was correct on both counts.

But all that was later.

I gestured toward the exit. "That Garfinkle guy who was just here?"

"Excuse me?"

"The doc with the Simon and Garfinkle hair."

"Oh. Dr. Klepstein."

"Yeah. The guy you were having coffee with."

"It was a meeting."

I got the point. No love lost there. "Does he work with Trout?" I fished.

"Hardly ever. Dr. Klepstein is a pediatrician. I suppose they would consult on a pediatric orthopedic procedure. But otherwise, no."

I pretended to write something else in my notepad. Something coppish. But it was just a note to remind myself Marie wanted me to pick up some kielbasa at Marek's in Tremont. Still, the act of scribbling had its desired intent. Toffoli was worried about something she didn't want me to know about. "Well, thanks for your time, Doc." I made a show of putting my notepad away in my coat and grabbed my cane. Luckily, I got to my feet without doing a pratfall.

"Sure, no problem."

I made like I was going but instead did my patented Stall. The one I perfected from watching a zillion *Columbo* re-runs. "Have you done your ER rotation yet?"

She looked at me like what would I care about her internship? I didn't. I cared about something else.

"Yes. Last fall."

"Lots of runaways come through. OD's and what have you?"

"Of course." I could see she was confused as to where I was going with this new line, so I took out my wallet again and flashed her the pic of Kimmy, next to my badge.

"This is unrelated to Trout. Take a look. Does this girl ring your bell?"

"No."

"Take a longer look, will ya? This one's for me."

I'll give her this. She did take an honest look at the pic of Kimmy but still shook her head. "Sorry."

"No worries, Doctor Toffoli. Just a shot in the dark." I tossed a fin on the table, along with my business card. "Coffee, and whatever that is trying to crawl out of your plate, are on me. Let me know if you ever run across the girl in the picture, or Dr. Trout. My cell is on the back. 'Preciate it. Merry Christmas."

As I gimped my way out of the cafeteria, I was struck by two things: how come she never asked why I was interested in finding

Trout, and why was she hiding that book about HIV under the *Plain Dealer* Sports Section? Yeah, I can read upside down.

CHAPTER 19

Drip Period

Nick sat on a throne of plastic and steel, and between grimaces recalled a lecture given by Professor Grayson in his Philosophy 101 class back at Kent State. Not that he gave a monkey's butt about philosophy, but it was one of those "core requirement" classes he needed to graduate. He remembered baldy Grayson rambling on about some old French dude named Montaigne. Nick hadn't retained much, but a quote came into his head that made him chuckle in between gasps.

And on the highest throne in the world,
we still sit only on our own bottom.

It was about humility. Yeah, well, Nick felt humiliated enough; what was one more reminder? Nick's throne was a riser over a shit-stained toilet in the bathroom of his hospital room. With his back brace Velcroed tight around him to keep him stable, physically anyway, he pushed and strained; each attempt sent him into another paroxysm of hurt as he tried his damnedest to give Demidova her dump. The dump that would get him out of this place.

Nick gnashed his teeth as he pressed his butt cheeks together so hard, he got dizzy and had to grab the side rails to keep from falling. Nick had never wanted anything so bad in his life than to heave this Havana. Hell, right now he would settle for a cigarillo.

Even a Virginia Slim. Anything to escape this prison of pain and the *memento mori* that was Trout, who Nick was half-convinced would enter the bathroom in his bloody snowman suit and, like a movie zombie, wreak his revenge. Nick was certain comeuppance was nigh. But wait: comeuppance for what exactly? What had he done wrong? Telling the man the truth? Goddamn, he even tried to catch the maniac when he hurled himself into space. Nick's rational mind realized that a flyer like that would surely kill anyone. More like *"memento* NO *mori."*

Nick's rational mind had also believed Trout's glib promises to make the pain go away, promises which proved to be nothing but lies. But who would believe Nick's truth? Just Julie. And look what happened to her. How fucking unfair. How *wrong.* One unholy Christmas Eve in a hospital and both their lives blown up. How could this happen? Trout going homicidal? Klepstein's arrogance and incompetence leading to Julie not only catching the blame for a kid's death, but also snagging a career and dream-ending disease? So why should he even care if he took a stupid dump or not? Like it was going to matter. Not with the lifetime sentences of despair and uselessness he and Julie were doomed to share.

Plop.

A Virginia Slim sliced through the water of the toilet bowl like a pebble in the pond of a Zen garden.

Holy shit! Nick couldn't have cared less if the Prize Patrol from Publisher's Clearing House had pranced into the bathroom and handed him an oversized check for twenty-gazillion dollars. Because the tiny turd floating in the bowl was priceless. It was his ticket out of this place.

Oh, and screw you and your humility, Michel de Montaigne.

* * *

Outside, Cleveland Mercy was deserted; Boxing Day had been kayoed by the relentless combo of nightfall and nonstop snow. The white stuff continued to accumulate in record amounts. The granite gargoyles at the hospital entrance were iced over beyond recognition. As was the adjacent park. All the playground equipment was buried.

Still, not a Snowboy in sight.

All was quiet on the eighth floor. The blinking Nurses Station was shrouded in shadow; the four-sided command post looked like an ectoplasmic spaceship. In the center, surrounded by the inconstant lights of the consoles and screensavers, hunched over the one active computer screen, which threw dancing pinpricks of light across his terrifying, alien face, Carmelo Iakopo RN sat alone, captaining the graveyard shift. His concentration was riveted on the flickering computer screen, as his right hand rhythmically moved up and down below his waist. With parted lips and shallow breaths, like a respiratory patient with an empty oxygen tank, Carmelo Iakopo interacted with his favorite Pornhub.com channel.

Until a Patient Light came on. Iakopo tried to ignore it but the buzzkill that was patient Gertrude Jepsen just wouldn't stop crying. Her frail voice crackled through his speaker.

"Nurse, please ... can you hear me? Nurse, I am in so much pain ... I need ... something. Please..."

Iakopo looked on the whiteboard and saw that Mrs. Jepson was just up from a double knee replacement. Why doesn't that bitch shut the fuck up? Tough it out, granny.

But she wouldn't. Gertrude Jepson was wailing worse than the fake screams of ecstasy emanating from the porn video. In fact, he could hear her voice all the way down the hallway.

"Please, nurse ... Please ... Oh dear God, I want to kill myself ... Please get me something. Nurse ... please ..."

Iakopo, furious, shut off his computer and slammed his fist on the Talk Button. "It's too early, Mrs. Jepsen. Chart says you have to wait one more hour. Dontcha call me again." Gertrude Jepson howled in protest but Iakopo cut her off. Still, her anguished cries echoed until they became intermittent sobs, until they became nothing at all.

Just when he tried to return to his video, another Patient Light came on. A glance at the whiteboard informed that this was a Mr. Will Meriwether, possessor of a brand-new plate in his skull. Iakopo again slammed on his mic. "Whatcha want, Mr. Meriwether?" The answer was the scratchy breathing of a sleeping old man who had rolled over his call button, as a Jeopardy rerun played on his TV.

"*Um … who was Doctor 'Jolly Jane' Toppan?*" queried a tentative *female voice.*

"*Yes! That is correct!*" *was the futzed reply from the eternal Alex Trebek.* "*Dr. 'Jolly Jane' Toppan was one of our earliest female serial killers. Fun fact: 'Jolly Jane' confessed to having derived a 'sexual thrill' as she fondled her patients in bed and watched them die from her poisonous concoctions. I don't know about you, panel, but I definitely would not want a house call from Dr. Toppan.*" *(Audience laughter.)* "*Well, that concludes the category 'Heels or Healers.' We'll be right back.*"

Iakopo shut off Mr. Meriwether's room, looked to the white-board and wondered how the Harvard pussy was doing. Not expecting much, he turned on Nick's audio and all at once was awash in a sea of tense voices. The first was the hoity-toity intern bitch. Julie emanated from the speaker like she was broadcasting from an AM radio station three states away. Her words went in and out and Iakopo had to strain to get it all. But he got enough.

"Maybe I should just disappear ..."

* * *

Nick lay on his side as Julie spoon fed him grape Jello. The only illumination was from the monitor lights and a thin sliver of ambient hallway fluorescence that cleaved through the partly-closed privacy curtain.

Agitated, Julie continued her thought: "Crawl under some rock where they can't find me." She slid another spoonful into his mouth. The remnants of the grape Jello on Nick's lips reflected in the pale light gave him the look of a gravely ill vampire.

He swallowed and protested, "Hell, if anyone should disappear it should be me. I mean what's going to happen when they realize Trout isn't around anymore?"

* * *

Oka e! This newsflash gobsmacked Carmelo Iakopo right in the middle of swallowing a handful of Adderall, prescribed for a patient named Gina Chen. Iakopo spat half-chewed tabs all over his console as he leaned toward the speaker, raptly listening to the Julie & Nick Hospital Room Mystery Hour.

"Absolutely nothing. There isn't a shred of evidence in his office that will link his absence to you. Just ditch the stupid Harvard lapel pin."

Oh man, Carmelo was hooked. Although he never had the patience to sit through stories with lots of exposition—even as an oversized toddler in his crib of palm fronds in his home village of Apai, he would cry like a bitch whenever his *Le Tina a lo'u Tina* (grandmother) tried to tell him about the legends of the Ancient Gods, until inevitably she'd throw up her hands and leave in a huff—this story tonight was one he'd die to learn how it ended.

His *Le Tina a lo'u Tina* would also tell little Carmelo to be careful what he wished for.

* * *

"I'll dump it just as soon as I'm safely out of here," said Nick.

"Safely? What are you talking about?"

"That *Phantom of the Opera* nurse—the freak who pulled out my catheter without any warning or anesthetic—he *saw* the pin and knows what it is. Worse, he moonlights for Muscat; more worse, the dude has a history of anger management issues."

"And you know this, how?"

"Because he told me! Jules, this guy scares the shit out of me."

Julie took advantage of his open mouth and jammed more Jello into it.

"Don't worry about him. If anything, they'll investigate that blackmailing psycho Russian bitch. That blackmailing, *murdering* psycho Russian bitch."

* * *

Iakopo's eyeballs all but bulged out of their sockets, like they were attached to a pair of Slinkies. He grabbed a pencil and began to take notes. The pencil snapped in his powerful hand, so he grabbed another but wrote with so much force it shattered and splinters embedded in his palm. But Iakopo felt no pain because— no offence to his beloved *Le Tina a lo'u Tina*—Julie and Nick's story was the best tale he'd ever heard. And potentially, the most lucrative. Nick's voice was next out of the speaker:

"Wait. *Demidova didn't murder Trout.*"

"*No? Her fingerprints are all over those French doors. Bummer for her, huh?*"

* * *

"Julie? You're really going there?"

"Why not? She is a murderer."

"What?"

"The sables. Who speaks for them? Do you know how many of them had to die to make her hundred-thousand-dollar coat?"

Nick tried to work that out. "Three?"

Julie glared at him.

"Five?"

Her glare escalated into a five-hundred-terawatt death ray.

"I don't know, I give up. Ten?"

"More like *sixty to eighty*. And do you know how they are killed?"

"Clubbed like baby seals?"

"No. They are shot in the face. So their pelts aren't ruined. Sables, they're kind of like Garfield except with more expensive fur and bigger teeth. But unlike Garfield, they can't speak for themselves. How can that woman call herself a doctor? She's a murderer. Just like Klepstein."

* * *

Klepstein! Him too? Iakopo felt like his head was gonna explode. Did all those docs kill Trout? Or could it have been just the Harvard pussy? But how? Da boy's in no condition. And it's not like Trout's body is in the middle of the lobby oozing blood and shit. All he did was not show up today.

Iakopo's brain was developing a bad itch. An itch he couldn't scratch unless he ripped his head off, and he remembered what happened the last time he tried that. Talk about a mess. Instead, Iakopo splintered the next pencil between his teeth. "Fuck me," he said as he chewed the pencil into kindling.

* * *

Julie, in a culmination of fear, frustration, and rage, yelled to wake the dead (and those soon to be dead) and threw the cup of grape Jello against the far wall. As it splatted and began to drip, tears welled in her eyes. But Julie wouldn't allow them to fall.

"Nick. What the hell am I going to do?"

"We. It's what are *we* going to do. Say the Western Blot proves to be worst case, which it won't, but if it is, I mean if you had to, couldn't you get a pathology fellowship or some other doctor job, like maybe at an insurance company where you could—"

"Think of reasons to deny people their medical care? Because the patient has a pre-existing condition? Or order a doctor to prescribe a less efficacious drug because it's cheaper? Become the in-house Dr. No at EZ♥Care for Jimmy Tom Muscat? No thanks."

"That's not what I meant."

"I'm sorry, Nick. I know you're trying to help but being the kind of doctor I want to be isn't going to happen. The question of why my residency was terminated will follow me everywhere. Second chances are scarce to none. Goddamnit!" She grabbed a second cup of Jello, this one peach, and threw that against the far wall too. The splattered peach joined the grape dribbling down the wall.

"Does your Dad know?"

"Of course, he calls every evening at nine, sharp. Really, Nick? Come on. The only communication I get from him is the occasional Guilty Dad Check from his beach house in Kauai. I mean ever since he married my latest stepmom, who I think is three months younger than me, it's like he's got Stockholm Syndrome. He let that skank get away with blocking my request to be his Skype contact. No, these days he just sits around his end-of-the-rainbow lanai smoking weed and drinking Myers rum. The only time he gets off his ass is to bury dead pigs in the sand when he's hungry. Our bonding days are over. It's you and me, Nick, unless you want to bounce too; call your folks and ask them to drive back from their eternal Winnebago tour of the country and take care of you."

Nick laughed but paid for it as cricks of pain rippled across his stitches. He bit his tongue. "Not fair. You don't get to make me laugh."

"I'm sorry. I'll tamp my drollery."

"Jules. Forget parents; it's you and I who will get through this."

"It's only fair I give you a chance to bail. Parachute out of the plane. Seriously. I'll only have a few hard feelings."

"Sorry. No."

"Think about it. Think what you could be giving up."

"Which would be everything. I go where you go."

"Wherever that is?"

"Yeah. Wherever."

Julie took both his hands, taking care to avoid touching the IV line above his wrist. "Except what if it's nowhere? Ever since I was four, I wanted to be a doctor. I used to 'cure' my Barbies. There were a couple of close calls; remember Glitter Hair Barbie? She was touch and go. But I never lost one single doll. And my Mom, my real Mom, she told me if I wanted it badly enough, if I tried hard enough, I could become the best doctor in the entire world. Her sitting on the edge of my bed is the only tangible memory I have of her. That, and how tired her eyes always were. Yeah well, sorry, Mom, wherever you are; sometimes trying hard isn't enough." She let go of Nick's hands. "I don't see any happy endings here." She gestured to Nick's untouched dinner tray of meatloaf, mashed potatoes, and broccoli with Hollandaise sauce. "Are you going to eat that?"

Nick shook his head and Julie blew out a sigh, picked up the tray, and flung it against the far wall as hard as she could. The tray clattered to the floor as meatloaf, broccoli, and mashed potatoes added to the multicolored Jello trickling down the wall. The mess looked like GMO Drip Period Jackson Pollock.

Julie sagged. "Sorry."

Before Nick could tell her it was okay, a distorted voice came through the speaker in Nick's remote, startling them. *"Every-ting okay in there, brah?"* crackled the voice of Iakopo.

Nick spoke into the remote. "We're good, man. Thanks. Just spilled my tray."

"Hey, no worries, brah. I'll call Housekeepin'. Lemme know if you need any-ting else. Any-ting at all. Carmelo Iakopo is here for you."

Nick palmed the remote so Iakopo couldn't hear and muttered, "Asshole." When he looked up, it was to see Julie putting on her coat and grabbing her stuff, including a couple of pills from an RX bottle which she dry-swallowed.

"Hey. Where are you going?"

"Home. I haven't slept for two straight days. The longer I stay around here, the more wired I get. Besides, I have to think." She paused. "You think too."

"I don't need to."

"Well, fine, but I can't stay because by the time the two Extra Strength Ambien I just swallowed kick in, my head needs to be hitting the pillow. If I'm not in bed, it'll be like the worst trip ever."

* * *

Julie, staring straight ahead but not seeing, her nerve endings electric, strode past the Nurses Station. Preoccupied with her own nightmare—and Nick's, as a not inconsiderable part of her would have to admit—she didn't notice Carmelo Iakopo lurking in the shadows behind the station.

Iakopo watched her walk to the elevators. He breathed through his nose and thought about the opportunity that had just presented itself. He had all this information (the parts he could understand, at least) but wasn't sure how to play it. It was too late to call Mr. Muscat, but maybe he didn't *need* Mr. Muscat for the idea that'd been bubbling like the molten lava in the Savai'i Volcano back in the homeland of his people. The one his *Le Tina a lo'u Tina* had told him was so powerful it had destroyed two-hundred villages last time it blew. No, he didn't need Mr. Muscat at all. He knew plenty about erupting and destroying. So why not take things into his own hands? Like right now? He knew he could get away with it. The Harvard pussy was alone and would be for the rest of the night because the emo intern bitch was wearing a winter coat, which meant she wasn't coming back till morning. So what's stopping you, Melo? Fuckin' nothing. Okay then: time to go all Savai'i over the punk in 822.

As he turned with purpose toward Nick's room, the telephone at the Nurses Station rang. Iakopo frowned. Thought about it for a second, and picked up. "Eighth Floor Nurses Station." As Iakopo listened to the fast-talking voice on the other end of the phone, the frown on his face grew darker and his serpents restless. "No, dat's okay. I'll help you guys out. I got two LVNs on the floor; they can handle things here. Be right down."

The frown had turned to frustration. The call was for all-hands-on-deck in the ER. Bus crash with multiple casualties and shit. Fuck. He gazed wistfully down the hall to Nick's room, but knew he had the rest of the night to do what he needed to do before the 7:00 a.m. shift came on.

He would just have to work a little faster. Skip the bubbling lava and get right to the eruption.

CHAPTER 20

In-box Me

Julie, buttoning her coat on the fly as she rounded the corridor to the elevator bank, arrived just in time to hear a ping and see Tick, the stoner cafeteria worker, wheeling a flatbed overloaded with cardboard boxes into an elevator car.

"Hold please," Julie called.

Tick turned, made eye contact with Julie with an expression akin to being busted transporting body parts scavenged from deceased patients to deliver to some mad scientist, the kind that lives in the bargain basement of VHS B-Movies.

Or in a "Closed Off" basement, thought Julie as she sprinted the final few steps to the elevator, which shut closed in her face and began its descent.

What is going on with these people? Julie had seen this furtive gurney-to-the-basement racket too many times now to put it down to coincidence. First Raven, the candy-striper from Nick's surgery dream, and again this wasteoid from the cafeteria. She looked up at the floor pointer and watched the progress of the car as it went *past* the Ground Floor, the ostensible end of the line, and stopped at its final destination: again, the closed-off B-3, the alleged sealed-off floor three stories below the Ground Floor.

Why? What's down there? On the other hand, who cares? What Julie needed to do was get into bed before the Ambien kicked in. Wake up with a clear head and consider her options. Hers and Nick's. That was way more important than going all Lisbeth Salander over the mysterious case of stolen cafeteria supplies. Why should she care? Especially now.

Because it really bugged her.

And she needed *something* in her life to make sense. Even something as stupid as this. Besides, it wouldn't be the first boundary she had crossed tonight. She pressed the Down button and waited.

Despite the laminated warning notice, Julie pressed B-3 upon entering the returned car. Amid the grinding and clanking of antique cables, counterweights, and pulleys that miraculously facilitated her controlled fall, Julie descended into depths unknown.

The landing jarred her as the car hit B-3 hard. Julie steadied herself against the side wall of the car and watched the elevator door slide open to reveal ...

Pretty much nothing.

Just an admixture of brick and decaying drywall and a dusty tacked-up sign that read:

WARNING: FLOOR NOT IN USE. NO EGRESS

Julie studied the brick and drywall and came to the conclusion that this didn't make any sense. Because she'd just *seen* the kid with a handcart full of boxes travel down *here*. To *this* floor. So, where was he? And for that matter, where did the candy-striper go with all those gurneys? Did these freaks wheel their carts *through* the brick and drywall via special effects into another dimension? A dimension not only of sight and sound but of mind? Next stop, *The Twilight Zone.* Cue the bongos.

Well, no. Memories of *Twilight Zone* re-runs aside, the laws of physics still applied in B-3. Didn't they? Julie lived in an empirical world, a world of objective reality. A world where magic didn't exist, except in Las Vegas showrooms. She contemplated the wall in front of her but it wasn't divulging its secrets. She reached out and touched it. To no result other than to streak her fingers with dust and grime. Julie grimaced and decided it was time to give up this ridiculous search of something that no longer concerned her and return to the Ground Floor, hurry home, and get into bed before she became another Ambien side-effect statistic* when she noticed the faint outline of a *handprint* on the far corner of the drywall, just above the filthy floor.

Why a handprint only six inches above the floor?

Just as Julie bent to find out, the elevator alarm clanged, startling her. She stumbled forward, her hand landing on the outline of the handprint, which resulted in the so-called sealed wall swiveling open as if mounted on a giant turntable. Julie found herself propelled into a world of darkness on the other side as the fake wall slammed shut behind her!

The no-longer-stalled elevator ceased clanging and Julie heard its gears grinding and its pulleys whining as it ascended, leaving her alone and trapped in the dark void of B-3 with no way out. No way out and no signpost up ahead that read *"Twilight Zone → Exit This Way"* that she could see. Just a vast black emptiness.

Okay, don't panic. Darkness is just an absence of light, and the other side of a wall is just the other side of a wall. So calm down, take out your cell and call Maintenance. They'll be here in no time.

---

* These side effects, according to the American Psychiatric Society and numerous legal proceedings, include sleep driving causing injury and damage, binge eating, sex with no memory of such, and aggressive behavior, including murder.

She fumbled for the phone. Held it up to dial. The phone dialed just fine, but didn't ring. Julie realized she was looking at a screen with zero reception bars and two words: No Service.

Okay. Don't freak. Be rational. Think this through. There must be another way out. As in staircases. Staircases that would lead up. Up and out of here. All she had to do was find one of them, climb the steps to the Ground Floor—and even if the staircase door was locked, her cell would work there, or at worse she could scream and bang on the door until someone from the hospital came and unlocked it.

An excellent plan. Now implement it. Julie stifled an Ambien yawn, enabled the flashlight app on her phone and saw she was in a corridor. A corridor that would inevitably lead to a staircase. So take a breath, a deep one, and start walking.

Julie held the phone out in front of her, lighting her way through a corridor, which was littered with Paleolithic medical debris: shattered cupping glasses, amputation saws, an original Écraseur,[*] a veritable museum of early twentieth-century medical arcana. She passed a door with a faded sign that read: Doctors Lounge.

My God, this was part of the original Cleveland Mercy, Julie realized, the area that was exempt from any OSHA regs because OSHA's jurisdiction didn't extend to the Underworld. Some of the doors opened to operating rooms with vintage tables still in place, surrounded by standing surgical lamps with rounded reflector shades and cast-iron bases; and over there, her flashlight revealed a patient ward that had once housed fifty patients on steel-framed cots in one cavernous room. This was incredible, a journey back to the hospital's roots. Roots that dated back to

---

* French for "The Crusher," an instrument with a chain or wire loop that was used to encircle and sever a protruding mass of diseased tissue, such as a tumor or testicles, by gradually tightening the chain or loop until the afflicted body part was removed. It hurt.

the post-World War I Spanish Flu pandemic that had turned Cleveland Mercy into a charnel house, despite the heroic efforts of doctors and the selfless Sisters. The ones with the hooded caps that tied under the chin with ruffles around the face, à la Florence Nightingale. Not thieving candy-stripers.

Julie was fascinated; this was like a medical archeological dig. If her heart wasn't beating like a Questlove groove, she'd have to admit this little sojourn was kind of cool.

And that's when her cellphone chirped a dead battery warning and her flashlight app failed.

Leaving Julie once again in the dark.

She forced herself to slow her breathing. Stifling another yawn (oh yeah, the Ambien), Julie reached into her belt clip and emerged with Plan B: her otoscope, the small flashlight doctors (and she was still a doctor, damnit) used to peer down reddened throats and into waxy ears. But better conserve the battery on this baby or she'd be dancing in the dark with the ghosts of Cleveland Mercy forever.

And as if all she had to do was *think* of ghosts, that's when she *heard them.*

They sounded like eerie electronic soundwaves blended with the banshee screams of shrieking females. In a foreign language. Maybe Japanese?

Great. Angry Japanese ghosts.

Stop it, Julie, she told herself. She might be in a spooky dark basement hearing some weird shit, but this was still a rational world where everything, if you looked hard enough for the answers, could be explained. The world you live in, remember? Objective reality. What you're hearing are not ghosts. There will be a logical explanation. For instance, the Ambien coursing through her bloodstream. She really had to get out and get out fast. Julie resumed walking down the corridor towards the source of the cacophonous sounds. So far, so good. She'd almost convinced herself that she wasn't going insane and everything was going to be alright until *something* brushed against her leg, causing Julie to fall backwards into a pile of stacked boxes, which tumbled all around her. Rising from the bed of boxes, she turned on her otoscope and pointed it at what had brushed against her.

Which was a large monster rat.

Literally.

The rodent she was gawking at was a four-foot, seventy-pound carpenter rat with platinum-dyed spiky back fur, a sniffling aqui-line nose redolent of a verminous cokehead, and two enlarged front incisors that frankly, Julie thought, looked professionally bleached. Okay Jules, now you are hallucinating. Real rats have yellow teeth and don't wear Michael Jackson circa 1983 faux military coats. Just close your eyes and count backwards and the rat will be gone. After counting down from five, she opened them again but the hipster rodent was still there. Not only was it still there, but his beady eyes ogled Julie as he pulled on a Gran Corona Cuban Montecristo and blew a wisp of aromatic smoke her way. A familiar scent that triggered a long-ago sense memory; the rat's cigar was the same kind of *el ropo* her Dad used to get across the border in Windsor, Canada, and smuggle home in bulk. Stuffed them down his Dockers along with the inevitable, "I feel rather well hung today" joke he always told to Julie's Stepmom Number Three—who'd pretend to be mortified, the bitch bleating like a demon sheep, as all the while Julie just wanted to bury herself in the backseat and turn up her Discman until her eardrums burst.

"Hey! Get that light outta my eyes! I'm standin' here!"

That's all it took for objective reality, empiricism, and palpability to seem like alien concepts to her—alien concepts on an alien planet drifting away into an undefined infinity, leaving her behind with shrieking Japanese ghosts and a giant rat with an even larger attitude. She lowered her otoscope and apologized. "Sorry."

"What? That's it? You're sorry? Don't you know I got low visual acuity in bright light? That hurts! What are you doing in my crib? Not that I mind." He limned a grin that highlighted the drool dribbling from his shiny incisors. "'Cept next time, in-box me, okay?"

"Okay."

"Ain't no thing but a chicken wing." He waved his Montecristo. "So how 'bout I show ya a really stellar cheddar? Or a gamey Gouda?"

"What?"

"Cheese, baby. It's what's for dinner. All those casomorphins. Dairy crack for my dairy queen. Whatcha say, cupcake?"

"Go away! You're not real!"

"Who says?"

"Me! Go away!"

"Ah, I get it. #Fem2. Whatevs. I can take a hint. Just be careful down here. Although there's been some gentrification, this hood is no place for a doll like you."

He blew a farewell smoke ring her way, turned and strode off. Julie watched him disappear into the darkness, his long tail whipping back and forth behind him, his voice echoing, "Be careful, Julie."

Julie's hand shook as the otoscope's flare fluttered like a search-light in an air raid.

Did he just call me "Julie"? No, impossible.

She was certain they'd never met before. Dead certain. She grasped for her impotent mantra: *Objective reality. Objective reality. Objective reality.* Until she realized her objective reality was not the hallucinatory rat but her utter terror, induced and enhanced by the Ambien. Christ, why did she take two of them? And Extra

Strength at that? Why didn't she wait till she got back to the apartment? Well, too late now. She shined her light on the boxes that had fallen around her when she'd recoiled from the smartass rodent. The boxes were the same ones the skinny kid had brought down here in his cart. All pilfered from the Cleveland Mercy cafeteria. Canned food mostly, some plastic utensils, and a dozen cases of anti-bacterial hand soap.

All definitely real, along with the growing realization she was not alone down here. Because the discordant electronic sound effects and the screeching Japanese girls had become much louder. Like, around-the-next-dark-corner louder.

Julie gathered herself and struggling to stay awake, trained the otoscope in the direction of the sounds, and moved on. As she got closer to an intersecting corridor, the beam from her light saved her from walking right into a crackling electronic panel protruding from the wall. The door to the panel hung away from its tenuous connection with the panel's hinges, revealing the exposed and (real) rat-bitten live wiring within. As if to prove the point, her beam illuminated the body of a deceased normal-sized rat; smoke emanated from its fried body and its yellow eyes were open in final surprise.

Julie steered clear of the sparking panel and headed down the intersecting corridor, where she further reacted to not only the continuing sound effects and screaming Japanese girls, but also the lights.

Electric lights.

No need for the otoscope here as a row of twenty-watt bulbs, encased in dingy steel mesh covers, bathed the new corridor in a pallid glow. There were also loads more boxes stacked everywhere. Some were labeled: "PHARMACY - DO NOT REMOVE." Adjacent to the boxes were brand new IV poles and other modern medical equipment: no amputation saws or Écraseurs here; instead there was an EKG machine, blood pressure monitors, disposable surgical kits, stethoscopes, even a portable x-ray machine, and lots more boxes of cafeteria food. On the wall nearby she saw a dusty fire extinguisher. The sign above it read, "IN CASE OF EMERGENCY BREAK GLASS" but the glass was already shattered into jagged shards on the grubby floor. And hey, over there, what was *that*? Could it be a certain familiar gurney?

Julie resumed towards the source of the dissonant sound cloud and came to a stop beneath a faded sign over a closed pair of double doors. The sign read "Doctor Jackson Ambrose Operating Theatre," the original lyceum of Cleveland Mercy. The same demonstration O.R. on a spot-lit stage surrounded on four sides by raised seating as depicted in the black-and-white photograph of Dr. Ambrose that Trout had showed Julie after Nick's surgery. Which now seemed like a zillion years ago, certainly a changed lifetime ago, but in reality, only two days.

The dissonance emanating from within had become deafening. Julie pushed the double doors open and slid inside like a burglar.

All the seats in the vast amphitheater were empty, save for two far below in the first row occupied by Tick, the cafeteria worker, and Raven, the candy-striper. The two of them manipulated game controllers with the intensity of NASA techs tasked with the responsibility of bringing home a hobbled spacecraft. They were playing a Japanese videogame, which was displayed on a freaking huge, hundred-inch video monitor, surrounded by ear-piercing speakers placed on the same hallowed stage where the venerated Dr. Ambrose had once displayed his surgical skills for the voyeuristic benefit of a hundred rapt medical students and doctors as he cut into the forever anonymous half-naked woman in that old black-and-white photo.

For Julie, it was like gazing into the depths of Hell. Because it sure seemed that's how deep this relic of a hospital was built underground, as if all the newer floors above were constructed on a foundation of malignancy. She stayed put at the top of the aisle and watched Raven and Tick as they competed against each other in a PS4 game called *Senran Kagura*, where a pair of voluptuous female ninjas fought throngs of anime villains; hence, the shrieking Japanese ladies. Julie surmised, via the help of the syntax-free subtitles on the monitor, the object of the game was to accumulate points by having your team of Ninjettes defeat as many of the bad guys, an endless supply of Yakuza mobsters, as possible.

On the monitor, one of the villains executed a slick martial arts feint to distract, and tore off the blouse of Raven's ninja, named Ryona, exposing a pair of architecturally implausible breasts.

A furious Raven manipulated the blouse back on her character and shut down the game. And with that, the noise Julie had been hearing throughout her basement trek, the soundtrack of her fears, ended. She watched as Raven, livid, bored a hole through Tick's skull with her Goth glare. "You perv! We agreed to disable 'Clothing Destruction!'"

"You agreed. I was just trying to rack up points. *Rack* up points," he repeated, in case she didn't get it.

"That's so funny I forgot to laugh."

"Hey, why are you so mad? If you remove clothing, you become more powerful. That's the game!"

"How about I remove your face? See how powerful you feel then, you sick twerp."

Tick backed off, "Raven, I'm sorry. For real. I won't do it anymore. How about we play just one more game? I promise …"

"Don't promise, Tick. You know you can't control yourself. Then you feel bad. Never promise what you can't deliver."

Well, this is awkward, thought Julie. Still, she'd better walk down the steps, introduce herself and get them to help her out of this basement before …

"Don't move, *putana*."

Julie gasped as a tall Afro-Caribbean girl, maybe eighteen, with an ultra-short coily hairstyle, which enhanced the ferocity in her dark-brown eyes, jammed one arm around Julie's chest and with the other held a syringe to Julie's throat.

"What's in that?"

"How badly do you want to find out?"

The girl wore a white hospital coat with a sewn insignia identifying her as a Pharmacy Aide and under that her first name, Jacinta.

Below, Raven and Tick turned toward the pair, both recognizing Julie from their earlier encounters.

"You," said Raven, as she headed up the steps of the lyceum, followed by Tick.

"Yeah, me. Hi. Could you ask your friend to remove the syringe?"

"No. What you are doing here? Why are you always following me? And how did you get in?"

"I don't know. It was an accident with the elevator and I'm having a really bad day and all I want is to go home and sleep."

"I think you just want to bust us."

"I have no interest in busting you." Julie yawned, slurred her words. "I am telling you guys the truth. I just want to go home." Half-asleep, she failed to clock the glance between Raven and Jacinta. A look that translated as whether to inject or not. Raven blinked her eyes in affirmation, but Tick put a restraining hand on Raven's shoulder.

"Wait. Don't."

"What?" Raven was still pissed off at him, and now this. "Why?"

"I think she's on the hundred. When I was working, I watched Dr. Klepstein fire her. A patient died because of some screw-up he did and he put it on her. I was pouring the dude his coffee so I know what I heard. Just sayin' maybe we should listen to her story first."

Raven could see that Julie was high on something; in fact, she could hardly stand. "Why should we trust you?"

"Why should you trust me? Because I asked politely? Also, now that I'm thinking about it, the reality is it doesn't much matter if your friend sticks me or not." Julie's eyes edged to the tip of the syringe. "Because whatever's in there, it can't be any worse than what's already been done."

At that, Julie's eyes closed and she collapsed into Jacinta's arms, fast asleep.

CHAPTER 21

A Scream Is Just A Scream

It was 4:00 a.m., the Hour of the Wolf. *"The hour between night and dawn, the hour when most people die, when sleep is the deepest, and when nightmares are most real."** So it was not odd that the shadowed corridor outside Nick's room was deserted; but what was odd was the closed door with a sign reading:

MEDICAL PROCEDURE IN PROGRESS

NO ENTRY

From within the room, a muffled scream was quashed before it could be heard. But so what? A scream in a hospital is unremarkable, a vocalization of pain as quotidian to the environment as a band-aid, a misread prescription, or an infected endoscope.

Because at Cleveland Mercy, or any hospital, especially in those wee small hours of the morning when the whole world is fast asleep, a scream is just a scream.

Unless it was Carmelo Iakopo RN who happened to be the one inducing said scream.

*　*　*

* From the trailer to the only horror film Ingmar Bergman ever made, *Hour of the Wolf* (1968). The original Swedish title was *Vargtimmen*. Somehow not as scary.

Nick thought he had survived the worst they could throw at him. Pills, procedures, Trout's "Full Isis," all of it. But now, with no one around except this psycho with his catcher's mitt of a hand clamped over his mouth, Nick knew this was his personal *Hour of the Wolf*. The hour he would die.

"This time, when I take my hand away, don't scream like a bitch," Iakopo whispered. "You unnerstand me?"

Nick's ping-ponging eyeballs indicated "yes" and Iakopo removed his hand. He wiped the saliva off on Nick's chest, on his posterior wound site, eliciting another whimper.

"Said keep quiet." Nick gagged as Iakopo leaned into Nick's face, breathing rancid poi. "There's a million ways for peeps to die in this hospital and nobody's gonna think nothing special if one of dem is you. I mean they'll check it out, but short of a gunshot wound, nobody's going to go all *CSI* and shit if you stop breathing. They'll go in the most obvious medical direction I point them. They'll feel kinda bad. For about five minutes, and den they'll move on like they always do. Yeah, no doubt your chick will feel bad too but in the end it's you who's gonna feel worse and after dat, you'll feel nothin'. Which is the direction this thing will go if you don't answer my questions. You feel me, brah?"

Nick croaked in the affirmative.

"Good. So where's Dr. Trout?"

"I don't know."

Iakopo blew out a frustrated sigh, sending another fetid blast down Nick's throat. "Bitch, I *heard* you and your chick talking about Trout 'not being around anymore.' What does that mean, xactly?"

"Look, all I know is he mentioned something about having to 'get away' or something like that. I was half-unconscious; I don't remember. Look, Melo, the dude's my doctor. I need him."

With his left hand, Iakopo reached into the trash can and emerged with Trout's Harvard lapel pin which he jabbed into Nick's bandaged wound. With his right, he blanketed Nick's face, causing him to gag. He leaned in close once more and hissed: "The Doc missed all his surgeries dis morning. Didn't call in. Didn't do his rounds. Didn't show for his clinic. Peeps round here are looking for him. You know why and you're gonna tell me."

Iakopo pointed the business end of the pin an inch away from Nick's eye. "What's more, dis Harvard pin *belongs* to Doctor Trout. Not you. Internet has you at Cuyahoga Community, then Kent State. Not Harvard. So I gotta ax the question: If you don't know where Dr. Trout is, just what the fuck are you doing with his pin?"

Iakopo released his hand to allow Nick to answer. "Maybe it came off his coat when he examined me. I don't know, man. I just found it here."

"And threw it in the trashcan *after* I noticed it?"

"It probably fell off the table. I was going to give it back to him."

Iakopo scowled and ripped out Nick's IV line.

"And I was going to cut off your morphine. No, wait. I just did."

Iakopo again jabbed Nick in the posterior wound site as his other hand smothered his cries. "Tell me, brah, what did your chick mean when she said they'll investigate that 'blackmailing psycho Russian bitch?' What you two got on Dr. Demidova?"

"Where do you come up with this bizarre crap?" Nick spoke through Iakopo's splayed fingers.

Iakopo's gaze directed Nick towards the in-bed all-purpose remote/call button. "Works two ways, remember?"

Nick sagged as if it was over for him, as if resistance was futile. "Okay. You win. One thing: Julie's got nothing to do with this, okay?"

"With what, brah?"

"All of it," Nick said. He feigned searching for the words as his left hand searched the bed for his iPhone.

"Not going to ax you again. Nothing to do with *what?*" Iakopo's tatt serpents looked poised to leap off his pockmarked face and bite him to death as Nick at last grasped the phone and fumbled for the Voice Memo icon.

"Let me breathe and I'll tell you. It's complicated."

"Listen, brah, I don't like the Trout either. Everybody round dis place thinks he's some kind a God. But I seen things. So I don't give a shit if you threw him out the fuckin' window, truth be told."

Nick tried to poker-face that one, but the guilty look in his eyes told Iakopo that he just hit the Trout Powerball Jackpot.

"Really?" Iakopo laughed. "No shit?"

Nick floundered for the damn Voice Memo icon.

"You *really* threw dat jackoff out the window?" Iakopo squinted as he reconsidered, "Nah, don't bullshit me. How the fuck did *you* do that? Ain't possible. Musta been your chick, right? Yeah. Tell me: she got pissed at him for messing up your surgery, right?"

"I said she stays out of it," wheezed Nick, as he got his index finger flush on the red circle on the Voice Memo icon. Thank God. At least, if this slobbering batshit mountain of depravity turned him into a pin cushion, it'd be recorded.

Starting. Right. Now.

"I want to talk to the police," said Nick, bluffing like a poker player holding a hopeless rainbow.

"No, brah. You're gonna pay me five Benjis a week or you ain't leaving dis hospital alive. And neither will your chick."

"Are you threatening Dr. Toffoli?"

"You pick up quick. And think about this: before I whack the bitch, I'm going to introduce her to Little Carmelo. I call him Little Carmelo cuz of the roids. I mean, who knew that shit would shrink your junk like dat? Neva-da-less, I'm gonna tap her ass till she can't walk. And den …"

Nick watched as Iakopo's eyes went from intense to intensely stunned as he vomited inarizushi, roast pork, poi, and a six-pack of Longboard Iron Lager all over his face.

As Nick choked and peeked through puke-covered eyes, Iakopo turned to reveal a hypodermic needle stuck in his neck like a Norwegian harpoon in a Minke whale's blubbery hide. Iakopo, dead-eyed, rolled off him and thudded to the floor, revealing …

… Tick and Jacinta, flanking a refreshed Julie, who addressed the inert lump that was Carmelo Iakopo:

"Your 'tapping' days are over, creep."

"Julie …" mumbled Nick.

"Hi, Nicky," she turned to the door, where Raven appeared and wheeled her ubiquitous gurney into the room.

"Let's take this tub of shit downstairs."

"Right."

Julie returned her gaze to Nick and examined his rainbow barf-covered face and said, "The Polynesian menu?"

CHAPTER 22

Carrots Peas Ativan

The original Doctors Lounge was stuck in a time warp circa 1959. Yellowing, frayed pinups of Anita Ekberg and Jayne Mansfield shared wall space with a Pan Am calendar depicting a Clipper on the runway of Honolulu International Airport. Grass-skirted hula girls placed leis around the necks of tourists in seersucker suits and straw-boater hats, as their wives concealed disapproving looks behind sunglasses and simulated smiles. On the mold-stained wall between Anita and Jayne, there was an Administrative Notice reminding the docs to wash their hands, except some long-dead joker had crossed out "Hands" and replaced it with "Cocks." It's good to leave a legacy.

Below the posters were ripped couches and easy chairs, long gutted of stuffing. They surrounded the center of the lounge where—absent a dining table—Julie, Raven, Tick, and Jacinta were seated in plastic chairs on either side of the gurney with the unconscious Iakopo still on it. He was in patient restraints, covered with a sheet, and snoring. The four used his wheezing gut, broad shoulders, and prodigious thighs as a makeshift table upon which sat a half-dozen cafeteria trays piled high with Styrofoam-encased meals and side dishes.

"Pass the peas?" Tick asked Julie.

Julie handed a carton to Tick, who pried off the lid and looked askance at the contents inside.

"What's wrong?"

"Forget it. I'm not blaming you."

"Uh, blaming me for what?"

"Tell her, Derpy," said Raven. "We all have to live with it. Tell her."

Tick displayed the carton to Julie. "See, the peas are mixed in with cooked carrots."

"Oh. That's no good."

"Thank you. At least, she understands. Unlike you two."

Jacinta took two pills out of an RX bottle in her pocket, dropped them in Tick's Kool-Aid cup, and said, "Drink."

Tick did so without protest.

Julie reacted to the meds. "What are you giving him?"

"Ten milligrams of Ativan."

"Really? Ten?"

"Tick has a humongous tolerance," said Raven.

"I work in the pharmacy," said Jacinta. "It's been trial and error but between these and the anti-depressant cocktail I've concocted, Tick's leveled out rather nicely."

"You're a pharmacist?" asked Julie.

Everybody laughed. Even Tick, who, with fork and knife, was separating the peas and carrots one by one. By one. By one.

"Not yet. Between my shifts as a pharmaceutical aide, I'm doing course work at Lake Erie College of Osteopathic Medicine. It's a long bus ride, but it's worth it. Two more years I'll have my license."

"That's great," said Julie.

"And best of all," Jacinta said, indicating Tick, "I'm getting practical experience one just can't buy."

Raven leaned close to Julie and whispered, "Tick's on the *spectrum*."

"I heard that. Could we talk about something else?"

"Like your incessant masturbation?" said Jacinta. She looked to Raven and gestured to the pin-ups of Jayne and Anita on the wall. "I told you we should've taken these down."

Julie opted for a change of subject. "Hey, I want to thank you guys for helping me with Nick." She reached for a Styrofoam carton of salad from atop Iakopo's gut, which was probably the closest a salad had ever come to it.

"Julie, it's totally cool," Raven said. "I mean, I thought you were trying to narc us out at first, but dude, what they did to you and your boyfriend really blows."

"Yeah. It does." Julie attacked the salad. She couldn't remember how long it'd been since she'd eaten anything. "How long have you guys been living down here?"

"Me, since last year," Raven said. "I was a senior at Kirtland High when I moved in."

"Why?"

"I couldn't take the pressure. At home. At Kirtland. All the AP classes. They make you do like a zillion hours of Community Service so you can become a more caring person but the real reason is to pad your resume so you can get into a "prestigious" university, like my Little Miss Perfect cousin did—Beverly Schechter—who wound up at Florida Southern getting knocked up by a lacrosse player, and I wound up volunteering at Cleveland Mercy. In the beginning it was a total drag. You wouldn't believe how many sick people are here! Like every day, there's new ones. This place is the anti-Disney World—the most depressing place on Earth."

"True," said Julie. "But how did you find *this* place? The basement?"

"It was last summer; school was out but I'm still doing my volunteer thing, piling up the credits, when I meet this really cool electrician, Ashanti, who was fixing the AC on the fifth floor."

"Fifth floor's Pain Management," Jacinta said.

"Yo, Jacinta, she already knows that," said Tick. "She works here."

"Not anymore," said Julie.

Tick and Jacinta frowned in commiseration as Raven resumed: "Anyway, Ashanti and me, not only was he drop-dead gorgeous but he *knew* stuff. I mean, like, more than just wires and plugs. Ashanti knew about the world, like civil wars in places I never heard of and refugees who drowned in the ocean trying to get to a better life and not be killed for just existing. He knew about it because Ashanti was one, a refugee. From torture. He, like, *lived* it. So, to make a short story shorter, we hooked up. I was sick of living at home with my parents who were always pushing me to "achieve." So I was going to run away—to LA or Frisco—but Ashanti, one day, he took me here. Said it could be like our secret place. Nobody would ever find us. Neither my parents or ICE. He rigged the fake wall to do that swivel thing so no one would ever get into the basement. Just us. Even the side doors to the staircases are cemented shut." She stopped in mid-story, squinted at Julie. "How did *you* figure it out?"

"You need to smudge out the palm print at the bottom of the drywall."

"Oh."

"So where is Ashanti now?"

"Gone." No one said anything further and Raven knew she'd have to elaborate. Either that or cry. "When HR found out Ashanti was working under a fake Social, that Josh creep, the CEO butt plug, instead of letting it slide or at worse just firing Ashanti, personally called ICE and got Ashanti deported back to Africa. And I haven't heard from him since."

"Why did Josh call ICE? This hospital is full of immigrant workers," said Julie. "They can't all be legal."

"Because Josh was hitting on me and didn't want the competition.

It didn't stop until he pulled out his tool in the elevator when I was taking a dead guy down to the Morgue and I kicked him in the nuts."

"Which comes out to four blue balls in one elevator," said Tick. He snorted at his witticism and a pea flew out a nostril.

Raven ignored him; her gaze remained fixed on Julie. "I had the presence of mind to snap a pic of Josh holding his sore nutsack next to the naked dead guy, which is why I'm still here. But the question was: Did I still want to be here? I mean I could've gone back home and been the robot my parents wanted, or stayed and helped out sick people. No extra credit attached. I didn't know what to do until I met these guys. They get minimum wage and can't afford rent anyplace decent."

"Tick and I were squatting in an abandoned house in Slavic Village and Raven kindly invited us to be her roommates," said Jacinta.

"So here we are. Cleveland Mercy is like its own ecosystem; we have everything we need down here."

"Except Wi-Fi," said Tick.

"Yeah, you have to go upside for that. But we have plenty of food, beds, video games. I don't miss the outside world at all. Because I found out I like helping patients. It helps me too, you know what I'm saying?"

"I do," said Julie, subdued.

"I need to cop some *zzzs*," said Tick, yawning, the Ativan getting to him. He closed his eyes and rested his tired head on Iakopo's pillowy paunch.

However, Tick didn't get much shuteye as, like the rumbling Savai'i Volcano back home, Carmelo Iakopo's stomach gurgled, his eyes slammed open, and the giant awakened with a mega-eruption that sent food trays flying. His open mouth reeked like a Honolulu sewer as the big guy roared, "Da fuck!" When he realized not only was he in restraints, but also being used as a dining room table, Iakopo flexed his calf muscles until the leg restraints snapped like toys.

Julie remembered the time she was similarly scared out of her wits as a child, while watching the original *Mighty Joe Young* with her Dad on the *Million Dollar Movie*, when the poor chained ape attempted his escape from the nightclub. The difference was Mighty Joe Young was an innocent creature, even though he was immense and threatening, while Carmelo Iakopo was just immense and threatening.

But not for long, as Jacinta, a syringe in each hand, jabbed them into Iakopo's stomach. Raven, even Tick, syringes also at ready, stabbed him in his thighs. But it was Julie's physician-accurate shot in his medial cubital arm vein—just before he could free himself and say, "I'm going to kill all-ya-all bitches!"—that made him heavy-lidded and, once again, unconscious. Moby Dick done in by a quartet of Ahabs.

"You guys okay?" asked Julie.

"Fabulous," said Jacinta, buzzed on adrenaline. "Better than that endomorphic asshole."

* * *

Carmelo Iakopo was "resting comfortably," as hospital press releases say. In reality, there is no such thing as "resting comfortably" in a hospital, or one wouldn't need to be in a hospital in the first place. That's like saying Jimmy Hoffa was "resting comfortably" beneath the fifty-yard line at MetLife Stadium. Because Jimmy Hoffa's maggot-sucked skeleton had a better chance of ascending into the Giants huddle than Iakopo did of ever getting up from his gurney—which had been moved to the center of a padded cell, known in less enlightened times as The Rubber Room. No flimsy psych restraints this time. In addition to Death Row grade handcuffs and leg chains, the four had sealed him in a XXXL straightjacket and tied a hockey mask over his face. Safe to say, Carmelo Iakopo wasn't going anywhere.

"Right?" asked Tick, still traumatized.

"Unlikely," Jacinta assured him, as she walked around the gurney, double-checking their mélange of subjugation devices. She looked to Julie. "I don't get it. I gave Jumbo here fifty mg of Propofol plus twenty of Dilaudid. I didn't want to go all Conrad Murray[*] on him but calculating weight and mass, that dosage should've been sufficient. Sorry about the scare, guys."

"You didn't account for the long-term use of Trenbolone and Deca-Durabolin this creep was taking," said Julie. "Those are the most powerful steroids out there. In fact, Trenbolone is only legal on livestock."

"You're, like, the real doctor here, right? So what do we do with him long term?" Raven asked.

"I don't know; I need to think this through. In the short term, though, we'll need to get an IV started, get him some basic nourishment."

"Right. I have all that stuff," said Jacinta.

"Do you have enough meds to keep him out for a while?"

"Do I?" Jacinta gestured toward the shelving in the hallway that strained under the weight of cases of drugs from the pharmacy storeroom.

"I'll also need a catheter."

"No problem." Jacinta went out into the hallway and rummaged through the boxes of medical supplies.

"How about a 16-C?"

---

[*] Michael Jackson's final doctor.

"Make it a 22."

"You're sure about that?"

"Definitely."

Jacinta winced, "I would not want to be his penis."

"Also, give me the biggest balloon you have."

"Would you like me to insert it?"

"No, this psycho is all mine." Julie walked over to the gurney, where Iakopo was moaning through the hockey mask.

"Payback's a bitch, isn't it? You don't mess with my man," she said. "Ever." Julie snapped on a pair of gloves, and the sound of fear echoed through the dank basement.

CHAPTER 23

The Americans With Disabilities Act

"These are from Mr. Muscat," said Edie, the nice lady who worked in Jimmy Tom Muscat's front office as one of his executive assistants, the nice lady whose knee had been shattered into splintered bone and torn tendon, whose head had been turned to mush in the ensuing fall from the bleachers—all because of her boss's heedlessly flung bat at last spring's company softball game. She was holding a handmade sunflower origami arrangement for Nick to see from his hospital bed.

"I could put it by the window so they could get some sun and maybe you could get the nurse to water them, but …"

"But they're not real sunflowers, honey; you made them out of gold foil origami paper, remember?" said Aggie, Edie's close friend at EZ♥Care, the HR VP and Nick's covert corporate supporter.

"Oh, of course," said Edie whose cloudy eyes briefly cleared.

"So, sun and water wouldn't do them any good. Besides, even if they were actual sunflowers, there hasn't been sunshine in this town since early November and it's still snowing like it's not going to stop till next May. And Nick, I don't have to tell you that deranged narcissist had nothing to do with this beautiful arrangement: Edie made them just for you. Except, as always, she's trying to make her boss look good, despite the fact his actions have left her strung out on opioids, anti-depressants, and anti-this and anti-that, all because he lost his temper over a child's game."

Nick, looking refreshed with some rest, morphine, and a bowel movement, said: "You know, ladies, there's no universe where I would've believed they were from Mr. Muscat in the first place; he's the reason I'm here. The guy hates me."

"No, he doesn't," said Edie. "You know how he gets sometimes."

"Yeah, we know how he gets." Aggie turned to Nick. "Despite the fact his big fat ego lost that game, he'll blame you until the day he dies, which frankly, I look forward to with great anticipation."

Well then, let's just add him to the list right under Trout, Nick thought. Instead, he said: "I've missed you two."

"Likewise, Nick," said Edie whose quivering hand held onto the origami arrangement as she maneuvered her way with the aid of a cane to the window, where she took great pains to set the origami on the sill at the perfect angle. Nick noticed that she hobbled across the room with a *please-don't-stare-at-me because-I'm-trying-to-ignore-it-and-you'd-better-too* limp.

"Six surgeries she's had," said Aggie, watching Nick watch Edie, "yet she still goes into the office."

"Aggie, EZ♥Care has been my life and sometimes Mr. Muscat can be awfully nice, at least he was in the early days." Edie shuffled over to Nick's bed and placed her hand tenderly on his. "And you can't beat the Health Insurance."

"Actually, you can," said Aggie. "Even after working in the front office for that poster boy for a corrupt CEO for twenty-six years, she's still had to dig deep into her 401K to make the co-pays." Aggie shook her head and resurrected an old argument, "I told you to get EZ♥Care Prime."

"Agnes, please. Besides, once he settles up for my injuries, we'll be more than okay."

"I'll believe that when the check cashes. I'm sorry, Nick, we didn't come here to have you watch us argue. You can see that at work. Speaking of which, how long did they say it would be before you can come back?"

"Just as soon as Doctor Trout …" Nick paused to correct himself. "They said a month or three for the wounds to heal, then lots of PT. Maybe late spring—latest, summer."

Or never.

Nick kept that part to himself as the image of Trout The Snowman flying into the night once again replayed in his head.

Aggie misread Nick's look. "Don't you worry about him not taking you back. Remember, I work in HR. You've got the Americans With Disabilities Act on your side."

"That's right. Mr. Muscat has to follow the law."

"Oh," was all Nick could muster, since he knew the last place he and Julie could remain was Cleveland. Their once rosy future had become somewhat less perennial and way more complicated.

A clipped "*Gud mor-nink!*" filled the room, as Demidova, trailed by the student posse, entered.

"Ladies," said Demidova, which was doctor-speak for Aggie and Edie to get lost.

Aggie took the hint. "We'd better be going, Edie, and get out of these folks' way."

Edie gave Nick's hand one last squeeze. "Anything you need, Nicky, just call. Anything. You know that."

"I do. Thank you so much."

"Don't forget to water the sunflowers," Edie said, with a Prozac smile. As the couple exited into the hallway, they passed an old man in a drab brown suit, leaning against a beechwood cane with a nickel-plated alligator's head handle. He politely tipped his fedora to them.

"Good morning, ladies," said Lieutenant Artemas Sikorski.

*　*　*

I watched the two old biddies pass me. Was rough to look at the one Muscat nailed with the bat hobble toward the elevators. Maybe what I planned on doing to him could help make up for it. Then again, maybe not. And to be honest here, what was I talking about: biddies? Get real, Artie: them "biddies" were younger than me. Another thing, they weren't so bad looking. Whoa. Don't even go there, big guy; I knew all too well how Marie could just look at me with her telepathic eyes and read every lecherous thought I ever had. So I wiped the image of me and the dames having a threesome in the handicapped-friendly penthouse at the Ritz-Carlton on West Third outta the IMAX in my head and peeked into the room where the Russian doc was explaining what's what to the junior docs.

"Nurse Iakopo noted on chart he observed fecal material in patient's toilet at 1:31 AM. Therefore, since young Nicholas has no fever, no infection, we will send him home today."

"Really? That's great," said the kid, who looked like … No wait! He didn't *look* like … he *was* the lefty with the sweet stroke who atomized the seagull and was later blindsided by that ass clown Muscat. Which also made him the boyfriend of that down-in-the-dumps doc I chatted with in the cafeteria. The one who told me her boyfriend was Dr. Trout's patient.

So where, pray tell, was Dr. Trout?

I turned up my hearing aids and leaned in to get the rest of what the Russki was saying.

"You will return to my office in one week for me to inspect your stitches."

"Your office?" the kid said, looking perplexed. "What about Doctor Trout?"

"I have temporarily taken over Doctor Trout's patients."

Not to mention Women's Tennis, Olympic Gymnastics, and select Swing State voting machines. I hung back, blended in with the rest of the defectives in the corridor, and kept listening.

"Do you have someone to take care of you when you are home, petal?" asked Demidova, then reeled that question back in the boat. "Of course, you do. I forgot, you have own personal physician." Comrade Demidova turned to Trout's toadies. "We are finished here." She was about to motorvate out the room when the kid in bed called out to her.

"Dr. Demidova?"

"Yes, petal?"

The kid bit his tongue, like he didn't want to make any waves. "About the nerve pain?"

"You still have nerve pain?"

"Yeah. Dr. Trout said it would go away fast. Except there's still this intense tingling and burning down my right leg into my foot. When I stand, it feels like my sock is soaking wet, like it's full of oatmeal."

"I see. Maybe you should not add milk to Quaker Oats you put in shoes."

Yeah, she actually said that. And worse, she got hearty laughs from her merry band of ass-kissers. And more worse, once those ass-kissers are full-fledged doctors, they'll be doing the same dumbass joke and even worser, *their* ass-kissers will be cracking it for generations. The upshot being untold multitudes of future patients will have to live with their hesitant claims of pain ignored for the sake of being a set-up for a callous punchline. Ha freaking ha.

Demidova licked the Maybelline off her lips and tried to take the edge off her brutal comedy stylings: "Yes, Dr. Trout *did* tell you nerve pain *should* decrease soon. But, remember, he also told you nerve pain can be unpredictable; it may take some time to calm down. And that is what you must do, petal. Calm down."

Some bedside manner this Sovietchik had. Although I'd bet a year of my impending pension that her bedside manner improved considerably when she was Trout fishing, because, strip away the Rosa Klebb* act and I could tell she was just as concerned about the whereabouts of "the best orthopedist in Northeastern Ohio" as was Nick Glass.

Not to mention me.

"Have patience, Nicholas. And be grateful you were lucky enough to have wonderful surgeon like Dr. Trout fix your back."

The kid shot her a look. The kind of look a patient doesn't dare lay on his doc. There was something *personal* going on between the two of them. I didn't know what it was, but damn straight I was going to find out.

A slight female Filipino nurse emerged from the cluster of elves and dumped a bunch of papers and brochures on Nick's side table. Demidova said, "Those are your post-op instructions, Nicholas. All answers to your questions, you will find in there. Including convenient manual for how to have sexual relations after back surgery. With either girl or boy."

Demidova was enjoying this. Well, she wouldn't be enjoy being such a bitchski in a few minutes, but that was gonna be then, and this was still now.

---

* Klebb, voted one of the "Ten Best Bond Villains" ever, was the SMERSH Colonel in *From Russian With Love*—the old lady with the poison blade in her Florsheims, played by Lotte Lenya. But I gotta go old school with my favorite Bond bad guy: Joseph Wiseman, the original Dr. No. Matter a fact, I saw him recently on a *Magnum P.I.* re-run called *The Birdman Of Budapest*. The original *Magnum P.I.* Accept no "re-imaginings."

"Follow directions closely, Nicholas. After all, you do not want to wind up back here, *da?*"

The kid's face flushed; the minions suppressed their cretinous giggles and it looked like this time, for sure, Demidova was finally exiting the stage. "Leave 'em laughing," Georgie Jessel used to say. Everyone thinks it was Milton Berle who said that, because Uncle Milty starred in this forties picture with Virginia Mayo called *Always Leave Them Laughing,* so you can see how it could've gotten mixed up through the years. Jesus, quit rambling, Artie. It's like your brain is one big footnote.

Speaking of notes, that's when something on the room's white-board caught Demidova's eye.

"Nurse Macaraeg," she pronounced it brutally, but on the other hand she probably got closer than I woulda. "Please to tell me when Nurse Iakopo signed out? I see no record on white board. And there is no end of shift report on computer from him. What is going on?"

Whoa, all of a sudden that nurse's kisser had a big-time guilty look on it. Like she was trying to cover for the missing nurse with the other unpronounceable name. "Very sorry, Dr. Demidova, we have no idea where Nurse Iakopo's change-of-shift report is."

"Why not?"

"Because we also have no idea where Nurse Iakopo is. He does not answer his pager or cell."

Demidova muttered some crap in Russian that didn't sound pleasant and cleaned it up for the English release: "When you see Nurse Iakopo, tell him I will have a word with his supervisor." With that, she finally left Nick Glass and his busted back to himself.

The elf pack was headed straight at me. They separated and galloped past like Comanches in an old Western, who would ride their horses around the camera and leave nothing but dust and high-pitched gibberish in their wake. In this case, the camera in the dust was me. Already, these pricks who probably didn't know which end of the thermometer to put up the ass had mastered the art of patient avoidance. Can't do no harm to what they can't see. But I didn't give a crap about them; it was in the Commissar Doctor's path that I planted me and my cane. That leaning tower of borscht wasn't going to get around me.

"Excuse me, Doctor Demidova?"

She paused and looked down at me; her head just about scraping the ceiling. Jeez, she had to go six-four at least. I wondered if she could dunk.

"If you wish to make appointment, please to call Lara in my office."

"Here's my appointment, Doc," I said as I badged her. A cheap-ass theatrical move, I know. But if you're wearing a tool belt, use 'em. "Lieutenant Artemas Sikorski, Homicide."

Even though she froze up like the ice on the windshield of my Caprice, despite Marie blasting it with her ConAir, I had to give Demidova credit for turning her Slavonic sneer into cool nonchalance without cracking one single facial bone.

"What may I do for you, Lieutenant?"

"Just a few minutes of your time, Doctor. I can see you're very busy."*

As I was about to go into my suave interro, I got distracted by some candy-striper, who looked like Elvira, Mistress of the Dark's granddaughter, zipping an empty wheelchair right towards Nick Glass's room. Except as soon as Elvira Junior clocked me holding my shield, she did a one-eighty back to wherever she came from. Yeah, was a strange move, but since I'd just bagged Demidova's

---

* My thanks to the late, great Peter Falk, or the unsung *Columbo* writer who came up with that gem. Can't tell you how many times that chestnut has worked.

undivided attention I wasn't going to get diverted by some siren spawn of Satan who was skittish around cops because she had a joint in her pocket or sacrificed a live chicken on InstaBook.

"Well, what do you want, Lieutenant? I must finish Dr. Trout's rounds."

"Does this look familiar?" I pulled a crumpled piece of paper out of the badly stitched pocket of my piece-a-crap JoS. A. Bank brown suit and handed it to her. She perused it with an admirable display of bewilderment.

"What is this?"

"A note to Dr. Trout, written by you."

"What makes you think I am writer?"

"Start with the tortured syntax and end with your signature on the bottom. I found it taped to the desk chair in his office. And if you don't mind me saying so, the tenor of your missive could be construed as rather threatening."

"Is personal thing."

"I'd say 'personal' is an understatement. Whataya say we go over the good parts?"

"*Nyet!* This is not your business."

"Actually, Doc, since Trout has dropped out of his life, leaving behind concerned colleagues, an anxious TV reporter who's supposed to interview him on 19 News tonight, a ward full of patients, an indifferent wife, and …" I subtly added, "… a definitely rattled paramour, I think it just might be my business. So tell me, when was the last time you saw Dr. Trout? Why are you seeing his patients today? Does the note have anything to do with his absence? Go ahead, take any one of those three. I got all day."

What did I expect? She gave me the stink eye and said, "I have no time for this nonsense. I have many patients to see. Call Lara for appointment."

This, as she stuffed the note in her coat, executed a Bolshoi-worthy pirouette, and tippy-toed after her students. Whatever. I let her take her *grand pas* down the hallway. But not without firing a parting shot across her tutu: "Go ahead, finish Trout's rounds. Keep the note, it's a Xerox. The original is at the Crime Lab. See you in your office. One hour."

"No! I am busy! Иди и порезвись с собою!" Being of proud Polish descent I don't understand much Russian, but I'll go out on a limb and guess she just told me to go fuck myself. She tossed that exit line over her long ballerina neck, one of those endless napes with the pulled-back hair that were so desirable to *artistes* like George Balanchine, who saw ballet and bulimia as an art form, not a contradiction. But what do I know? I got jaded from years of being dragged to my daughter's ballet recitals and then listening to the blow-by-blow, explaining every fancy move as I tucked her into bed all those nights.

All those nights I wished I had back.

This, despite the fact I could never get past my first impression that ballet was just a visualization of how to kick dog shit off your shoes, set to music.

"One hour," I called after her. "And if you don't show, we can move our chat to an interrogation room downtown."

Hell if I was gonna let Dame Kareem Abdul Fonteyn stiff me. I turned and gimped back down the corridor. For some reason, the image of the panicked candy-striper with the Elvira hairdo and the alabaster skin popped back into my head. Something strange about her. Yeah, of course, strange; but I'm talking *something bugging me strange*, except I didn't know what it was and put it out of my head, as I had bigger fish to fry.

Or so I thought at the time.

* * *

Raven, disguised in dark glasses and pink scrub cap, glanced over her shoulder for any potential danger—like more cops— and pushed her wheelchair-riding patient into an elevator. She sagged in relief when the door slid shut and the elevator began its clunky descent.

Nick was the patient in the wheelchair and he was going home. He wore sweats and a huge look of relief. He was preoccupied with balancing the plastic bag on his lap that read "Patient's Belongings" and therefore didn't see Raven's floor selection. Which was B-3. Good for him he hadn't noticed or he wouldn't have been grinning like a fool. As far as he knew, he was on an elevator ride out of this horror show of a hospital where just about everyone seemed intent on either maiming, exploiting, or killing him. And whether these assaults were in dreams or reality, it no longer made any difference because Nick had reached the point where he couldn't tell which was which.

He pictured Julie waiting curbside in her primer-patched three-cylinder '97 Geo Metro hatchback that he kept threatening to take to the Earl Scheib on Pearl and bring back in her favorite color. Which was … blue? Or was it green?

Because of the anesthesia still clouding his head, he couldn't remember.

What he could remember was that Julie was in a kind of pain that dwarfed anything he was going through. The two of them would go back to the apartment, and together they could figure out how to deal with her HIV issue and Klepstein's play to kick her out of Cleveland Mercy. Hell, it still might not be an HIV issue at all. The whole thing could be overblown, the kind of tragedy that only happened to Other People.

Right?

Just like getting stabbed in post-surgical wound sites with a Harvard lapel pin wielded by a depraved, blackmailing Samoan nurse was something that also only happened to Other People.

Right?

And who in the world was ever a victim of an unnecessary operation, performed by a greedy bone surgeon, later dressed in a snowman suit, whose blind rage—literally, *blind freaking rage*—had sent his Hippocritic ass flying out a penthouse balcony to certain death in a vain effort to silence his patient?

Other People?

No.

The correct answer to all of the above was him and Julie.

Nick had the feeling there was no way he could plausibly rationalize any of this. Because at Cleveland Mercy, implausible was just the jumping-off point. He looked up at Raven, thinking this was the slowest moving elevator in the world. "So, my friend is waiting for me?"

"Julie? Yeah."

Raven took her scrub cap off and ran her fingers through her Audrey Tautou hair—her Audrey-Tatou from *Amelie* hair.

Which caused something to spark in Nick. Something about this candy-striper seemed familiar. But what, he couldn't quite grasp. Must be the drugs.

The drugs! That's it! When he was under anesthesia. She was the candy-striper who was gunned down in his dream by the security guards with the reindeer antlers sticking out of their caps! The one who offered to clean the blood off his dick and then squished it around her mouth like some kind of wine connoisseur. And here she was in real life! Holy shit!

Wait. She was still talking. "I know it's lame that the hospital makes you split in a wheelchair but it's way better than leaving with a toe tag."

WTF? Nick no longer trusted anyone and confirming his paranoia, he turned and saw they'd *passed* the Ground Floor and were headed to the depths of the Basement. B-3.

Where the sign on the elevator said you couldn't go.

Nick sunk his head in dismay. Was he dreaming this too? Was everyone who worked at this hospital insane? Could Cleveland Mercy be like that Edgar Allan Poe story Mrs. Ong had made him read in English Lit called The System of *Doctor Tarr And Professor Fether*? The one where the staff of the nuthouse were really the inmates who'd taken over the place?

Nick winced as the elevator came to a jolting stop. "Chill, dude," said Raven, as she placed a restraining hand on his shoulder. "Everything's cool."

No, nothing was cool. Nick watched as the elevator door slid open, revealing the cracked brick and drywall along with the dusty sign that read:

WARNING: FLOOR NOT IN USE. NO EGRESS

Nick attempted to fling himself out of the wheelchair, yelling at Raven: "Where's Julie!? Take me back!"

"Dude! Chillax! She's right here!"

She took her hand off Nick's shoulder and bent down to the now discreet outline of the palm print at the bottom of the drywall, placed her hand on it, and said, "*Voy-la!*"

The floor swiveled on the turntable and sent them into the basement, where stood a disheveled Julie holding a flashlight up to her face. She wore a pea and carrot-stained doctor coat and an otherworldly look.

"Hi, honey."

Nick slumped back in the wheelchair and closed his eyes. How could any of this be real? But when he opened them again, Julie was still there.

"Slight change of plans," she said.

*　*　*

"My Dearest Snowboy, if you do not leave bitch wife immediately, I will call and tell stupid cow everything! EVERYTHING! Also, I will go to Humane Resources and—"

"Enough!" interrupted Dr. Irina Demidova, sitting behind the desk in her small, windowless office, a world of status away from Trout's EZ♥Care Limited Edition Penthouse Suite. There were patient charts and papers everywhere: piled high on her desk, chairs, even on top of the filing cabinets—and who used filing cabinets anymore? Demidova also had scores of yellow sticky notes written in Cyrillic affixed to almost every surface of her computer, as if she didn't trust the magic box's ability or inclination to remember what needed remembering.

The only personal artifact in the office was a framed and auto-graphed photo of the 1980 Soviet Union Winter Olympics Ice Hockey team. The team who memorably lost to the gutty under-dog American amateurs, the *Do-You-Believe-In-Miracles!* guys. Oblivious to the multiple tragedies to come, Irina Demidova's father, Gennady, a bottom-six winger for the Soviets, third from the left in the back row, smiled the smile of a winner into camera. Later, in that fateful game against the determined Americans, Gennady would clank a wide-open shot, a certain goal, off the post. Like most of the team, Gennady was an active duty Red Army soldier and would soon find himself transferred to the frontlines in Afghanistan.

The last time Irina had seen her *Papasha* had been some twenty years ago, on a platform in the Paveletskya Station in the Moscow Metro. A half-blind, prematurely old man in a frayed woolen coat, Gennady's torso—minus hands and legs, blown off by an IED in Helmand Province—was secured, via rope, to a piece of plywood attached to roller skate wheels. From here, the disgraced hero, begged for kopeks to buy more rotgut vodka to kill the phantom pain where his limbs used to be. Gennady's unseeing eyes never recognized his daughter, who each week faithfully placed half her meager stipend, earned as a medical student at the Sklifasovskogo Hospital, into his tin cup.

But today and for always, his boyish face, etched in self-assurance and the knowledge that the future was his, looked down on his special little girl from the signed photo above her desk.

"Enough!" Demidova repeated.

"Enough what?" asked this grandfather of a policeman leaning on his super ugly cane from the other side of her desk. No way would she move the files off the chair so this crippled *xyecoc*[*] could sit! He was not even making an effort to hide his amusement at her note to Templeton. How stupid of her to leave it taped to his chair! *Da*, she'd been, she admitted, drunk and angry, but still this was an idiotic mistake to leave it for this уёбок[†] of a policeman to find. She watched as Sikorski scanned the note with a feigned look of confusion.

"You are dirty old man."

"No, Doctor Demidova, I'm a soon-to-be-retired cop, working my last case. If this even is a case. So help me out here: I don't care what you and Trout had going on. What concerns me is

* cocksucker
† fuckface

why he went missing right after you left this pastiche of poorly written threats taped to his office chair. By the way, it's Human Resources, not *Humane* Resources. Next time you want to have your ultimatums taken seriously, hire an editor. But back to the question, is there a cause and effect here? Anything you'd like to confess?"

Irina's answer was to turn on the waterworks.

The funny thing was, even as her tears flowed like the River Don in a spring rain, Irina knew in her heart Templeton had never been serious about leaving his bitch wife and marrying her. He only wanted a second "wife," a younger and prettier version. After they "met cute"—Templeton had explained this American romantic comedy trope to her while they watched VHS of *Not To Have Sleep In Seattle* in his suite at the Kempinski seven years ago at that orthopedic convention in Berlin—on that romantic December evening when they fell in love, or *she* fell in love, a detail Irina only belatedly realized, Templeton had promised to "pull string" with old Harvard "bro" at the State Department and bring her to Cleveland USA.

And so he had. Templeton also had assured Josh Przybylowicz, the CEO who would do anything to retain his rainmaker Trout, that Irina was licensed to practice medicine in the States and, fortuitously enough, the State of Ohio. Therefore, Josh hadn't looked too closely at her credentials and, acting upon his recommendation, the Board of Directors had unanimously approved her appointment to the Cleveland Mercy staff.

And then what?

After years of being on call—in every sense of the word—years of promises made and not kept, years of kinky sex (having to put her head in the snowman pouch was least of it), the lying мешок дерьма* Templeton runs away like a coward. Not like her father who was a true Hero. So yes, it was not so hard to cry in front of this *dedulya*, this rude policeman.

"I have nothing to confess, Lieutenant. Other than I loved him," she said, as she wiped away a final tear. "But if I see him again, I will kill three-timing bastard with bare hands."

"As a homicide detective, I can't condone that." Sikorski headed for the door. "I'll be in touch. Oh, Dr. Demidova, just one more thing …"

She gazed at him through bloodshot eyes. "What?"

"Don't leave town."

* sack of shit

CHAPTER 24

One Ticket To Paradise

"Hey! Where da fuck am I?"

This and more spewed out of the goalie-mask-covered yap of the straightjacketed, tortured body and soul of Carmelo Iakopo. "Don't fuck wid me like dis! It ain't right!"

The door to the padded cell opened and Julie and Nick entered. Julie wore a crisp white doctor coat and Nick carried a plastic cup. Julie graced the immobile giant with a cheery, professional smile. A smile that indicated she was willing to go that extra mile for him, even if that extra mile could terminate in a very dark place.

"How are we doing today, Carmelo? Would you like some cane-sweetened applesauce?"

"Fucking bitch."

"I think he said 'yes,' Nick."

"I think so too." Nick dumped the contents of the cup through the bars of the goalie mask, causing the giant to sputter like Daffy Duck having a stroke.

"Calm down, *brah*." Nick tossed the cup and took out his iPhone. "Calm down and listen."

"Listen to what?"

"The amount of trouble you're in. And your way out of it." Nick hit Play on his phone.

Nick's futzed voice emanated from the speaker: *"I want to talk to the police."*

And Iakopo's reply: *"No, brah. You're gonna pay me five Benjis a week or you ain't leaving dis hospital alive. And neither will your chick."*

"Are you threatening Dr. Toffoli?"

"You pick up quick."

Nick pressed Stop as Julie said, "We cut the last part to save you the embarrassment of the world hearing about your steroidally shrunken testicles in open court."

"What do you want?" Iakopo spat through the mask.

"This isn't about what we want. This is about what you want. We can call the police, give this to them, and you'll wind up doing ten or twenty years at Chillicothe Correctional."

"Which would be a real pain in the ass," said Nick.

"Or, because we believe in second chances, not to mention prison reform and reducing the rate of recidivism, you can enjoy our limited time offer of freedom by taking the one-way ticket to Paradise we reserved for you on Trip Advisor."

"Honolulu. Coach. Middle seat," said Nick. "And you can go wherever the heck you want after that."

"Except back to the Mainland. You don't ever come back here again," added Julie.

Iakopo began to laugh but gagged on the applesauce. "'Cept what if I do come back? Like when you least 'spect it? Come back and mess you up. Whatcha gonna do bout it?"

"Not being complete dunces, we thought you might be so inclined," Julie said. "But here's the deal: if in the future—next week, next month, next millennium, whenever—either one of us are not accounted for, even for an afternoon, this recording will be delivered by a third party unknown to you, to the police and the District Attorney. Then, I assure you, you will go to Chillicothe."

"Deal or no deal?" asked Nick.

"Deal.'Cept there's something you ought to know before laying all this grief on just me."

"What?"

"Your boss, Mr. Muscat, he's the one who told me to make your stay here 'unpleasant.' Dat's the word he used. Told me to use my 'discretion.'"

"You don't have any discretion, Carmelo. You enjoyed every second of it," said Nick. He looked to Julie. "Told you he was Muscat's boy." Nick leaned into the mask. "Take a look up, Carmelo."

"Up where?"

"The ceiling. Tell me, do those cracks look like Baby Jesus with a woody?"

"Oh fuck me," said Iakopo, whose eyeballs instead went to his catheter bag full of piss as he realized a ticket to Paradise wasn't such a bad thing.

* * *

A wheelchair containing Iakopo, handcuffed to the arms but no longer straitjacketed, was pushed by Raven along the dim corridor leading to the secret elevator portal. Also, instead of the hockey mask, Iakopo's face was swathed in thick white bandages replete with eyeholes and a mouth opening, giving him the appearance of a crazed but cultured burn victim, as he had a *New York Review Of Books* carryall ("Free With Paid Subscription!") on his lap. Jacinta and Tick, wagging flashlights, led the way while Julie walked beside Raven and the wheelchair.

Julie leaned over to Iakopo. "I put eight hundred and seventy-three bucks in your knapsack. Enough for the ticket, one checked bag, and a pupu platter for the plane." She pointed at Tick and Jacinta up ahead. "My friends will drive you to Cleveland-Hopkins

International. And don't even think about trying anything on the way, because the young lady with the syringe will put you down like a rabid dog."

"Woof woof," Iakopo barked.

Jacinta hung back and gave Iakopo a glimpse of the horse-sized syringe in her coat. "Just try me. This is a combination of midazolam and hydromorphone. The last time Ohio used it for capital punishment, it took the condemned man twenty-five excruciating minutes to die; even the executioners were so horrified they left the last batch on the shelf."

"Where'd you get it?"

"Off the shelf."

"Okay, you win. I'll send you freaks a postcard from Paradise." He smiled at Julie, "Say goodbye to your pussy boyfriend from me."

"You're so sweet," said Julie.

"Dat's me …" Just as Raven turned the wheelchair into another corridor, Iakopo leaned his body hard left, overturning the wheelchair and his massive frame into Julie, knocking her head against the wall where she collapsed, bleeding and unconscious. "… sweet," he finished.

Roaring, Iakopo flexed and snapped the left cuff off his wrist but had no time to do the right side as Jacinta was coming straight at him with the Death Penalty syringe. He rose to his feet, and with his right hand still attached, swung the wheelchair at her. The footrest scored a direct hit to her face and Jacinta was likewise out before her head hit the floor. Her hypodermic needle clattered away into the darkness.

With his free left hand, Iakopo ripped off his head bandages, liberating his rainforest of hair. Tick threw his flashlight at him and turned to run, but didn't get far as Iakopo, with his incredible wingspan, grabbed Tick by the neck and lifted him off his feet.

Raven, standing her ground behind the wheelchair, screamed: "Let him go!"

Tick's legs kicked uselessly as Iakopo eyed Raven's keychain. "Unlock da other cuff, or I will choke dis gink till his nuts come out his eyeballs." Indeed, Tick's face was already eggshell blue and his legs now limp.

"Okay. Just let him go." Raven, shaky, cycled through the key ring.

"Hurry it up!"

"I'm trying!" Raven fumbled for the correct key.

"Fuck dis!" Iakopo let the unconscious Tick drop to the floor and grasped for the key ring in Raven's hand ...

... just as he was blasted point blank in the grill by a stream of baby-shit brown fire retardant. Iakopo's howl echoed throughout the basement as the extinguisher foam burned and blinded him.

Raven jumped back to find herself next to Nick, who unsteadily wielded the antique fire extinguisher he'd grabbed off the wall—the same extinguisher Julie had passed on her Ambien journey through the catacombs.

"I knew he'd try something," said Nick, on the verge of collapse.

"Oh shit!" This from Raven as she grabbed the extinguisher from Nick and whirled to give the returning Iakopo another blast.

The sightless giant screamed again. Crazed and disoriented, pinwheeling the wheelchair like a discus, Iakopo careened through the corridor spewing fire retardant and a promise. "I'm gonna kill all-you-all—"

Iakopo didn't complete the sentence, as the spinning wheelchair made contact with the open—and still sparking—electrical panel where Julie had seen the incinerated rat. Iakopo's free hand blindly reached out, only to grab the salad of live wires. An intense current coursed through the big guy's body and he burst into flames, lighting up like a Waikiki Beach New Year's fireworks show. His hand, intractably adhered to the sparking wires, caused him to jerk and twitch like Fred Astaire performing a Saint Vitus dance, with the electricity-conducting wheelchair playing the part of Ginger Rogers. Flames consumed Iakopo's magnificent hair like a Malibu fire on a Santa Ana day as he toppled to the floor, where his crisped and smoking body convulsed a few times before coming to a full stop. The acrid smell of burning Samoan melded to the melted metal of the wheelchair was overpowering.

The others, bruised and in various states of shock and acuity, staggered to their feet. It had become quiet in the B-3 corridor, save for the intermittent buzzing of electricity. Jacinta, featuring a purple gash on her forehead from impact with the wheelchair leg-rest, crawled on the ground through the carpet of fire retardant and retrieved her precious syringe. Raven let the fire extinguisher clank to the floor with a hiss and moved to examine Tick and his neck. Nick stifled a breath as his wound sites throbbed. Julie, with a line of blood dripping from her ear where she hit the wall, came over and held him. All in all, everyone had come out of it okay, except Carmelo Iakopo, who had opted for one ticket to Paradise Lost.

"Whoa, this dude really *is* a burn patient now," croaked Tick. His nascent laugh turned into a nasty coughing jag and then a scream as Iakopo's blackened arm reflexively grabbed his leg.

And wouldn't let go.

Julie, Raven, and Jacinta stomped on Iakopo's dead, grasping arm with its live nerve endings until they severed the appendage from Tick's leg.

"OMG!" said Raven. "What was that?!"

"A spinal reflex. Happens about thirty-nine percent of the time after brain death," explained Julie. "It usually occurs within the first twenty-four hours but in some cases—"

"Okay, Julie, whatever. But how about explaining *that*!" interrupted Jacinta, as she pointed in amazement at Iakopo's penis. Scorched, smoking, and fully aroused, Iakopo's immense member protruded through his burnt and torn pants like a one-eyed mahi-mahi done up Cajun Style À La Muscat.

"That's one smoking hot dick," said Raven.

"Also not an uncommon phenomenon," said Julie. "Priapism can be a result of traumatic death. It has to do with rapid blood flow and the final spasms of the nervous system. In some cases, the membranes become more permeable to calcium and the cells don't expend as much energy to push the ions out, so the muscles contract. This leads to rigor mortis and sometimes even ejaculation."

"Ah, TMI," said Raven.

"For example," Julie continued pedantically, although the reality was she was babbling in a state of shock, "This is what happened to the Prophet Mohammed upon his death. Mainstream Muslim folklore concerning The Prophet's death said he died of poisoning by a Jewish woman, which, even though I was raised Catholic, is utter nonsense. Scientific consensus concerning Mohammed's death indicated he suffered a brain embolism leading to a postmortem erection. That's where the seventy-two virgins in Heaven comes in, because in most of the ancient interpretations of the Koran it is promised the erection is eternal."

"Fascinating, no doubt, Julie," said Jacinta. "Except what do *we* do with a six-foot-nine, three-hundred-and-fifty-pound corpse fused to a wheelchair?"

"Bury him?" suggested Raven.

"Even if we could find a spot in the woods or wherever, the ground's frozen solid," said Nick.

"So's the lake," said Jacinta. "We can't put him in the water until it thaws. Which, with this winter, will be weeks and weeks."

"Is there a floor freezer here?" asked Julie. "A really big one?"

"In the old commissary," said Raven.

"Okay, we have to get him in there before rigor sets in. Come on, give me a hand, guys."

Tick proffered Iakopo's severed hand to Julie.

"Sorry," he said to a universe of angry looks; he dropped the hand and began to cry like the traumatized kid he was. Raven and Jacinta put sisterly arms around him, telling him it was going to be okay, and after a while Tick stopped sobbing. Still, his anxiety was reflected by the question mark forming on his face.

"Is it okay if we don't put him next to the peas?"

*　*　*

Alone in the smoky corridor, Julie delicately hugged Nick. As they parted, she caught a look at her watch.

"Hey. It's midnight. Happy New Year, honey."

"You too. Next one's gotta be better, right?"

"How do you figure?"

"I don't know. I guess I'm defaulting to optimism."

"Still? After everything that's happened?"

"Why not? Maybe we can change things up by sharing our annual New Year's resolutions. You first."

"Really? Okay … I resolve not to get any more of my blood on you."

"And I resolve not to kill anyone else."

"Kill?" Julie cut short a bitter laugh. "You didn't kill either one of them, Nick."

"Sure I did. I mean, not on purpose."

"No, what killed those creeps was Karma. Sorry, but you don't get to take all the credit."

Part Two

PART THREE

Five Months Later

"Don't mind them, just keep walking"

(What the ghost of Virgil said to Dante in *The Divine Comedy*)

CHAPTER 25

The Resurrection of Templeton Trout

Although the longest winter since The Great Blizzard of 1978 had ended, the Great May Thaw was even crueler. Thousands of Clevelanders found themselves stranded in malls, offices, and on the roads as the city and its environs melted. Even the snow-drifts that had frozen over the playground equipment at the park adjacent to Cleveland Mercy had thawed enough so that a brave band of tykes—the children of parents visiting sick relatives, of hospital employees with nowhere else to stash their kids, or neighborhood preschoolers who had gone sugar crazy in cramped apartments—were out on the monkey bars, see-saws, and swings while their half-attentive adult supervision huddled in cliques over coffee and soggy sinkers.

The three dozen kids, jacketed and galoshed against the chill and melting snow, roughhoused on the playground equipment; their taunting and laughing, punctuated by ear-piercing shrieks, combined to drive the moms, grandparents, and the occasional unemployed dad as far away from them as possible and still be considered responsible adults.

A crew of daredevils lined up at the slide for their seven seconds of action but were gridlocked by a smallish boy with threadbare mittens and thick black glasses, with one temple held together by surgical tape. He sat immobile at the top, unable to bring himself to push off. The boy, whose name was Leon, stared down the length of the slide toward a mountain of ice turned into a mound of dirty snow and had visions of crashing into it and being swallowed whole, never to see his mom again. Something he hadn't considered when he'd raced the other kids to the slide and been the first to climb the steps.

Leon's wavering pissed off the other kids. Particularly, the six-year-old playground bully, Lance, who was next in line with a Timberland boot poised on the top step and North Face gloves grasping the ladder. "Whatcha waiting for, Four-Eyes? Come on, let's go!" he screamed. "Come on!"

"Yeah, whatcha waiting for, Four-Eyes?" the kid standing behind Lance echoed this riposte as all the others joined in. "Whatcha waiting for, Four-Eyes? Let's go, Four-Eyes," they urged in annoying sing-song.

Despite peer pressure, Leon still couldn't bring himself to take the plunge. He and his mom had just moved into the neighborhood when she scored an x-ray tech job in the hospital. This was Leon's First Day in the playground with a whole group of new kids and he hadn't a friend or ally among them. Leon began to sniffle, as the kids below ridiculed him without mercy.

"Out of my way, wuss," said Lance, pushing his way to the top next to the teary Leon. "I'm goin' first!"

Lance, whooping all the way, hurtled feet first down the icy steel into the mound of snow at the bottom which exploded into a shower of white. As the slush settled, Lance found himself staring at a newly revealed, winter's-long buried snowman, who stared back at Lance through shattered glass eyeballs.

Lance squinted in surprise and laughed. "Hey, it's Frosty! It's Frosty!"

The other kids laughed. How cool was this? A buried snowman. "It's Frosty! Frosty!" They echoed Lance like playground Pips. Even Leon joined in, relieved they'd forgotten about him. Lance stared at the snowman and thought something was weird. "His stupid head's on backwards," Lance laughed, and reached out to remedy the situation.

It was at this point that the cohort of adult supervision reacted to a blood-curdling scream. A scream that was much more than typical playground communication. This was a scream of profound terror and the genesis of years of therapy for poor Lance.

Beanie-covered heads swiveled and coffee was spilled as the adults ran as one toward the slide, wondering which one of them was responsible for the kid who had surely bashed his or her head open. *Please let it be someone else's*, was the collective thought.

They arrived to see a shrieking Lance face-to-face with the now headless snowman. Well, not exactly headless. The newly revealed human head protruding from the snowman suit was a mummy-grade African American male of about fifty. But it wasn't only the expression of indignant and profound surprise etched on the dead guy's face that freaked out Lance …

No. The vision that would appear each time Lance closed his eyes for the rest of his life was the parade of defrosted yellow maggots crawling out of Templeton J. Trout's vacant eye sockets.

* * *

"A true-life mystery that has baffled authorities since last Christmas has finally been solved by none other than that all-knowing sleuth Mother Nature herself, as Northeastern Ohio's long winter has thawed into a spine-chilling spring for a group of tots and their parents at the children's park at Cleveland Mercy Hospital, where the body of renowned orthopedic surgeon Templeton J. Trout has been found—much to the horror of one traumatized six-year-old boy. Dr. Trout's corpse, impeccably preserved in a sarcophagus of ice, was unexpectedly unearthed as the unwitting youngster flew down that slide into the frigid fright of his life."

Betsy Nguyen's plucked eyebrow directed her cameraman, Derek—the auteur who had shot the video of Nick's spinal fusion—to swing off her close-up and get a shot of the playground slide, which was subsumed by the CSI Cleveland circus: a coroner's wagon, forensics team, cop cars with flashing lights, along with a gaggle of grief counselors comforting distraught kids and their annoyed adults, who had better places to be than shivering in this park all damn day.

Also in Derek's shot was the sobbing Lance in the arms of his splenetic mother, who had told Betsy Nguyen on camera this would be, *"the last fucking time we come to this fucked-up place. This fucking hospital won't have one shit-stained bedpan left when I'm done suing their goddamned balls off."* Which would have made great TV except that the amount of bleeping necessary to clean up Lance's mom's statement, much to Betsy's vexation, reduced the interview to unairable adjective-free gibberish.

At the edge of Derek's frame, an old man in a wind-whipped brown overcoat and fedora supported himself on a cane as he listened to the protestations of a younger man, wearing a cashmere topcoat over a mohair and wool suit. Josh Przybylowicz waved his arms up and down like a deranged marionette as Lieutenant Artemas Sikorski implacably took in the show. Derek tightened frame, eliminating both men from the shot, and zoomed to the still whining Lance just as his angry mom bomped him one, but good.

"The young boy, whom we will not identify because of his tender age, is being consoled by his concerned mother," reported Betsy over the tender images of child abuse. (Although this footage was not suitable for air either, Derek would make sure to add it to his reel.) He swung the camera back onto Betsy just in time for her big finish: "The exact reason as to how and why Dr. Trout wound up in his icy cocoon is at this moment still unknown. *That* mystery has yet to be solved."

Betsy paused, looking at once perplexed, empathetic, and gorgeous, as she tossed the story back to the studio in her Every Anchor accent. "Betsy Nguyen, 19 News. First. Fair. Everywhere. Melinda and Tiago, back to you."

"Three, two, one, and we are out," said Derek as Betsy blew out a breath, frowned, and handed him her wireless mic.

"You know, I downloaded this public speaking app. It's got, like, similes, metaphors, alliteration, all kinds of helpful goodies," she said. "Except do you think 'sarcophagus of ice' was too literary? And I'm not too sure about 'flew down into the frigid fright of his life' either. Too many Fs?"

"What? No. Great stuff," said a preoccupied Derek. "They're going to pixilate my shot of Mommie Dearest slugging her kid, aren't they? Dammit. It's fucking gold."

* * *

"Give me a break. You already searched Trout's office, Lieutenant."

"Yeah. Five months ago. Right after that humdinger of a Christmas party he hosted. Forensics found more semen than on a Princess Cruise."

"Well, we have a new tenant in there. What do you expect to find now?"

The fuck? Here I was freezing my nuts off and this uncooperative slick in the fancy cashmere overcoat was skating on a rink called Obstruction of Justice, not to mention Obstruction of Warmth.

Question was why. I looked up to Trout's penthouse office, which was a big mistake because something cracked in my neck that didn't sound so good.

"Maybe a clue as to who pushed him out the window."

"Who says he was pushed?"

"The stiff is down here. His office is up there, and who commits suicide in a snowman suit? I ain't Hercules Poirot but call it a working theory. Give me the key, Przybylowicz. By the way, am I pronouncing your name right?"

"Close enough, but you can call me Josh P."

"Thanks, Josh P. You can call me Lieutenant Sikorski. Now give me the damn key."

"Lieutenant, isn't it obvious Dr. Trout wound up, uh, where he wound up because he was falling down drunk?" said Josh P, apparently not realizing he'd uttered the most inappropriate laugh line I'd heard in my forty years of asking incisive questions.

"In that case, who closed the window afterwards? His inconsiderate party guests?"

"The cleaning crew?"

"You're really going there? The cleaning crew? Everybody always blames the cleaning crew. Well, sorry, Josh P, but they had Christmas Eve off. I checked. My fingerprint guy is on the way. Oh wait, before I head up there, I need to ask you about another missing hospital employee."

Josh P groaned like he was getting fisted by Lenny Goldstein, my conscientious urologist. "There are no other missing doctors, Lieutenant."

In other words, he didn't answer my question.

"That's good. Because I was going to ask you about an RN who works here. Big Samoan guy? The catcher on your softball team. We had an inquiry from his grandma in Honolulu. The guy hasn't been heard from since around the holidays either—shortly after Trout went missing. Carmelo Iapoopoo or something like that."

"Iakopo," Josh P corrected me. I guess with a name like Przybylowicz, you get sensitive regarding pronunciation. "And no, we have no idea where he is either. He just disappeared in the middle of his shift one night. Weird."

"Definitely weird, Josh P, because I checked the logs for that night and Iakopo was the RN in charge of yet another figure outta that softball game. A guy who happened to be a patient."

"What patient?"

"A kid who played for the EZ♥Care team. You'd remember him, the lefty who hit the ground rule seagull. A year later, Trout does a spinal fusion on the kid, soon thereafter falls out his window, winters in the park, and the catcher—the lefty's nurse—goes missing. I'm not a huge believer in coincidences, so it'd be helpful if I could find him."

"We'd like to find him too, Lieutenant. We owe him a paycheck and he owes us an explanation as to why he walked off the job with no notice."

"Owes his landlord an explanation as well. He left all his stuff there. Makes you wonder."

"Wonder what?"

"About the endless realm of possibilities. Except right now, all I got to play with is the stiff I got. So if you'll give me the damn key, I'll go upstairs and wait for my fingerprint guy."

"I don't think that's wise."

"Why is that? Why would you want to make me get a warrant?"

"See, the guy we leased Trout's suite to—"

"What about him?"

Przybylowicz looked over my shoulder and gave me a smug look, like a divorced dad who bought six-year-old junior a drum set to drive his ex insane. "He's also from the softball game."

I turned to see a black Escalade with illegally tinted windows pulling across two handicapped spots between the kids' park and the back of the hospital. Classy. I was about to call Traffic and have the fuck towed—but who gets out of the Escalade but the guy I been trying to get face to face with for about a year now: Jimmy Tom Muscat. He slammed the door of the Escalade, gave the alarm two beeps so none of the squirts would steal it, and headed straight at us with purpose. His cowboy boots crunched across the snow like he was walking on a carpet of potato bugs.

Muscat didn't recognize me. Must've been the fedora. He went straight to Josh P, as if the slick worked for him. Which I was beginning to think might not be a stretch.

"Josh, I just heard the terrible news."

"Yes sir, the whole hospital is struggling with how to deal with the shock of it all."

Muscat lowered his voice. "Did you find anything?"

"Um," said Josh P who was definitely uncomfortable having this conversation around me. He kind of twitched in my direction to shut Muscat up, but it wasn't working—it mostly looked like he'd come down with a sudden case of Lou Gehrig's Disease.[*]

"What's wrong with your face, son?"

"Nothing, Mr. Muscat. It's just ..." He squinched at me again, trying to clue him in.

"You better see a doctor about that tic. I hear there's a shitload of 'em here." Muscat hee-hawed at that knee-slapper.

"Right. Will do," said Josh.

---

[*] The Iron Horse hits .340 with 493 dingers, almost 2000 ribbees, a 112.4 WAR (yeah, I keep up with that modern sabermetric lingo), and six-time World Series champ—and all anybody remembers him for is a horrible disease and a speech I still get misty-eyed over.

Muscat went on—still oblivious to me, the old man in the fedora. "Did Trout leave a note?"

"No."

The boys were entertaining but it was time to interrupt. "You know, fellas, collecting clues is my job."

That's when Muscat recognized me. "You!" He just about went all Tasmanian Devil and I thought (okay, I hoped) he'd get a stroke right then and there. But no such luck.

"Yeah, me. Been a while, Jimmy Tom. You cancelled the last three depositions. When are you gonna quit hiding behind your *Court TV* mouthpieces and face the music?"

"I had no idea he'd be here, Mr. Muscat," Josh P sniveled.

"Neither did I," I said. "But since I am, I suggest you not cancel the next deposition or you'll find yourself dragged into court on a Bench Warrant explaining to Judge Grabarkewitz—a real law and order guy whose wife's speeding tickets I just made go bye-bye—how come you keep cancelling."

"That's illegal!"

"So's being a party to an unlawful death."

Josh wanted no part of this. "I was just explaining to Lieutenant Sikorski that he needed to ask your permission to enter your suite, Mr. Muscat."

"Fuck no. Stay out of my office, you duplicitous prick."

"I don't think so. It was Dr. Trout's office at the time of his flyer. Therefore, I'm searching it in my official capacity as CDP Homicide. This has nothing to do with our civil matter. You want to argue about it, I'll get the warrant emailed to me in two minutes. I know you don't respect official documents, Muscat, but not complying with a search warrant sends your ass straight to jail and I'd be delighted to drive you there myself." I held out my palm to Josh P. "Now give me the goddamn key, Junior, I'm freezing my gonads off out here."

Josh P threw his arms up like he was doing Jazz Hands in the chorus of *Sweet Charity* and tossed me the key.

"Thanks. See you at the deposition, Muscat." I turned and tottered my way towards the back entrance to the hospital.

I no sooner made it to the safety of the sidewalk when I noticed over by the rear loading dock one of those sheet-draped gurneys that kinda look like a regular hospital gurney, but they're not. The low-hanging sheets are there to conceal the compartment *beneath* the gurney, which exists to stash a stiff. That's because no hospital can have the public watching dead folks getting wheeled through the corridors; bad for business. Not that the Icebox employees who were loading the deceased into the back of a Cleveland Mercy meat wagon for the Last Ride to the mortuary were fooling me. The other dead giveaway, so to speak, was the patients who were lucky enough to survive this place, they left by the front entrance in a wheelchair with either a look of relief or drool on their chin. Or both. I watched the two attendants—a skinny guy with hair to his shoulders like a chick and an actual chick with a watch cap pulled down over her ghost-white face—load the gurney into the back of the wiener mobile. The girl with the watch cap kinda looked familiar, but don't ask me how. They got in the back as a young black chick drove the bone wagon past me. Right about then, my teeth began to itch. Because there was something about watch-cap girl that was bugging me. And I almost had it, too, until I was interrupted by a voice I knew better than Marie's.

Well, almost better.

"Excuse me, Lieutenant Sikorski? Betsy Nguyen, 19 News."

Ah, the harmonious tones that trilled out of the face that fronted every personal tragedy or inspirational triumph I'd seen on TV for the last seven years. Like the blinded Afghan war dog who ran away from Camp Pendleton and made it 2,385 miles cross-country to reunite with his paraplegic handler, only to be run down outside the VA by a FedEx truck. Only Betsy Nguyen could make that a feel-good story. Betsy looked smaller than she did on TV, like the camera took ten pounds *off* her. Marie always swore Betsy Nguyen had an eye job. Frankly, I don't give a damn, but Marie's been obsessed with news people's plastic surgeries ever since I bought her an eighty-inch Ultra HD at the Micro Center in Mayfield Heights.

"Lieutenant, could you give us a comment on Dr. Trout's tragic death?"

"Nope. Talk to those two," I pointed to Josh P and Muscat who were strategizing their damage control. "Maybe you could ask Mr. Przybylowicz why he leased out the late Dr. Trout's suite before the doc's body was even found? And why is Mr. Muscat slumming here when he's got his own big fancy building in the Circle? Kinda suspicious, if you ask me." I winked bye-bye to Betsy and went inside the hospital where it was warm and welcoming. More or less.

*   *   *

Josh Przybylowicz and Jimmy Muscat remained in intense conversation as the CSI team wheeled Trout's bagged body towards a waiting coroner's van.

"The cop asked me about Iakopo," said Josh P.

"What did you tell him?"

"The truth. That Nurse Big-And-Crazy split without a trace."

"Which I still don't get. He didn't even leave me a message. I called his cell a dozen times. Just went straight to voicemail, then not even that. I wonder if he had anything to do with Templeton's 'fall'?"

"I doubt it. No one at Trout's Christmas party saw him, and Iakopo's hard to miss. No, I think Templeton offed himself."

"Why"?

"Maybe he got cold feet," Josh said.

"Save the humor, son. Something's wrong here. Templeton wasn't the type. He enjoyed being who he was too much. Now he's dead; plus my clean-up hitter and eyes and ears here is missing; plus Klepstein loses all of us a cash cow; plus that fucking cop is getting on my nerves. I don't like any of this, Josh. I suggest you run a tighter ship here or—"

"Mr. Przybylowicz? Could I get a comment?"

Betsy Nguyen, trailed by Derek, approached, cutting short Muscat's threat. Didn't matter; Josh got the gist. He pasted a troubled look on his face, which under the circumstances wasn't a stretch.

"Dr. Trout was a fine family man, a wonderful doctor, a saint who walked this Earth. And as soon as we have more information, you'll be the first to know, Betsy. Promise."

Betsy, frustrated, signaled for Derek to cut and as soon as he did, Muscat crunched over the snow to Betsy.

"Hi, Jimmy Tom Muscat. EZ♥Care. I love your work, Miss Nguyen, and was wonderin' if you had any plans tonight?"

"You get right to the point, don't you?"

"If the point is giving you exclusive information on this tragedy, well, I plead guilty. Just don't make me plead for dinner at the Marble Room." Muscat's eyes gleamed like a lion sizing up a gazelle with a broken leg.

CHAPTER 26

Easing Back Pain During Sex

by
Templeton J. Trout M.D. - F.A.C.P. - F.A.A.O.S - F.A.B.O.S
and
I.M. Demidova M.D

A junker Geo Metro, whatever color it used to be obscured by geological strata of primer paint, pulled up in the slush outside a soot-coated building on Literary Road, a vestige of the Tremont neighborhood's bygone past as a college town. Now, to some of the more erudite residents, the street sign was just a punchline.

The ground floor of the building was taken up by Marek's Fine Meats and Ukrainian Market. The lights were off for the evening, the steel grates pulled down, and the CLOSED sign dangled behind the security-barred front door. The Metro appropriated a parking spot marked "Customers Only" and a gaunt woman wearing a parka with a faux fur collar exited. She pulled the collar tight against her neck, where it met the sharp edges of her close-cut, light-brown hair, and paused to allow her oversized raspberry-colored glasses to defog from the warmth of the car, before heading toward the residents' entrance next door to Marek's Fine Meats.

Keys in hand, illuminated by the light fixture above the door, an almost unrecognizable Julie Toffoli let herself in.

* * *

They were in a space without light.

A chasm suffused blue by Coltrane's penetrating tenor in the dark, playing "What's New?"

Answer: everything.

*   *   *

In darkness.

"This is almost like doing it with somebody else."

"I wouldn't know," said Julie.

"Think of it as polygamy without the stigma."

"Monogamy for morons?"

"Well, you have that right. Because it appears I'm not holding up my end of the deal."

"Sweetheart, don't whine. Nick Glass doesn't whine. I think we need to look at that stupid book again."

A match flared and a candle was lit, revealing Julie's new glasses next to a Bluetooth speaker adjacent to a dozen prescription bottles pushed aside on the night table to make room for Trout and Demidova's rainbow-colored sex manual for post-op paralytics.

Julie blew out the match, grabbed the booklet and settled back in bed next to Nick. With her short haircut and weight loss, she looked hardened, severe. It was only when she smiled, which occurred rarely these days, was she unmistakably Julie. She pulled the jumble of covers to their shoulders as she read aloud from the booklet: "'*Easing Back Pain During Sex.*' by Templeton J. Trout and I.M. Demidova. Now there's a collaboration from Hell."

"Literally."

"Half-literally," Julie corrected. "Trout may reside there but that witch still practices at Cleveland Mercy. And I don't."

Nick slid closer for a better look at the manual. Over five months out from surgery and two corpses later, he'd put on a little weight and grown the beginnings of a beard. But if his expression still looked pained, he couldn't help it; that's where he lived and his body wouldn't let him forget. Still, he made a conscious effort to not let the hurt define every damn minute. But that was a losing battle and the mask he put on didn't fit so well. Julie's mask—her change from the girl next door to the chick with chips on both shoulders—was an even tougher fit, as her low T-cell count and compromised immune system only fueled her anger. Still, she tried.

They both tried.

They tried because neither could conceive of any other way to get through it. Not without the other.

"Have you heard back on any of the Fellowship applications or are you keeping them secret?"

"It's more like they're keeping it secret from me. Now's the time they should be flooding my mailbox. Interviews need to be scheduled, all that."

He touched her shoulder, turning her face towards his. "Klepstein, sabotaging you from coast to coast. How is that even possible?"

"Because those guys—and the vast majority are guys—they're members of an exclusive and privileged club. They go to the same conferences, the same conventions, they cover for each other when they screw women who aren't their wives. They probably even have a secret handshake. Christ. My med school grades were impeccable. I have great L.O.R.s from my profs. So, I guess, yeah, one asshole can wipe out the last five years of my life. If he's motivated enough. And he is."

"File an EEOC Complaint."

"Not an option. Filing a discrimination suit is a for sure way of never seeing the inside of a hospital again. Except as a patient. Or in my awesome disguise."

She turned her face back to the book. "Hey, Nick? Right now? Let's not talk about this. We've supposed to be doing funner things, right?"

"Right." He flicked a thumb on Trout's author picture, a post-humous bitch slap. In retrospect, not as satisfying as watching him soar off a building. Still, living in a 24/7 purgatory of nerve pain that cut through his leg like a scythe, and back pain almost as raw as the day he was cut—Trout's legacy of agony—it was scant satisfaction.

In the author's photo, Trout had opted for a visual facsimile of concern and compassion blended with his default *If-there-is-a-God-then-you're-looking-at-Him* mien.

"I can't help thinking about it. What do you think happened to him?"

Instead of answering, Julie wriggled out of her Cavs sweatshirt and said, "Turn to page nine. That looks promising."

* * *

Their nude bodies faced each other on their sides. The long scar on Nick's back shimmered scarlet in the candlelight. Their fingers, their faces, their lips, touched, comforted, and after all these years, still explored.

Coltrane had given way to Johnny Hodges, whose sensual alto caressed the intro to "I Got It Bad (And That Ain't Good)." Julie stared past Nick's face at the booklet she had nestled on his shoulder. It was open to a page with a diagram of a couple likewise on their sides in the identical intimate position. The bed was now surrounded by a shrine of flickering candles, illuminating their studio apartment, which looked like it was furnished and decorated by Goodwill Industries in close collaboration with a medical supply house.

Julie read from the book: "*If a back problem lingers for weeks or months, you may feel like pain is running your life. When it hurts to move, fear of pain—as much as the pain itself—can keep you from trying even normal activities.*"

"I did not know that."

"Please. I'm doing foreplay here." Julie continued reading: "*As disappointments and frustrations add up, you may wonder if you'll ever be pain-free again. These worries can make it harder to deal with your partner. And if pain keeps the two of you from enjoying sex, you may both feel so dissatisfied that your relationship begins to suffer.*" Julie paused. "Is our relationship suffering?"

"No, I think ... I think it's ..." Nick couldn't finish his thought as a wide-breaking grin creased his face. Or was it a grimace?

"Nick? Are you okay?"

Blowing out shallow, rapid breaths, he found it impossible to answer.

"Oh. Yes. You're okay. You're way more than okay," said Julie as their bodies pressed together. She let the booklet drop to the floor and reached over to the night table and grabbed a ready condom. She put it on him with the dexterity of a surgeon and pulled him inside her.

"Thank you, Jacinta," she whispered.

"Yo? I'm Nick."

"The blue pill she got us. The one I gave you with the green tea? It's working!"

Until it wasn't. Nick winced as a light went out in his eyes. He closed them and began to thrust faster, faster, and faster, but soon the only thing he could do was stop.

After an eternity of silence, Julie whispered, "Nick, we have nothing but time."

"I can't get past the hurt. Even when it's not so bad, all I have to do is wonder for how long and it always tells me. Always."

"Stay still." From the speaker, "I Got It Bad" ended and the raucous "Jeep's Blues" began. "Just stay still and don't do anything else."

She kissed his neck, his chest, and disappeared under the covers. Ellington's big band built to out-and-out ecstasy as the brass section joined Hodges's alto.

After two verses, Nick opened his eyes and watched as Julie reappeared. He punched the headboard and groaned as he sagged to his side, turning away from her.

Julie leaned over and gently kissed his scar. "Nick? You know what? You were you again. We both felt it. It's going to happen. Sooner or later. Anticipation is the best part, right?"

"It's too much in my head. Without any warning, my brain hits a panic button. Does Jacinta have a pill for that?"

"Nick, we just need more time."

"But what if time's not the problem? My back isn't healing like they said it would. Not even close. What if I can't ever be normal?"

"Nick, please, let's not talk about normal." Julie picked the wrinkled condom off the bed and tossed it away. "It's because of me you have to wear this … impediment."

"Well, the rubbers from the Dollar General on Superior didn't stop us in the backseat of my Dad's DeSoto back when … Screw it. That was a long time ago."

Nick maneuvered back on his side, grimacing. He started to speak, but Julie put a finger on his lips.

"Nick, I've loved you since we were thirteen years old and we were slow dancing to Celine singing "My Heart Will Go On" in the Mayfield Middle School gym. And that will never change."

"Not for me."

"Then it's settled."

"Maybe this pain management guy can help tomorrow morning."

"Which one is it?"

"Dr. Karaoke."

"Ganapur? Why him?"

"He was the only pain guy EZ♥Care would cover. The rest were 'Out Of Network.'"

"At least he gave you some fascinating dreams. Anyway, as long as I'm with you, he can't do any more damage."

"Yeah. Because Trout got there first. You know, I'm glad that bastard's gone. It was his own damn fault. The only thing better would've been if he survived the fall and was ripped apart by a pack of urban coyotes as he crawled through the snow on two broken legs." Nick half-smiled. "Too harsh?"

Julie wiggled her hand. Maybe, maybe not. Nick took it and held on. "I wonder where he wound up. I mean it is weird."

"Nick, enough. Let's reconcile to the fact that we're never going to know. Okay?"

"Okay."

He knocked a few of the RX bottles on his night table out of the way and retrieved a universal remote. He turned off the music and aimed the remote at the TV as Julie pulled the Cavs sweatshirt over her head, shivering against the cold.

The twenty-seven-inch Zenith on the dresser across the room buzzed to life. On screen was the pixilated footage Derek had shot of the crying kid, Lance—the bully who'd discovered Trout's body. The chyron at the bottom of the screen read:

BREAKING NEWS:

MISSING DOC FOUND DEAD IN TOMB OF ICE

That holy shit storm of a visual was followed by Derek's film school one-hundred-and-eighty-degree shot beginning with the onlookers at the park watching CSI bagging the corpse and concluding on a close-up of Betsy Nguyen, who sold this drama as if she were the spawn of Edward R. Murrow and Laura Ingraham.

"—inexplicably, the world-famous surgeon was wearing a snowman suit. What, if anything, was the significance of that? Was he role playing? Was he pushed or did he jump? The only certainty is CDP's most highly decorated homicide investigator, Lt. Artemas Sikorski, assured me he would not rest until he finds the answers. I'm Betsy Nguyen, reporting from Cleveland Mercy Hospital. Tiago and Melinda, back to you."

Nick clicked off the TV. The fading light from the burnt candles glinted across their faces. They looked like kids who'd just heard their first ghost story around a campfire.

CHAPTER 27

Off The Tallahatchie Bridge

The "borrowed" red-and-white Cleveland Mercy ambulance—headlights off, raspy windshield wipers on—drove by moonlight through a cold mist along a narrow exurban road well outside of town. Accompanying the rhythmic hooting of a Great Horned Owl was the unfluctuating sound of the nearby Cuyahoga River, whose surging spring current was freed from the cloak of ice that had silenced it over the long winter.

A grove of tall river birch gave way to a right-angle turnoff that led to a blocked-off viaduct bridge. Attached to the two A-framed traffic barriers with blinking yellow lights was a sign that read NO ENTRY. With good reason, as this deteriorated and disused bridge, which dated back to the Roosevelt WPA of the thirties, had outlived its utility as a means to transport anything heavier than a Model T. Beneath it, ran the Cuyahoga whose national claim to shame was it caught fire in 1969. *Time Magazine* contemporaneously described the polluted Cuyahoga as *"the river that oozes rather than flows,"* further going on to presciently point out, *"a person does not drown in it, but rather decays."*

Which was Raven, Jacinta, and Tick's thinking, as they had decided the viaduct was the perfect spot to dump the still-frozen big guy. Worst case, from an environmental perspective, he'd thaw out at the bottom of Lake Erie and give a school of yellow perch a bad case of aquatic acid reflux.

Raven and Tick darted out of the ambulance and removed the blockades with the precision of commandos, as Jacinta inched it onto the creaky viaduct. Once on the bridge, she braked and waited for Raven and Tick to return the barriers to their original positions. The two, exhalations trailing them like confessions, completed the job and clambered back inside. Jacinta drove on for another hundred yards and came to a stop at the middle of the bridge.

The rear door swung open. Tick jumped out as Raven nudged the sheet-draped gurney toward him. Tick held onto the front with every bit of strength he had as Jacinta exited the driver's door and moved to the rear of the ambulance to help him out.

"Hang on, Tick," Jacinta said, as she bent down and lowered the wheels. "You can do it."

"No problem," said Tick. Followed by, "Oh crap!" as his foot slipped out from under him.

Tick's tenuous hold gave way and the tilted gurney knocked him backwards onto the wet and crumbled pavement. Raven leapt out, but too late to prevent the cart from pinning Tick against the railing where, upon impact, gravity (plus three hundred and fifty pounds of frozen Samoan) blew open the corpse compartment door, and Tick found himself staring eye to eye with Iakopo's flash-frozen, black-and-blue post-electrocution stiffy.

"Tick!" yelled Jacinta, as she and Raven managed to roll Iakopo's body off him and onto its back at the edge of the railing. Tick hyperventilated like an improvisational Lamaze instructor.

"You okay?" said Jacinta.

"His *thing* touched me."

"Hey, Jacinta, little help?" asked Raven, who had pushed the corpse compartment door closed and needed assistance lifting the gurney back inside the ambulance. Jacinta left Tick and helped Raven slide the cart back inside and shut the doors behind it.

Raven blew out a vapor cloud and said, "Okay, let's get him over the side before anyone shows up."

"As if that will happen at three in the—"

The sound of an approaching car put the brakes on Jacinta's presumption. "Quick! Grab him!"

"I'm trying!" said Raven, struggling with the frozen blue, gigantic, naked corpse.

"What can I do?" said Tick, getting to his feet.

"Yank and lift," said Jacinta.

The approaching car's headlights swept the beginning of the span, a hundred yards away.

And stopped.

"Why are they stopping?" said Tick.

The swirling blue and red lights on top of the car answered the question.

"Five-O," said Raven.

"No no," moaned Tick.

"Come on. Hurry. Tick, we need you! On three," said Jacinta. "One … two …"

The trio lifted Iakopo. Tick, riding fear and adrenalin, didn't think his part through as he inadvertently grasped Iakopo's chilled member, which snapped off in his hand like a Thanksgiving wishbone.

From the entrance to the bridge, they could hear the scraping of the traffic barriers as they were moved aside. Tick, frozen, gaped at the detached dick in his palm.

"My God, Tick, pitch the pizzle!" said Jacinta.

"What?"

"Toss the tool!" said Raven.

Which Tick did, accompanied by a primal scream that caused birds to flee their nests and forest animals to trample through the underbrush.

The orphaned boner was soon followed over the side by the dickless Iakopo, as Raven and Jacinta managed to get him over the railing an instant before the Cuyahoga County Sheriff car's headlights illuminated them.

The enormous crash and splash Iakopo made as he hit the fast-flowing water was masked by a brief burst of siren from the cop car.

The three, shaken, turned as twenty-one-year-old Cuyahoga County Sheriff's Deputy, Harley Pollard—anxious to solve his very first crime—exited the black and gold-striped cop car.

At a generous five-six, one-thirty, which liberally stretched the minimum physical requirements of the Sheriff's Department, as well as possessing a boyish face with close-together darting eyes, Harley more or less presented as a suspicious fourteen-year-old dressed in his father's uniform on Bring-Your-Kid-To-Work Day—that is, if Pops was Sergeant Pablo Picasso. However, the Glock he was pointing at them more than made up for his lack of heft.

With his other hand, Harley shined his tactical flashlight on the trio. He squinted at this odd group wearing parkas over hospital scrubs; it couldn't have been more weird if he had pulled over a starship full of Xyrillians.[*] He aimed his light on the Cleveland Mercy ambulance, then back to the three. Reluctantly, he holstered his Glock.

"You know, this situation reminds me of the song my Granny used to play all the time when I was a kid and it drove me totally

---

[*] See *Star Trek: Enterprise*, Episode 105.

mental," Harley said in a post-pubescent voice that he tried to keep from cracking. "You know, the one where this girl and this guy named Billie Joe McAllister threw something off the Tallahatchie Bridge?"

"'Ode to Billie Joe.' Bobbie Gentry. 1967. Ranked number 412 on *Rolling Stone*'s '500 Greatest Songs Of All Time.' Capitol Records. Eight Grammy noms and four wins." Tick said all that in a monotonic five seconds.

"Yeah. That's the one, Rain Man." Harley let his flashlight linger on their faces, one by one. "Hated that song."

Jacinta nodded in agreement, "Me too, Officer. All that twangy redneck rubbish."

"No, it wasn't the twangy redneck 'rubbish' that bothered me— which you should open your mind to, or at least give it an honest try; there's some exceptional roots musicians like Bill Monroe, Hazel Dickens, or Arthur Alexander you'd probably enjoy. In fact, Arthur Alexander was an African American country singer who had the distinction of being the only artist ever covered by The Beatles, The Stones, and Bob Dylan on three different songs he wrote."

"Why are you looking at me when you say that?" asked Jacinta.

"What? Sorry, I don't mean nothing."

"Just because this Arthur Alexander is black? Are you patronizing me, Officer?"

"No, ma'am, I'm not. I was trying to say it wasn't the so-called twangy redneck rubbish that drove me mental, it was the *words* that twisted my brain all into knots. That is, until I was old enough to go into an AOL Chat Room—that's what my Grandma called them back then, Chat Rooms—devoted to deciphering what the song really was about. There's plenty of theories out there: the most popular is Billie Joe and the Narrator Lady, Miss Gentry, were throwing an aborted baby off the Tallahatchie Bridge. Could've even been an interracial child." He shot Jacinta a quick look, "No offense."

"You are doing it again," said Jacinta.

"I'm sorry, ma'am. I'm only trying to make a point here. Which is how the theme of the song illustrates the indifference we, as a society, show towards human life."

"Then why are you a cop?"

Raven shot her a look. Jacinta shrugged. "It's a fair question."

"Ma'am, things have changed a lot since the sixties," said Harley.

"How exactly?" asked Jacinta.

Raven jumped in for the save before this went any further south: "Indeed, the sixties were a turbulent decade in our history," said Raven, lifting this wooden pearl straight from a CNN documentary called *The Sixties* which she'd watched during the course of one of her assignments as a candy-striper. Josh P had designated Raven to keep close company with an iconic female folksinger who'd collapsed on stage at her induction ceremony at the nearby Rock and Roll Hall of Fame. For six weeks, as her song slowly faded out, the guitar-picking granny was suspended in a purgatory between Cleveland Mercy and Rock & Roll Heaven. Her deluxe private room was paid for in cash: *Cash on the catheter*, as Josh P sensitively put it. Upshot was, between the osmosis of the CNN documentary and all the "groovy" things the folksinger told Raven she had experienced—including "balling" Joe Cocker (whoever *that* was: Jeesh, it sounded like a porno name to Raven) at the Chateau Marmont on the Sunset Strip—well, Raven could hold her own on anything sixties. So maybe she could talk this hick cop into letting them go before Jacinta got them all arrested.

"That's what my grandma says," Harley replied. "She said people were goony back then. Didn't even wear shoes half the time.

But listen, I'm freezing my butt off here and I bet you guys are too, so tell me what you all are doing on this bridge at three in the morning?"

"Clearly, we took a wrong turn," said Jacinta.

"Now you're insulting me, ma'am. You had to move the traffic barriers to get the ambulance on here. So, I guess the better question is just what *exactly* did you three throw off this bridge?"

"Nothing," they replied in ragged unison.

Deputy Harley Pollard and his asymmetrical eyes frowned in disappointment.

"Okay then. My apologies and all. And we were having such a nice exchange of views, too. Licenses and registration, please, because I'm going to have to take you all down to the station."

CHAPTER 28

Perp Walk

If Julie's primer-coated Geo Metro was the burial ground of all color, for one jaywalking tabby it was also the executioner at dawn.

"Did you hear that?"

"Hear what?" Julie's tone was less a question and more a posture of defiance.

Nick slunk deep into the passenger seat. The steady scraping of the Metro's worn wipers over the rain-pelted windshield was the soundtrack of tension.

"Nothing. I thought I heard something."

"If you think I ran over that cat, why don't you just say so?"

"Was probably a pothole."

"No, it was a cat. I was speeding. I can't see well through the windshield and I was preoccupied. The poor thing darted into the street. I had no time to react."

"It wasn't your fault."

"Fault's got nothing to do with it. You can't carry guilt for what you can't control. It's not healthy. Was it your fault Trout got himself killed because he tried to get rid of the evidence of his lies? Whose fault was it that psycho nurse electrocuted himself while trying to kill all of us? Was it my fault the cat was reckless, and I didn't slam on the brakes because you're not wearing a seatbelt because it cuts into your anterior scar? No, we're total amateurs when it comes to being moral deficients."

Julie flicked on her turn signal and waited to veer onto Pearl. The wipers kept scraping. Nick took advantage of the pause to shift to another position that in five minutes would hurt just as much.

"The professional here is Muscat. He had no problem wrecking your back over a freaking *softball* game. Just so he wouldn't *feel* bad, so he wouldn't *look* bad. Hell, he carried a grudge for a whole year and used Iakopo as his stooge until the big ugly decided to freelance. All this because Muscat couldn't hit a ball and you can."

"Could."

"Could. Fine. Muscat also had no problem taking out his frustrations by throwing the bat that crippled his devoted assistant. Bad luck for Edie. She was sitting in the wrong seat. Even when she heals, she'll have severe arthritis for the rest of her life, continuing neurological deficits, all because Jimmy Tom Muscat does not give a damn what damage he causes to other people. No matter how much loyalty they give, it doesn't matter. The ethos for assholes like him and Klepstein and Trout and Iakopo is: *Does what I'm doing in the moment make me feel better or does it make me feel worse?* Consequences are irrelevant. That's why they call them sociopaths."

"It'd be nice if they *all* could die."

"It would, but we're not murderers. And Karma is not going to get all of them."

"Do you want to go back and check out the cat?"

"I would have already, but then you'd be late for the Ganapur appointment. My priority is you."

"That goes both ways."

A look of disquiet creased her face. "Hey, check my phone again? The burner?" Julie laughed. "Christ, I'm even talking like a criminal now. *Burner.*"

"Yeah. You're right out of The Low-Rises."

As Julie laughed again—a refreshing sound for Nick—he poked around in her purse, pulled out an old flip phone and examined the screen.

"Nothing."

"Which worries me."

"Maybe Raven didn't want to wake you."

"No. She was supposed to leave a text after they dumped Iakopo in the river. Holy crap, I just said 'dumped Iakopo in the river.'"

"You said it because it had to be done. Raven knew I had a doctor's appointment—it was late and she probably decided to let you get some sleep. It's not like you don't need some."

"What? Are you saying I'm not looking fabulous and gorgeous lately? I knew it."

"Jules … I don't care how you look."

"Suave, Nicky. Maybe you could rephrase that in the form of a compliment?"

"Um, you have an adequate personality?"

It got a laugh, and that's all Nick needed: "Look, what we talked about, leaving Cleveland after Ganapur does whatever he can do? If anything. Going somewhere new, starting over? Well, I thought of something. Maybe it's stupid, but—"

"I'm sure it's not stupid," Julie interrupted. "But it's difficult to talk about the future when we're both neck deep in the present."

"Maybe not."

"Nick, please. I can change my appearance, but I can't change the reality that Cleveland Mercy dumped me. And I can't change what's inside me."

"Those are hindrances, not dead-ends. I've been playing with an idea. A place where you can be a doctor and I could be ... I don't know, something that doesn't involve lifting anything."

"Nick. Save it for now. Please. We're here." She turned the wheel and aimed for the five-story parking structure adjacent to Cleveland Mercy. "Hand me my meds?"

Nick reached inside her purse and emerged with a plastic pill box. He snapped open the compartment marked *"Friday"* and emptied a half-dozen multi-colored pills and capsules into her palm, followed by a water bottle.

"Thanks, sweetheart," she said. "Oh wow. Look at that."

That being a half-dozen local news vans parked in front of the hospital. Nick bit his lip. "You think they're here for us?"

"I highly doubt it. A SWAT team with a No-Knock warrant would've come to our place and kicked the door in at three in the morning or something dramatic like that. Maybe Raven's folksinger warbled her last lullaby. Or, more likely, they're just milking Trout."

"Fish don't lactate."

"Thank you, Mr. Science." Julie grinned but nevertheless drove carefully past the news vans, and into the parking structure.

*   *   *

At the front entrance to Cleveland Mercy, a crowd of about a hundred plus, bundled against the cold and wet, surrounded a phalanx of plastic-protected media, gawked as a young and unsmiling police detective, with soaked red hair pulled back in a bun and a CDP raincoat over her business casual suit, supervised two uniformed officers as they executed quite the splashy arrest. The female uniformed cop who had a grip on the forearm of Dr. Irina Demidova was short, stocky, and not gentle. Her shiny wet cap and immaculate uniform contrasted with her statuesque prisoner's sable-covered, blood-stained scrubs. They looked like The Village People, distaff version, as they sloshed towards a parked patrol car. The young male cop in front of them nuzzled the top of his holster as he scrutinized the onlookers—just in case the mob of cancer patients, amputees, or brain surgeons decided to dispense vigilante justice. But no such violence was forthcoming from this crowd, who savored this unexpected break in the Cleveland Mercy routine of life, death, and breakfast.

Demidova spat venom at the old man with the cane who accompanied the young red-headed detective.

"You are worse than KGB! I have patient on table now!"

"One day, he'll thank me," said Lt. Sikorski.

"Why do you do this?!"

Sikorski shot a quick glance to see that Betsy Nguyen—in the center of the line of TV reporters and cameras—was rolling, and grandstanded his answer for the benefit of the local media. Might as well cap his celebrity cop career in style.

"Because the State Medical Association has informed us you are not licensed to practice medicine in the Buckeye State. In fact, according to the AMA, you're not licensed to practice anywhere in the United States."

"You lie!" said Demidova. "Dr. Trout arrange all my licenses! Everything is in order!"

"Then I'd say killing him was a helluva of a way to say thanks."

Oohs and aahs from the crowd as Demidova wailed, "*Akhineya!* How could I kill the man I love?" Demidova's white-hot glare would have made the sun cower, had it been out.

"Save it for the jury, Doc," said Sikorski. "Along with the reason your fingerprints were all over his French doors to oblivion."

"He ask me to open!"

That begat woofing from the bystanders, who'd taken on the singularity of a reality show audience.

"Maybe. But I doubt he asked you to close them behind him after you pushed him out. By the way, thanks for confirming my theory in front of all these witnesses." Sikorski gestured to the young, redheaded female detective next to him. "You *do* remember the part where my colleague, Detective … Detective …" Sikorski trailed off, apparently having forgotten his junior partner's name.

"Corbin, sir," Detective Debbie Corbin whispered to him.

"Right. I was holding back for max effect, Detective," Sikorski whispered back. "Thought a rook like you might appreciate having your name on the TV. No charge."

"Yes, sir. Thank you," Detective Debbie Corbin whispered back, although it was clear neither she nor her abundant freckles believed him.

"Anytime." Sikorski turned it up again for the crowd and media. "I was reminding you, Dr. Demidova, Detective Corbin has read you your rights. Anything you say may be used against you in a court of law. So please feel free to continue."

"*Schas po ebalu poluchish, suka, blyad!*" Demidova hissed.

Sikorski scanned the crowd. "Is there a Russian in the house?"

An aging refugee from the 1970s USSR and likewise seventies American fashion—a balding hipster with a ponytail, paisley slacks, and a tight turtleneck—stepped out from the crowd and raised his hand.

"She say, 'I will fucking kill you, bitch motherfucker.'"

"Thanks," said Sikorski as the Russian guy waved for the TV cameras and took out his cell to call his girlfriend to tell her to DVR the news.

Chants of *Artie! Artie! Artie!* rose from the crowd. This was the Red Trash version of a Springer episode, except with better production values and a hotter antagonist.

Hiding behind a nearby rebar-reinforced concrete planter—the kind that are *de rigueur* at soft targets like hospitals or sports arenas—was Josh Przybylowicz, who was watching his CEO career blow up like a Russian space station before his eyes. Hell, two sets of quintuplets switched at birth would've been better PR for Cleveland Mercy than this freaking circus act. Why did that senile cop have to pimp his bust for every camera in Cleveland? Couldn't he have taken Trout's slutsky out the back way? Discreetly? Would that have been so hard? Josh reached for his cell. But unlike the seventies Russian guy, he was not calling his girlfriend.

Sikorski moved closer to Demidova. As did a half-dozen zoom lenses.

"Use your phone call wisely, my little tractor. See you at the station." Sikorski motioned to the female uniform, who got up on her tippy-toes, palmed Demidova's head, and guided her into the backseat of the waiting cop car as the male cop and Detective Debbie Corbin got in the front. Sikorski watched the patrol car drive away, lights flashing, and turned to limp his way through the cheering throng toward his parked Caprice.

Head down, careful not to slip on the slushy pavement, Sikorski passed a cluster of bystanders near the front entrance. Concealing themselves behind the looky-loos were Julie and Nick. They were about to enter the hospital but had stayed on as keen observers to the arrest.

Julie watched the police car clear the circular drive and exit onto the street. "You know what's in that car?"

"Our Get-Out-Of-Jail-Free Card?"

"Yes, that. But also Karma." Julie's eyes were hard and unforgiving. "That sable-cidal bitch is getting what she deserves."

Nick didn't reply. He knew, they both knew, that was an innocent—well, *legally* innocent—sable-cidal bitch being driven to jail. Sure, Julie was correct: Demidova *did* deserve all that because of her complicity in the destruction of Nick's back, and, by extension, their lives.

Still. She didn't murder Trout.

After all these years, Julie could read his mind. "Don't worry, we'll send the old cop a postcard later; she won't get the chair. Let's get inside or we'll be late for Ganapur."

She turned to help him into the lobby but abruptly stopped. "Crap, I forgot to 'prime' the parking ticket."

"What?"

"A new thing. Another one of Josh P's revenue-producing schemes. It's predicated on the fact there will always be enough people too stressed out, or don't read English well enough, to forget to input their time of arrival and what parking spot they're in before coming downstairs. If I don't do it, we have to pay the all-day charge of thirty-two bucks."

"What an asshole."

"Yep. That he is. Hey, don't worry, Ganapur always triple books his appointments. You'll still be waiting when I get back."

"What if they take me early and he wants to give me a shot or do a procedure or something like that?"

"Won't happen. This is a consult. That way, he can bill insurance for this visit on top of any subsequent treatments. So, if he wants to put you on his schedule for something, fine. We can always cancel." She kissed him on the cheek, turned to leave, but paused to take the "burner" out of her purse. Julie opened it, frowned, and snapped it shut.

"She probably just flaked."

"No. Not Raven. I'll call after we're done here. Be right back."

Julie made her way through the remnants of the crowd towards the Lego-like parking structure, an edifice that looked incongruous adjacent to the stately Cleveland Mercy, a monument from another century. Hand carved by master artisans between the gargoyles were the Latin words:

Misericordia - Novus - Fiducia

Which roughly translated to: Compassion, Innovation, and Trust. Nearby, the stenciled words over the parking structure read:

EASY♥PARK @ CLEVELAND MERCY
POWERED BY EZ♥CARE™
NO ATTENDANT ON DUTY - PLEASE PAY AT MACHINE

Which translated to: If you're interested in receiving Cleveland Mercy's commitment to "Compassion, Innovation, and Trust," you first have to pay the cover charge at the door.

CHAPTER 29

Dr. Ganapur's Chamber Of Horrors

An elevator opened on the lobby level. Nick stepped inside, only to immediately back out as if he'd just stepped into the fire pit of Hell. "Sorry. Wrong way."

"Hey, Nicky Glass! This is *exactly* the right way! Don't you recognize me? It's Jen Kovačic from Admitting."

Like he could forget Mrs. Bride of Frankenstein, the hagfish lady who'd rushed him through the electronic signature process that had included his alleged permission to give Betsy Nguyen and 19 News the right to broadcast his spinal fusion which, thankfully, due to Trout's vanishing act—not to mention the minor detail that the op was a failure—had never aired. And now, never would. Too depressing and ghoulish even for local news.

With a wizened claw, Mrs. B of F pulled Nick back inside the elevator and off they went.

"I see you didn't get my phone message."

"What message?"

"The one canceling your appointment with Dr. Ganapur today. His seminar in Pakistan got pushed up a day, so he's jamming to get all his out-patient procedures done before he leaves tomorrow night. It's slam-bam-thank-you-ma'am up there."

"Uh, I'm just here for a consult."

"I know that, silly. But there's no reason for you to suffer for two more weeks. I'll get him to examine you in one of the pre-op rooms in between his procedures."

"Thanks," said Nick as he watched the elevator indicator point them closer to the Out-Patient Surgery floor.

"Anything for you, Nicky." She lowered her voice even though they were the only occupants of the elevator. "Darn shame about Dr. Trout."

Nick did his best to look pensive. "Tragic."

"I hope they fry that Commie impostor. Dr. Trout was a god among mortals."

*   *   *

Julie, her Metro on the roof of the parking structure in the last available spot, pulled up her hoodie against the rain and hustled to the covered Pay Station adjacent to the elevator and staircase. She flashed frustration, as there were three parties waiting in line in front of her. Couldn't this move any faster?

As Julie cursed under her breath, a computer voice—that sounded a lot like the AOL guy who used to say "You've Got Mail," but now in retirement was reduced to working multilingual parking lots—directed a Nicaraguan mom with a hyper five-year-old boy to take her ticket. The problem was there wasn't any ticket to take. Yet, the AOL guy was insistent, bordering on petulant, Julie thought, as he hectored the woman in Español: *Por favor tome so boleto. Por favor tome so boleto.* The group waiting in line grew restless.

"Excuse me," said Julie. "Maybe I can help." The mother nodded her thanks as Julie pressed LANGUAGES on the screen, selected ENGLISH, and the AOL guy immediately accommodated: *Please take your ticket,* followed by the magical appearance of the ticket.

With the relief of someone who'd just won a minor lottery, the lady again thanked Julie, took the ticket and her son to the elevator where she pressed the Down button. And waited. Pressed it again. Nothing until the elevator alarm blared like a klaxon on a submerging submarine. Everyone in line reacted, as the floor indicator showed the elevator was stuck on the second level.

"*Apúrate, hijo*," the mother said and pulled the kid toward the interior staircase. "*Vamos a caminar.*" But after one step, Mom stopped short and pulled her kid close because spread out on the landing of the staircase was the inert body of a homeless guy. Filthy, disheveled, maybe sixty, maybe seventy, surrounded by plastic bags full of crap, and guarded by an off-leash pit bull. The speckled pit's ribs were showing, but he still ran a good seventy pounds and his teeth were sharp and his jaw hardwired not to let go. He growled low at the intruders.

Julie didn't need to translate for everyone to understand no one was getting past the pit.

* * *

"The sad fact, Nick, is you have FBS: Failed Back Syndrome."

Dr. Ganapur held up his iPad for Nick to see, as he scrolled through the slices from Nick's latest MRI. Nick, legs dangling off the edge of a gurney in a pre-op cubicle, tried to comprehend what Ganapur was showing him—those MRI "slices" that might as well have been shots from the faked moon landing.

"Look at this sagittal image here," said Ganapur, pointing. "It's obvious the fusion has failed to adhere. And after this amount of time, it should have. No question."

"Thank you, Dr. Trout."

"Hey, hey, Nicky. My man." Ganapur closed his iPad and sat next to Nick on the gurney, as if they shared this phantasmal nightmare equally. "It does no one any credit to speak ill of the idolized departed. Dr. Trout was using his most excellent and expert judgment and skills. There are many reasons beyond his control why the fusion has not held."

"Reasons like he was deciding who he wanted to screw more: Betsy Nguyen, the TV camera, or me?"

"Of course not. Anybody would choose Betsy Nguyen, hands down," he laughed but Nick didn't, so Ganapur exchanged his comedy stylings for empathy. "Nick, I understand how you must feel. But there could be many reasons the operation did not have a positive outcome. Perhaps it was what we call a 'hardware fracture.' Or inadequate bone material placed into the fusion area. Or perhaps excessive motion on your part caused the pedicle screws to fatigue."

"Wait. You're saying this is my fault?"

"Nick. Please disabuse yourself of such pejorative concepts as 'fault.' There is no 'fault' in medicine, just as there is no crying in cricket. It is what it is—an unsuccessful outcome. Please understand, in extremely rare cases even an artist such as Dr. Trout does not achieve perfection. But I do have excellent news for you."

"You're the guy who can fix it."

"Me? Of course not. No one can. The fusion has failed. You have three choices. One, see another EZ♥Care surgeon and take your chances on a second fusion; the risks are a weakening of the adjacent segments which can lead to further fusions and or spinal cord injury. Of course, spinal cord injuries can cause neurological damage, sexual dysfunction, paralysis, and death. Two, do nothing. Learn to live with the pain; between structured conservative therapies and medication, that is a possibility. Or, give me twenty minutes and I can completely eliminate *all* your pain. I guarantee it."

* * *

Julie had called 911 and help was on the way. But she couldn't wait as one way or the other, she had to get to Nick. The alarm from the stuck elevator continued to shriek as the trapped parking cohort huddled in the rain far away from the staircase and the deceased homeless guy. Foam dribbled down his stubbled chin, his bladder and bowels had voided, and his loyal pit growled at Julie as she took a cautious step toward him.

The group watched with apprehension and then shock as Julie took a canister of pepper spray out of her purse and advanced toward the dog, whispering to him in a soothing voice, "I'm sorry, boy. But I really need to get down those stairs. Forgive me."

The pit began his leap as Julie gave him a blast of OC in his snout. The dog yelped and staggered back. Julie bounded over the dead man and ran down the stairs, her boots clanking on the metal slip-proof stairs.

* * *

Nick, wearing a light-blue surgical gown topped by a polypropylene cap, was positioned on his stomach on a table in Ganapur's freezing operating room. An IV line flooded his bloodstream with mellow juice and his brain with déjà vu as Marty Ganapur talked him through the procedure in his soothing Urdu-accented English.

"With the implantation of the Spinal Cord Stimulator, I am going to make you a functioning young man once again. One hundred percent pain free. And you can take that to the bank."

As Ganapur spoke, a surgical assistant opened and inspected the SCS that would soon take up residence in his spine.

Nick whispered, "Swear on your mother's grave?"

Ganapur, who was sneaking a peek at what appeared to be the device instruction manual, lifted his head sharply. "What did you say?"

"Said you wear cool aftershave," Nick mumbled into his oxygen cup.

Ganapur pursed his lips. Okay, he'd buy that; after all, he *had* heavily sedated Nick, having learned his lesson with this troublesome young man when Doctor Trout performed his reality show spinal fusion. That was the first time in his career that Marty Ganapur not only had a patient wake up, but sit up and scream, right in the middle of a procedure! Thanks be to God, everyone had been cool and no one squealed to the Patient Advocacy Department. But, no more. No more would he leave anything to chance in an O.R. From now on, when Marty Ganapur put a patient out, they were going to stay out!

And this time, no hootenanny allowed.

"Nick, I want you to count down from ten. Starting now."

"Ten … " Before Nick could get to *nine* he was comatose.

"Okay, let's get the IPG in," said Ganapur to the O.R. nurse, who was old friend Connie Smith, also from Nick's original spinal fusion team. It was like the band had gotten back together again. Except for Trout and Demidova, of course; but John and Yoko could go suck it because this time Marty Ganapur was the front man.

"Excuse me, Doctor Ganapur? Aren't you going to place temporary electrodes in the epidural space to see how the patient does for the week? You know, leave the IPG taped to the side of his butt? I don't need to tell you, Doctor G, but it's S.O.P. before we insert the Spinal Cord Stimulator permanently."

Ganapur gazed at her like that was the most ridiculous thing he'd ever heard. "Look, Connie, I've got a long-ass flight to that conference in Karachi tomorrow night. You know and I know we might as well just cut to the chase with this chucklehead. The boy is a dead-ender."

He held out his hand. "Sharp metal thing, please."

* * *

The elevator alarm was still clanging when Julie reached the ground floor exit to the parking structure. She stepped aside as a team of paramedics, followed by two Animal Control officers carrying a cage, rushed past her. At the exit, she paused to pull up her hood before dashing outside across the circular drive to the hospital entrance, when both her cellphones rang at once. She took them out of her coat, sent the call on her personal cell to voicemail and answered the "burner."

"Raven! Thank God!"

But it wasn't Raven on the other end. Julie listened and said, "Excuse me, Sergeant, I thought you were a colleague. Yes, this is the Cleveland Mercy Morgue. And yes, this is Doctor Chatterjee speaking."

A pair of boys shrieking ghost noises so they could hear their voices reverberate throughout the parking structure, ran past Julie and out the door, where they continued to holler as they jumped and splashed in every puddle. On their tail were angry parents, who ignored Julie and yelled at their kids to keep it down and quit getting their shoes wet if they knew what was good for them. The parents followed their spawn out the door as Julie cupped the phone and explained, "I'm Doctor *Melissa* Chatterjee, Sergeant. Dr. *Ganesh* Chatterjee is my husband." Julie did a fake laugh at whatever the cop on the other end said. "You've got that right; Ganesh always says the family that fillets together stays together." She listened some more. "Oh *that?* No, none of my corpses have come back to life. Um, what you heard is an elementary school field trip." Julie listened and replied: "I thoroughly agree. It's altogether inappropriate to bring children into a working morgue; I can't tell you how many times I've brought this up to the school district and the hospital. But I suppose you're calling about our missing ambulance?"

After hearing him out, Julie responded, "Thank God. We've been making calls everywhere. Yes, those three are most definitely Cleveland Mercy employees—for now at least." Julie laughed an *I'm-only-kidding-but-maybe-I'm-not* laugh as she resumed: "They were transporting a decedent to a mortuary in Middlefield or Mesopotamia, I forget which exactly … Yes, all the way to Warren, that's right. They were supposed to return late last night, however my graveyard shift assistant received a text saying they'd had some mechanical problems, but certainly they should have been back by now …"

Julie, growing nervous, listened to a brief summary of the arrest and broke in: "On a bridge? Really?" She sighed theatrically, "My guess is they were smoking marijuana and tossed it over the side. But no, no charges; you can cut them loose because, frankly, we need that ambulance back. I assure you, Sergeant, we will take care of this matter internally. Thank you so much and our sincere apologies for your trouble."

Julie clicked off, pulled the other cell out of her pocket and hit Voicemail. What she heard on the other end was a puzzled voice saying: "*Hello? Hello? Can you hear me? Oh, this is voicemail? Right. Anyhoo, this is Jen Kovačic from Cleveland Mercy? Nick Glass left this number as his emergency contact.*" Julie felt a sharp pang in her stomach as Jen continued: "*Just want to let you know Nick came through the procedure like a champ and is doing great! He's all ready to be fetched!*"

WTF? *What* procedure?

"*He's at Out-Patient Post-Op on the tenth floor. Bye!*"

Julie's face journeyed from anger to dismay to guilt in the time it took to slice an incision or enter a billing code. She put her phones away and walked out into the rain to the hospital to retrieve The Champ.

* * *

Late night, the street outside the apartment was dead—not a sound, save for rain lashing the windows. Nick, encircled in a fortress of mismatched pillows, lay in bed as Julie, back in her Cavs sweatshirt, gently rubbed a cream onto the newest branch of the tree of scars on his back.

"You know, I'm wondering if I was cut out to be a doctor in the first place. Maybe it was just a starry-eyed little girl's dreams. What else was my Mom going to tell a four-year-old? That I'd better learn how to make a good Horchata Almond Milk Frappuccino?"

"Chill with that, Jules. I'm the one who owns self-pity in this relationship and I don't feel like sharing."

"Selfish."

"That's me. And why did we have to spend eighty bucks for this special cream for the new scar? I've got tons of the stuff."

"Because this cream contains CBD."

"Weed?"

"Sorry to disappoint but CBD is a cannabinoid within the marijuana plant that produces zero psychoactive effects. THC is the ingredient that gets you high. This stuff promotes healing on an anatomical level by targeting the body's endocannabinoid system. It's good for pain control, the immune system, and sleep regulation."

"Sounds like doctor gibberish to me."

"I think you've had enough doctor gibberish. Besides, if I was a real doctor, I would've stayed on the roof and did CPR on the homeless guy till help came. Instead, I pepper-sprayed his dog and ran down to join you and Ganapur. Which, of course, I was too late for."

"Which wasn't your fault. None of it was. In fact, what's totally impressive is your restraint in not mentioning once that you think I let Ganapur scam me ."

"No, no; that's on me; I told you it was just going to be a consult."

"But you didn't tell me to allow Ganapur to hotwire my back. Maybe he did scam me. But I reacted in the moment to what he was proposing. What with him leveling with me about Trout's fusion being a failure, he earned some credibility; the Spinal Cord Stimulator fix sounded plausible and since he's leaving the country tomorrow night and it was get it done right now or wait two weeks in more pain, I went for it. Whatever, the thing isn't activated yet. That's at ten in the morning with the company reps who will program it. He said I would feel 'substantial and immediate relief' and if it doesn't work, he'll take it out when he gets back. 'No harm, no foul.'"

"Let's hope."

"Hey, at least you sprung Raven, Jacinta, and Tick from the Mayberry RFD jail. And yes, I've been watching too much METV lately."

"We both have." Julie put away the cream and helped Nick into a t-shirt. She walked into the bathroom and washed the gunk off her hands. "I think Ganapur's big hurry to put the SCS in your back was motivated by bucks. He didn't want anyone else doing it while he was away." She returned to the bedroom to find Nick attempting to re-arrange the pillows.

"Stop. Let me do that." Nick acquiesced as Julie retrieved her thought: "Not only his cut, but also a nice chunk of change for EZ♥Care's device plus Cleveland Mercy's bite. You've been a gold-chip asset to all of them."

"My dream come true."

"Ha."

"You know where I screwed it all up, Jules?"

"Not getting out of Muscat's way?"

"No. Way before that. It was the blinders I had about playing pro ball in the first place."

Julie crawled into bed, wrapping her arms around him. "What blinders? You were really good."

"But I never considered alternatives because it never occurred to me I might not be good enough. High school and Kent State were nothing but pro scouts in my living room, the prospect websites touting how I was a five or at least a four-star can't-miss; so it had to be true, right? Until I get to Rookie League and the guys I played against were the best players on *their* high school or college teams. By the time it became obvious my ceiling was some other dude's floor, it was like a lifeline when Muscat offered me the job after The Tribe cut me. Shuffling papers, playing softball, being the Local Hero face of EZ♥Care sounded like a way better option than being assistant manager at Seti's Polish Boys. Until I realized what an absolute scum Muscat is."

"Well, at least he subsidized your degree in Health Admin. Not to mention your lifetime EZ♥Care Prime."

"Which was something I thought I'd never ever need. I mean, all the years I played, not a sore arm, a strained hammy, nothing. I didn't know what pain was. And that's why, when Muscat wrecked my back and EZ♥Care sent me to Trout, I was like a canvas that not only hadn't been painted on, but hadn't even been stretched. What was I going to do, not listen to him? He was the big-leaguer in that relationship."

Julie kissed the back of his neck and said, "You're right. You do own the self-pity in this relationship. I feel lots better now. Thanks for that."

She kissed him again. Nick struggled to turn his body to meet hers. The streetlight, diffused in the rainy mist, illuminated their faces in a panoply of shadows.

"Anytime," he said, and returned the kiss.

CHAPTER 30

Long Snake Moan

The new day broke bright and clear. The rain had moved out and a high sun in. It shone down on a moisture-beaded, black-and-gold Cuyahoga County Sheriff's cruiser parked on top of the viaduct bridge, the one from which Raven, Jacinta, and Tick had heaved Iakopo's body into this tributary of the Cuyahoga River, forty feet below. Windows were rolled down on the cop shop as the radio blasted Late-Period Elvis's "You'll Never Walk Alone." Deputy Harley Pollard was nowhere to be seen. But you sure could hear him.

Harley, partly obscured by rising mist, was under the bridge in the hard-running creek, wearing a pair of hip waders. He slogged through the marsh along the shoreline as he piped along with The King's creaky baritone. He thought he sounded close enough to Elvis (maybe better, if you want to be blasphemous about it) to wonder what it would've been like for him if he were born sixty or eighty years ago. In the America of his grandma's youth, it was received wisdom that if you had the talent and tenacity you could be anything you dared to dream. Well, Harley's twin passions were music and fighting crime—just like Elvis, who had met with President Nixon and asked to become an undercover FBI agent, only to pay for it with his life. At least that's what Harley believed, having subscribed to the internet exposé which definitively proved that the Black Panthers, in cahoots with The Weathermen, upon discovering The King was a secret Feeb, had slipped him a lethal cocktail of morphine, Demerol, and Quaaludes that fateful night at Graceland in 1977, then bought off his doctor to cover up the cause of death, listing it as a heart attack due to chronic constipation. Just another true fact the Deep State didn't want you to know.

Well, Harley had wanted both careers as well: a singing crime fighter. But unlike Elvis, Harley had run up against a veritable border wall in his quest to make it in the music biz—this, despite having sent scores and scores of homemade demos to record companies, publishing companies, and country stars like the Zak Brown Band, Lonestar, and heck, even Little Big Town. Harley's Hotmail inbox was peppered with automated rejection epistles and worse, ninety-nine percent of the artists never even returned his demo cassettes—despite him enclosing self-addressed stamped envelopes in the unlikely event Blake Shelton or The Kings Of Leon or Cassadee Pope, who can't even spell her name proper, didn't think his stuff was *right* for them.

That left crime fighting as Harley's remaining career path. And now, fresh out of the Academy, he wasn't getting much of an opportunity to do that either, as his senile Sergeant had assigned him to cruise the lonely back roads of Cuyahoga County on the graveyard shift five futile nights a week.

Until his solid police work resulted in the arrest of those three scrub-wearing punks on suspicion of throwing some kind of contraband off the bridge. Only to have it all come to dogshit in the morning while he was catching up on his *zzz*s with his earplugs on—because his grandma was binge-watching the complete seventh season of *The Gilmore Girls* with the volume turned up to a hundred earsplitting dBs, because she was as deaf as a blue-eyed cat—and he missed the phone call from his dumbass Sarge, who'd cut the trio loose just because the hospital morgue vouchsafed for them. Heck! Releasing them without even *verifying* just what they were doing on that bridge at three in the darn morning! Well, Harley *knew* the suspects were doing *something* illicit. You could tell they were some kind of integrated gang, the kind you see on TV cop shows. So, like life imitating art—in particular his own years-long quest to determine what Billie Joe McAllister and Miss Bobbie Gentry were tossing off the Tallahatchie Bridge—here he was, under the decrepit viaduct in this stinky marsh, which smelled like a passel of bear dumps, investigating a potential real crime. All Harley needed was to find what those smartasses had tossed off the bridge in that flash of a second before he shined his cruiser's light on their guilty-as-sin faces. Still, it sure would've helped if he had some idea of what the heck he was looking for. Stolen guns? Hillbilly heroin? A fetus? Or …

That's when Harley Pollard saw the snake.

It was a rare Canebrake rattler, wrapped around a floating log, and it had something bluish in its mouth. Harley knew the Canebrake was on the ICUN Red List of Threatened Species and therefore, as Federal law stipulated, it was *"illegal to harass, kill, collect, or possess"* the suckers. But if this wasn't an extraordinary exception, what was? That blue thing between its fangs could be the evidence he was looking for. Therefore, Harley had no problem putting three bullets in the serpent's prefrontal scales and blowing the slimy sonofabitch in half.

Harley advanced toward the dead-as-dirt snake, taking care to avoid having the Canebrake wreak posthumous venomous revenge. He gingerly extricated the blue thing out of the serpent's maw and held it up to the radiant sunlight like an offering to Jesus.

It wasn't any kind of creature Harley could recognize. He examined it every which way from Sunday and it wasn't until he pulled back a little piece of something that might've been some kind of skin, did he come to the realization that he was staring into the peehole of an uncircumcised and limp pecker.

With the sounds of PJ Harvey's "Long Snake Moan" emanating from his radio in the cruiser on the bridge, Harley reached into his pocket for the Ziploc bag he purchased at the Aldi in North Randall (because you never know) and dropped the snakebit tallywacker inside, sealed it, and waded through the marsh back to shore.

Heck, this was way better than those Rascal Flatts douches ignoring another of one his demos.

CHAPTER 31

Remember The Ghaznavids

Marty Ganapur had designed his office space in the **EZ♥CARE LIMITED EDITION PENTHOUSE SUITES @ CLEVELAND MERCY** as a paean to 1980s Americana meets 980s Ghaznavid Dynasty, Pakistan. Framed Cruise and Schwarzenegger movie art shared wall space with a pictorial hanging Persian carpet, which recounted the epic ass-kicking of the Samanids by the Ghaznavids—a conflict celebrated by poets as long forgotten as the Ghaznavid Dynasty itself. The Ghaznavids were a powerhouse that once dominated all of Persia, Afghanistan, and Pakistan. An empire that in order to fund its foreign-based armies, collected taxes from traders, artisans, peasants, and even the scribal class. All this, according to the explanatory plaque mounted to the side of the pictorial rug. Julie thought maybe those scribes would have been better off if they'd invested in poppy futures, as she turned her gaze away from the rug and back onto Marty Ganapur, who stood behind his chrome and glass desk waiting for an answer.

Which he got.

"No," said Julie.

Ganapur, dressed for travel in a pair of stretch chinos to accommodate an emerging gut, a loose polo shirt, and a look of fake regret, zipped an overnight bag closed and stuffed bound papers into an obscenely expensive Hermes Carbon Fibre briefcase equipped with eighteen-karat gold-plated locks.

"No?" he repeated.

"No," added Nick, who had gravitated from the framed *Risky Business* movie one-sheet on the opposite wall.

"Look, could I help it that the EZ♥Stim reps failed to show this morning to program your spinal stimulator? Clearly, there was a communications mix-up. I would assume, because of the spontaneous nature of Nick's procedure yesterday, his name was not on the list sent to EZ♥Stim."

"Translation: you forgot to let them know," said Julie. "So no, you don't get to walk away."

"As you can see, I am flying away. A colleague and I are being picked up by Towncar at 7 p.m. to be taken to a private jet. However, I have emailed EZ♥Stim, and their reps will contact you for the next available appointment."

Julie took a menacing step toward him. "One, it's 11 a.m. so you're not going anywhere for eight hours, and two, do you really expect Nick to walk around with that electric device in his back, which is only there because you manipulated a suffering patient, who's appointment was for a consult, into agreeing to an ad hoc procedure—a procedure you 'guaranteed' would eliminate his pain—while you go gallivanting around the world? I don't think so. Program it yourself, Dr. Ganapur. Now, please."

"Look, whoever you are—"

"I'm Nick's Patient Advocate and if you don't program the stimulator our next stop is the Office of Fair Practices. I hear you are somewhat familiar with them." Julie hoped to hell Ganapur wouldn't recognize her. Sure, they didn't know each other but he could be recalling her face from the checkout line in the hospital cafeteria, or her presence at the weekly Morbidity & Mortality conference (where Marty Ganapur was often the Inquisitee), but still there was no way he should recognize her now. Not just because of Julie's new harsh look but also because of the way she projected—angry and hostile. The fresh-faced, pony-tailed, intern formerly known as Doctor Julie Toffoli had long since left the building.

Ganapur extended his palms in piqued surrender. "Okay, okay. I won't leave you in the lurch, Nick. But we must go through the programming quickly as I have much to do before I leave." He moved from behind his desk, past his Globetrotter James Bond Special Edition Luggage Set on the floor, all packed and ready for international intrigue, and faced Nick. "Please take off your shirt."

Nick did so, revealing a battered torso that looked like ten miles of East Terrace Road, considered the worst street in Cleveland, if not the entire USA. But nothing out of the ordinary for Marwan Ganapur who'd driven over far worse back home. "You have the remote control?" he asked Nick.

Nick handed him the small remote which featured the EZ♥Stim logo.

"Excellent. With this, you can regulate the amount of amplitude, width, and frequency of the electrical pulses. The trick is calibrating it to your own personal sweet spot."

"And it really isn't going to hurt?" asked Nick, whose evolved default was to expect the worst. Julie picked up on his vibe and moved to a protective spot close by.

"Of course not. Once we ascertain the correct settings, the most you'll feel is a mild pulsing sensation, not unlike the Magic Fingers at the Motel 6 on Engle Road at the end of a long day."

Julie recoiled as this sleaze actually *winked* at Nick. Right in front of her. Ganapur made a couple of quick adjustments on the remote and handed it back to Nick. "Okay, I have it on very low. In fact, it's probably too low. Just press the Power button."

Nick looked at the remote control in his hand and froze.

"Come on, Nick. Magic Fingers, remember?"

Nick sighed and switched on the power button, only to instantaneously scream and tumble to the floor where he uncontrollably writhed, his body jerking spasmodically. "Stop! Make it stop!"

Ganapur bent to Nick, pried the remote out of his hand and turned it off. Nick slumped on his stomach, moaned in agony. A widening liquid stain appeared on the carpet where he lay.

"What did you do, Nick?" said Ganapur, pissed at the piss all over his plush Persian Merino rug with the famous Weeping Willow design.

"I turned it on, like you said."

"Electrocution is impossible." Ganapur fiddled with the settings as if he were disarming a ticking bomb. The red wire, or the green one?

"Ah, I see the problem. It is a matter of adjusting the frequency *and* the amplitude. They must work as one, in harmony. We can't have the frequency one way and the amplitude another. Did you not read the literature I sent home with you yesterday?"

"There was no literature," said Julie. "I drove him home. He had nothing. Just the cattle prod you implanted in his back."

"Of course," Ganapur realized. "The EZ♥Stim Reps have the literature."

Julie helped Nick back to his feet. Ganapur adjusted the remote and looked Nick in the eye, graciously not acknowledging the stain on his expensive carpet—although, beyond a doubt, Nick would see a proportionate reflection of Ganapur's displeasure reflected in his co-pay.

"With the adjustments I've made, all future pain signals will be blocked," reassured Ganapur as he held out the remote to Nick. "Consider the onramp to the I-90 of pain and suffering closed."

He thrust the remote in Nick's twitching palm. "Please note the new settings and power it on."

Nick, still tremulous despite his brain telling him to tough it out, cradled the remote. His index finger quivered over the power switch like a tuning fork.

"I do not have all day, Nick."

Okay. Okay. Nick told himself he'd faced worse before. Much worse. Like a zillion surgeries and "procedures," which he knew were euphemisms for volitional torture. Still, just follow the doctor's instructions. It'll be okay. It'll work. *It had to.* Nick knew he needed to believe. To trust these guys. He blew out a breath and flicked the switch.

The result was the classic definition of crazy. Again, electric currents surged through him, causing him to crumple to the floor, screaming and squirming. His shrieks sent the pigeons on Ganapur's window ledge flapping skyward as Julie intervened.

She grabbed the remote out of Nick's hand and hit the Off Button. It was like turning off a light switch; Nick at once stopped spasming. Nevertheless, he lay sprawled on the stained Weeping Willow rug whimpering in pain.

Ganapur stared at Nick in disbelief. What had he done wrong? What had he *ever* done wrong? "Nick, please enlighten me. What exactly did you feel?"

"An electric shock going straight through my dick and up my back into my brain."

Ganapur tried to bring the intensity in the room down a few notches. Humor always worked. Humor like: "You would not be the first man in history to have his brain commanded by his *phunno.*"

"That's not funny," said Julie.

"I am sorry, *Miss*, but we have an almost one hundred percent success rate with the implanted Spinal Stimulator. However, even in the rare case when they do not function as well as hoped, they still do not cause electric shocks. This is unheard of. Impossible.[*] I will have the company reps expedite the appointment and give you all the time you need for instruction in the proper use of the unit. Or …" Ganapur reluctantly allowed, "… perhaps the remote is a lemon and the reps can program another one. At any rate, go home and wait for the technicians to call. I really have to finish preparing my papers and pack my briefcase."

"No! What you will do is put Nick into an O.R. right now and take that Satanic piece of steel out of his back."

"Impossible. I told you—"

"Do it," said Nick. "It took twenty minutes to put in, it should take twenty to take out."

"Look, I simply cannot remove the device today. I am scheduled to fly with my colleague Dr. Klepstein tonight to attend a week-long conference on Pediatric Pain Management at the Aga Khan University in Karachi. It is sponsored by EZ♥Care and it is most important for their expansion into South Asia."

Julie's outrage vanished. At once she was stone-faced, expressionless. Ganapur made the mistake of not reading that, as he blithely continued: "So, Nick, if you cannot tolerate the device even after tweaking by the reps tomorrow, I will order a procedure to be put on the calendar ASAP and one of my colleagues will remove the Spinal Stimulator while I am away."

---

[*] Not so impossible. A year long Associated Press investigation flagged more than 80,000 adverse reactions since 2008 to these spinal stimulators, including spontaneous electric shocks, life-threatening infections, severe battery burns, and at least 500 deaths. More than half of the patients interviewed by the AP said they felt "pressured" by their doctors to have the procedure, with some of the doctors promising "100 percent pain relief." The procedure—not including hospital costs—can run up to $50,000 dollars.

"Wait," said Julie. "Did you say Klepstein?"

"Yes."

"Kasper Klepstein? Pediatrics?"

"Yes. As well as my most esteemed colleague, Dr. Klepstein is a dear, dear, friend." Ganapur regarded Julie quizzically. "Do you somehow know Dr. Klepstein?"

Dear, dear, friend was the clincher, as Julie recalled Klepstein and the night of the Code Blue—the most devastating moments of her life and the final moments for young Charlie.

"Nope," replied Julie. "Never heard of him." And with a diversion Magic Castle magicians would die for, Julie wound up holding a syringe to Ganapur's carotid artery.

Ganapur's eyes pinwheeled like Scrooge McDuck on acid. "No, not the carotid! You will shut down one side of my brain!"

"Correct. Unless you take the Stimulator out right now."

Ganapur stared at the syringe and back to Julie and that's when it hit him. "You are the intern with HIV."

Julie almost stuck the syringe in him right then and there. "How do you know this? That is confidential information." Then she realized how: "Klepstein told you. Your dear, dear, friend. Get Nick into an O.R. now!"

Ganapur, terrified, nodded in acquiescence. "Okay. But first I need Nick's insurance approved. I cannot conjure an O.R. without going through channels." He gestured at his desk phone. "May I?"

Julie released him but stayed close, needle poised, as Ganapur picked up his phone and dialed. Nick moved next to her.

"What else? What else can these quacks do to me?" he said, as Ganapur muttered numeric choices and attempted to scale the electronic escarpments of EZ♥Care Customer Service. "My entire body is either some kind of deranged science project or a crime scene. What else?"

"Nothing else. I won't let them touch you again." Julie took his hand. "Except to get Old Sparky out of your back."

Ganapur hung up, smiling, making no pretense at concealing the sweet *schadenfreude* the phone call had just provided. "I am sorry to inform, but Nick's insurance has been denied. His benefits are maxed out. Too many procedures."

"That's insane! You people ordered all of them! Besides, Nick has EZ♥Care Prime. His insurance doesn't max out until one million dollars."

"Then I'm sure it will be news to both of you that Nick, in fact, owes Cleveland Mercy, plus its various physicians and vendors, four-point-seven million dollars. Therefore, I cannot legally take the Stimulator out of his back until he is insured. Unless, of course, you have cash—say, forty large—on you. No? Didn't think so." He pointed to the door. "Bye-bye."

Nick freaked. "No! This is impossible! I *work* for EZ♥Care! Call Mr. Muscat, my boss!"

"With all due respect, Nick, acting as your health insurance advocate does not fall under my job description."

"Do no harm," said Julie. "Right, Dr. Ganapur?"

"Of course."

"Well, in my case, as you well know, I no longer have that obligation."

Julie jabbed the needle into his neck. Ganapur's eyes dimmed like dying stars. She withdrew the syringe and Ganapur crumpled to the floor like one of the fallen Ghaznavid spearchuckers in his hanging rug painting.

Julie spoke to his inert form. "Who's the big man on hippocampus now?"

"Good one, Jules," said Nick as he heroically stepped over his puddle of piss.

CHAPTER 32

Dr. Julie's Chamber Of Horrors

Blinding lights on cast-iron stands spot-lit two side-by-side gurneys in the otherwise darkened basement O.R. The gurneys each supported a surgically shrouded, anesthetized body lying on its stomach. Shrouded, except for the identical operating site on each back that gleamed bright yellow from the Chloraprep antiseptic solution. The layout had the chimeric feel of two twin beds in those chaste fifties romcoms where Doris and Rock weren't allowed to be seen in the same bed together—as if that could ever have been a thing. From the basement boom box the adagio movement of a haunting Shubert piano trio accompanied Julie, decked out in full surgical regalia, assisted by Raven, likewise garbed, as they worked back and forth between the two patients. Julie threaded the leads via catheter into the epidural space in the back of one of the patients. Since there was no scar, that had to be Ganapur.

As Raven sponged the site she said, "I bet I could do this for real. I mean the nurse part."

"I bet you could too. Generator."

Raven had it ready and placed it in Julie's palm.

"You sterilized it, right?"

"Of course. I put it in the microwave under the Popcorn Setting."

She continued to keep the operating area clean as Julie looked up at a stolen fluoroscopy screen and maneuvered the spine stimulator to connect it to the leads in the epidural space. "Alright. One Spine Stimulator out of Nick, one into Marty Ganapur. Let's close this lowlife up."

"You are so awesome at this."

"Yeah, well, thanks. I know I should've just thrown the damn thing away, but even if it's just for a second, Ganapur needs to feel a fraction of what he did to Nick. Still …"

"Look, Ganapur put the thing in Nick to make beaucoup bucks and so his Pakistan trip wouldn't be inconvenienced, and you did it because he tortured the hell out of Nick and didn't even care. It's like the Golden Rule, weaponized."

"Still," Julie repeated as she put the remote control for the stimulator into Raven's front pocket, "when you wheel Ganapur back into his office, put the remote in the briefcase on his desk along with the note I wrote, informing him of what's in his back. He'll need it when he eventually wakes up in Pakistan."

"Really? You mean—"

"Yeah. Along with the internal anesthesia, Jacinta also injected eighty milligrams of extended release Oxy and fifteen milligrams of Xanax. Ganapur will sleep through his Towncar ride to the airport and probably all the way to Pakistan. Once there, Klepstein can take the stimulator out of him. Although personally, I'd rather put my trust in Edward Scissorhands."

"Wow. So in the meantime, Klepstein will think Ganapur's blotto?"

"That's the idea. Until he reads my note and realizes he'll have to be a real doctor. Anyway, I'm sure when all is said and done, the boys will have a good laugh. Still … "

"Hey, Julie, you didn't do anything wrong here. We didn't do anything wrong."

Julie didn't reply and Raven, possessing the perception and empathy that made patients trust her, said, "Something else going on, right?"

"I need to ask you something."

"Anything."

"That old cop with the cane? The one who arrested Demidova, who's been around for months asking all these questions?"

"I'm not a huge fan of cops. Old or young. What about him?"

"Back around Christmas time, Sikorski cornered me in the cafeteria, asking about Trout. I played dumb and he bought it. Except he asked me for a favor."

"Yeah well, never do cops a favor. Because it's never a two-way street."

"I didn't. I just want to tell you he showed me this couple-of-years-old photo of a high school girl who kind of looked like you. Except not how you look now."

"So what? I don't know him and I haven't done anything against the law." She looked at Ganapur's inert frame and her basement hideaway in general. "I mean, majorly against the law."

"He said finding the girl had nothing to do with his job, that it was personal."

Raven processed this, shook her head dismissively. "Sorry. I've never seen him before, not until he started coming around the hospital."

"Okay. It's just that when Nick wakes up, we need to get out of Cleveland quick. I thought I'd mention it."

"Thanks. But I don't know this cop. I do know my life is better now than it used to be. I also know I can't live in this basement forever, and Jacinta and Tick can't either, but right now it's what I need. Same with them. They come from some pretty messed-up life situations. The three of us have a safe thing going and I don't want anything to screw it up."

"Okay. Just stay careful. I'm really going to miss you guys."

"Ditto. Promise you'll inbox me when you can."

Julie had a flash of the hallucinatory rat saying those exact words but thought it best to keep that to herself. "Of course," she said.

Raven looked to the snoring Ganapur. "I better get this loser dressed and upstairs before his Towncar comes." She grinned with sudden inspiration and took a phone out of her coat, "Except first, I'm going to get a pic of his crooked little knob and have Tick upload it onto the Cleveland Mercy website. Give the doc a new 'head' shot. He'll be famous."

"Um, you don't want I.T. tracing it back to you guys."

"No prob. Tick could fake a Pakistan ISP. He's already changed about a million doctor bios. And the FAQs. They're hilarious."

"Just be careful, okay."

"Always." Raven paused, then gave Julie a long, close hug. "You and Nick, too," she said as she let go, grabbed the gurney and wheeled it out of the basement O.R. before Julie could see that she was crying.

The Schubert trio continued as Julie leaned over Nick's gurney and gazed at him. He was still asleep, and for one of the few times in the last year and a half his face seemed at peace; she could imagine him as the old Nick, the boy who she grew up loving and who loved her back with all his heart. Dreams derailed, mind and body degraded, but he was still there, and so was she. Who could ask for anything more?

She leaned over and kissed him. "I love you, Nick. None of these bastards will ever hurt you again. I promise."

The last Schubert chord resonated like a bittersweet ending to a black-and-white movie. The kind you walk out of brushing back a tear.

CHAPTER 33

Call Me Marwan

Slivers of moonlight pierced the glassy waters of the Arabian Sea, reflecting the shadow of a large nocturnal bird whose song was a tuneless mechanical whine. The bird was a Gulfstream G550 corporate jet emblazoned with an EZ♥Fly logo on its fuselage, and it was making its final descent into Jinnah International Airport in Karachi, Pakistan.

The jet brushed the tarmac on the blue-lit runway at Jinnah like a feather floating from the heavens. The perfect landing was wasted on the only two passengers in the luxuriously appointed cabin. Wasted, because the two Cleveland Mercy docs—after sixteen hours and twenty-one minutes of flight time, with one brief and unnoticed stop in Dubai for refueling—were equally wasted. Marty Ganapur, seat-belted to his sofa bed by a conscientious stewardess, was unconscious, honking like a dyspeptic goose. Opposite him, stretched out on a plush aniline leather recliner, also buckled up, his batwings matted with alcoholic sweat, his butt chin coated with vomit that had dripped onto his unbuttoned shirt and chest, was a dead drunk and asleep Dr. Kasper Klepstein. The battle of their snores sounded like a wildly successful sleep lab.

Once the reverse thrusters had slowed the plane, the stewardess emerged from her tiny service compartment and scooped the two dozen miniature bottles of Glenfarclas Single Malt strewn around Klepstein into a garbage bag. As the Gulfstream crept towards the terminal she slipped on her hijab and, not so gently, shook the docs awake and said, "Welcome to Karachi, gentlemen." Klepstein took one look at her and shrieked like a patient abruptly awakened from anesthesia. Once he realized where he was and what was on his chin, he accepted the wet towel from the stewardess without a word. He stared at her hijab as if she was the one sporting the puke-stained garment.

The EZ♥Fly Gulfstream advanced in a stately crawl along runway 25R/07L towards the Jinnah East Satellite Terminal, normally the entry point for international flights. But not at 3 a.m. Instead, the jet made a gradual left onto a turnoff tangent and another left onto a narrow taxiway before slowing to a stop adjacent to a nondescript one-story structure. Soft yellow light illuminated an open-air guardhouse in front of the building. A uniformed Immigration Officer sat within, smoking and reading a dog-eared copy of *A Case Of Exploding Mangoes* by Mohammed Hanif. Nearby, four armed soldiers stood desultory guard. A sign identified the building as "VIP Terminal J," the private secure entry to Pakistan for the rich and discreet.

The door at the rear of the cockpit was pushed open and the airstairs unfolded by the co-pilot. Deplaning first was the soused and cranky Klepstein. He had put on his necktie and suit jacket in an attempt to hide the chunks encrusted on his shirt, but this sartorial faux pas would prove to be the least of his Third World gaffes.

Once Klepstein had carefully traversed the six airstairs to the tarmac, he turned and looked back to see Marty Ganapur, risen from the dead and clutching his distinctive Hermes briefcase, poised at the top. Marty woozily held onto the side rail with his other hand. The co-pilot and stewardess moved to steady him but he shook them off.

"S'all right. I'm good." Marty gazed in confusion at his colleague below. "Damn. Kasper. What the hell? Did I really sleep for sixteen—"

Before he could complete the question, Marty lost his footing and face-planted onto the dusty tarmac. He rose with a bloody lip and a sheepish grin; he didn't feel a thing. Neither did the Hermes, which was indestructible and intact.

"Jesus H. Christ, Marty," said Klepstein, as he picked up his colleague and briefcase. "Wake the fuck up." Clutching his arm, Klepstein led Marty toward the guardhouse that featured a small sign in English (the official language of Pakistan) reading: "VIP Customs & Immigration" and underneath that, Klepstein guessed, some foreign chicken scrawl probably saying the same thing.

As the two staggered across the runway, like Marge and Gower Champion doing their famous dance "I Might Fall Back On You" from *Show Boat* (that is, if Marge and Gower were on Quaaludes), Marty couldn't stop yawning. He shook his head, trying to clear the vestiges of the veritable pharmacy injected into his system by Jacinta. Behind them, a couple of soldiers in camo retrieved their suitcases from the plane, shared a laugh with the stewardess, and brought the luggage into the Customs building.

"What the hell's wrong with me?" asked Marty.

"You want a clinical diagnosis? You're loaded! And you've been loaded since fuckin' yesterday!"

"No shit?"

"Hell, Marty, when I went by your office to fetch you, you were out cold on your ass; you sounded like my wife spitting my jizz into her CPAP mask. Don't you remember me waking you up? Had to half carry you to the Towncar."

"Kinda. I guess. But this is really odd. I mean, I didn't even *take* anything. The only thing I'm feeling besides being incredibly tired is some crazy back pain from God knows where, but—"

Klepstein, walking and talking while drunk, interrupted, "I, Kasper K. Klepstein, God of all things Aesculapian,* *do* know from where. It's from you lying in the same damn position for almost an entire day. My fuckin' back would hurt too."

He gestured to the Immigration guard shack and the officious, splendidly mustachioed official behind it. Clearly, not a guy to be trifled with, but Kasper Klepstein wasn't feeling too clear at the moment. He thought he was whispering as he breathed the stench of alcohol and barf into Marty's ear and said, for all to hear: "How long is this going to take? I want to get to the goddamn hotel and get a shower; tell Osama over there to hurry it up."

Marty blanched. "Kasper. Please don't say that word."

"What word?"

Marty sotto-voiced the word as he shot an anxious glance at the Immigration Officer.

"What, Marty? Shower? Why can't I say shower?"

"*Osama,*" hissed Ganapur.

"Oh, I get it," laughed Klepstein. "These turbanators are still sensitive about Abbottabad, right? When good ol' Seal Team Six did their little *incursion?*" He addressed the Immigration Officer. "Am I right, homie?" Klepstein began to doctor/rap, replete with drunken dance moves:

I got the clearance/To run the interference/
Into your satellite/Shinin' a battle light!

---

* Aesculapius was the Greco-Roman God of Medicine who might have been more famous had he bothered to write his own Oath.

He gracelessly pirouetted into Marty, almost falling on his ass, then gathered himself and began to pace the tarmac like Pacino on the sidewalk outside the bank in *Dog Day Afternoon*, yelling, "*Abbottabad! Abbottabad! Abbottabad!*"

This thespic homage got the attention of the soldiers standing at their posts by the building. A couple of fingers slid toward selector switches on their weapons. Marty, sobering, grabbed hold of his blitzed colleague.

"Kasper, please. Calm down."

"Alright, alright, I'll be 'sensitive,'" Klepstein air-quoted. He brought his arms down and whacked Marty flush on the (unknown to him) surgical site on his back.

Marty howled as Klepstein looked at him curiously. Why would a love tap on the back make him scream like a little bitch? "Alright, fine. 'Great Satan' will behave." Again, he accentuated the negative with more air quotes.

By now, Marty Ganapur was becoming way more concerned about this mysterious and excruciating pain in his back than Klepstein's racist xenophobia. "Kasper, there's really something wrong with my—"

"Gentlemen. Passports, please," the Immigration Officer demanded.

Marty opened his Hermes, pushed aside a paper with the warning PLEASE READ! and grabbed his passport. As soon as he handed it over, a soldier seized the case and took it to the shed.

"Hey!" Marty protested.

"It needs to go through Customs with the rest of your baggage," said the Immigration Officer. "There is a sign; perhaps you gentlemen did not see it." He proceeded to take his sweet time examining the American physicians' passports as he typed info into his computer. Klepstein whistled the *Jeopardy* theme song; Marty gingerly reached around and tried to locate the source of the pain in his back, wondering what the hell was wrong.

Inside the Customs building, a circular luggage carousel groaned into action as Klepstein's and Ganapur's bags and lastly, the Hermes briefcase, traversed past the x-ray machine. From his perch, a uniformed Customs Inspector watched as the docs' stuff went through. All routine, until *something* in Ganapur's briefcase caught his eye. Among toiletries, an emergency change of bikini briefs, and a thirty-six pack of Trojans, was the Remote Control Unit for the Spinal Stimulator implanted in Marty's back. However, without that important bit of context, the damn thing sure looked like a detonator to a bomb.

The Customs Inspector, who'd lost his second cousin Ghafoor in the 2010 terrorist attack on Jinnah International that had killed thirty-six people, fumbled for his walkie. A blast of frantic Urdu followed as the Inspector's eyes stayed riveted on the detonator that was surely going to send him to the Seventh Heaven of Naraka to prematurely meet Ghafoor who, although a true martyr, died owing him twenty-eight thousand rupees. A debt he was not ready to collect on just yet.

Outside at the guard shack, right hand poised in mid-air, the Immigration Officer with the fabulous mustache was about to stamp Marty's passport, when the crackling from his walkie on the counter, accompanied by the Customs Inspector's terrified warning, caused him to step on the brakes. The Immigration Officer's face contorted into an expression of shock. His mustache curled, like a caterpillar looking for a prefab cocoon.

"What the fuck, Marty?" said Klepstein. "What's taking Paki Magnum P.I. here so long?"

"I don't know. It's been a long time since I … Oh shit …" Marty trailed off. He had understood enough.

The Immigration Officer clicked his walkie twice and pointed them toward the Customs building and the soldiers guarding it. All of them had unslung their weapons. Klepstein's wrecked brain began to absorb their situation as something less than normal. "You sure this is the VIP Terminal, Marty?"

"Would you gentlemen wait over there with my colleagues, if you may be so kind?" asked the Immigration Officer.

"Fuck no!" said Klepstein. "You listen to me, Paki Magi P.I. We are *world-famous* physicians. And you and your shithole of a country should be on your knees five times a day facing Cleveland O-H-I-O and thanking me and Marty here for flying an entire fucking day to keynote an international medical conference, the purpose of which is to help heal your crippled Third World rug-rats, most of who are just gonna grow up and blow themselves and innocent civilians to shit anyway. So what I'm saying, asshole, is, do you want me to make a phone call to the Minister Of Health, wake the greasy sonofabitch up, and tell him the stupid pricks running this so-called VIP terminal are a bunch of power-tripping little martinets? Do you? Do you really want me to call him, Paki Magi P.I.?"

"Go to the building, Doctors," said the Immigration Officer, his 'stache now bristling.

Klepstein turned to the now terrified Marty Ganapur, "Christ, you'd a thunk these fucks would've had belly dancers and snake charmers waiting for us. I mean what's up with these elephant jockeys?"

A Heckler & Koch MPF submachine gun (proudly and locally manufactured by the Pakistan Ordnance Factories) appeared at his head, pointed by one of the "elephant jockeys."

Klepstein sobered up quick. "Right away, General."

The soldier and a comrade, his H & K also pointed at them, escorted the two American docs—although Marty was merely a Permanent Resident Alien and wondered if he should mention that to the guy in the mustache and also tell him Magnum P.I. is an esteemed personage in the US—toward the Customs building, out of which emerged a Very Senior Officer in full dress uniform, replete with a fruit salad of medals and ribbons pinned to his chest, and a suspicious look on his weathered face, which sported the biggest mustache of them all.

"Whoa! Now *this* dude is the real Paki Magnum P.I.," sputtered Klepstein, reduced by alcohol, anger, and ennui to pure id. Whatever filters his soggy brain possessed, which even when lucid were few, had been disabled.

"My back hurts, Kasper," whined Marty. "It really hurts."

None of that was of any concern to the Very Senior Officer who held out the remote-control unit for the Spinal Stimulator implanted in Marty's back.

"Dr. Ganapur," said the Very Senior Officer.

"Call me Marwan," interrupted Marty, grimacing through this inexplicable pain. How could his patients deal with this kind of misery day in and day out and not become mental? He couldn't, that's for sure.

"*Doctor* Ganapur," the Very Senior Officer resumed, "Would you be so kind as to explain this device which we discovered in your briefcase? What is its purpose?"

"How should I know? It's not mine."

As the Very Senior Officer frowned, Klepstein whispered in Marty's ear. "Typical Third World shakedown, eh?"

Again, Klepstein *thought* he was whispering, as every soldier—their collective integrity impugned, and by inference their entire culture and country—glared at him with pure hatred.

"Aw, fuck it!" said an oblivious Klepstein. "How much do these Abba-Dabba-Doos want?" He reached inside his suit pocket for his wallet.

The sounds of submachine guns switching from safe mode to burst caused Klepstein to quickly remove his hand and hold it up for all to see. "Hey. Just getting out my wallet, guys. Jeesh. American dollars. Who wants some? This'll go a long way for a down payment on a nail salon in Dearborn."

As Klepstein continued his Ugly American act, a tiny glimmer of discovery—like the earliest Edisonian twenty-watt light bulb—strained to traverse the journey from Marty Ganapur's prefrontal cortex to his diaphragm, which assiduously attempted to force enough air into his trachea to produce a human sound. A lucid thought into speech. Finally, the light bulb, after dimming and flickering, summoned the power to stay on.

"Ah," said Marty. "May I see that?" He snatched the remote from the Very Senior Officer's hand and nodded with recognition. "This, my friend, is a remote control for a Spinal Stimulator. For a pain management patient. Perhaps I mistakenly packed it, although I have no recollection of doing so. At any rate, it is harmless. I will show you. Observe, please. You will see—nothing untoward will happen."

That is, not until Marty flicked on the power switch. Which activated the Spinal Stimulator implanted in his back. His subsequent scream was a rocking ten on the Pain Scale; in fact, he sounded much like his patient Nick Glass did when he first tried out this miracle pain control device, back in Marty's office. Simultaneous to his scream, Marty danced about the tarmac like Baryshnikov in the throes of a grand mal seizure, as he internally and continuously electrocuted himself. What he couldn't do, because he was high and hurting—*and had never been a patient in need of this device*—was to have the cognition to stop the fireworks show inside his body by simply pressing the OFF button. Instead, as he fell victim to the advances of cutting-edge pain management, Marty did what any panicked animal with opposable thumbs would do: he threw the cause of the pain, the remote control unit, as far away from himself as possible.

Of course, that didn't alleviate his agony and, unlike Nick, he didn't have Julie with him as his Patient Advocate. All Marty Ganapur had was his drunk, bigoted, arrogant colleague, Kasper Klepstein, who just wanted to get a shower and go to sleep. Neither of which would prove to be necessary.

"Ooohhh!!! Ooohhh God!!! No!!! Aaahhh!!!" and similar wailed from Marty as he thrashed about on the runway.

Klepstein looked askance. "What the fuck? Marty? Why are you break dancing? Honestly, man, that's not going to impress these guys. Let's just pay 'em."

But Marty continued to shriek and flail as he stumbled into one of the startled soldiers like a human bumper car. He howled at the guy like a coyote feasting on a Maltese at the front yard koi pond. Which would've been okay, embarrassing but excusable, if he hadn't made his next mistake.

Marty reached out to steady himself. Except, what he grabbed was the business end of the soldier's submachine gun and in the process pulled it toward him.

Any objective observer would agree: Marty was attempting to wrest the weapon away from the soldier. And that's what the *Top Secret ISI Report* would later state.

Who could blame the soldier for panicking? Who could blame him for firing a burst into Marty's head and turning it into a bloody pulp? A bloody pulp whose mouth kept moving but even more remarkably, so did his feet, as the Spinal Stimulator kept him bouncing off various soldiers as the dead-on-his-feet Marty Ganapur continued his macabre dance. Klepstein panicked and turned to run back to the plane but didn't get far, as the Very Senior Officer cut him down with a single shot from his sidearm.

Klepstein, at least, appeared dead. But Marty's body, although having more holes in it than your average NBA defense, kept on shaking and baking.

"Cease fire!" ordered the Very Senior Officer, who walked over to Marty Ganapur's still-gyrating form. A body whose head and all four appendages were tenuously attached to his dancing torso. It didn't make sense. How could this corpse still be moving? The Very Senior Officer raised his .44 Smith & Wesson Model 29, a gift from the CIA Station Head for his sixtieth birthday, and put one last shot, the coup de grâce, into Ganapur's skull. What brain matter that was still left inside the cranium exploded pink, but the bullet-riddled body kept writhing. The frustrated Very Senior Officer emptied the rest of his rounds into the vivacious corpse, but to no avail.

With a shout, the Immigration Officer came running with the remote control in his hand and an idea in his head. He explained it in Urdu to the Senior Officer who shrugged his okay. At this point, why not? The Immigration Officer aimed the remote at the dead-dancing Marty Ganapur, hit the OFF button and the pain doctor danced no more.

The Very Senior Officer wondered, *How? Why?* But he didn't have time to further contemplate this fiasco as the other American proved to be still alive. Alive and crawling toward them, pleading for help. Klepstein's batwings were stained red, foam flecked his lips, and blood fled his guts.

"Please take me to an ER. Please. My life can still be saved. AB Negative. Just tell them Code Blue … Code Blue … "

The Very Senior Officer and the Immigration Officer exchanged a silent communication, culminating with the Immigration Officer walking over to Klepstein. He regarded the bloody, groveling dog at his feet, stroked his magnificent mustache, and said, "Aloha, asshole," before putting a bullet in Klepstein's temple.

The Very Senior Officer turned to the gathered soldiers, white smoke wafting from their spent weapons and said, "Scrape them off the tarmac before the passenger jets arrive. The Board of Tourism will shit elephants."

PART FOUR

"Gone - glimmering through the dreams that were"

Lord Byron

CHAPTER 34

Security

"I am so sorry we didn't invite you to our wedding," said Edie. She was wearing a Yukata kimono with a pattern of oversized pink blossoms on a background of black as she limped without her cane, which hung on a hook by the front door of a light-filled, open-spaced condo overlooking Lake Erie in Avon Bay. She placed a tray with two cups of tea and a plate of McVitie's Digestives chocolate biscuits in front of Nick and Julie. The two were seated at an artisanal wooden table near a glass door, which led out to a small balcony. But neither were enjoying the view at the moment. Not that there was much to see, just the usual endless expanse of gray lake blanketed by low gray clouds.

"Nothing personal, but we didn't invite anyone," said Aggie. She was hunched over a laptop at a corner oak desk in an alcove. Next to the laptop, a printer spewed out pages. "What we did was take an extra hour of lunch, went to the Cuyahoga County Courthouse, took out a license, and got a licensed officiant—my brother, who is the Superintendent of the State School for the Deaf—to marry us, and we were back before anyone at EZ♥Care was the wiser."

"Why didn't you guys tell anyone?" asked Nick, wincing as he singed his lips on that first swallow of tea.

"Be careful, Nicky, the tea is very hot," said Edie. "You should always let it steep, dear."

"Thanks, Edie." He dabbed at his mouth with a cloth napkin. "But hasn't same-sex marriage been legal in Ohio since 2015 or something?"

"Nick. How they did their wedding is their business," said Julie.

"Well, sure. I just—"

"Truth be told," said Edie, as she sat next to Julie, "We would've loved to have had our friends and families at a proper wedding and reception, but you know sooner or later the news would have gotten back to Mr. Muscat."

"Who wouldn't have approved," said Aggie, as if she gave a damn what he thought.

"So screw him," said Nick.

"Not interested. The bottom line is the man signs our checks. Not to mention The Big One, the settlement with Edie that paid for this condo."

"Besides, we're only there for a little while longer," Edie added. "Just until we're eligible for our full pensions. And I can't tell you how much I wait for that day."

"Because that's the day we will have our reception," said Aggie. "Hope you both are free. In the meantime, could you imagine— despite the protection of the law—Jiminy Cricket Muscat for one second tolerating a gay *and* interracial marriage in his company? In his Administrative Offices? No, we didn't think so either."

"He'd have kept us in litigation forever, not wanting to pay us the same retirement benefits he would a traditional couple," said Edie. "And we don't have forever."

"Who does?" murmured Julie.

"Hey you, cut that out," said Aggie. "Didn't you see the sign on the welcome mat that read 'No Misery Beyond This Point'?"

"Isn't that insensitive to the truly miserable?"

"No more insensitive than how you pronounce the heart in EZ♥Care."

"And how does one do that?"

"One doesn't. Because the heart in EZ♥Care is silent."

Julie, in spite of not feeling anything close to it, laughed.

"Good one, Aggs," said Nick.

"Did I tell you I like your hair, sweetheart?" said Edie to Julie.

"Please. My fugitive look? My *I'm-no-longer-a-doctor* do?"

"No way that should've happened," said Aggie. "Not only Klepstein framing you, but also manipulating your Program Director to approve it."

"All because she wouldn't …" Nick paused in order to phrase his words for polite company. "All because Julie wouldn't 'go out' with him."

"What?" said Aggie, perplexed. "I don't know anything about that. From where I sit, the reason Klepstein held Julie liable for the passing of that child was because Klepstein told Muscat somebody had to take the fall for the demise of their 'cash cow' and it wasn't going to be him."

"What? What cash cow? That can't be right," said Julie. "Charlie was born indigent. His mother was an addict with HIV who abandoned him in the Flats."

"True," said Aggie. "But his *grandfather* is a moneybags recluse, who for years has paid Cleveland Mercy, EZ♥Care, and Dr. Klepstein a fortune to keep him alive."

"But his chart … "

"Honey, I've seen the paperwork."

"Who is this grandfather?"

"I wish I knew. The name is pseudonymous, like a Donald Trump porn star NDA. No doubt somebody rich and powerful.

The payments are structured through a web of shell companies. All I know is the grandfather needed a living heir so the cash would stay in the family and not go to the IRS; therefore, the man paid whatever it took to keep the boy alive. Why else would Josh P keep Charlie in a single room all those years? Certainly not on Medicaid bucks."

"But that's just cruel. And not even realistic. Charlie, if that was even his real name, was lucky he lived as long as he did. If you want to call that living."

"So the way out for Klepstein was to blame Julie," said Nick. "Except 'blame' meant ruining her career."

"Which is why he kicked the student out of the room and had me run the catheter line—and not warn me about the second defib," said Julie. "He knew what would happen. That sonofabitch *knew*."

"I'm so sorry, dear," said Edie, as she placed her hand on Julie's arm. "It's wrong but it's not the end. You have to think outside the small box that is Cleveland Mercy. It's a big world out there and somewhere in it is a place for you and your skills. You will have choices."

"Thank you. I keep telling her. There's no reason she can't practice medicine. Just not here. Which is why the minute Muscat reinstates my insurance and deletes the bogus four-point-seven-million-dollar invoice, we're gone."

"To where?" asked Aggie.

"Yes, well, Nick has some sort of secret plan which he promised to explain to me at dinner. Until then, I guess I'll just have to trust him—like I have ever since we were thirteen."

Edie kept her hand on Julie's arm. "Listen to me, dear. Wherever you go, I know you'll find your place. You're a healer. That's your calling. You saved my life before the ambulance came. The EMTs said there was no doubt about that. Do you understand what I'm telling you?"

"Things are different now."

"What's different is there are more obstacles. But what's the same is you *are* a doctor. And you cannot let anything change that," said Aggie.

"Which is why, sweetie, we're glad you called us. Because with what we're going to give you, you're going to be able to nail that cocksucker Muscat's balls to the wall with a rusty gutter spike."

"Damn, Edie. I think your repression issues are in the rearview mirror." Aggie laughed and pulled a flash drive from her computer, rose from her desk, and collected the papers out of her printer tray. She brought them to the dining table and joined the other three. Aggie handed the drive to Julie and pushed the papers across the table for her and Nick to peruse.

"Nick, with this information, Muscat will have no choice but to reinstate your health insurance. Permanently. The short version of what's here are documents that detail a years-long relationship with Josh P at Cleveland Mercy, involving Medicare fraud, ripping off patients by illegally limiting their access to exclusively 'In-EZ♥Care-Network' physicians, fake charges, unnecessary surgical procedures, *phantom* surgical procedures. A number of doctors, including …" she looked pointedly to Julie, "Kasper Klepstein, along with Trout, and that pain management quack Marwan Ganapur, were involved and it's all in that flash drive. It took years of us skulking around after hours to compile this stuff. It's rock solid."

"What it is," said Nick, glancing up from the hard copy, "is criminal. Jules, look. Cleveland Mercy charges a patient seventy-seven bucks for a seven-dollar box of gauze pads, while Josh P's compensation is three-point-five million and holy shit, Mr.

Muscat pulls down forty-four mil! Plus performance bonuses and stock options!"

"Exactly. I'm sure the FBI, FDA, IRS, and whatever other initials you threaten Muscat with, will be quite interested. It's because of scum like him and his crew, sixty percent of the bankruptcies in this country are because of healthcare bills. Yet, somehow, we're thirty-first in life expectancy. *We*. The U-S-of-A. The only country in the developed world that does not guarantee healthcare for all our citizens, where the third leading cause of death is medical error.[*] And it's not going to get better until leeches like Muscat and Trout are gone."

"Aggie, Trout is already gone," Edie said.

"You know what I mean. Look, EZ♥Care owns the companies that make everything doctors stick into people, as in what Ganapur put in Nick's back. Except Muscat's cost is twenty-five percent of what he sells them to Josh P and Cleveland Mercy for. Then they split the difference on the insurance reimbursements and outrageous patient co-pays, which is what keeps the local Cadillac and coke dealers in business. There's a reason our entire health insurance 'industry' sucks up more Benjamins than the domestic GDP of France."

"Aggie please, stop aggravating yourself. Your blood pressure, remember?"

"Sorry, honey. It's just that these parasites piss me off so much, I wouldn't mind seeing them all dead."

At that, Nick and Julie exchanged a quick look. The ladies, however, didn't notice.

"That flash drive is your real insurance policy." Aggie slipped her hand into Edie's. Their matching fourteen-karat white-gold

[*] Johns Hopkins Study (2016)

wedding bands reflected the sunlight now breaking through the low cloud cover onto the lake and into their condo.

"Thank you," whispered Julie.

"We're happy and blessed to do it," said Aggie. "Just be careful. I mean that. Muscat might come off as a buffoon, but don't underestimate him. Because everything is *personal* with him. *Everything.* Consequences of his actions are irrelevant to him. Do you understand me?"

"Too well," said Nick.

"Good," said Edie. "Then go kick some Jimmy Tom Muscat ass."

CHAPTER 35

The Wrong Woman

I resisted it at first when six weeks ago my Captain asked me to "mentor," whatever the hell that means, a rookie detective, a scrub who passed the Detective Exam after serving maybe five minutes in Patrol, possibly because she happened to be the favorite niece of Commander Chris Corbin, head of the Bureau of Special Investigations—which includes Homicide. I mean what was I gonna do, even though everybody knows I work alone? I haven't had a partner since I punched out the last one, that annoying prick, Billy Shamet, who wouldn't stop cutting big wet ones with the windows rolled up. He went whining to HR and told them that a snarling German Shepherd was more sociable than me, so they transferred him to the K-9 unit. Last I heard, Shamet was at Metro Health recovering from multiple dog bites. Me, I'm on Rover's side on that one; Billy Shamet shoulda been riding a short bus, not a CDP plainclothes vehicle.

But Detective Debs, with flaming red hair and freckles that scrunched up like a colony of fire ants when she was thinking real hard, was alright. I took her to the Demidova bust to pop her cherry and she handled the collar just fine. Besides, the Department isn't completely nepotistic; if Debs couldn't cut it during her probationary period with me, I could kick her butt back to Patrol or

Remedial Parking Tickets or wherever. But so far, I had no reason to. I wouldn't admit this to anyone, except maybe Marie, but I also discovered this mentoring business worked both ways: Detective Debs has been teaching me lots of stuff I didn't know before. Like not to take Josh P at face value when he told me there was no security footage from the night Trout chose to hibernate in the park. Nope, Josh P wasn't lying; like usual, he was just ignorant. Turned out he thought the security footage was something they taped over every two weeks, like they do at Goldie's Doughnuts. But as Debs figured out, Cleveland Mercy stored the stuff on a cloud—and I didn't even begin to want to know how they did that. The only clouds I know are Cumulus and Nimbus, who were suckled by a she-wolf and went on to found Ancient Rome. My point is Debs got her hands on evidence I never would've known even existed. Not in a million years.

Which told me two things: one, it really was time to pull the plug on my storied career, and two, before I did, it would be the bee's knees to get my mitts on the video starring Demidova, live and in color, going into Trout's office the night of. That, on top of her prints on the French doors, would give even our witless D.A. an unlosable case.

Here again, I gotta say, Debs came to my rescue and taught me how to use the joystick she uses to play video games to get me through all the footage quicker. Hey, hold your joystick jokes because this gismo worked as easy as returning a baby's smile. I bet you thought I was going someplace disgusting there, but I'm a grandpa and there is one particular little girl's smile I really miss. Which was the whole point of me putting off retirement just a little bit longer.

Enough with the mush. Once Debs put the little silver thing in the computer and schooled me on how to make the images go backwards and forwards and sync it with all the other Cleveland Mercy cameras, I was ready to watch the surveillance video from Dr. Trout's penthouse floor on that silent night, holy night, he did his impression of a flying snowman. So far, though, all I saw was a bunch of medical riffraff, including Demidova, going to his party. I skipped ahead a few hours and watched them all stagger out.

Except Demidova.

Then it was a bunch of nothing for the next councla hours until I woke up from a little snooze and was rewarded by the incriminating sight of a zonkered Demidova stumbling out of Trout's office with a pissed-off expression on her mug. She had changed from her doctor duds to an unbuttoned fur coat over a lewd angel costume replete with a bent-to-shit halo on her head—about as appropriate as Mother Teresa wearing a thong in the Swimsuit Edition of *Sports Illustrated*. Yeah, sorry. I'll pause a second so you can get that image out of your head. Okay? Is it gone? Good. So back to my target, Dr. Irina Demidova: her angel costume reminded me of Glinda, The Good Witch of the South in *The Wizard of Oz*; that is, if Glinda gave ten buck lap dances.

My God, I remembered how I used to watch that picture every Easter on WOIO with Kimmy until she more or less grew out of it. But never mind that: right there, on the surveillance footage was the evidence that put Demidova at the scene of the crime at about the time Trout took his flyer.

I toggled (see, Debs even taught me the lingo) to another camera angle, the one by the elevators, and picked up Demidova jabbing at the button with the business end of her halo like she was trying out for the Russian fencing team. The elevator came and she stumbled in and was gone, except for the tail-end of her fur coat which got clipped by the elevator door like Marek slicing a pound of *salo* in Tremont. I noticed the time stamp on the screen: 11:37

p.m. I was about to shut it down, but who pops out from behind a Christmas tree across from the elevator—wearing a hospital gown, Kent State Baseball t-shirt and back brace, and leaning on an IV pole—but Nick Glass, seagull killer and Julie Toffoli's boyfriend, the jittery young doc I questioned in the cafeteria way back in the beginning. Holy moly! What was Glass doing up there? At that time of night?

I went back to the camera angle pointing at Trout's office, and there he was. The kid moved like he was in godawful pain. In fact, Glass moved so slow, he reminded me of Travis Hafner, the slowest Cleveland Indian of all time. Good Lord, it was painful watching Haf run the bags.* Just like it was painful watching how long it took for *Nick Glass to walk right into Trout's office.*

Huh?

Back up, Sikorski. On its face, Glass going into Trout's office proved nothing. Trout could've been long gone out the window, but the kid was sure in there a long time. At least a half-hour. But the clincher for me was what came later on. After Glass left, the other camera picks him up getting in the elevator; then forty-five minutes later, his girlfriend, Dr. Toffoli, comes *out* of the elevator.

Pushing a janitor's cart with a bunch of cleaning supplies on it.

Then *she* goes to Trout's office, pauses at the door to snap on a pair of gloves, and heads inside.

What would Toffoli be doing in Trout's office with a cart of cleaning equipment unless she was cleaning up *for* someone? Like her boyfriend who somehow offed Trout?

I hit Stop and went back to the beginning. The more I saw all this traffic, the more it looked like the stateroom scene from *A*

---

* Travis Hafner in his illustrious twelve-year career that included four-thousand, seven-hundred and eighty-two plate appearances, stole a grand total of eleven bases. And I don't remember any of them.

Night at the Opera. You know, the Marx Brothers: Groucho, Chico, Harpo, and the humorless one with the beard, Karl. Except what wasn't so funny here, in fact was pretty damn disappointing, was it appeared Nick Glass, with Dr. Julie Toffoli's assistance, had been the instruments of Dr. Trout's demise. And as regrettable as that was, I had to believe that took Miss Vladivostok 2008 off the hook.

I grabbed my phone, started punching in a number, when there was a banging on the door and Detective Debs barged in. She held a baggie in her hand with something grayish blue in it, like one of Marek's *kaszankas* gone bad in the sun.

"Thanks, Deb, but I already had lunch."

"What?" Her freckles crinkled up, all confused like. "Oh no, Lieutenant, this isn't a sausage. It's a penis."

"Look, Detective, your social life ain't my concern." Then it hit me: "What the heck did you just say?!"

"This penis, Lieutenant. It was sent over by the County Sheriff's Department. They found it in a creek."

"And why would I need County's wayward dongs?"

"They thought you might be interested because DNA identified it as belonging to Carmelo Iakopo, the RN who's been missing since the day after Christmas. Since his last assignment was supervising the care of Nick Glass, I thought there might be a connection."

"More like a disconnection. But good thinking, Debs. Let's saddle up."

"Where to, Lieutenant?"

"For starters, Nick Glass and Julie Toffoli's apartment. Those are our new suspects."

"Yes sir."

She was about to charge out the door but put on the brakes and asked, "What about Dr. Demidova?"

"She's what we call a Red herring. Call down and cut her loose on the homicide charge. No way she killed Trout. If she can make bail for practicing medicine without a license, fine. But we do murder in this department. Just tell the DA's office to hold onto her passport. I trust her about as much as I trust the Grilled Cheese Pretzels at First Energy."

I put on my coat and grabbed my cane. I didn't know whether to thank Debs or whack her with it as she held the door open for me, like she was helping a blind man cross that insane five-way intersection at East 55th, Woodland Road, and Kinsman in heavy traffic.

As we entered the bullpen, she held up the baggie. "Lieutenant? What should I do with this, um, penis?"

"Ah jeez. Put it in the freezer for now. Just make sure you write 'Evidence' on the baggie or it won't be here when we get back."

"Yes sir."

CHAPTER 36

Customer Service

Julie's Geo Metro looked as out of place on the bucolic tree-lined Burton Trail in Chagrin Falls as the Queen of England's Bentley touring an Eritrean refugee camp. Even if Julie's sub-compact wasn't patched together from various dead Geo Metros like a mechanical Frankenstein's monster on four bald tires, it still lacked the cachet to be anywhere near the elegant enclave of Marcourt Farms. The mere presence of the born-again junker tooling past eight-figure mansions surrounded by acres of groomed green, guarded by Old Money growths of sixty-foot Yellow Buckeyes, was an aesthetic affront in and of itself. Yet, onward the Metro groaned, backfiring along the rolling hills towards a serene river of blue.

"It says to go straight, then cross the Chagrin River," said Nick in the passenger seat to Julie, as he checked the directions on his phone.

"Chagrin River. Someone had an epic sense of irony."

*   *   *

Julie, outside the idling Metro, pulled open a white-painted gate, beyond which a gravel road led toward an imposing riverfront mansion. A castle built on the EOBs (Explanation Of Benefits) of the multitudes of the sick and sicker fortunate enough to have an EZ♥Care health insurance policy. She returned to the car and started up the road to Muscat's Xanadu. Despite the righteousness of their mission, the two gazed in awed intimidation at the looming manse ahead.

"How does just one guy live there?"

"I assume you're being rhetorical," said Julie, as they passed a waterfall splashing into a series of layered ponds, followed by horse stables, a driving range, and an enclosed batting cage next to an acrylic-coated basketball court. Ahead, Muscat's black Escalade was parked on the circular stone driveway near the faux Greek-columned entry. However, before they got that far, Julie turned onto a side driveway out of view from the main house.

"Let's hope Aggie and Edie were right about this being the staff's day off," Nick said.

"They've been right about everything else." Julie pulled to a stop at the side of the manor where an alarm panel was embedded in in an electrical panel. "Let's do this."

* * *

The direct-from-1992 sounds of "Let's Get Rocked" by Def Leppard blasted from in-ceiling speakers in Muscat's indoor gym. On one wall were shelves of golden trophies. Solid gold, not that cheap gold-plated crap they give to losers just for participating. No, Jimmy Tom's shelves sagged under the weight of twenty-four-karat gold trophies that depicted Muscat, golden bat in hand at the apex of a perfect swing, gazing into the heavens. Other golden trophies depicted a Greek God version of Jimmy Tom Muscat running, swimming, and biking his way to countless EZ♥Care Ironman Triathlon first-place finishes.

Opposite the trophy wall was a floor-to-ceiling tempered-glass window that looked out onto the river and countryside beyond. There was not a single other mansion to spoil the view. Muscat, however, was not looking out the window, or perhaps he might have glimpsed the approach of the avenging Metro.

Instead, he was running in place on his Technogym Artis® Run treadmill, replete with Bluetooth, web connectivity, and built-in interactive IPS screen. Perhaps the coolest trophy of them all, however, were his kicks. Muscat, blonde-streaked hair matted with discretionary sweat, ran hard on his rare Nike Hyperadapt 1.0s—sneakers that Nike had nicknamed E.A.R.L., which stands for a technology called "Electro Adaptive Reactive Lacing." That's right, a shoe that laces itself once it feels weight on the heel. Or, conversely, can unlace. The midsole glowed an otherworldly blue thanks to a wireless bi-weekly recharge.

His treadmill screen was tuned to 19 News. The closed-captioning on the treadmill screen was enabled so Muscat could read the news as he sang along with Def Leppard vocalist, Joe Elliot. The only difference between Joe Elliot and Jimmy Tom Muscat was one of them sounded like a chicken being beheaded.

* * *

Nick, reading off a cheat sheet provided by Aggie, punched a series of numbers into the alarm panel that resulted in a reassuring chime. He turned to Julie, who stood at the rear of the Metro, hatchback in the air, a duffel bag at her feet. "Nick," she said. "We can still turn around."

"Why?"

"Why indeed," she said as she pulled an IV pole out of the Metro and latched the door to a close.

* * *

Muscat, recharging his beta-endorphins, kept on running and singing. His Richard Simmons tank top and Dolfin short shorts were swamped in sweat as Nick and Julie, like Norman Rockwell ninjas, appeared on each side and cuffed him to the safety handles of the treadmill. Julie picked up a remote and sent Def Leppard back to the nineties, as Muscat, running in place, looked to his cuffed hands.

"What the fuck, Nick! This isn't funny!"

"Who's laughing?"

"What the hell are you doing here?"

"You mean how can I be walking, when your Samoan goon was supposed to cripple me? I mean, worse than you and EZ♥Care already have?"

"What? I've had zero contact with him." Muscat squinted at Julie, and not recognizing her with her new look, lowered his voice, "Who's the box cutter?"

"I'm his advocate," said Julie. "Box cutter? Really?"

"Sugar, if the dildo fits …"

"Shut up, Muscat. Shut up and listen."

"Whoa. Look who grew a pair. Okay, Nick, I get it. Except if we're going to talk, turn the damn machine off and uncuff me. Then you can tell me what you want."

"How about I tell you what I want and you just do it."

"Say *cheese*, Muskrat," said Julie as she aimed her iPhone at him.

"Hey! You can't video me. That's a crime!"

"We'll get to the crimes, but just to be legally accurate: Ohio is what's known as a 'One Party Consent State.' So, Nick, do you consent to me videoing this piece of human excrement?"

"Sure. Action."

"Yeah, well, Nick—you see all those Ironman trophies behind you? I can run all day and night if I have to. I'm like one of them Calumet Farms thoroughbreds."

"Who's about to be gelded."

"Good one, Jules."

"Thanks. And we're rolling."

"What do you want, Nick?"

"One, reinstate my health insurance as required by law. Two, zero out the bogus four-point-seven-million-dollar debt ..."

"What's 'three'?"

"We'll get to that. First my insurance."

"Okay. No problem. Your insurance is reinstated. The four-seven was a clerical error. The Russian doc, when she wasn't too busy murdering Trout, forgot to officially discharge you. The system had you hospitalized for one-hundred and seventy-nine days and maxed you out. I'll fix it."

"Okay. Fix it. On *paper*."

"I just gave you my word."

"I prefer paper."

"We'll accept the top sheet," said Julie. "Signed and countersigned."

Muscat glared at them with a growing rage. Something deep within began to transform. Like Dr. Bruce Banner, blasted with gamma rays and becoming The Incredible Hulk, Muscat was mutating to his core essence. As perspiration streamed down his face, his cheeks flushed crimson—less from the exertion and more from being told by this traitorous punk and his somehow familiar "advocate" what to do. Because no one tells Jimmy Tom Muscat what to do. No one.

"Are you referring to the policy that's cost me seven figures because of all your damn surgeries and shit? That policy?"

"I'm an employee and I'm entitled to it."

"Not anymore. I changed my mind. Your EZ♥Care Prime policy's canceled."

"On what grounds?" said Julie.

"On the grounds that on Nick's original application, he made one whopper of a material omission."

"What material omission?"

"Concealed your pre-existing condition. Your bad back."

"What! I didn't have a bad back until you ran me over!"

"Sorry, but your bones were bogus. I had it checked out. And hey, maybe the 'collision'—that *you* caused because you didn't get out of my way, which everybody saw—didn't help things, but Dr. Ganapur informed me his study of your medical records, plus his hands-on professional examination, led him to the indisputable conclusion that you've had a back on the brink since childhood. Probably why Cleveland released you. Whatever, it's a pre-existing condition you unlawfully concealed and Ganapur will testify to that in court. Therefore, your insurance is null and void."

"Ganapur's a quack and liar!"

"He's a respected staff physician at Cleveland Mercy. And as any medical litigator will tell you, you'll need a physician of equal stature in the field willing to testify in court against him. Got one of them? Nope? Then consider yourself fired and uncuff me."

"Maybe you'll think differently after you look at this," said Julie. She inserted Aggie's flash drive into a USB port on the treadmill computer.

"What's that?"

"Material *commissions*," said Julie as 19 News on the treadmill monitor was replaced with spreadsheet after spreadsheet scrolling in front of Muscat's widening eyes. He was looking at dates, numbers, and names. Names like Przybylowicz, Trout, Klepstein. And Ganapur.

"What the hell is this?" said Muscat.

"Evidence detailing the millions of dollars you've stolen from the State of Ohio, Medicare, Medicaid, your customers, and your shareholders. Oh, check it out: here comes documentation of your kickback arrangement with Josh P and certain Cleveland Mercy doctors."

"And here are the documents detailing the existence of Klepstein's deceased 'cash cow' along with his subsequent motive for framing Dr. Julie Toffoli," Nick added.

"Who's me. Remember? And I apologize for taking such a long time to mull over the offer you made at the picnic, but after due consideration, I've decided against taking any position at EZ♥Care. Mainly because what you do is a conflict of *everyone's* interest."

"That's the third thing, Mr. Muscat," said Nick.

Muscat squinted at Julie. "Hell, I knew you looked familiar. Listen, I had nothing to do with—"

"Holy shit! Jules! Look!" Nick pointed to the screen, where the spreadsheets were jostled for picture-in-picture space by Betsy Nguyen doing a live stand-up at the entrance to Cleveland Mercy. The BREAKING NEWS chyron at the bottom of the screen screamed:

TWO LOCAL DOCS KILLED IN PAKISTAN TIGER ATTACK

A PR shot of a stern Kasper K. Klepstein M.D. was shown in an inset above Betsy, soon joined by one that read Marwan Hussein Ganapur M.D. However, instead of Marty's handsome face, his Cleveland Mercy web photo was a cellphone pic of a crooked penis with a mushroom head. Raven wasn't joking. On screen, the photo insets were quickly deleted.

Julie grabbed the remote and turned up the volume. "…although a Pakistani Army spokesman stated the escaped zoo tiger, a rare white Siberian named Lloyd, has been euthanized, no further details are available at this time," reported Betsy. "Josh Przybylowicz, CEO of Cleveland Mercy, has just issued a statement, reading in part, 'Our thoughts and prayers go out to the families of these two dedicated physicians. Doctors Kasper K. Klepstein and Marty H. Ganapur exemplified the best of Cleveland Mercy. Hope, compassion—and yes, mercy.'"

Julie stared at the screen. A palpable doubt creased her face. She and Nick exchanged a questioning look. Another pair of villains dead because of them? Sometimes a tiger is just a tiger. Right?

Muscat, slack-jawed and breathing hard, kept running in place, getting nowhere fast. "Tiger attack? I thought those striped fuckers were extinct."

"Apparently not," said Julie.

"So about my insurance," said Nick. "You said Ganapur was going to testify about my so-called *pre-existing condition*? Maybe you have a Plan B?"

"Water," croaked Muscat. "Please."

"Water? We have way better," said Julie.

*   *   *

Me and Detective Debs pulled up and parked in front of Marek's on Literary. As we stepped out of my Caprice, I wondered how a street could come to be called Literary Road? What? Did the crosswalks and traffic lights know how to read? Wasn't it supposed to be the other way around?

I rang the bell at the building entrance. Not surprisingly, neither Glass or Toffoli answered. So I kept buzzing different apartments until some stoner who just woke up from a twenty-hour nap croaked, "Who's there?"

"Rascal House Pizza delivery." I winked at Debs to show her how it's done.

"Fuck off," said the futzed voice on the other end of the intercom as it disconnected.

I wished I could've taken my wink back when Debs put her hand on the door knob, turned it, and walked inside like she lived there. How was I supposed to know it was unlocked from the get-go? I sheepishly showed Debs what was left of my choppers as I led the way through the dark lobby and up the creaking stairs. Debs looked at me with some concern. The stairs were okay, it was my knees that were creaking, but she wasn't going to hear that from me.

Debs knocked on their door, but no answer. So I took my some-would-say-illegal lockpicks out of my coat and went to work. Debs' eyes bugged out, most likely because she had visions of her career ending before it began. Hey, whatever. If every cop played by the rules, what kind of world would we live in? For the record, that was a rhetorical question. First, I tried the torsion wrench, then the twist flex, the offset diamond pick, the ball pick, and just about the time I was sure Debs was either going to report me—or worse, later laugh at me over a microbrew with her friends in some hipster "pub"—I got lucky with Old Reliable, the trusty hook pick. What? Like she thought I'd never done this before? I pushed open the door and went inside. Debs' scruples didn't quite cross the threshold with her; nevertheless, the rest of her followed me in.

Of course, I knew nothing we'd find here would be admissible in court but I had a buffet of baffle on my plate: one splatted spine surgeon in a snowman suit, one missing Samoan nurse who himself was missing his *schmeckle*, and now, having just heard the news on the way over, two *other* Cleveland Mercy docs, one of them my buddy Garfinkle, lying on a slab in a Karachi morgue mauled by a Siberian tiger named Lloyd. Therefore it was imperative I find Glass and Toffoli before the city of Cleveland began to feel a shortage of medical professionals.

As Debs put on a pair of gloves and opened drawers and cabinets, I went to the mail piled on the kitchen table, where I found an opened envelope with the return address reading EZ♥Care Health Solutions. Yeah, sometimes it's just that easy. I perused the missive inside and saw it was EZ♥Care's version of a Dear Nick letter: the sons-of-bitches had terminated the one thing that kid really needed, his health insurance.

"Detective, get me Muscat's home number."

Debs pulled out her phone and whizzed her fingers on it like Pearl Bornstein from the Secretarial Pool used to do on her Underwood Five. Now, *that* was a keyboard. Anyway, Pearl's gone and so's the Secretarial Pool, which is another reason I'm retiring. Wait! What's this? Three seconds later and Debs was dialing Muscat without even punching in any numbers? How the heck does that work? I was about to compliment her on her phone skills when Muscat's voicemail interrupted:

"Hey hey! It's Jimbo! H M U and I'll get crackalackin' back atcha in a jiff. Beep!"

Followed by an electronic beep. I couldn't decide which beep pissed me off more. In the end, it wouldn't matter.

"Mr. Muscat," I said into the phone. "This is Lieutenant Sikorski CDP. You know, the guy who's suing you for Wrongful Death? Well, this isn't about that. I'm calling in my capacity as a public servant because we have reason to think there may be some trouble headed in your direction. Please lock your doors and wait for us. We're on the way."

I hung up, turned to Debs. "I need his address ASAP."

She held up her phone. "Already programmed in. Along with the route."

I grinned. I knew she'd make a good cop. "Then let's get the crackalackin' heck outta here. And keep calling him."

She grinned back. Gotta love the way her freckles danced.

*   *   *

The muted whirring of the treadmill was white noise compared to the nonstop thump thump thump of Muscat's digital sneakers. The new accoutrement was the IV Julie and Nick brought with them. The bag dripped yellow-green nourishment into Muscat's arm—as God forbid, he'd get a heart attack or stroke. Not on their watch. The two sat on a pair of EZ♥Physio exercise balls and waited for Muscat to acquiesce, only to be startled by the ringing of a cell left on a weight bench. Muscat's ringtone was "Wake Me Up Before You Go-Go" by George Michael and Wham! Thankfully, it stopped. But the respite was only temporary; after a moment, it started again. And stopped. And so on. Julie and Nick ignored it as they were mesmerized by the lightshow flashing from Muscat's sneakers.

"Hey, Muskrat," Julie asked, "what's the deal with your kicks?"

"Thought you'd never ask," he wheezed. "They're one of a kind. Nike rolled 'em out in 2016. Hyper Adapt 1.0s. Originally cost $720. But they turned out not to be a thing. Was a limited run and they dropped out of circulation. But I found these babies on Alibaba for what? Eight K? Score!"

"What's so special about them, besides the stupid blinking LED light?"

"The shoes are *self-lacing*."

"What?" Julie was shocked. "Eight thousand dollars for a pair of sneakers that lace themselves?"

"And *un-lace*. They respond to pressure. And speaking of pressure, you think you're in the driver's seat but one thing you amateurs might want to consider is what's going to happen when my security guy, Crispin, comes back from his lawn bowling tournament. I know, I say 'Crispin' and 'lawn bowling' and it sounds like he's some kinda English rose, but he's ex Brit SAS and those motherfuckers make the Navy Seals look like Jerry's Kids. And don't get me started on them—those disturbing little tards cost me a fortune over the years. So, have you gamed out what's going to happen when Crispin comes back? Have you?"

"Nope," said Nick. "Because we know you give your staff every third Sunday off."

"There's no one coming to get you out of this, Muskrat. You might as well give Nick his policy. It'll be way more painless than watching JAIL-TV tomorrow and seeing yourself nailed on 19 News by Betsey Nguyen."

"For your information, I already nailed *her*. The night they found Trout's body. Right between Sports and Weather."

Julie whispered to Nick, "Ha. See? You never had a chance."

"Jeez, Julie. How could you even think that?"

Her answer was a devilish grin, which was replaced by a look of frustration. "I'm getting tired of this clown. Time to move the ball down the field." Julie rose from her exercise ball and kicked it across the room next to Muscat, who could do no more than jog in place and like it.

"In one minute, we, our fingerprints, the flash drive, the video, along with my—what did you call them at the company barbeque when we met? Chesticles? Yes, *chesticles*. Like, what are you, ten years old? Well, we're out of here and taking our news scoop to Betsy Nguyen. So enjoy your run, Seabiscuit."

Muscat sputtered, "Chesticles! Jesus! I *whispered* that to Nick, for Chrissakes."

"No. You don't whisper, Mr. Muscat." Nick got up, also kicked his ball across the room, and joined Julie. "You shout, you bully, you drool. You don't give a damn who sees or hears you. Well, nobody's going to hear you now."

"No! You can't leave me like this!"

"You're right, we can't." Julie pocketed Muscat's cell. "We'll call Crispin once we're at the station and he can use his SAS skills to cut you loose. The two of you can make a nice cuppa, turn on the telly, and watch your reputation and freedom go down in flames. Bye-bye, Muskrat."

"See you in the Loser's Circle, Mr. Muscat. You can apologize and make restitution to Julie then. Let's go, Jules."

Muscat gasped for breath. "Okay, I'll reinstate the damn policy! Was a system error that generated the termination letter in the first place."

"You know, Mr. Muscat, the real system error is guys like you, guys who don't bring anything to the table, making millions off of sick people."

"Oh, grow the fuck up, Nick." The man couldn't help it. Combativeness was in his DNA. "Grow the fuck up and think about your career and the generous salary I pay you."

"Right. And out of that generous salary, I pay taxes. In return, I get cops when someone jacks my car; I get firefighters when my house burns down; hell, I even get a library card to improve my mind. But what I don't get is what the rest of the civilized world already has: healthcare. For that, I'm dependent on parasites like you."

"Hey, Nick, can we talk about your conversion to Democratic Socialism another time and you guys cut me loose?"

In answer, Nick pumped up the speed on the treadmill. "First, you get Customer Service to reinstate my insurance right now. We can do it from here. Remember that program I wrote last year, the one you said was brilliant? How a customer can video conference with Customer Support? Face to face with a real human being?" Nick punched the interactive screen on the Artis®-Run's computer.

Within seconds, an annoying three-note dialing tone pinged from the speakers. All the while Muscat continued running. Tears welled in his eyes. Tears which were replaced by laughter. Insane laughter, like a Bond villain who just launched a thousand nukes at Boise.

"What are you laughing at?"

"Last month … last month … I moved Customer Service to the Philippines!"

"So?"

"So no one can understand a single word any of 'em say. And that's if you can get one of those tailless monkeys to pick up the fuckin' phone!" Muscat screeched like a Rhesus and kept on running.

Nick whispered to Julie, "What's wrong? He's acting like he's drunk."

"Runner's high. He's manic."

The tones ceased their knelling as the call was answered by an animated avatar of a Customer Service Agent who looked like Kristen Stewart. "Hello and welcome to EZ♥Care Customer Service. If you have a life-threatening emergency, hang up and dial 911. Please listen to all the options as our Menu has recently changed." An animated sombrero appeared on the head of the avatar who said, "*Para Español, marque siete.*" The avatar lost the Español (and sombrero) and continued in bland American English. "To file a new claim, press one. To inquire about the status of an existing claim, press two. To pay your bill, press three. To—"

"Oh Jesus," interrupted Muscat. "I gotta take a piss."

"I'm sorry; I do not recognize that command," said the avatar. "To switch to Touchtone only, press nine."

"A piss! I gotta take a freaking piss!" cried Muscat to Nick and Julie.

"First my insurance."

"I'm sorry, but I still do not understand you," said the avatar. "Let's start over. Perhaps we'll try this another way."

"Oh shit. Now I gotta take a dump too. Please, take me off this machine. Please!"

Nick and Julie, although supremely grossed out, remained immune to Muscat's begging. As did the avatar: "For new claims, please press one. To inquire about the status of an existing—"

"Nick, hit zero!" yelled Muscat. "That always works!"

"I'm sorry, but that is not a valid command," said the avatar.

"Fuck if it ain't!"

"Sorry, but I.T. deleted that option, remember? Customers were getting wise to that trick and you told me to make it harder to speak to a human being."

"Well, why don't you fucking *tell* me how to speak to a human being, Nick!"

"Say six, six, six."

"Six, six, six!" yelled Muscat. Those were the magic words, as the Kristen Stewart avatar was replaced by a real human: a coffee-skinned male Filipino with a roundish face, flat nose, dark, deep-set eyes, and a bountiful head of thick black hair. The Customer Service rep had a masters in philosophy and in his free time was struggling with his doctoral thesis on Spinoza and his opposition to Rene Descartes' rationalist doctrine of mind-body dualism. However, he had to buy school books and pay the rent; hence, the always exhausted Catapang Abaday worked the graveyard shift in the Manila EZ♥Care Call Center. He introduced himself as "Anderson," his more palatable American work name. Catapang's first language was Tagalog; his second, Spanish, and to complete the trilingual trifecta, he spoke thickly accented English.

Which translated to Muscat that he was speaking to some Third World dimwit.

"May I have your customer number, please?" asked Catapang.

"Customer number? I'm your goddamn boss, Anderson, or whatever the hell your real name is."

"Excuse me, sir?"

"I want you to generate a document stating Nicholas Glass is insured by EZ♥Care."

"Prime," Nick said.

"In perpetuity," added Julie.

"I will need the customer number, Mr. Glass."

"Get this straight! I'm not fucking Glass, you dog munching dink! I'm Jimmy Tom Muscat, your fucking boss!"

"Excuse me, sir. My boss is Scott. He works in the next cubicle."

"Well put 'Scott' the fuck on!"

"I'm sorry, sir. Today is Scott's day off and his boss, April, is taking her child to school. Now, if you will be so kind as to give me the customer number—"

"How many times do I have to tell you! I don't *need* a customer number! I'm the CEO of the goddamn company! I pay your pathetic little salary, you fucking asswipe!"

Despite the abuse, Catapang (which means "Brave Fellow") followed his script, because one never knew when they were testing you. No way was he going to give them any reason to fire him. "The customer number, sir?"

Nick, concerned this exchange was not going to end well, crawled adjacent to the treadmill, just out of the shot, took out his EZ♥Care I.D. card and whispered to Muscat. "It's 3-W-2-4-X-1-7-9."

"What? Say that again, bitch!"

"The customer number, sir."

"I wasn't talking to you, dumbass! I'm about to get you Glass's number. Hang on!"

Muscat scowled at Nick, "Give me that fucking number again, you pathetic loser, so I can—"

"Sir, without a customer number, I cannot help you. If there's nothing else …"

"Yeah, here's something else, Anderson. You can choke on ten inches of my red, white, and blue dick!"

"… then thank you for calling EZ♥Care and have a nice day."

"No! Wait! Wait! That was a joke! Just a—"

Before disconnecting, Catapang said goodbye in his own special way: "*Anak ng kamote*."*

Catapang vanished and was replaced by the EZ♥Care Customer Care home page, where the patients were all vacant smiles.

Nick shot a downcast look to Julie. "Now, what do we do?"

Before she could answer, Muscat screamed worse than the Wicked Witch of the West during her "I'm melting!" death scene. In Muscat's case, he was screaming: "My kicks! My kicks!"

"Oh my God," said Julie. She and Nick watched in shock as Muscat's suddenly strobing sneakers *unlaced themselves* and went rogue, tying themselves into crazy knots, whipping themselves around his milky white ankles. The result being Muscat tripped

---

* Son of a sweet potato. Which in Tagalog is about as nasty as it gets.

over the laces and smashed his face into the computer monitor. Repeatedly. With each hit, shards of glass pierced his face, obscuring his features in rivulets of red. A two-inch piece of glass protruded from his left eye.

Nick found the OFF button as Muscat slumped forward, blood spewing from his face. Julie felt for a pulse, and shook her head.

"Oh man, not another one," said Nick. "We killed him."

"No. We didn't kill him, Nick. His eight-thousand-dollar sneakers did."

"Hell. What do we do?"

"Uncuff him, get our stuff, and leave."

"Really?"

"I don't know, Nick. He's dead. No one's going to believe his sneakers did this. What else can we do?"

Before Nick could answer, a weary but commanding voice, a voice used to calling *safe* or *out*, cut through the gray areas: "For starters, you can put your hands up," said Lieutenant Artemas Sikorski.

Jolted, Nick and Julie turned to the doorway and saw Sikorski and Detective Debbie Corbin blocking their egress. Detective Corbin motioned with her Glock 19 for Julie and Nick to do as her Lieutenant said.

CHAPTER 37

Confessions

That sonofabitch Muscat was as dead as the battery in his unanswered cellphone. As dead as a rejected health insurance claim. Entire forests have been cleared to create the EOBs dropped from the high windows of the EZ♥Care executive suites, like so much confetti onto the parade of suckers who were under the delusion that if they paid their premiums on time, their health needs would be met. Except when they weren't.

Who knew the cancer drug prescribed to keep my daughter alive was deemed *Off Label?* Therefore:

Benefit Denied.

Who knew that the ER on Detroit Avenue, where I'd taken *her* daughter, Kimmy, my nine-year-old granddaughter, after she sprained her ankle in a soccer game, was *Out Of Network?* Therefore:

Benefit Denied.

Denied, even though the freaking hospital was four blocks away from the soccer field. Yeah, yeah, I know they call it a *pitch*, not a field, but I'm still not down with the notion that if you can't use the arms you were born with, how is soccer even a sport? No offence to the billions around the world who are addicted to this stupid game; no sir, I aim all offence at the departed dirtbag on the treadmill, who was no longer in any condition to stamp: *Benefit Denied.*

Meantime, the only ones who could explain why Muscat's life had been denied were the two kids cuffed to a piece of equipment Debs told me was called the "Vibro Gym," a high-tech piece of junk that models and actors and other professionally thin people stand on for ten minutes a day to get their exercise. Huh? Losing your gut fat by getting vibrated? It sounded like a load of crap to me, but Debs told me the Vibro Gym "Diamond" model, which of course was the one Muscat had to have, was top of the line. Featured sixty-five thousand Crystallized Swarovski Elements encrusted into the equipment's vibration plate—whatever Swarovski Crystals are, or for that matter, whatever a vibration plate is. I'm sorry, but Debs lost me at the embedded six-hundred hyacinth-colored stones. Personally, I could think of lots better ways to spend seventy-grand to stay in shape, like hiring Rita the Receptionist at the Station to compliment me every morning by saying, "Have you lost some weight, Lieutenant?" as she handed me my glazed sinker and cup of black joe with three cubes.

Even before Debs could finish Mirandizing them, both Bonnie and Clyde readily confessed. Although, the two did plead extenuating circumstances. And plead they did. They pleaded more than the flop-sweat spraying Godfather Of Soul, James Brown himself, wailing *"Please, Please, Please"* as his Famous Flames threw the velvet cape over him and tried to drag him off the stage at the old Akron Armory that one spring night back in 1971, when Marie and me …

Never mind. Here I am digressing from my digressions. So, without further irrelevancies from me, here's how they pleaded their case:

"I took every medical precaution possible," said Toffoli. "Not only was the IV bag glucose-based but I added magnesium, calcium, vitamins B1, B3, B5, B6, B9, and of course, B12."

"Bingo," I said.

"That's not funny," said Toffoli. Even Debs groaned. "I also added a small amount of fluid from the inside of a coconut. Studies have shown that coconut milk, especially from an immature fruit, is an excellent intravenous electrolyte. We drove to the Whole Foods in Rocky River to get just the right one."

"You know, Lieutenant, what was in the IV doesn't even matter," Glass took the baton. "Muscat's stupid electric sneakers killed him. It was an accident. Hell, they were *all* accidents."

Whoops.

The two of them looked at each other like they'd been caught stealing quarters from Saint Malachi's poor box, as everything just got a whole lot more interesting. Until *interesting* became *mind-blowing mesmerizing* when Toffoli handed over the little silver flash drive. After that, I couldn't shut them up.

One thing that never changed over decades of listening to assorted barf bags so overwhelmed by the guilt they was carrying, it was always like a high colonic for their souls when they finally got to blow the gaff. Hell, I've heard 'em all, like the traveling salesman who, under the harsh lights of Interrogation Room Number Two, admitted to chopping his wife into little pieces and putting said body parts into his Samsonite and sending it to Paris because she said one too many times he never took her anywhere nice.

Easy. Case closed.

Except these two kids, Toffoli and Glass, it seemed to me, didn't *technically* murder with aforethought any of that deserving crew of frauds, sadists, and thieves. Lesser crimes, sure; although I'm not positive there's a statute that covers snapping the frozen johnson off an already deceased felon.

I needed to mull over what it was I would—and should—charge them with. And since HQ said there'd be at least a four-hour wait till the crime scene ghouls got here, I told Debs to keep Muscat's corpse company while I took these two in and booked 'em myself. Debs thought it'd be better if I waited for some uniforms to do it, but I blew her off. I've been booking miscreants since before her Pops promised her Moms he'd pull out in time.

Debs, of course, thought she'd heard the whole story in Muscat's fancy gym. And she had.

Nick and Julie's story.

But there was a little bit more that needed to be confessed today. From me.

I just didn't know how to do it. Or even if I *should* do it. I had to decide if today was the day I'd cap my illustrious career by tossing it down the crapper, or do nothing and settle for the gold watch and the go-go dancers at my retirement party at Clancy's Cop Stop.

Both choices had their downsides. I mean even the easy way out wasn't so easy: Take the dancers. Please. I was on a first-name basis with most of them, having busted them multiple times over the years. That, and *not* having busted them multiple times over the years—because once in a while they'd help out with a tip or I felt bad for one of their kids having to walk to school through the snow with holes in their soles. So bye-bye to the occasional double-sawbuck which I knew I'd never see again. Marie never said nothing when I'd come home on payday one bag shy of a homer. We never did talk about the Job. Still don't. It's like an unmarked border, one that isn't on any map, but still one that neither of us ever crosses—which is why, I suppose, we're still married after forty-three years. And most of 'em, damn good ones. So no, I didn't know how I was going to play this but I knew Marie would have my back. Even if I chose to do it the hard way.

Sure, I took an Oath. I've taken a few oaths in my life and I've done my damnedest to stick by them. Except, what do you do when two of them smack into each other like a 3 a.m. smash-up on the southbound I-77?

If you survive, then it's time to buy a new car. Say you've narrowed down your choices between a Ford Escape versus a Mitsubishi Outlander. One's American-made, but the other's cheaper. But the company that makes the cheaper SUV used American POWs as slave labor in WWII, including my Pop; while at the same time Henry J. Ford used French POWs in his German factory in 1940 and was referred to by Hitler as his "inspiration." In fact, Adolf kept a life-size portrait of Henry J. next to his desk.

So which car do you buy?

Holy crap, I gotta stop with these internal Socratic dialogues. I mean, who died and anointed me Saint Artemas of Shaker Square?

Just figure it out, old man. Because it really ain't about the car, it's about the driver.

CHAPTER 38

The Vanity To Dream

Julie and Nick—cuffed in the front as a courtesy, although they didn't realize it—flanked Sikorski as the lieutenant led the way to the parked Caprice. He leaned on his cane, and his shoes crunched on the muddy gravel drive.

"You two tell a tragic tale."

Nick and Julie didn't respond. Just kept slow walking with the old man to the Chevy.

"After all these years, nothing much surprises me anymore. Takes a lot to move the needle. Except this story … it's more depressing than the time I popped a Cialis end of shift on a Friday, bought Marie a dozen roses, only to find my mother-in-law decamped in the adjoining bathtub for the weekend."

"Do we have to listen to you trivialize what's happened, Lieutenant?" said Julie.

"What's trivial about throwing away eighty bucks?"

Julie turned her head away in disgust.

"Alright. I'm sorry, Toffoli. This whole thing is bugging the hell out of me. All these lives, either ruined or ended or whose fates have yet to be determined and I'm trying to work out why you're the ones wearing the bracelets."

"That part is on you," said Nick.

"Tell me you didn't sneak over to Karachi last night and unlock Lloyd the Tiger's cage at the zoo."

"No. Wasn't us." Nick looked up as a v-shaped skein of Canadian geese flew above their heads, over the Chagrin River to the Great North. Going home. Sikorski too, glanced at the sky but kept walking. One stab of his cane at a time.

"Listen, you two. I get it. Maybe all this death and destruction was the world wreaking some kind of payback against those shitheels for screwing up yours and who-knows-how-many-other people's lives. Problem is, I gotta go by evidence. What I can see, hear, touch, whatever. Metaphysical retribution doesn't count as an extenuating circumstance. Juries want every story wrapped in a bow, because they're spoiled by how it works on TV. But I know after forty some years of doing this, the real truth isn't always what you see, hear, and touch. Sometimes getting where you need to be isn't the logical outcome of dialectical discourse."

"Do you have a point, Lieutenant?" asked Julie. "Other than impressing us that you know a big word?"

"Just ride with me here."

"Where?"

"I don't know. We'll see. Nick, you're a ballplayer …"

"Was."

"No. You're a ballplayer. I remember seeing you when I took my granddaughter to see The Golden Flashes play Ball State some years ago. I think you played short. For sure I saw you play last year when you took out that seagull. You know, I *wanted* to call it a dinger because no way that ball was getting run down, but the Rules say it's a ground-rule double. So that's the way I had to call it. You follow me?"

Nick didn't reply. Kept his head down against the cold wind and continued his careful walk on the slippery drive to the Caprice.

Sikorski, annoyed, lifted his cane and tapped Nick on the shoulder, stopping him.

"Really. Lieutenant. What is your point?" said Julie.

"That ground-rule double call was black and white. But there's other situations where the rules aren't so clean. Ambiguity, which leads to subjective judgment, can become determinative. For instance, Nick, tell me, at the conclusion of any given play on the bases, a runner is either gonna be safe or out, am I right?"

Nick stared at the geese.

"Asked you a question, Nick."

"Yeah. I guess."

"Well I can't guess. Say you're playing short, and a right-handed batter slices a rope down the right field line and it kisses the chalk—should be an automatic two-bagger. Except you know your right fielder's got a cannon, and you know the hitter is a two-hundred-and-forty-pound catcher who can't run worth shit. And you also know that the catcher's an ass can, the kind of prick who every time you've been at the dish has been busting your balls about your mom's sex life. And you know why; he's trying to mess with your concentration. But you ignore him because you're zoned in on the pitcher and what he's gonna throw because you've already stroked two hits, which only pissed the catcher off more, so now you know he's gonna come into you at second with his spikes high."

"This is utterly fascinating," said Julie.

Sikorski ignored her. "So you go to the bag, you yell for the second baseman not to cut because you know the right fielder's hanging the ball to you on a clothesline and you've got a shot. The catcher and the ball are gonna get there about the same time, so you block the bag with your right leg as you stretch for the throw and swipe tag the sonofabitch across his face just as he spikes you in the knee. You feel the blood and know you're looking at stitches as soon as you're off the field. But for the briefest of instants, the ball was in your glove when it made contact with his mug while your back foot was still on the bag. But the ball dribbles out just as you're reaching for it. Now, there's no cameras, no super frame-by-frame slo-mo replay. The base ump's maybe an old guy trying to make a buck to supplement his Social or a kid who's saving up for college or an herb. Whatever, he's wearing blue so he's gotta make a call. So what's the call gonna be?"

"What he saw," said Nick.

"What he *thinks* he saw." Sikorski resumed his careful limp to the Caprice, his prisoners on either side of him.

"I'm still waiting for a point," said Julie.

"The point, my dear, is … Aaaggghhh!"

Which was the sound Sikorski made as his cane lost traction on the slick gravel and he fell toward the wintery-hard ground.

To Nick, it looked like Sikorski was going down in super slo-mo, frame-by-frame. Although he was cuffed with his hands in front of him, Nick dove to make the play. The play being breaking Sikorski's fall.

Which he completed. Sikorski landed on Nick's back and rolled off grunting, but unhurt. Nick, however, had just taken two hundred and ten pounds of Sikorski on his fusion. He yelled as that familiar sharp stab from Devil Pain said, *Hi, remember me?*

Julie watched helplessly; all she could do was flail with her cuffed hands at a bunch of air.

Detective Corbin ran out onto one of the balconies of Muscat's mansion, her face flushed with the sharp bite of the cold afternoon wind. She shouted, "Lieutenant! You okay?"

Sikorski got back up in slow arthritic stages. He steadied himself, reached down, and with everything he had, pulled Nick to his feet.

"Thanks," Sikorski croaked, trying to catch a breath.

"Lieutenant?" cried Corbin as she started down the steps toward them.

"Stop! I'm fine. Go back inside, Detective, and wait for the techs."

Detective Corbin, unsure, hesitated. "Shouldn't I—"

"No, you should make sure CSI arrives to a crime scene as virginal as a novitiate on her first day. Thank you, Detective." Sikorski brushed slush off Nick's jacket. "You okay?"

"Yeah. I've fallen on it before. You get used to it."

"Jesus, Nick. You didn't have to do that. For him?"

"He could've broken his hip."

"So what?"

"Yeah, well, I appreciate it, son. That was a gutsy move. But I still gotta bring you guys in and hold you for Involuntary Manslaughter on Muscat, scum that he was."

"You should've let him break his damn hip," said Julie.

"I'm sorry, both of you. I am. But that's how I saw the play."

"Christ. You could've arrested us without the long and pointless baseball metaphor, Lieutenant," said Julie.

"Sorry, Toffoli, it was my way of working through it. Look, promise not to run off, and I'll uncuff you for the ride. It'll be a little easier, especially for him."

Julie shook her head in disgust. "Like where's he going to go?"

Mixed in with the white noise of the nearby Chagrin River gushing to Lake Erie, there was the distant honking of another skein of geese. Flying north ten thousand feet above the three small figures below.

*   *   *

Nick and Julie were once again cuffed, but this time to each other; an attachment as inevitable as breathing. But for how long, Julie wondered? They were alone on one of the slatted backless benches in a barren holding tank, a dank empty room, which smelled of stale sweat and bad choices. Julie couldn't help but think about how they got there. Once upon a time, she and Nick had been like everyone else who bought into the mythology that if you believed, that if you worked hard enough, your dreams and aspirations would come true. But now, their dreams were no longer theirs, snatched away by a capricious universe, a cosmic jokester they never saw coming.

She tried to move her cuffed hands a bit, but realized Nick had fallen asleep against her shoulder; one of those rare, fickle moments when the invisible weights on his eyelids forced them closed and his body gave in to its need for regeneration, as fitful and brief as the moment might be. So Julie kept her cuffed and sore hands still, ignored the chafing pain as she rebuked her gone-rogue mind for wondering what might have—no, what *should* have been. Which inevitably led to wondering where and how the rest of their lives would play out from here. From this bench, no place good. Separate cells in separate prisons, to be sure. In separate but similar states. States of despair and disillusion, to be self-pitying about it. Well, screw it. Cue the violins. How else was she supposed to feel?

The answer was it didn't matter because Life-As-Planned was over for them, obligatory as the final shot of a doomed couple in some old black-and-white French film noir, flawlessly framed heartbreak: their punishment for having the vanity to dream.

From another room, behind a closed door, voices indistinctly murmured, phones jarringly rang. No ringtones here, just Old-School strident bells that wouldn't have been out of place in a good old *Policier Américain*. The American noir where Sikorski would've been played by fellow Clevelander Brian Donlevy; no discussion of American film noir would be complete without mentioning tough-guy actor Brian Donlevy, who often played hardnosed cops, sometimes with a faintly discernible heart. Well, Sikorski wasn't Brian Donlevy; Sikorski was a poser, a third-rate throwback, with about a third of the brains of the blacklisted Hollywood scriptwriters who'd pseudonymously laid bare their despair on the blank page. And despair was never a good beginning, just an inescapable end.

The door opened. Sikorski limped in, ten-year-old flip phone held in the crook between his neck and ear. Julie thought he mumbled something like, *"Yeah, I'll try; that's all I can do,"* before snapping it closed. One hand gripped his tasteless cane, the other clutched a couple of Dave's Market plastic bags. His white overgrown crewcut was damp, as if he had run his hands through it with tepid water from the sink in the men's room.

Nick felt the disturbance in the air and woke up. He looked around, for the moment not registering where he was, but bit his lip as he remembered.

Julie said, "We both need to take medications, Lieutenant."

"I thought that might be the case."

Sikorski reached into one of the plastic bags and emerged with their pill bottles; he placed them on a wooden table marked by decades of despair and defiance carved onto every available surface. He limped over and reached for Nick's arm to help him up. Julie ignored Sikorski's proffered hand, yanked Nick up with her cuffed hands and walked with him to the table, where they crumpled onto a bench. Sikorski shrugged—*okay, fine by me*—and helped himself to the bench across from them.

"What? Do you need to watch, Lieutenant?" said Julie. "Afraid we're going to go all Romeo and Juliet on you so you don't get your promotion for arresting Cleveland's Most Wanted?"

"No more promotions for me. What'd I tell you back in the cafeteria when we first met, when you still seemed to give a damn, about this being my last case?"

"*We* are your last case? We weren't even on your radar back then. You were looking for Trout. And some runaway, remember?"

"I do. I still am. Do you know where she is?"

"No. See, we're here with you."

"That you are. How are you feeling, Nick?"

"Thanks for asking, Lieutenant," said Julie. "But we don't need any new friends."

"Yeah, well, I suspect you two will have thousands of them when news of Muscat's demise hits."

"What do you care?" said Nick, more alert, present.

"It's his job, remember?"

"No. Whatever you may believe, Toffoli, it's more than that. Do you see me shedding tears? You saw me serve his ass with a lawsuit at the ballgame."

Julie was in no mood, no mood at all, to cut the old cop any slack. "Aw, what happened? The evil medical-industrial complex Eisenhower warned us about failed to cure your old-man arthritis? No, wait—that was the military-industrial complex. My bad. Guess you're going to have to get used to that limp. Get your hip replaced, maybe a knee or two. Better hope the medical devices they jam in you aren't contaminated because of poor quality control. I would hate to see you get an infection and go into fatal septic shock. I can already see the motorcycle cortege featuring every Harley-fetishizing cop in Ohio; they'll shoot their rifles in the air and scare the Canadian geese and, in a week or three, everyone will forget who you were, outside of the missus. And possibly your dog."

"I don't have a dog. And you're too young to be a cynic, young lady. Cynicism needs time to be accumulated. Earned. And no, this isn't a so-called old-man limp. Happened when I was twenty-seven. I fell off an icy roof trying to rescue my little girl's three-legged cat."

"Bet she's forever grateful," said Julie.

"I wouldn't know. She's dead. You can ask Jimmy Tom Muscat about that. No, wait. You can't. Thanks to you guys, he's burning in the fires of everlasting Hell. At least, one can hope there is such a place, not just the hell we inhabit."

Julie and Nick exchanged a look. Nick said, "What? Is this some kind of new interrogation technique? Good cop, gooder cop? Empathy for the accused?"

"Wasn't that a Stones song, Nick? My Dad had it on vinyl."

"You're thinking of 'Sympathy for the Devil,'" said Sikorski. "And I don't have either one for Muscat. Empathy or sympathy. You might as well know I believe *Raven*, as you call her, is my dead daughter's kid. Runaway, two years now. Her real name is Kimberly Davinow. That is, if I'm correct that it's her. And everything in my cop's gut tells me I am."

"What happened to your daughter?" asked Julie. She couldn't help but ask. It was as if her internal hard drive had crashed and the screen had gone black, but now was glimmering back to life. Despite banging on the Escape key, she was re-setting to the factory-default Julie. In the start-up flickering of that screen, Julie allowed herself to wonder who she was becoming—or who she had become. Answer: ultimately, she was still Julie. This reboot was measured in nanoseconds—the time it took to ask Sikorski about his late daughter.

"She died of colorectal cancer. Thirty-six-years old."

"I'm sorry, Lieutenant."

"Yeah, well, the doctors they were all sorry, too. But not all that much. At least, most of them."

"That's not fair. It's the disease that's not fair. Doctors … most of them do care. They're under tremendous—"

"Don't talk to me about tremendous pressure and don't talk to me about fair. First guy Karen saw was some smug EZ♥Care-approved internist who thought Karen was a little hysterical. You know how women get? Neurotic housewives? Always on the rag? He gave her some anti-depressants and Tramadol and told her to check back in three months. But her gut still hurt, so the next guy from EZ♥Care, a gastroenterologist, threw a dart and guessed Irritable Bowel Syndrome. A bland diet, some Bentyl combined with Klonopin oughta clear things up. I mean, Karen was in the middle of a divorce from the *jabroni* who got me this stupid cane. And you know how women have a hard time coping with stress."

Julie didn't rise to the bait, instead played it like a quarterback going through progressions, or a doctor gaming the possibilities. "Why didn't the GI just cut to the chase and give her a scan? Those kinds of cancers are usually curable if treated early."

"Yeah well, the third schmuck did give her the scan. I mean by that point, *someone* fucking had to. If the first guy ordered it, maybe they would have caught the Beast in time. I don't know that, but I'd like to think she might've had a shot. But you know how it goes. From day one, none of them would listen to a complete sentence out of Karen's mouth—instead they'd cut her off after five words and treat her by algorithm. You know the EZ♥Care 'guidelines,' Toffoli? About two seconds after Muscat's bitch, Josh Przybylowicz, was made CEO, he adopted them at Cleveland Mercy: eight minutes of 'face time' per patient, so the docs can make their thirty-patient quota for the day. So who has time to really *listen*? What Marie and I saw with Karen was a series of gender-based judgments: that's the correct jargon, right? But when every 'Let's try this for a few weeks' fix turned into a couple of months of *not* fixed—no, not fixed at all—everything changed and there was a whole chorus line of white coats, tap dancing and shufflin' their feet like The Four Step Brothers and their 'Eight Feet Of Rhythm' live on the EZ♥Care main stage, except they weren't twirling top hats and clickety-clacketing their way to the Big Finish. No, they were stumbling and tripping all over each other in their rush to get out of the spotlight, as they needed to pass her off to the 'Exact Right Guy For This,' or 'The Best We Have.' Well, that's how we found ourselves in a mahogany wood-paneled office on the twelfth floor—the VIP floor—listening to another kind of specialist, an oncologist, who spoke slow and solemn like an undertaker pricing coffins. This fuck used phrases like *'Fighting chance'* and *'Advanced Directives'* and finally *'Putting affairs in order.'* He might as well have been wearing a cowl and carrying a scythe. But it turned out he was just the warm-up act for a new troupe of headliners whose act was to dole out scintillas of hope while bleeding us of every fungible asset we had. Karen was a goner; we all knew it by then, but we didn't want to believe it. Who would want to? Who *could?* She was thirty-six fucking years old and I was still paying off her student loans. Whatever … the important thing was: the racket that kept Jimmy Tom Muscat in putting greens and killer Bluetooth sneakers was those last somber fucks. Stage Four? No, more like Stage Green. In human terms, kind of a bummer, but Stage Four cancer is the real rainmaker. They gave Karen three months. Scared the shit out of her, and of course scared the shit out of Marie and me. So we did whatever they told us, no matter how useless, no matter what the cost was, whether financial, physical, or to our hearts. First there was the chemo, then the chemo *cocktails* because who can stop at just one? No sir, no closing time at the EZ♥Care Watering Hole. Open 24/7. The friendly bartender topped them off with bottomless radiation shooters. And when Karen finally stumbled out of that dive, just down the block there were the last-ditch All-You-Can-Eat-Never-Say-Die '*Experimental Trials.*' The ones that came with the '*Unknown*' side effects, which begat more tumors, which begat more surgeries. Let me count the body parts: lymph nodes, guts, brain. Wherever the Beast wanted to go, those heroes chased after it, cutting off its tail, except the Beast was like a fuckin' lizard, the tail always grows back, right? After sixteen months my little girl looked like a pin cushion. She wanted to die, but she wouldn't. Because Karen didn't want to lose Kimmy … *Raven* … or whatever the poor kid now calls herself."

"God," whispered Nick.

"God got nothing to do with it. If he wasn't too busy picking sides in football games or letting wars play out, maybe he would've paid attention. Maybe there wouldn't have been so many of those days when Karen came home from the latest 'Trial' of some voodoo drug, crying her guts out because she was *burning* from the inside out; yeah, *that* three-grand-a-month wonder drug was the one that caused the soles of her feet and the palms of her hands to turn black from heat. Karen couldn't walk and she couldn't turn a doorknob without screaming like she was being tortured in her own personal hell. Toward the end, she could only walk across a room on her *fucking knees*. Took ten minutes to get ten feet. I think the one and only good day Karen had, was the day she closed her eyes for the last time. Only thing, by then, Kimmy had bolted without leaving a forwarding address. The cheerleading, student council president, perfect kid—my granddaughter who I taught how to drive a stick—couldn't handle it anymore; she was sixteen years old and she was gone."

Sikorski banged his cane on the floor, hard. "And now, after two years of wondering what kind of life's horrors she fled to, what kind of evil's chewed her up, I'm guessing she's in that hospital, of all places. Helping people for free. Living god-knows-where." He took a deep breath, pulled it together. "I think they call that irony."

"I am so sorry."

"Yeah, everybody's sorry. I had no leads on her whereabouts, until I met you."

"That's bullshit."

Sikorski flared like a match striking the wall of a black cave.

Julie quickly snuffed that angry flame out.

"No! That's not what I meant. Not at all. What EZ♥Care did to your daughter was bullshit. Me, I thought becoming a doctor would be the best way to live a life. For *me* to live a life. Because a good doctor needs to be like Sherlock Holmes, like you probably were before *you* got cynical. When you were the guy who discovered the clue the rest overlooked or took for granted. Well, that's what becoming a doctor was going to be like for me. I wasn't going to practice medicine by algorithm, by shortchanging the patient with my time or my brain. No. I was determined to figure out what my colleagues couldn't—what the online medical journals, who, after two months with their links already obsolete, couldn't—not fall back on the throw-shit-against-a-wall moneymaking tests, endless meds, or the value judgments of a patient's worth. The value judgments of a patient's *moral* worth. No, that wasn't the way I was going to do it. Because if you don't treat each human being as if they're worth something, you're worth nothing yourself." Julie looked at the scarred table and said softly, "But as you know, I can't do that anymore."

"You know that's crap, Julie."

"Maybe you're right, Nick. You keep saying it often enough. But this little therapy session is irrelevant. Isn't it, Lieutenant? Let's get it over with. Process us. Our TV plays cop shows all night long; I know how this works. Where's the matron who's going to stick her gloved fingers up my body cavities? One thing, though, just make sure they don't hurt Nick anymore. Will you do me that favor?"

Sikorski didn't answer. His expression, unreadable.

CHAPTER 39

Doki-Doki Mode

Deafening electronic J-Pop, booming bass, jackhammer drums, high-register SFX, and nonstop Japanese echoed through the candlelit basement operating theater three stories under Cleveland Mercy, where Tick and Raven, wired and bleary-eyed, riveted by another anime game, hunched forward on the springy old couch. An overnight debris-field of crunched cans of Red Bull and Snickers wrappers were strewn atop a swayback cigarette-burned ping-pong table; the two manipulated their haptic vibration-creating joysticks no less expertly than a pair of Navy drone pilots at an anonymous base outside Vegas who were blowing up a Taliban wedding in Kunduz. No collateral damage here, except to young brain cells.

The all-nighter had taken its toll on Raven, who rubbed a blood-shot eye. The thing about living like subterranean rats was that the concept of night and day became meaningless, except when it was time to pull a shift up in the hospital. Raven slumped back on the couch, a speed freak crashing into a wall of exhaustion.

"Hey," Tick whined. "Why'd you stop?"

"Because we've been playing for, like, ten straight hours. Dude, I'm tired."

"Not cool, Raves."

"That I'm falling asleep?"

"No, that you let me reach *Doki-Doki* Mode when I didn't earn it."

"Too bad. I'm crashing. You win."

As Raven powered down the game the realization something was wrong hit them both: the booming sounds of deep drills and jackhammer blasts continued to rock the old O.R. theater *after* the video game had ended. Reflections from the flickering candles danced across their faces like an encroaching forest fire; it felt like the entire third-level basement floor had become its own theme-park ride.

"Dude, do you *feel* this?"

Tick didn't answer. Instead, his gaze went to the ping-pong table where cans of Red Bull were jumping ship. The joystick fell from his hand.

"Raves? Is this an earthquake? Do they even have earthquakes in Cleveland? I thought seismic events only happened in LA or Sumatra. Or Japan. *Japan*! Do you think something *inside* the video game somehow caused—"

"Shut up, Tick!" she said, as the double doors to the theater banged open, further startling them. Jacinta appeared, smartly uniformed for her early AM shift upstairs in the hospital pharmacy, and it looked like she could use plenty of what they had up there because the look on her face was one of dread.

"What's going on?" asked Raven.

"The way out has disappeared. I was just there. Ashanti's turntable has been destroyed. Instead, they've built a floor-to-ceiling cement wall blocking our way to the elevator."

Tick began to shake. Raven grabbed him. Jacinta, herself shivering, leaned against the door frame for support. "We're entombed. And no one in the world knows it."

"Except Julie and Nick."

"And to state the obvious, they are long gone."

*   *   *

Julie and Nick, still in the holding pen, still cuffed together on the bench, were again alone. No other prisoners had joined them and the only sounds were the still-ringing phones and indistinct voices emanating from the adjacent room. Nick, asleep, occasionally mumbled something incomprehensible and one time even broke out laughing but just as quickly was again quiescent. Julie remained still, not wanting to move her cuffed hand and wake him. Her sore wrist had become downright painful and she wondered why Sikorski hadn't booked them yet, much less why he hadn't allowed them to call a lawyer. After his little therapy session, Sikorski fixed the two of them with that sphinx cop stare of his and left the room without saying anything else. Maybe he was a diabetic and needed a quick fix of Krispy Kremes. At this point though, Julie didn't care if Sikorski's blood sugar was being sucked up by a hypoglycemic alien cocooning deep within his intestines. *Que será.* No wonder Raven ran away.

What was Sikorski to her or Nick anyway? Nothing but another judgmental obstacle. As Julie began to kill time by making a mental list of who else their world could do without, the door was pushed open and, with some effort, Sikorski reentered the room. He placed more weight on the cane as he moved toward them. His face offered neither explanation nor warmth.

His actions, though, another thing, as he reached in his pocket for a key, uncuffed Nick from Julie and freed the dangling cuffs from her hand, which she shook to get blood flowing again.

"This way." He motioned for the two to follow him to the opposite door. However, Julie remained where she was and Nick stayed with her.

"No. First, we demand our phone call," said Julie. "We have a constitutional right to—"

"There's a pay phone out there." Sikorski opened the door, revealing not a cop bullpen but the main terminal to a bus station. The constant drone of voices punctuated by ringing phones, Julie and Nick's soundtrack for the last two hours, were all part and parcel of a functioning Greyhound bus station.

Nick blinked, trying to process what was in front of them. "Wait. You drove us to the police station—I saw it—and you put us in here. An annex, you said."

"It is, after a fashion. The police station proper is around the corner on Payne. Out there is the Greyhound terminal on Chester. In fact, my *dziadzia*, that's grandpop in Polish, helped build it back in '48. Thing of beauty, ain't she? Late art-deco in the Streamline Moderne style; was the final Greyhound designed by architect William Strudwick Arrasmith. I guess neither of you ever heard of him or give a shit but at one time he was a big deal and Cleveland had the most famous bus station in the country. Which means they'll soon tear it down, pave paradise and put up a parking lot. Well, fine, just as long as they do it after I'm croaked."

Nick persisted: "What have we been doing here then?"

"Waiting. I'm tight with management and they let us use this overflow waiting room for off-the-record conversations certain sworn officers of the law may want to have with certain citizens."

Sikorski's cell vibrated. He took it out of his coat, saw who it was, and tapped back a one-character reply.

"We still want our phone call," said Julie.

"To *who*, Toffoli? Here I was thinking you two weren't dim. I'll speak slowly; try to follow. The reason I kept you in this room is I had to make a few arrangements and, now that I have, what's gonna happen is I'm gonna put you two on a bus. Any bus. Your choice. Take it somewhere where you can start over. Make sure it's nowhere obvious. That also means get off of social media and stay off. It means toss your credit cards. Buy new cellphones. Buy new identities. Use what's in this."

This was a bulging manila envelope that Sikorski stuffed inside Nick's jacket.

"Nick. First, get your back better. Do your rehab exercises or whatever the hell your doctor here tells you to do. Be religious about it. Then I want you to use that degree in Health Administration to do something different other than separate sick people from their money and kick their asses out the door." He turned to Julie. "You. Go and be a doctor. That's what you are, yes? Good. Yeah, I'm aware of your condition: I was, from the first time I met you, and saw the cover of the book you were hiding. Yeah, I can read upside down. I bought a copy too, so I know the trade-off for longevity is kidney and bone toxicity and a bunch of unpleasant side effects; but more important, I know you'll still be able to do your job because you're smart, you're stubborn, and when you're done moping, you'll move mountains to complete your calling. I want to give you the chance to do that. Wherever that might be. Look at it this way, Life itself is one big side effect. Last, Toffoli: tell me where to find Kimmy. Or, if she prefers now, Raven. I give you my word all I'm going to do is talk to her. I will not make her do anything she doesn't want to do. I'm not doing this as a cop; I'm a *dziadzia* myself and I want, especially for Marie's sake, to have some peace of mind about our granddaughter. Besides, after today, I'm either retired or brought up on charges. Hopefully, I can skate the latter. I've dodged my way out of way worse situations since the last century and I still have some goodwill in this town. Also, I have Betsy Nguyen on my side, and how Betsy Nguyen goes, so does Cleveland."

"What do you have going on with Betsy Nguyen?" asked Nick, with perhaps a twinge of envy.

"I did her a favor once. Leave it at that." Sikorski glanced at his watch and said one word to Julie: "Kimmy?"

Julie scrutinized his craggy face, looking for a tell. She scoped the bus station for waiting SWAT teams ready to pounce on her and Nick. No SWAT. Unless they were disguised as indigent families, homeless, or servicemen passing through. She returned her look to Sikorski. "Why are you doing this?"

"You two aren't criminals, you're victims who stood up for yourselves. And on my last day carrying the shield I've done my best to honor forty-some years, I don't want my legacy bust to be you two. If I did, I'd be leaving you to the tender mercies of an ambitious DA who will not give a damn about anything else but framing a pair of trophies to his wall. I'd be spending the rest of the retirement Marie and I got planned not able to look in a mirror without seeing a sap whose last decision was chickenshit wrong."

"I'm still looking for a catch," said Julie.

"Jesus H. Christ." Sikorski looked to Nick. "What do you see in her?"

"Everything."

Nick placed a hand on Julie's shoulder. "Jules. There's a hundred grand in this envelope. Let's tell him what he needs to know and get out of here."

"Wait." She looked Sikorski in the eye. "I believe you. But I also believe you are giving us your retirement money. We can't take it."

A slow-growing grin, one of the first ever, at least the first ever seen by Julie, spread across Sikorski's face. "Tell me, Toffoli, do you think I'm crazy?"

Nick and Julie exchanged a glance but neither replied.

"I'll take that as a yes. But no, this isn't my retirement money. What it is, is some loose change I found in Muscat's desk drawer." Sikorski patted Nick's pocket where the envelope protruded. "Consider it your parting gift from EZ♥Care. And consider this—the next time you two are feeling invincible or stupid or both, besides the hundred G's, Muscat also had a Glock 19 in that drawer. Which means you can also consider yourselves friggin' lucky you snuck in there while he was exercising and not sitting behind his desk counting his money and calling one of the hookers I saw in his contacts. This dough is your stake. No one else knows about it. Not even Detective Corbin, who has spent the last two hours removing every vestige of your presence there. I'll thank her for you. She didn't have to play along."

"Thank you. Truly. But there's one more thing."

"You're in no position to be making any demands, Toffoli."

"Two things. Two people. Two kids. They live with Raven in the basement. They've got real jobs at the hospital. They work hard and have no place else to go. I don't know where they came from but it can't be anyplace good and if you run them through your computer, I'm sure their IDs will come up bogus. I want you to promise me, Lieutenant, that you won't put them into the System. Please leave them alone. They've had nothing—well, almost nothing—to do with any of this."

"That's it?"

Julie nodded.

"I'm not interested in them. Just tell me how to find Kimmy."

"Do you have a piece of paper? Better if I draw it."

Sikorski gave her his cop field notebook and the Number Two pencil that fitted in between the metal spirals just right. As Julie scribbled, Sikorski spoke to Nick in a low voice.

"I put my card in the envelope, along with the phone number of a guy who can help with the IDs. My cell is also on the back. Let me hear from you one of these years."

Nick nodded. *Okay. He would.*

Sikorski's phone buzzed. It was a text. He replied, one thumb at a time. Julie handed him back his notebook, noticed him texting, and defaulted to paranoid.

"Who are you texting?"

"My partner, who just drove that piece-of-shit Geo Metro out of Muscat's driveway and dumped it in the bottom of the lake. You okay with that?" He gestured them toward the Greyhound. "Now go. Good luck to both of you and don't disappoint yourselves."

CHAPTER 40

Thriller

Me, I didn't know where Nick and Julie went after they got on the bus, but I knew where I was going. I waited as a bunch of babbling docs and nurses banged out of the elevator, and then I got in. I made sure I was alone and pressed B-3, like Julie said, and took a deep breath as I felt myself dropping. Except the feeling I had was more like the anticipation I felt when me and my buddies were inching *up* on The Thriller, the old wooden coaster at Euclid Beach Park they closed down in '69. I think it was '69. I wasn't here; I was on a frigate in the South China Sea. Anyway, The Thriller would clack up the wooden slats so slow that halfway to the clouds your heart would already be in your throat because you knew any second you were going to be flying into a dizzying space of colors, the wind would be sucking the air out your of your cheeks, everybody would be screaming their lungs out, and you knew you were gonna die but somehow you never did. That ride was the best feeling ever.

Which was kind of how I was feeling right now, taking this slow boat down to B-3.

The elevator hit the bottom of the third level of the basement like a pallet of bricks dropped off a roof, sending an electric spike of pain up my spine. And to think Nick felt like that all the time.

In spades. Whatever. His story, at least my part in it, was over. I was here to see my granddaughter.

Except, when the elevator door opened, what I was looking at wasn't a mix of fake brick and drywall with a handprint on the bottom that you pushed and presto chango, the turntable swirled you into the basement—which was what Toffoli promised I'd see. No, what I was looking at was a fresh-painted, still wet, still smelling like someone cooked carrots in ammonia, solid concrete wall. From floor to ceiling, from side to side. No way anyone was going to get through that rock.

Shit. I couldn't believe, after all the gut spilling, Toffoli would lie to me. At least, lie to me over something so *personal*. But lie to me she did. Right to my face. Hell, she was better than Meryl Streep in that Abba movie Marie made me see. Where the hell was my never-wrong Artie Sikorski radar? My gut feeling that could always tell the difference between amateur lying sacks of shit, professional lying sacks of shit, or someone who was giving it to you straight? Fucking Toffoli. She and Nick, kids who once had it all in front of them for the taking. But what they took was me. They took from me my last bit of hope just like I took the hundred grand from Muscat, or whoever his undeserving heirs were. Except what Toffoli and Nick did was worse. The hell with the money; what they stole from me, after a career of looking at the dark side of people, was whatever capacity I had left to see anything different.

I stared at the shiny cement wall which was painted the color of an all-day sucker. Me.

I turned around, thinking what kind of plausible story to tell Marie, a story that still had the possibility of some kind of happy ending in it, when I heard this *tapping*.

From behind me.

I let the elevator go and walked to the cement wall and listened like a hungry owl trying to hear a mouse sneak across a barn on a moonless night.

And there it was again. *Tap tap tap.* Except it wasn't tapping, it was somebody or somebodies on the other side of the wall, and they were banging on it with what sounded like an iron pipe, or maybe just their bare fists.

I called out Raven's name. I called it out louder.

The tapping got louder.

*   *   *

The rain-dappled Greyhound pulled out of the bus station in Eau Claire—the terminal sharing space inside a MacDonald's, where they'd stopped for a ten-minute break and picked up another couple of passengers before rejoining westbound I-94. It was still late afternoon, but the headlights were on as the bus drove through a hilly area surrounded by clusters of pine and birch, fronted by copses of highway billboards advertising weekend gun shows, the upcoming Blue Ox Music Festival, and cheese. Lots of cheese.

Julie and Nick were seated in the two rear seats opposite the bathroom with the busted door that didn't close all the way, which accounted for a part of the rancid smell around them, but at least they had privacy. No one within four rows of them. The Egg McMuffin Julie wolfed down complemented their own fetid piece of Americana. She watched Nick, slumped in the window seat, enervated by this endless day of death, money, and a half-dozen Percs, dozing open-mouthed, wiped out from a long ago morning that began with tea with Aggie and Edie and extended to the execrable dead body of an execrable excuse for a human being, culminating with the intervention of a certifiable cop—bent as they come but at the same time as mushy as Aunt Eleanor's undercooked meatloaf—who granted them their freedom, along with a purloined hundred grand, and put them on this reeking bus to various points west. Julie washed down the McMuffin with a gulp from her high-alkaline-content water bottle, as if the ionized Icelandic Spring stuff would counteract the effects of the Yellow Dye Number 6 on the processed American cheese in the McMuffin, which, when she thought about it, was sacrilegious— what with them traveling through America's Dairyland and all.

She wondered if Nick could stay asleep; at least, till they reached Saint Paul.

*   *   *

I stood jammed against the back of the elevator car with a jittery Josh P beside me, like we were lined up to be executed. All that was missing was the last cigarette. In Josh's case, it would be an e-cigarette. The staccato reports resonating in front of us did sound like a firing squad. Except this one wore Hazmat suits. So did Josh and I. We stood behind them and watched the goggled-up, ear-plugged, and masked Cleveland Mercy maintenance guys undo their handiwork as they jack-hammered and sledge-hammered their way through the brand-new cement wall at B-3. A portable genny powered the standing lights that illuminated the yellow-tinged dust cloud. It soon got to the point where I couldn't see shit but it didn't matter because I knew I'd be seeing Kimmy soon enough.

I knew Josh P wasn't sharing in my excitement. Still, coming off like Geraldo Rivera finding jack in Al Capone's secret vault was way better for him than taking up residence in Capone's former cell in Alcatraz. Yeah, yeah, I know, Alcatraz is closed, but you get the idea. And so did Josh P when me and Debs braced his ass about an hour ago. The pit stains on his four-hundred buck Armani dress shirt spread like the Metroparks Zoo Flood as Debs put the flash drive in his computer and navigated him to the documents implicating him in Muscat's rip-off schemes. All his co-conspirators were now deceased, except for Demidova, who'd pawned various trinkets from Trout, jumped bail, and vanished to Vladivostok or wherever the hell she came from.[*]

After Josh envisioned decades of residency at the Ohio State Penitentiary, not to be confused with the university of a similar moniker and similar types of citizenry, he was quite receptive to my deal, which was, either he busts open his new wall in B-3, or I bust him.

My last official assignment was to find Trout. Done. My last unofficial assignment was to find Kimmy. Almost done. Just as soon as she came walking out from behind the rubble, I could call it a career.

By the by, Detective Deborah Delaney Corbin could call it a career too: the beginning of a helluva career. Tomorrow I'd be recommending her for a permanent slot in Homicide. Didn't matter her uncle was head of the Bureau of Special Investigations, Debs passed the Artemas Sikorski Detective Field Exam with flying colors. The major thing Debs nailed was the guiding principle of my entire career: *There's justice, then there's what's just.* Anything else was peppered milk gravy on a chicken-fried steak.

Debs got that.

Josh, he got it too. As he damn well shoulda, because the only other *request* I laid on him was simple. Just give those kids who'd been living in the basement a rent-free, three-bedroom apartment

---

[*] For the record, I ain't buying the official story that Klepstein and Ganapur were eaten by a runaway tiger named Lloyd. No offense to Karachi's finest, but what self-respecting carnivore would deign to eat those rancid quacks? Whatever, Karachi wasn't my beat. Cleveland was.

in the building across the street that Cleveland Mercy owned, the apartment complex with a gym, heated indoor pool, restaurant, and movie theater. The building where they stashed all the nurses and doctors he recruited from out of state, and when I say out of state, I mean way out of state, since most of the nurses and doctors were assorted foreigners on rather dubious visas. Upshot, the kids (and Kimmy, if she wanted) got the apartment, plus they got to keep their jobs. Along with a twenty-five percent raise.

Oh yeah, Josh also agreed to open a Free Clinic as an adjunct to Cleveland Mercy. A place where anyone who needed help could get it. Especially at-risk youths. Josh said no problem, he'd break ground right away. Like in two weeks. I told him to call Betsy Nguyen and give her an exclusive; announce he's personally donating one million dollars of his own bank. If he played it right, she'd have him coming off like the Albert Schweitzer of Cleveland.*†

It was amusing to see Josh P roll over like a slobbering Saint Bernard at the Westminster Kennel Club after the judge squeezed his balls. Still, got to hand it to him; Josh had no problem signing a perpetual lease for the Free Clinic. Hell, what with all I had on him, he would've signed away his own mother to the Du Roc Crips.

Wait. All this yakking in my head, and I didn't notice how quiet it suddenly got. The yellow smoke hung like an inversion layer of smog as three dust-covered figures appeared out of the haze. They stood on the other side of where the wall used to be, like statues nailed to the floor. They reminded me of those poor people from 9-11, the ones who stumbled out of that hell looking like ghosts.

One of *these* ghosts was Kimmy.

* Yeah, I knew all this was a bit more than I promised Julie, but I knew she and Nick would appreciate it.
† Google Schweitzer. I don't have time to explain everything; Kimmy was about to be freed.

I'd know her anywhere.

I ripped the plugs out of my ears, tore the goggles off my face, and pushed my way past Josh, past the light-stands, bumped past the workers who were picking up the rebar, and limped as fast as my cane could propel me to Kimmy. She looked at me kinda dazed but I didn't care. I dropped my stick into the debris and grabbed her shoulders with both my hands.

"Sweetheart, me and Marie, we missed you so much. Thank God you're okay."

The smoke was clearing a bit and I could see her dark-brown eyes searching my face. I could see confusion in them. Of course, it was understandable, having been through what she and her two pals had experienced, the terror of being left to rot away without anyone ever knowing.

To this day, what happened next still blows my mind, like when I was six years old and I was sitting on our front stoop bouncing my Spaldeen up and down, waiting for my Pops to come home from his shift at Republic Steel, 'cause he promised when he got home he'd take me to the candy store as a reward for the first (and probably last) "A" I got on some first-grade test, the highlight of my academic life, when all of a sudden, *there he was*. Standing at the end of the block, his clothes streaked with grime, face blackened with soot. I ran to him, my thin cotton shorts stuck to my little pencil legs on a humid September day, and I jumped up and hugged him and laughed and kissed him until I looked into his eyes and saw, behind all the soot, the guy wasn't my Pops after all, it was Mr. Davis who lived in 2-B. No. Wasn't my Pops at all.

Just like the girl I was hugging now wasn't Kimmy.

I wanted to tear my heart out. I guess I wasn't the detective I thought I was. Because Kimmy didn't have dark-brown eyes. Never had. Kimmy's eyes were deep blue.

Wait. Unless she was wearing brown contacts …

No, she told me. She didn't wear contacts or glasses and her eyes had been brown all her life.

Oh my God, this girl who I had just wrapped my arms around wasn't Kimmy. She didn't have the eyes of her mother, my Karen; she didn't have Karen's face; she wasn't the beautiful little girl I used to take to Jacobs Field to see Cliff Lee throw his unhittable cutter. No, this ghost standing before me, scared and shaking, wasn't the granddaughter I'd been searching for these long and painful last two years.

And, as if to clinch that brilliant deduction, she pushed away a tear or two from her dust-painted face and asked me if it was okay if she could call her mom.

Her mom in Kirtland.

Of course, it was okay. The three of them could do anything they wanted to do. After all, that's the deal I made with Josh P and I was going to stick by it.

I suppose where it all got screwed up in the first place was back in the cafeteria when I showed Toffoli the high school picture of Kimmy, and with her doctor's eye she *looked* for a similarity. In retrosight, Toffoli scanned the pic like she *wanted* to find a similarity. And probably, because of the sad-sack story I told her at the bus station, she felt bad for me and told me what she thought I wanted to hear. Hell, I'm sure Toffoli believed it herself. After all, the photo I showed her was a couple of years old, from high school, color fading, and Kimmy was just a sophomore. But if you looked real hard there *was* a resemblance between the two girls. You couldn't tell the eyes were a different color. I woulda made the same mistake if I didn't know any better.

And I *did* know better.

Still, I invited the three dust devils over for a shower, a place to flop if they wanted. I told them I'd get them some clothes, Marie would make a home-cooked meal. Her special *gulasz*. I even promised the squirrely kid with the twitch he wouldn't have to tolerate cooked carrots touching his peas.

I didn't even *want* to know what the hell that was about.

As I watched them walk to the elevator, Jacinta, Tick, and ... Raven ... I couldn't help but think retirement would give me a lot of extra time. And since I had a functioning flip phone, plenty of shoe leather, and what remained of my brain, I knew one of these days I would find Kimmy. I'd find her for Marie, for Karen, and myself. And I wouldn't rest until I did.

PART FIVE

Two Years Later

CHAPTER 41

Nowhere Obvious

A covered ATV weaved like an ant through sugar as it down-shifted on a snowy trail approaching a small community of a dozen or so cabins. A layer of caribou skins was latched to vertical aluminum poles, which gave the occupants of the ATV some protection against the elements, which today was just the cold, the stubborn late-spring cold. The ATV slowed in front of the last cabin on the outskirts, a more expansive building than the others, but like the others it had a sloped corrugated iron roof and was on stilts. Framed behind this isolated community were groves of Western hemlock and Sitka spruce, which thinned as they ran up against the Great Alaskan Range many, many miles in the distance.

A Yupik man and woman, wearing caribou-hide coats, wolf-fur hats, and whale-skin boots, exited the ATV. The woman held a blanket-swathed infant close as they walked past another ATV parked in front of the structure and took the steps up to the door. From somewhere, a pair of Malamutes barked, but their hearts weren't in it. There was a red medical cross on the weather-beaten door. Although painted only two years ago, the cross was already fading. One had to know it was there.

Seated at a homemade wooden desk behind a counter, wearing

thick glasses, was a twenty-year-old Yupik named Amliqq, although she was known as Elisabeth. Like most of the Yupik in the area, she preferred using an Anglo name. Elisabeth looked up from an antique nineties desktop with a CRT monitor as the couple with the baby entered. She removed her glasses and asked in Yupik what the problem was, but quickly realized she didn't need the details as the Yupik woman held out the baby for examination. The little girl, four months old, was feverish and trembling. Elisabeth told them to have a seat on the plastic chairs in the waiting area and she hurried into an inner office. The waiting area was stocked with a few toys for the kids and a stack of well-thumbed magazines; except these doctor office periodicals weren't the requisite *Entertainment Weekly*'s or *People*'s, but old issues of *Mother Jones*, *The Nation*, and *Cat Fancy*—upon which sat a fancy tabby, licking her paw and wiping it across her striped forehead.

The headline on the *Nation* had to do with how Trump was ignoring a new virus from China. Called it some kind of hoax. The subhead had to do with some passengers testing positive on a cruise ship. All this, far, far away from here.

The inner office was filled with books, just about all of them thick, medical, and fighting for shelf space. Dr. Julie Toffoli's nose was close into one that had the word Orthopedics on the cover. Even with two sweaters under a lab coat, she sat, freezing, as she inputted notes into an iPad, when Elisabeth entered the room. Julie looked up from the book. The remarkable thing, among many remarkable things, was that the last two years had turned her into Julie again. Her light-brown hair had grown out and was pulled up into a top knot and the oversize raspberry glasses had been dumped at a bus stop in Chilliwack, British Columbia, a stop on the Trans-Canada Highway. With a stethoscope around her neck, Julie pretty much looked like she did back at Cleveland Mercy. Just a little older and a lot colder.

"Liz. What's up?"

"A baby with a high fever."

Julie put down the book and went to a sink to wash her hands. In the middle of her thorough wash, the cell on her desk vibrated and skidded along the well-worn wood. Julie glanced at it but because her hands were cleansed couldn't touch it. She left it on her desk. Elisabeth slipped on a glove and took the phone with her as she followed Julie out the door.

* * *

The sign on the wall above the exam table in Room Number One read:

FULL DISCLOSURE

I AM HIV POSITIVE.

BUT I POSITIVELY WILL NOT INFECT YOU

OR YOUR LOVED ONES. THANK YOU, DR. JULIE

Both mother and father masked apprehension as they watched a gloved-and-masked Julie concentrating on the baby's heartbeats through the stethoscope. The only other sound in the room was the crinkling of the exam paper as every now and then Julie would change the baby's position.

Elisabeth, standing just behind Julie, explained, "They say she has stopped breathing at least ten times since yesterday."

"How long do these incidents last?"

Elisabeth asked the parents and translated their answer. "Sometimes twenty-five or thirty seconds."

"Does she gasp or choke?"

Julie didn't wait for Elisabeth to translate, instead acted it out for the parents, who gestured yes and began trading off sentences to Elisabeth who relayed the information back to Julie.

"They don't know what to do. She is their first child."

"Diarrhea?"

The mother indicated yes.

Julie thought aloud. "Lucy was born in the thirty-fourth week, right?"

"Yes," said Elisabeth, chart in hand.

"Six weeks early. Apnea of prematurity?" Julie wondered to herself. Then to Elisabeth: "Ask if she vomits after eating."

Lucy's mother understood. "Yes."

Julie turned to Elisabeth, "Weight loss?"

Elisabeth looked at Lucy's chart. "Fourteen ounces since the last visit, three weeks ago. She's twelve pounds, fifteen ounces."

"Okay." Julie checked off the symptoms and her options. As she did so, her cell, which Elisabeth had brought in with her and placed on a shelf, vibrated once again. Julie, working through a decision, continued to ignore it. She turned to Elisabeth.

"Tell them Lucy is going to have to spend the night. I need to stay up with her and monitor respiratory function, heart rate, and pulse oximetry. Of course, they can both stay as well. Let's begin Lucy on 100 milligrams of amoxicillin every eight hours and prepare an injection of a low dose intranasal corticosteroid. Meantime, ask Mrs. Kashatok to keep Lucy's head raised for two hours after she nurses. They can make themselves at home in Exam Two. Bring in a couple of cots. Is that okay with them?"

The parents got most of it even as Elisabeth translated.

"Yes, we will stay. Thank you, Doctor Julie," said the mother.

"Of course."

As Julie squeezed Mom's hand, she reacted to the cell vibrating once again. Mrs. Kashatok picked up Lucy, and Julie, the cell. Five texts had come in since the family's arrival. "Excuse me," said Julie and exited the exam room.

She hurried down a narrow hallway toward a door with a sign that read "CLINIC MANAGER." She opened it and charged inside, calling.

"Nick?"

"Jules."

A pretty much unrecognizable Nick, with almost two years of beard and an unpruned growth of long, uncombed, sweat-matted hair, was sprawled on the floor and, even though buried in multiple blankets, he was drenched and his face was flushed with fever. His cellphone lay next to him.

"Why aren't you in bed?"

"Too soft. The floor is better."

"And colder."

"Coulda fooled me. Jules, I'm burning up."

"Stupid question? But where does it hurt the most?"

"Where it should hurt the least." Nick shivered and pulled the blankets up to his eyes.

"Nick. This is Day Five now and my special combo plate of Vancomycin and Clindamycin hasn't made a dent in this infection. You may have the opioid tolerance of an elephant but toughing this out is no longer an option. No way around it, sweetheart, something's going on with your fusion and you need an MRI."

Just those three letters, it wasn't even a word, brought a shudder to him. He tried to joke it off. "Yeah, but we don't have one."

"No, but the regional hospital does. I'm calling Regis and getting you medevacked down there right now."

"You're not coming?"

379

"Of course I am. But not till tomorrow morning. A preemie with a serious breathing issue just came in."

"Lucy Kashatok?"

"Yeah. I need to stay up with her all night, and you needed that MRI yesterday. I shouldn't have put it off."

The beard and hair and blankets obscured everything except Nick's eyes. They had the wary, frightened, and angry look of a bear caught in a trap. Julie lay down next to him. She ran her hand through his sweat-saturated hair. She kissed him on the cheek. A hand emerged from under the blanket and Julie put it in hers.

"Nick, I can't leave this baby."

"I know. Don't worry, I'll be fine."

Julie kissed him. "I'll see you tomorrow morning. I promise."

*   *   *

The evening sun reflected off the silver skis fitted on the bottom of the Cessna 208 as it ceded contact with the Earth and flew towards the low-slung clouds.

On the ground, Julie stood alone at the edge of the landing strip. She couldn't see the plane any longer, but she still could hear it. After the engine sounds dissipated into the wind and the Malamutes' distant barking took over, Julie turned and plodded through the snow back to the village and her clinic, a quarter of a mile away.

Only now, with the panoramic overview of the outpost she and Nick called home: the landing strip, the snow-covered meadow, the river on one side bordered by a grove of Yellow Alaskan cedars, and finally the village itself in the far distance with the mountain range beyond, was it plain Nick and Julie had settled at the remote outpost featured in the television exposé of the illegal "sports" hunts that she and Nick had watched, sickened, in his hospital room after the spinal fusion back at Cleveland Mercy.

Another lifetime ago.

Since Julie and Nick had migrated to the Great White North, there had been only one other such illicit hunt in their new home. And that hunt was over before it began, aborted by the waiting presence of Alaska Fish and Game officers along with State Police, acting on an anonymous tip from Julie and Nick. Those rich dilettantes who so enjoyed mugging for the camera with their arms around their slaughtered trophy animals—the creatures who were the lifeblood and sustenance of the indigenous Yupik—were, after a cycle of media shaming plus payment of massive fines and restitution, sent packing back to Texas where they were reduced to massacring pen-raised quail while at the same time trying to avoid—with the notable exception of a former vice-president—shooting one another in their beer-soaked grills.

* * *

Julie reclined on a patched ottoman in Exam Room One. A colorful handwoven blanket was draped around her shoulders. She had one eye on the book she was reading, a dog-eared textbook titled *Pediatric Resuscitation: A Practical Approach,* and the other on little Lucy in the adjacent bassinet. Lucy had stabilized, her breathing had slowed a bit and the fever had gone down incrementally.

Yet.

Yet, the baby still seemed fitful, every once in a while, startling Julie with a heartbreaking cry.

Adjacent to the exam table, just in case, was a blue crash cart. Julie didn't even want to go there, as no matter how much time had passed, no matter that Charlie's death at Cleveland Mercy wasn't her fault, she still couldn't, still wouldn't get the Code Blue out of her mind. Nor would she ever. Julie had asked Elisabeth to bring in the cart and have it ready *after* Lucy's parents had gone to bed in Exam Room 2.

Elisabeth didn't second guess Julie about the crash cart even though she thought it was a bit paranoid. She owed Julie more than unquestioned constancy; she felt she owed Julie everything she had or ever would have for giving her the chance to learn from her, and not only that, the promise of a loan to help attend the University of Alaska at Anchorage and after that, unthinkable as it sounded for a rural Yupik girl, medical school. Elisabeth would be the first from her village to even contemplate going to university. No, Elisabeth would never second guess Julie.

* * *

Eleven in the evening. Julie's cell buzzed. Nick, Julie was told via email from Kika, a night shift RN at the regional hospital, had his MRI and was asleep in a room. He was being pumped full of strong antibiotics and doing better. Julie had made the right call medevacking him down. Also, Julie needn't rush as the results wouldn't even be seen by an orthopedist until tomorrow afternoon soonest as the doctor was still en route. Julie thanked her, and wrote she'd be there by mid-morning.

Julie's buddy, Regis, daredevil medevac pilot, who'd had his leg saved by Julie last year after a violent landing in a whiteout snowstorm, was coming back for her at first light. As far as Regis was concerned, anything Julie needed was on the house. In fact, when Regis had picked Nick up the previous afternoon, he'd proposed to Julie that he drop Nick out the door at ten-thousand feet so the two of them could live happily ever after. Anything for her. Julie laughed and reminded Regis he was already happily married, concurrently to three different women, and had eleven children. Regis shrugged it off and said, "So you're saying I have a chance?"

Julie laughed in her sleep and opened her eyes. It was six in the morning and Elisabeth was standing over her, holding a cooing little Lucy, who had made a remarkable turnaround.

"Oh no. I …"

"You fell asleep," Elisabeth said. "I thought you would, so I let you. You needed it. I watched Lucy the rest of the night. The good news is she had zero non-breathing episodes and the better news is her fever broke, and the best news is Regis just radioed and will be here in twenty minutes to take you down to Nick."

* * *

The clock in the O.R. read 6:15 AM. The heavy vibrato of Native-Canadian Buffy Sainte-Marie crooning how she wanted to be a country girl again emanated from a boom box on a shelf. It drowned out the soft, indecipherable murmuring of a duo of surgical assistants as they prepped the O.R. Scalpels, forceps, clamps, etc. were placed in neat rows on trays. Machines were calibrated. Toward the rear, a sedated patient, face hidden by a blue curtain, was monitored by an anesthesiologist as a nurse used a sterile sponge stick to paint an antiseptic solution on the patient's back before putting the fenestrated drapes in place.

The murmuring was further obscured as a middle-aged Inuit RN sat at a small desk in the front of the O.R. and read from a chart into a micro-recorder. The RN was all business, her voice a monotone, as she read:

"The patient is a twenty-nine-year-old Caucasian male who presented in hospital last night with infection and back pain. The subsequent MRI, read by a visiting orthopedist at midnight, revealed a previous lumbar fusion located from levels L-1 to S-1. The fusion, estimated to be about two to three years old, *had never properly fused*, although the patient had learned to cope with the issue. However, over the last week, the patient had developed an allergic reaction and according to the visiting orthopedist, had subsequently *rejected* the donor cadaver bone. The orthopedist called it a 'Black Swan' event and concerned over the viability of the patient, scheduled emergency surgery as soon as a team could be assembled. The entire fusion will be removed and replaced using the patient's *own* bone material, to be harvested bilaterally from his hips. The bone material will be fused to a new structure which will encompass all lumbar and thoracic levels. All seventeen levels are dangerously weakened; therefore, the patient's entire back up to the cervical discs will be immobilized. The orthopedist informs that a procedure of this complexity will require an estimated six hours."

The RN grimaced, turned off the recorder, and muttered to herself, "Poor boy."

Her attention went to the green-scrubbed surgeon who briskly walked into the room. Almost jauntily, in fact.

"Good mor-nink," said the surgeon to the room. "Are we ready?"

"Yes, Doctor …"

"Fedorova," said Dr. Irina Demidova. "Anastasia Varya Fedorova. And I would say …"

Demidova paused to look at the chart before continuing. "… young Nicholas is lucky I missed boat to Vladivostok last night."

She leaned over and whispered something into Nick's ear.

*   *   *

As before, in the O.R. at Cleveland Mercy, it defied logic that a fully anaesthetized patient on an operating table could hear Demidova's—or anyone's—words.

But Nick was special. He heard *something*.

A familiar voice. Those accented fragments of speech that made their way to deep inside his superior temporal gyrus.

Nick dreamed he heard Dr. Irina Demidova whisper to him, *"Hello, petal. Did you miss me?"*

* * *

Julie entered the hospital at a run. She headed to the young receptionist at the information desk.

"Nick?" It took her a second to remember Nick's new last name. "Nick Charles?"

The receptionist called it up on her computer.

"Just got out of Recovery."

"Recovery! What? The orthopedist wasn't supposed to arrive until this afternoon!"

"Yes. But a different surgeon showed up in the middle of the night."

"Just showed up? Who?"

"Honestly, I have no idea. She said she was on her way home. Wherever that is. All I know is everybody's saying it was some kind of miracle. She saved his life."

"She?"

Before the receptionist could answer, Julie heard the rolling of a gurney. She looked up and ran to meet it. The patient, Nick, was still out cold. Julie took his free hand. Two IV bags dripped into a port above his wrist on the other hand.

"What happened?" Julie asked the orderly pushing the gurney.

"Dude got a brand-new back. His old fusion almost killed him. They're waiting for him in ICU."

Julie bent to see Nick's droopy, unaware face. "Where's this surgeon?"

No sooner was the question asked than the answer became apparent as Julie heard the clickety clack of high heels echoing behind her. Julie turned around to see a pair of six-inch stilettos and most of a sable coat swinging out the front door.

The orderly said, "The weird part was the surgeon knew him from the Lower 48, said that she *owed* him—for the last one. No charge."

Julie could only gape. Although Demidova was out the door and gone, Julie could still hear the echo of high heels resonating in the hallway.

"Jules?"

Nick's eyes had opened. They were clear. The bear had vanished, cut loose from his trap.

"Where are we?"

Julie looked back from the front door to Nick.

"In a good place."

∗   ∗   ∗

ACKNOWLEGEMENTS

In the universe of this novel, the story ends just as the first hint of the Covid-19 virus is starting to hit the media's consciousness, and my characters in rural Alaska are not yet aware of it. So, it's not a thing. Well, as I write these words on the last day of 2020, the pandemic is very much a thing. The grief I've given to a few fictitious medical professionals in the story should do absolutely nothing to detract from the heroism and humanity of the frontline medical workers who have given their all, and in many cases their lives, to fight this scourge. They are the best of who we are.

I'm overwhelmed by the support and inspiration I received in writing this novel, especially from Stefanie Leder and Dr. Garson Leder who were enormously honest and helpful with their input.

A huge thanks to Stephen C. Beck, M.D. for his invaluable contributions which went beyond medical suggestions and corrections as Steve is an accomplished writer in his own right, with the career to prove it. His insights were vital. All medical errors and a tweak or two for dramatic purposes are mine alone.

I want to thank the people who read early and sometimes multiple drafts. Their feedback, likewise, was essential. Thanks, George Beckerman, Phil Combest, Richard Jewell, Don Klein, Mimi Leder, Robbin Miller, Stephen A. Miller, Richard Stanley,

Rick Tuber, and John Lisbon Wood. Likewise thanks to Geraldine Leder, tied for best sister ever.

I regret this wasn't finished in time for my Mom, Etyl Leder, to read. She would ask me literally every time we spoke or met when I'd be finished, and she made sure that everyone in her orbit knew about it. She passed away at the age of ninety-seven.

Sabine Havelka-Leder had a lot to do with me deciding to write this book. Parts of her story, and all of her spirit, are on every page. *Ich vermisse dich so sehr.*

I also miss my Dad, Paul Leder. After all this time, it pains me that he's not around to read it and tell me how I could make it better.

Who is around and helped make YOU MIGHT FEEL A LITTLE PRICK way better is Foyne Mahaffey. Foyne tirelessly read and helped edit endless drafts, contributed some great lines, and most important of all, rescued me from (most) of my worst instincts. She is a truly awesome partner. I couldn't be luckier.

Some housekeeping:

In case any Nike lawyers have read this book, I can attest, to my knowledge, in real life there have been zero cases of Nike Hyperadapt (E.A.R.L.) sneakers going rogue and doing what they did to Muscat. If anything, I'm sure Muscat must have bought a pair of counterfeits. Real Hyperadapts just don't do this.

This is a work of fiction and Cleveland Mercy, of course, does not exist; it is, however, a stand-in for various other institutions of healing I've had the pleasure of patronizing. Employed at Cleveland Mercy are a number of physicians and other medical characters who are painted less than sympathetically and I admit, are hyperbolically drawn. But not entirely as much as one might think, as in certain scenes I've repeated verbatim what I had heard or witnessed. Some are based on real life counterparts, albeit heavily disguised or are composites—and I didn't mind killing them off. However, it's also essential to mention there are plenty of caring and skilled healers who have invested their lives in service of rest of us. One, in particular—whose idealism and professionalism prominently made it into the story—represents and exemplifies the best in medicine. There are others in real life who are similarly selfless and dedicated professionals. I know; I've met them. They, indeed, deserve stories of their own.

But not this time.

Reuben Leder lives in Los Angeles

CPSIA information can be obtained
at www.ICGtesting.com
Printed in the USA
LVHW010307290421
685921LV00002B/2/J